PROTECT AND DEFEND

**Center Point
Large Print**

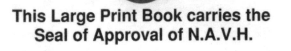

**This Large Print Book carries the
Seal of Approval of N.A.V.H.**

PROTECT
AND
DEFEND

VINCE FLYNN

CENTER POINT PUBLISHING
THORNDIKE, MAINE

To
Thomas Patrick Tracy

This Center Point Large Print edition
is published in the year 2008 by arrangement with
Atria Books, a division of Simon & Schuster, Inc.

The text of this Large Print edition is unabridged. In other
aspects, this book may vary from the original edition.
Printed in the United States of America.
Set in 16-point Times New Roman type.

ISBN: 978-1-60285-091-0

Library of Congress Cataloging-in-Publication Data

Flynn, Vince.
    Protect and defend / Vince Flynn.--Center Point large print ed.
        p. cm.
    ISBN 978-1-60285-091-0 (lib. bdg. : alk. paper)
        1. Rapp, Mitch (Fictitious character)--Fiction. 2. Intelligence officers--Fiction.
    3. Iran--Fiction. 4. Terrorism--Fiction. 5. Large type books. 6. Political fiction. I. Title.

PS3556.L94P76 2008
813'.54--dc22

2007036535

ACKNOWLEDGMENTS

To Emily Bestler and Sloan Harris, my editor and agent, for your friendship and many talents. To David Brown for being the best publicist in the business. To Jack Romanos, Carolyn Reidy, Judith Curr, and Louise Burke, and the rest of the Atria, Pocket, and Simon & Schuster family; thank you for all of your hard work and support. To Sarah Branham, Laura Stern, Kristyn Keene, and Niki Castle, thank you for being so good at what you do, and for being nice while you do it. To Jamie Kimmes for making life significantly less cluttered, which to a writer is no small thing.

To Rob Richer for your friendship and wisdom. To Judd Stattine and Bob Olson for your integrity and professionalism. To Dr. Jodi Bakkegard for taking such good care of me. To Chad Harris at thethirdoption.net for keeping things rolling. To Sunny Wicka and Brad England for your generous contribution to the fight to find a cure for Duchenne Muscular Dystrophy, and to my wife, Lysa, for being my classy, calm partner in an otherwise chaotic life.

1

Mitch Rapp ran his hand along her smooth, naked thigh, up to her waist, and then down along her flat stomach. His body was pressed against hers; front to back, her head resting on his arm. This moment had not been part of the plan, but it shouldn't have surprised him. There had been signposts; furtive glances, comments made only half in jest. The tension had built for the better part of a year. Each of them silently wondering. Neither knowing for sure if it would ever go to that next level. And then they arrived at the private villa overlooking the tranquil beach. The warm, humid air, the crashing surf, the shots of tequila; all coalesced to create a situation of overwhelming sexual tension.

Rapp kissed her bare shoulder, nudged a lock of her silky, black hair with his nose and listened to her breathing. She was sound asleep. He lay still for a long moment, completely intoxicated by the smell and touch of the beautiful woman lying next to him. He hadn't felt this alive in a long time, though guilt was still hovering in the recesses of his conscience, waiting to come rushing back at any moment. He could sense it gnawing at the edge of his psyche. Trying to get back in. Forcing him to think about things he wished he could forget, but knew he never would.

Pulling himself away from her, he rolled onto his back and stared up at the ceiling fan. Candles danced with the breeze and threw a faint light on the slow-turning blades and the dark, stained timber rafters above. Beyond the open balcony doors the waves rolled onto the beach. It had been two years since a bomb had destroyed his home on the Chesapeake Bay, killing his wife and the child she was carrying. Not once since that tragic day had he slept soundly, and tonight would be no different.

They'd come for him on that fall afternoon—not her. His guilt over her death drove him to the heights of rage and the valleys of sorrow. He had been a fool to think he could settle down and have a family. There were too many enemies. Too many relatives of the men he had killed. Too many governments and powerful individuals who would like nothing more than to see Mitch Rapp lying facedown in a pool of his own blood. There had been moments—moments of deep despair where Rapp had quietly wished one of them would succeed. He welcomed the challenge. Just maybe, someone would get lucky and put him out of his misery.

The odds of that happening tonight, however, were slim to nonexistent. Contrary to what his current prone position and the woman lying next to him suggested, Rapp had not traveled thousands of miles for a romantic getaway. Simply put, he had journeyed to this tropical location to kill a man. A narcissistic political operative who had selfishly put the needs of his party and himself above those of America. His scheming had changed the course of the last presidential election and resulted in the deaths of dozens of innocent people. With each passing week, it become more obvious that the man thought he had gotten away with it. In fact, only a few people did know of his involvement, but unfortunately for the target, they were not the types to let treason go unpunished.

Rapp and his team had kept an eye on the man for the better part of a year. At first the surveillance was extremely passive. He was on one coast, and Rapp and his people were on the other. They tracked him electronically through his credit cards and ATM withdrawals. As the months passed, and the target began to let his guard down, they stepped up the surveillance. Listening devices were placed near his home, office, and boat, and his cell phone calls were monitored. Spyware was installed on his computers and they began tracking his every move, looking for a pattern or an opportunity.

That was how they discovered the trip he had planned, a month-long excursion from San Diego down to Panama and back. The target was planning on putting his brand-new two million–dollar boat through his own personal sea trial. Rapp got his hands on the complete itinerary for the trip and sent an advance team to scout the ports of call. Terminating the target in a remote Third World country was infinitely better than doing so in America.

It turned out Puerto Golfito was the perfect location.

Relatively small, the fishing village had a growing tourist industry. Cruise ships now dropped anchor a few times a week to disgorge their passengers. Commerce was on the up, real estate was booming, and the entire city was in a state of flux. It was the perfect environment for two people to come and go unnoticed. As far as operations went this one was not all that challenging. Even so, one aspect of the plan was giving Rapp some concern. The naked woman lying next to him was adamant that she be the one to send this man to his grave.

Maria Rivera had been the logical choice to accompany Rapp. Fluent in Spanish, she was highly motivated where the target was concerned. A little too motivated, possibly, which in addition to one other thing made Rapp a bit hesitant. She was more than capable of taking out the target, either by hand or with a gun, but she lacked practical experience. There was a reason why professional killers typically came from either the Special Forces or the mean streets. Both groups of men were desensitized to violence. They looked at it as a way to achieve an end. The formula for success was often no more complicated than meeting violence with superior violence.

The lovely Latina beside him had seen neither the mean streets of a ghetto nor the rough, covert world of Special Forces operators. Quite to the contrary, she had spent the last decade working for one of the world's premier law enforcement agencies. Maria Rivera was a second-degree black belt and a former

Secret Service agent who was an expert marksman with a pistol. She had been destined for greatness until a bomb tore apart a motorcade she was assigned to protect. The internal investigation that followed cleared her of any incompetence or blame, but in a business where success went unnoticed and failures became documentaries on the History Channel, she was quietly ushered off the fast track and stuffed away in a basement cubicle where her ambitions began to atrophy like the unused muscles of a comatose patient. Rapp knew she wouldn't last long, so he offered her a chance at a new career.

Officially, Rivera worked for a private security company headquartered in McLean, Virginia. She was given the title of vice president and put in charge of personal protection and threat assessment. Her salary was three times greater than what she had earned with the Secret Service. The war on terror was good business for private security firms. Much of the company's work was legitimate, but more and more Rapp was using them to do things that Langley needed to hide from the press and Congress.

This little south-of-the-border excursion was a perfect example of such an operation. Individually, Rapp would have had no problem getting a select number of senators or congressmen to sign off on the operation, but getting an entire committee to agree and not leak was impossible. Ego and political ambition trumped national security for far too many elected officials.

Rapp turned and looked at Rivera. Even though this

operation was fairly simple, there was absolutely no room for mistakes. It had to look like an accident, or there would be too many questions. He wondered if she really had it in her, or if the years of law enforcement training would kick in and give her reason to pause. Killing a fellow human being was not always as difficult as one might believe. Give someone a minimal amount of training and put them in a situation where they are forced to defend either themselves or their family and most will rise to the occasion. Give someone like a Secret Service agent hundreds of hours of training and they will efficiently, and without hesitation, use lethal force to stop a gun-wielding presidential assassin.

Ask one of those same agents to kill an unarmed civilian and you have now moved into the unknown. Even if guilt is confirmed, and the punishment fits the crime, few law-and-order types relish the role of executioner. The agent is no longer being asked to react to a threat. An entirely new skill set is needed. Essentially you are asking a person who has only played defense to now line up on the other side of the ball and perform with the same level of proficiency. To change one's role so quickly is nearly impossible. To kill cleanly, and make it look like an accident, was the domain of the rare, tested assassin.

Rapp checked Rivera again. She was sleeping soundly. Slowly, he slid his right arm out from under her neck, pulled back the sheet, and slid out of bed. As he covered her with the sheet her head stirred slightly and then settled back onto her pillow. Rapp backed away and walked across the cool tile floor to the balcony. A soft, humid breeze ruffled the tops of the palm trees below. He looked out across the bay at the bobbing masts of the sailboats and searched for the sleek cruiser that belonged to the man they had come to kill. The boat had arrived late in the afternoon and dropped anchor a convenient 200 feet from the nearest boat. The 63-foot Azzurra with its bright red stripe was easy to pick out among the other white hulls.

The man was scheduled to stay in Puerto Golfito for two nights. He had yet to deviate from his itinerary, which made Rapp's job all that much easier. The plan for this evening was to watch him, but Rapp was beginning to have second thoughts. He looked up at the quarter moon and the approaching clouds. In an hour the conditions would be as good as they would get. The forecast called for clear skies the following evening. A quarter moon on the water provided more light than most people would think and more light increased the odds that they might be seen.

Rapp glanced back at Rivera. This one was going to be up close and personal. There would be no detachment through distance and the scope of a rifle. Even though the target was no threat physically, this was for many the most difficult kind of kill. The biggest psychological test. Bare hands. No knife. No gun. Just you and the prey wrapped in a death spiral like an anaconda squeezing the last breath from some warm-blooded animal it had plucked from the bank of a stream. She would feel the heat of his body, smell his scent, hear his muffled cries, and quite possibly see the pleading fear in his eyes. No, he decided, it was too big a test for Rivera.

Silently, he walked over to his bag and pulled out an encrypted Motorola radio. He turned it on and left it across the room on the dresser. With the rest of his gear in tow he slid out of the bedroom and made his way down the hall to the living room. The large sliding doors were open, covered only by sheer white curtains. Rapp headed for the middle, found the seam in the fabric, and stepped out onto the patio. He put on a pair of black swim skins and walked down the path to the water. The house sat on five acres and had its own private beach.

Rapp reached the tree line and checked the expanse of sand. It was empty. He slid a Motorola radio and a collapsible headset under the swim skins and strolled casually across the beach with his fins, snorkel, and dive mask. There was no sense in trying to be sneaky at this point. If anyone saw a person in black slinking suspiciously across the beach at this late hour they were likely to call the police. Rapp waded into the water, getting a fix on the boat. He lined it up with a dip in the tree line at the opposite end of the bay, finished putting on his mask and fins, and began slicing through the water toward the boat and its owner. He was going to squeeze the life out of Stu Garret, and he knew from experience that he wouldn't feel the slightest bit of compassion.

2

ISFAHAN, IRAN

T he cigarette smoke hung thick in the air as the three men eyed each other with a mix of contempt and suspicion. Azad Ashani did not want to be here. The fifty-one-year-old head of Iran's Ministry of Intelligence and Security knew what was coming. Sooner or later the bombs would fall and the facility where he sat would be destroyed by an American onslaught. There was of course a good chance it would be the Israelis, but in the end would it be any different? The Israelis, after all, would be flying American-made planes and dropping American-made bunker-buster bombs.

Ashani studied the concrete walls and ceiling of the cramped office. They were fifty feet underground in the Isfahan nuclear facility. Ashani had been reassured by engineers and bureaucrats alike that the facility was impregnable. Above them sat a surface building with a rebar, interlaced, two-meter slab of superhard concrete supported by a skeletal frame of massive steel I beams. Ten feet beneath that sat a one-meter-thick span of concrete and rebar and more I beams. Ten feet beneath that the same thing, and so it went all the way down to the fourth subterranean level. The engineers had told him ninety-nine percent of the American arsenal would be stopped by the massive ground level slab. The second floor was touted to be one hundred percent effective against the one percent that just might be able to get past the first barrier.

This may have comforted many of Ashani's fellow government officials, but Ashani was a born skeptic, not a blind religious fanatic. The American defense industry was constantly churning out new weapons capable of bigger and more amazing feats of destruction. When American ingenuity was pitted against his own government's boisterous propaganda, a sane man was left with an easy choice of who to believe. On his original tour of the facility he asked the chief engineer, "If the second subfloor is one hundred percent effective, why bother building the third and fourth subfloors?" The question was never answered.

Ashani had no doubt the facility was marked for destruction, and he was increasingly convinced it would happen within the month. He had firmly, though respectfully, argued against its ever being built. The hard-liners had won, however. They had now poured more than a billion dollars into this facility, the one at Natanz and several others, all while the Iranian economy grew increasingly anemic. Officially, the program was for the peaceful development of nuclear energy. The entire world knew this to be a lie, for the simple fact that Iran was blessed with massive oil and gas reserves. Economically, it made no sense to spend billions developing a nuclear program when cheap oil and gas were abundantly available. What they needed were refineries.

With each passing day Ashani felt a greater sense of impending doom. It reminded him of the feelings he'd had as a graduate student back in 1979. He could see the fall of Shah Mohammad Reza Pahlavi coming as clearly as he saw the ascension of the religious fanatics. Grounded in math and economics, Ashani was pragmatic. There was no denying the fact that the shah was a puppet dictator who raided the national coffers to pay for his opulent lifestyle. This dislike, however, had to be tempered with an acknowledgment of the fanaticism of Ayatollah Khomeini and his band of blackrobes. While in graduate school at Shiraz University, Ashani had watched the religious zealots draw his fellow students to their cause. In time, they boarded buses and headed to Tehran for the protests. Ashani remembered thinking that they had no idea what they were getting themselves into.

Revolutions were a tricky thing, and this one would be no different. Hard-line clerics fanned the flames of the populace's rage and created in the shah a villain far greater than the facts would support. Young students and professionals who wanted to throw off the censorship and yoke of the shah's secret police had no idea that they were making an alliance with a group that was no friend of free speech, feminism, and the enlightenment of Persian education. The youth of the country, however, was swept up in the storm of change like an angry uneducated mob. Very few bothered to stop and think what things would be like after the shah was removed. Ashani knew, though. In the end, revolutions were almost always won by whichever group was most willing to slaughter any and all opposition. Nearly three decades, a marriage, and five daughters later it was clear to Ashani that many of those students regretted what they had done.

This was Ashani's third trip in as many weeks to the underground facility. He had been ordered by the president to escort Mukhtar himself this time, as if somehow their mere presence would help protect the place from the impending aerial bombardment. Ashani had absolutely no authority over Iran's Atomic Energy Council or the Supreme Security Council, both of which oversaw the operation of the half dozen not so secret facilities that Iran had invested so heavily in. Nonetheless, they imagined spies at every facility and they wanted Ashani and his secret police to catch them.

That was the reason they gave for demanding more and more of his time, but Ashani knew the real reason. It was classic politics. The writing was on the wall, and the leaders were looking to hedge their bets. There was now a consensus that the Americans or their surrogates would attack. A couple of well-placed bombs could bring billions in investments and talent to a catastrophic halt. Unemployment was over twenty percent, and close to half of the country was at or below the poverty line. All of this while sitting on massive reserves of natural gas, oil, and coal. They were in the third decade of their vaunted Islamic revolution and the people were faring no better than they had under the shah. This nuclear gambit was in danger of bankrupting the government, and if Ashani knew anything about the religious zealots, it was that not a single one of them would accept blame. They were now lobbying for his support. Those who had championed the development of nuclear weapons were now telling him that they had always held reservations.

The second reason Ashani had been asked to make the trip was sitting next to him. Very few people made Ashani anxious, but Imad Mukhtar was one of them. The Lebanese-born terrorist was the most ruthless man he had ever met. Cold, calculating, and full of hatred, there was nothing he wouldn't do for the cause. One of Ashani's least favorite aspects of his job was dealing with Mukhtar, but there was no avoiding it. As the leader of Hezbollah in Lebanon the man had become a crucial part of the broader Iranian strategy.

The third man in the meeting was Ali Farahani. He was in charge of security at the Isfahan nuclear facility, and he did not like visitors from Tehran. Especially these two. Farahani leaned back and put his feet up on the metal desk. He took a long pull from his cigarette and announced, "The Americans do not have the balls to attack us."

Ashani had subtly warned the Supreme Security Council that Farahani was not up to the job of running security at the nation's most important facility. His family was very well connected, and as was often the case in Iran, nepotism had played a significant role in his posting. Ashani turned to the master terrorist beside him to see how he would handle the brash confidence of a fleshy bureaucrat.

Mukhtar's already narrow eyes grew more so, as he studied the silly man across from him. He leaned back and said, "So you don't think they will attack?"

"No." Farahani shook his head and scratched his heavy black beard. "They have been mauled in Iraq, a divided country half our size. They do not want to pick a fight with the rising Persian Crescent."

"And the Jews?"

"Let them come. The new S-300 anti-aircraft missiles from Russia are in place. The Jews will not get within a hundred kilometers of this place."

Mukhtar glanced sideways at Ashani, who gave him nothing but a blank expression. Turning back to Farahani, Mukhtar said, "I trust those Russian missiles as much as I trust you."

Farahani paused and then in a reasonable voice asked, "Why do you insult me?"

"Your security doesn't impress me. I saw half a dozen lapses on my way in, and I haven't even started my surprise inspection."

"Inspection?" asked a shocked Farahani as he pulled his feet off his desk. "No one said anything about an inspection."

"That is why it is a surprise, you imbecile!" Mukhtar stood so fast his chair shot backwards, scraping across the concrete floor.

A nervous Farahani stood as well and after a moment regained enough composure to say, "Under whose authority?"

"The Supreme Council's," Mukhtar snapped.

Farahani looked to the head of Intelligence and Security for confirmation. His own brother sat on the council! How could it be that he had failed to inform him?

Ashani nodded and said, "Our friend from Hezbollah specializes in unconventional warfare. He is here to see how vulnerable you are to things other than aerial bombing . . ."

"A ground assault?" The head of security sounded incredulous. "Impossible."

Mukhtar started for the door. "We shall see."

Ashani looked at his watch and kept his disdain for the two men in check. This was going to be a very tedious day.

3

PUERTO GOLFITO, COSTA RICA

The half-mile swim out to the boat took just under twelve minutes. Rapp could have done it in less time, but he was more interested in stealth than speed. He circled around to the bow, only his head above water. A dim light glowed from two of the portholes. The others were all dark. Under the cloudy night sky he was nearly impossible to see. Rapp took off his mask, snorkel, and fins. One by one he stuffed them into his swim bag and tied the bag just beneath the watermark to the anchor line. He then swung around the starboard side, close to the vessel, listening for any hint that Garret or his wife might be up and moving about. When he reached the stern he stopped and peered around the corner to check the swim platform. It was large, fifteen feet across and six feet deep. More importantly, its teak deck was empty.

Rapp had spent a lot of time in and around water over the last fifteen years. In terms of clandestine operations it offered many advantages, stealth being chief among them, but there was one big drawback. Noise traveled great distances and with great clarity on a relatively still night like this. Now, as Rapp listened, the only sound he heard was water lapping up against the sides of the boats and the occasional clanging of a line against the mast of one of the sailboats anchored in the harbor.

He slowly pulled himself out of the water until his upper body was resting on the teak platform. The boat was big enough that he didn't need to worry about rocking it as he climbed onboard. His chief concern was that some insomniac stargazer on a nearby boat might catch a glimpse of him. He listened intently for several minutes and kept his eye on a sailboat and cruiser anchored several hundred feet closer to shore. Satisfied that no one was watching, he eased himself entirely onto the platform. Staying on his stomach, he rested his head on his forearms and remained motionless.

Rapp had played this one over and over in his mind's eye for months. He'd envisioned a variety of scenarios where Garret might meet his death—some more satisfying than others. The efficient practitioner in him wanted to play this one safe. Take no risks. Hit him before he even knew what was happening and get it over with. But there was another part of him that desperately wanted to see the fear in Garret's eyes. The man was a disgusting narcissist who hadn't lost a wink of sleep over the innocent people he'd had a hand in killing, and the many more who were physically disfigured and emotionally scarred from the blast. Simply putting him out of his misery would be letting him off too easily.

Everything about this operation had to be analyzed with two main objectives in mind. Garret's wife could not be harmed, and his death needed to look like an accident. With the advances made in forensic science these were no small tasks. Rapp had focused on Garret's affinity for boating almost from the start. Thousands of people died every year in boating accidents—collision, fire, drowning, electrocution, or simply disappearing were all options.

Each time a new surveillance report arrived from the West Coast, Rapp took the time to read it thoroughly and in the context of his options. After a while a pattern began to emerge. Wanting to see things for himself, Rapp traveled to San Diego on a private plane. He arrived after dark and left before sunrise. From the balcony of a rented condo he spent an entire evening watching the marina where Garret kept his boat. That one night confirmed the opening that Rapp had detected in the surveillance reports.

For several months now, Rapp had imagined killing Garret more than a dozen ways, but only two stood up under scrutiny. When they found out about the trip he was planning with the new boat, everything fell into place. Even after he told Rivera that she would take point, Rapp continued to play the two scenarios in his mind. He thought of killing Garret so often that it almost felt like a memory.

Virtually every time he closed his eyes he pictured himself exactly where he was right now—on the aft swim platform of Stu Garret's yacht. His low profile would rouse no suspicion. Under a clear moonlit sky he would look no different from a rolled-up tarp. On a night like tonight he would be nearly invisible. All that was left to do was wait for Garret.

4

Isfahan Nuclear Facility, Iran

The janitor pushed the cart down the hallway at a slow pace that appeared to be the result of either an injured left leg or a lack of enthusiasm for his job. He was wearing faded green coveralls with his security badge clipped to the flap of his left breast pocket. His black hair and beard were shot with gray. Over the last year and a half he had swept, scraped, scrubbed, and mopped virtually every room, hallway, and stairwell in the facility. He was respectful to his superiors, upbeat, and in general, well liked by the other people who supported the important scientific work that was being done.

The name on his security badge was Moshen Norwrasteh. He was sixty-six years old. Born and raised in the southeastern Iranian town of Bam, he had lost his wife, two children, and three grandchildren in a devastating earthquake that had killed over 30,000 people in 2003. Norwrasteh had struggled for years to find work after the quake, and then one day a cousin who worked for the Atomic Energy Organization found him a job at the Isfahan Nuclear facility. At first, his coworkers did not accept him. With unemployment rates so high the competition for any job, even janitor, was extremely intense. The locals whom he worked with were resentful of this outsider taking one of their jobs.

Within a month or two, though, he began to win them over. Norwrasteh had the penchant and the desire to fix almost anything—especially if it was powered by electricity. People brought in their phones, radios, toasters, vacuums—anything with a plug and he would fix it. On the weekends and in the evenings he went to people's houses to help rewire and update their electrical service. He never accepted money, only a warm meal and some much needed companionship to help fill the void left by the death of his entire family.

Norwrasteh had even been to the home of Ardeshir Hassanpour, the famous Iranian scientist who oversaw the country's uranium enrichment program. Hassanpour had come to his ramshackle shop on the ground level and asked him if he could drop by his house and fix a few things. Norwrasteh said that he would be honored. After installing a ceiling fan and fixing two broken lamps, he received neither an offer of payment nor a simple thank-you. Sitting down for a warm meal, even with the house servants, seemed out of the question. Norwrasteh remembered leaving the house and thinking to himself that he would feel no empathy for the man when the hammer fell. For the others, though, the ones who had shown him compassion and friendship, he would do everything in his power to make sure they made it out of the facility unharmed.

Moshen Norwrasteh's real name was Adam Shoshan. He had volunteered for this operation three times before the director general of Mossad and the prime minister finally relented. From the very beginning their greatest reservations lay in the fact that Shoshan himself was volunteering for the mission. The man simply knew too much. He was a senior officer, not some fresh recruit who'd been plucked from the Israeli army.

A twenty-seven-year veteran of one of the world's most feared and respected intelligence agencies, Shoshan was Mossad's resident expert on all things Persian. He was fluent in both Farsi and Arabic, and, most important, he had spent the first twenty years of his life living in Iran. Born in Tehran, Shoshan was the son of a wealthy diamond merchant who was very influential in the Persian Jewish community. As the

Iranian revolution began to gain momentum Shoshan's father grew increasingly nervous, and in 1979 he sent his wife and children to live in Vienna with relatives. Once things blew over he planned on bringing the family back. Unfortunately, they never did. Five months after sending his family to safety, Shoshan's father was accused of espionage and sedition and put on trial. The sham of a legal proceeding lasted less than five minutes. He was denied representation and was not allowed to speak on his own behalf. A guilty verdict was handed down and Shoshan's father was taken out back and shot in the head.

Adam Shoshan was the only surviving male relative. Against the wishes of his mother, he moved to Israel and enlisted in the army right as things were once again heating up in the region. A new group called Hezbollah was on the rise, and the PLO was asserting itself in the occupied territories and beyond. In 1982 he was on the front lines of the invasion into Southern Lebanon. While he was on foot patrol his military career was cut short when a Hezbollah suicide bomber blew himself up in the middle of Shoshan's platoon. A hot piece of shrapnel sliced through his left leg and damaged his hamstring beyond repair.

He was still in the hospital when Mossad came calling. It turned out they had had their eye on Shoshan practically from the moment he'd enlisted in the Israeli Defense Forces. Hezbollah was on the rise and Israel's top spy agency needed people who could analyze and dissect Iran's involvement in the Middle

East's newest terrorist organization. Shoshan did exactly that for the next two decades. He went from Collection to Political Action and finally Special Operations, where he rose to the number two position. He had been involved in the planning and execution of dozens of assassinations and paramilitary operations, and he had helped recruit and run spies from Tehran to Damascus and beyond.

The idea of sending someone to Iran who was well past his physical prime was not taken seriously. At least not at first. Shoshan had not participated in an actual field operation in almost a decade, and at no point had he done long-term undercover work. With few alternatives, though, and Iran inching closer to becoming a nuclear power, Shoshan's idea started to look less ridiculous. It was bold, yet simple, and the director general slowly began to see the wisdom of the plan. There was one glaring problem, however. If he was discovered the Iranians would torture him, and contrary to the statements of Amnesty International, torture worked. No matter how tough the individual, a skilled interrogation team always got what they wanted. Shoshan would be operating deep behind enemy lines with almost no backup. It was a huge gamble, but Israel had few choices.

Shoshan rounded the corner with his cart out in front of him. His posture was hunched and submissive but beneath his bushy black and gray eyebrows his eyes were alert, scanning the hall ahead. The signal had been given. Fifteen months of living a lie was about to come to an end one way or another in the next twenty-four hours. Shoshan wouldn't even allow himself to think about his extraction. The mere thought of seeing his beloved Israel again was enough to entice him into abandoning this underground tomb today and to hell with the mission. He'd come too far for that, though. He needed to see this through to the bloody end. Even if it meant his own bloody end.

Up ahead, a door on the left opened and two men stepped into the hallway. Shoshan glanced at the first man and then the other. The man on the left he recognized instantly. He ran the MOIS or Ministry of Intel and Security. His name was Azad Ashani. The man on the right was a ghost. Someone he had been chasing for nearly a quarter of a century. A man who had killed thousands of Israelis with his reign of terror. Shoshan gripped the handle of the cart tightly in an attempt to control his shock. Could he really be so lucky? Shoshan got control of his nerves and looked up for a second glance. He studied the eye sockets and the forehead, two features that were nearly impossible to change. It was him. Shoshan's head began to swirl over the bizarre gift he had been given. He had hunted Imad Mukhtar across three continents, coming close only twice, and here they were, face-to-face in the dank hallway of an Iranian nuclear facility on the very day that it was marked for destruction.

"I have not been impressed with your security thus far," the man on the right said in Farsi.

Shoshan slowed to a near crawl. Ali Farahani, the

security chief, joined the two men in the hallway and completely blocked Shoshan's path. Shoshan nudged his cart toward the wall and took on the most passive posture he could muster, which was not easy, considering every fiber of his body wanted to grab a screwdriver from his cart and jab it through Mukhtar's eye socket.

"I want to start with the reactor," Mukhtar stated in a commanding voice.

Shoshan was shocked by the mere mention of the reactor. Iran had gone to great lengths to make the rest of the world think that it was located at the Natanz site some 120 kilometers away. He knew it was beneath them, but he had never heard anyone in the facility speak of it so openly.

Farahani closed the office door. He had a look of extreme discomfort on his face. "That area of the facility is off-limits to you."

"Nothing is off-limits to me. If you would like me to call the president, I will do so, and then I will tell him how incompetent you are and I will make sure you get transferred to the Afghan frontier, where you will spend the rest of your career dealing with those savages."

Farahani hesitated. A defeated look fell across his face as he debated his options. After a moment he relented. "Follow me."

The three men started down the hallway, walking right past Shoshan, neither man paying him the slightest notice. Shoshan breathed a slight sigh of relief and checked his watch. He was supposed to wait for confirmation before he set things in motion, but how could he refuse this gift? Imad Mukhtar, the man responsible for so many indiscriminate bombings and countless deaths, had walked into a facility he was tasked with destroying. It was an opportunity he could not pass up. Surely, his superiors back in Israel would understand. Shoshan picked up his pace. There was much to be done. Especially if he wanted to catch them in the reactor room.

5

PUERTO GOLFITO, COSTA RICA

Stu Garret was not known for his patience. In his mind this was the singular trait that had propelled him to such great success. He was a decisive taskmaster who worked people as if they were his serfs. He wanted positive results and nothing less, and compliments to subordinates were almost unheard-of. In the world of political consulting and campaign management he was king. No other living person had successfully managed two separate bids for the Oval Office. His ability to orchestrate a campaign had taken on an almost mythical aura in the media and Democratic circles. His opponents, on the other hand, thought of him as the most underhanded, unethical jerk ever to stalk the wings of American politics.

Garret wore this reputation as a badge of honor. If

his opponents were dumb enough to follow the rules, that was their fault. He was a practitioner of all the most underhanded techniques. To him politics was guerrilla warfare. Hit-and-run tactics were the marching orders he gave his staffers and operatives. Go on the offensive and never let up, and absolutely never ever admit any wrongdoing to the press or your opponent. Elections were a competition that took place over a relatively compressed period of time. Garret often carried the day by sheer inertia, like slowly moving a rugby scrum toward the goal line. This bullish attitude and uncompromising vision served him well in politics, but was about to fail him in another arena. One with a far more serious endgame.

Garret and his wife were asleep in the master cabin that was tucked up in the bow of his brand-new Baia sixty-three-foot Azzurra. Garret rolled over, his left leg dangling off the side of the king-size bed. His eyes opened, blinking several times. Slowly the blue numbers of his bedside digital clock came into focus. It was 2:11 in the morning. He let his eyelids close and rolled onto his back. Occasionally, if he changed positions it would take the pressure off his bladder and he could fall right back asleep.

People all over the world are creatures of habit and Garret was no different. He liked to start his day with several cups of very strong black coffee and end it with a bottle of Chardonnay—sometimes two. These habits and an enlarged prostate made a certain nightly ritual inevitable. At roughly 3:00 a.m. and 6:00 a.m. he awoke to alleviate the pressure on his bladder. Simply cutting back on the coffee and wine would have been an easy solution, but Garret didn't like depriving himself of anything he liked. The way his mind worked, getting up to relieve himself wasn't the problem. It was falling back asleep. The magic bullet he'd found was sleeping on the water. When on land Garret found it almost impossible to get a good night's rest. On the water, however, he could relieve himself as many times as his swollen prostate required and the motion of the ocean was guaranteed to rock him back to sleep.

The other benefit of boating lay in its solitude. The older Garret got, the more he realized he simply didn't like people. Most he found to be irritating and obnoxious, but even the endearing ones wore thin over time. He'd made a small fortune getting men and women elected to public office. Professional charmers who could change personas to fit each potential voter. Even these chameleons found a way to get under his skin. After a while their feigned can-do attitude and politically correct speak became intolerable. Garret was at his core an irascible man who believed everyone acted in their own selfish interests.

The evangelist who spoke of his love of Christ did so not out of adoration for his savior, but out of a need for others to hold him in high regard. Garret had met one too many Hollywood types who professed their desire to save Mother Earth, while ensconced in one of their several ten-thousand-square-foot homes of which they were the sole occupants. Did they really believe in global warming or were they simply hypocrites? The town had its fair share of sanctimonious phonies, to be sure, but most simply wanted to be accepted and to be thought of as enlightened, intelligent, and compassionate. Garrett had no such need. He yearned for the acceptance of others about as much as he wanted a sturdy kick in the groin.

The visual brought a sly grin to Garret's face. He was very happy with the way his life had turned out. Especially in light of how things were going just a year ago. He'd just finished running his second successful presidential campaign. Having helped orchestrate one of the greatest come-from-behind victories in the history of the country, he was flushed with a sense of omnipotence. Manufacturing a victory was probably a more accurate definition of what he'd done, but he wasn't about to go there.

The important thing was that he had done his job. Politics was a rough game, each side willing to do the most unseemly things to win. None of it surprised Garret. History was filled with examples. Over time untold numbers of siblings had poisoned and been poisoned while jockeying for the throne; civil wars fought over mere ideas had killed millions; there'd been too many assassinations, bloody coups, and revolutions to even count that had upset entire continents. Julius Caesar had been stabbed twenty-three times by a cabal that included some of Rome's most learned and intellectual senators. Hitler burned the Reichstag to the ground and blamed the Communists. The examples of men lying, cheating, and murdering their way to power was long and illustrious.

For Garret, if there was any lesson to be learned from history, it was that victory went to whoever was bold enough to take it. Pitted against some of history's more sensational power grabs, Garret felt that what he had participated in was pretty mild. After all, he would have never joined in the plot if the photos hadn't been thrown in his face—a clear effort by the other side to play dirty. Garret knew it had been his old nemesis Cap Baker, who had sent him the pictures. Garret's candidates, presidential nominee Josh Alexander and his running mate Mark Ross, were getting their asses handed to them by the Republicans. Money was drying up and the time left to close the gap was shrinking quickly, but they still had a chance. That was, until the photos arrived.

There were a lot of obstacles Garret could overcome, but the wife of his candidate caught on film having sex with a Secret Service agent was not one of them. Garret showed the photos to Mark Ross, Alexander's vice president on the ticket. Ross nearly lost his mind, but after a good thirty minutes of a profanity-strewn tirade, he composed himself. He was not prepared to quit so easily. He had fought too hard to see his lifelong ambition destroyed by some little slut. Ross had contacts from his days at the CIA and as Director of National Intelligence. He went to work on finding a way to neutralize the problem, and in less than a week had reached a deal with a very shady expatriate named Cy Green.

Now it had been a little more than sixteen months since the attack on the motorcade that had killed Jillian Rautbort and fourteen others, including the Secret Service agent who had been sleeping with her. Garret had deluded himself into thinking that his role in the entire matter had been that of a bystander. He had neither condoned nor criticized the plans that had been set in motion. He had merely followed orders.

Garret remembered the shock and surprise he'd felt when the bomb attack had worked. The press, the public, even law enforcement bought the entire thing. A splinter terrorist group took credit for the attack on the motorcade, and the hunt was on to track them down. The voters rallied behind Alexander and Ross and several weeks later they rode the tide of sympathy to victory. Everything was going smoothly up until the week before the inauguration. That was when Mitch Rapp, Langley's top counterterrorism man, had somehow managed to track down the assassin who had detonated the car bomb. In just a few short days, everything they had worked so hard for began to unravel.

Just days before the inauguration the two men who had helped them pull off their miraculous come-from-behind victory disappeared, never to be seen by anyone again. That was unnerving enough, but mild compared to the shock Garret felt when he received the news that Vice President–elect Ross had died of a heart attack the morning of the inauguration. In the Oval Office, of all places. Garret knew Ross had a history of heart problems, but he found it hard to accept the timing of his departure. He had no real evidence that Rapp was to blame, but the odds of all three conspirators dying in the same week were impossible to swallow. Garret's gut told him the CIA was behind the entire thing, but he was hardly in a position to run to the authorities or the media. He left Washington and promised himself that he would never return. A year later, however, he was already rethinking that decision.

He missed manipulating the media and the voters. He missed outfoxing the Republicans and watching them complain about his dirty tactics. President Alexander's people were courting him as if it was a foregone conclusion that he would run the reelection bid that would begin in a little over a year. No man in the history of the republic had ever managed three successful campaigns. Being the first, and likely only, man to do so would be hard to refuse.

Garret threw the sheet off himself with no regard for his wife lying beside him. He placed his feet on the floor, grabbed the edge of the recessed bookshelf, and stood. As was his habit, he was buck naked. He began walking across the cabin toward the open door. A strip of lights along the floor illuminated the way past the bathroom. Garret used the onboard toilet as little as possible and never for a simple piss. One of his other defining traits was that he was cheap, and he'd be damned if he was going to pay the extortionate rates the marinas charged to pump his waste tanks.

He reached the door that led topside and undid the lock. As he climbed the steps he thought of the adrenaline rush he got from running a presidential campaign. Maybe it was time to get back in the game. Surely, if they were going to kill him they would have done it months ago.

Garret stepped into the spacious cockpit with careless confidence, blinded by his own lack of patience. It was simply unthinkable to him that anyone would wait to do anything. He walked over to the port side and along the narrow passageway that led down to the swim platform. Reaching out with his right hand, he steadied himself against the side of the boat as he moved down the steps. His knees and back were stiff. When he reached the expansive platform he turned immediately to his right as he always did.

Garret moved his toes to the edge and grabbed hold of himself. He flexed his knees several times and let out a yawn while he waited for his prostate to release its grip on his bladder. As he was looking out across the bay at the lights of the small town, he noticed a slight tremor beneath his feet. He started to turn his head to look over his shoulder, but before his head moved more than an inch a gloved hand clamped down on his mouth. A startled scream leapt from his throat but never made it past his lips. Garret felt the warmth of the attacker's breath on his right ear and then he heard a voice. It was a growl, barely louder than a whisper, and it sent shivers down his spine.

"One fucking peep, and I'll snap your neck like a toothpick."

6

ISFAHAN, IRAN

A dam Shoshan rounded the corner with his cart and counted the paces. To his satisfaction the long barren hallway was empty. He located the faint pencil mark at waist height and unfolded his small footstool. Reaching under the cart, he retrieved a metal box and yanked the wax paper off the back, exposing a sticky surface. After looking over both shoulders, he limped his way up the stool and pressed the device firmly against the wall, securing it in place. With no time to spare he folded up his footstool, set it on top of his cleaning cart, and was off.

Shoshan's mission had evolved in ways no one had predicted. He had been sent in as a spy in the most classic sense of the word. His mission was to surreptitiously collect intelligence on the Isfahan Nuclear Facility and nothing more. No unneeded gambles or risks were to be taken. He was to monitor who came and went and at what time. He was to build dossiers on the key scientists, and most importantly he was to ascertain the capacity of the centrifuge facility buried deep underground. Almost as an afterthought, the air force weighed in with one request. If it was possible, they wanted to get a look at the blueprints of the facility. After all, they would be the ones who would be called on to destroy it, and the more they knew about where to drop their bombs the better their chances were of succeeding.

Shoshan was under strict orders to move cautiously, take his time and make sure he passed on accurate information. This was not to be a quick in-and-out operation. The ops people back at Mossad anticipated he would be in country for a minimum of one year. Shoshan accepted all of this with a sense of duty and honor. Every time the maniacal Iranian president appeared on television and expressed his desire to see Israel consumed by a nuclear fireball, Shoshan was reminded just how much was riding on his ability to sell himself as a Persian.

He blended in and did his job. He cleaned toilets, washed floors, and kept his eyes and ears open. At first he had been extremely cautious. Surprise inspections were not unusual and the security people were unusually hard on the newcomers. The small room where he kept his cleaning supplies was tossed twice in the first month. This caused the already cautious Shoshan to be even more careful. After the second month he learned that the guards inspected his closet not to look for evidence of espionage, but to pilfer supplies. In the passing months Shoshan got to know them better and their suspicion of the newcomer dissipated. In a breakthrough that no one could have predicted, it was Shoshan's lifelong hobby of tinkering with all things mechanical and electric that would prove to make the difference.

Shoshan was cleaning the guards' break room one day when he happened to overhear the men complain about the poor reception of the television. He asked them if he could take a look at it, and they consented. After a quick inspection Shoshan located the problem and fixed it with a few turns of his screwdriver. In the eyes of the guards this elevated him to near-godlike status. In no time at all he was fixing broken TVs, microwaves, radios, and pretty much anything with a circuit board. Word spread quickly that the new janitor was a very handy man to have around. Even Ali Farahani, the head of security, came calling. The hot summer months were upon them, and Farahani's air conditioner was not working.

Shoshan went to Farahani's house and located the problem. He ordered a part and the following weekend installed it free of charge. Farahani was very grateful and asked Shoshan if there was anything he could do for him. Shoshan said there was, and showed the head of security his storage closet at work. In addition to the cleaning supplies, brooms, mops, and buckets, the room now contained haphazard stacks of household appliances that were waiting to be fixed. Farahani was at first enraged, thinking that the janitor was being taken advantage of by the other employees. Shoshan assured him that was not the case. He had no family to go home to. They had all been lost in the earthquake. The work helped him pass the lonely hours in the evening. What Shoshan wanted from Farahani was permission to stay after his shift was over so he could work on the appliances. Not only did Farahani give him permission, he found the janitor a much larger, unused storage room on the third sub-level where he could set up his makeshift repair shop. At the time, Shoshan knew he had reached a critical breakthrough, but he never could have dreamed just how advantageous this single move would turn out to be.

In the months that followed, Shoshan spent many evenings and weekends at the facility. He explored the corridors by day while pushing his cleaning cart from one room to the next. The guards now paid him only a passing glance as he came and went with boxes of tools, circuit boards, batteries, tubes and all of the other stuff he needed to stock his repair shop. It was during this time that Shoshan got to know Cyrus Omidifar. Omidifar was the chief engineer for the entire facility. He was the man who made sure everything worked properly. The power plant, the elevators, the ventilation systems, the plumbing, the guts of the place, it all fell under the purview of Omidifar. Like Shoshan, he loved to tinker with things.

At first Shoshan did not grasp the importance of Omidifar and all that he oversaw. Shoshan was too busy focusing on the scientists and nuclear program to stop and think about the actual bricks and mortar, or in this case steel and concrete. That all changed one evening when he went to visit Omidifar in his above-ground office. There on the table was a set of blueprints for the entire facility. Shoshan remembered the request from the air force targeting specialist and immediately cursed himself for not having his tiny digital camera with him. He stood over the prints, trying to grasp as many details as possible while his friend finished up a phone call.

When Omidifar was done he joined Shoshan at the table and announced, "An impressive feat of engineering . . . isn't it?"

Shoshan agreed.

"It is designed to act as a series of nets." Omidifar flipped the top page over and revealed a side elevation of the ground floor. "The top floor is two meters thick with six interlaced layers of rebar. If the Americans drop their bunker-buster bombs, we are very confident this first line of defense will stop them."

Shoshan wasn't so sure. Before going in country he'd been told that the Americans had their best military minds developing a new series of bunker-buster bombs that would get the job done. Shoshan looked at his friend. "And if it doesn't?"

Omidifar shrugged. "There are three more floors the bombs would need to penetrate. They are not as thick as the first floor, but they don't need to be. The first floor will stop or slow even their heaviest bomb. If one happens to get through, it still has to penetrate three more floors. Each of them one meter thick with interlaced rebar. The only way the Americans could destroy this facility would be to use a nuclear weapon, and they would never be so reckless."

"What about the Jews?" Shoshan asked. He'd learned to take a perverse joy in playing role of Jew hater.

The question made Omidifar pause. He was a practical man not prone to spewing anti-Semitic remarks. "I am not so sure about the Jews. I advocated conducting this entire operation in secret, but our fearless president likes to taunt our enemies. Now we have made ourselves a ripe target."

Shoshan smiled and nodded. His eyes returned to the print and his inquisitive mind went to work, not as a spy, but as someone who was endlessly fascinated by how things worked. "How did you support all this weight?"

Omidifar flipped several pages to a new sheet that showed a different cross-section of the facility. "We basically built an underground skyscraper. There is a steel skeleton that supports the entire structure."

That was when it hit Shoshan. He had never been allowed access to the fourth sublevel where the reactor and the centrifuges were located. He had assumed it was built into or under the bedrock. From the air the facility was impervious to all but a nuclear strike and despite the hawkish attitude of some, Shoshan felt that neither the Americans nor Israel would play that card. Isfahan was a city of over a million people. There was no way either country would drop a nuclear weapon in the vicinity of so many civilians. If Shoshan's instincts were right, however, no air strike would be needed. Something far simpler could cripple the entire facility. As Shoshan looked at the prints on that afternoon he paid particular attention to the size and gauge of the steel that had been used. By the time he left Omidifar's office a new course of action was forming in his mind. Shoshan was ready to make the transition from spy to saboteur.

Months later Shoshan was struck by the irony that the destruction of the Twin Towers was what opened his eyes to the facility's central weakness. He did not think of the towers in their pre–9/11 form and the way they dominated the southern tip of Manhattan. He didn't think of them as piles of rubble and twisted steel. His mind fixated on a five-second clip of each building as it collapsed under its own weight.

After leaving work that night Shoshan did not sleep. He played the clip of the towers imploding on themselves over and over in his mind. He knew he had stumbled across the bare underbelly of the dragon. His mind raced ahead, making a list of what he would need, and how he would sneak it into the facility. On that night nearly a half year ago the whole thing seemed crazy, but what bold action didn't at its inception. The next morning he put everything in an encoded report and left it at his dead drop. While he waited for an answer from Tel Aviv, he found an excuse to go back to Omidifar's office and this time he brought his camera.

It took two months of back and forth as the experts

debated the merits of Shoshan's plan. The deciding factor ended up being the air force's lack of confidence in their own ability to take out the facility with anything other than a nuclear strike. During those two months Shoshan furthered his plan, exploring the recesses of the third subfloor, locating and photographing as many steel I beams as he could. He passed everything along anticipating the questions before they came. During that time Shoshan also began construction on a false wall in the back of his storage room, foreseeing the necessity to hide the materials he would need to conduct his sabotage.

Shoshan spent countless hours alone with his thoughts trying to piece everything together. Simply striking at one or two points would not do the job. The plan would have to be comprehensive, and that meant it would take hours to carry out. Charges would need to be placed. He would be exposed the entire time, as would the explosives. Even the most witless guard would be likely to stumble upon the devices.

The solution came one afternoon when the facility suffered a brief power outage. Shoshan was cleaning a rest room on the second subfloor when it happened. The room went pitch black for a few seconds and then the emergency lights came on. Shoshan stared up at the square unit attached to the wall just below the ceiling. It consisted of two adjustable floodlights mounted near the top of a beige metal box approximately a foot and a half long by a foot and a half wide. Shoshan left the bathroom and looked down the long hallway. He counted four more emergency lighting units in this area alone. That night he photographed the lights and wrote down the make and model number. The next morning he informed Mossad that he had found a solution to their problem.

Five weeks later the first shipment of a dozen units left Haifa for Mumbai, India. After clearing customs the shipment was repackaged and sent up the coast to the Iranian free trade zone of Chabahar. From there it made its way inland to Isfahan. Two more shipments followed the same route. Each day Shoshan would pull up to the main gate of the facility on his motorbike, which had two saddlebags and an old plastic milk crate strapped to the back fender. The milk crate was almost always filled with parts. The guards had come to expect this. Inside each saddlebag, though, was a counterfeit emergency lighting unit. Not once in a month's time did the guards ever ask him to open the bags.

Following the schematics Shoshan had been through countless dry rehearsals. The experts back in Israel had thought of everything. Instead of using C-4 plastic explosives they packed the devices with relatively new thermobaric explosives. The thermobaric explosives would work extremely well in the underground confines of the facility, literally sucking all oxygen from the air and creating an enormous vacuum effect. They weighed less than conventional explosives and packed nearly three times the punch. Having the devices detonate at precisely the same time created another problem. Running det cord between each of the two units was dismissed immediately. Detonating the devices remotely was also impractical. There was no way for a radio frequency to penetrate all the concrete and steel. The solution was to install a highly accurate clock within each device. Via a master remote Shoshan had the ability to set a designated time for all of the devices to detonate. He did this in his storage room before putting them in place.

Twenty-six devices weighing eight pounds apiece. Just 208 pounds of explosives. Demolition firms used far more explosives to bring down buildings in nice neat little piles. That, however, was not Shoshan's objective. He was not trying to topple a building, and he certainly wasn't worried about how they would haul the mess away. His objective was much simpler. He was going to blow out the main support columns between the fourth and second subfloors. The loss of structural integrity would set off a pancake effect, bringing the upper three floors crashing down on the roof of the final subfloor. All that weight, falling with such force, would snap the vertical steel beams at the bottom of the structure. The four floors would end up pressed together like a stack of pancakes. The entire centrifuge facility and reactor would be smashed into a radioactive mess.

Shoshan limped down the hallway and checked his watch. He had just under thirty minutes to clear the facility. Done placing the devices, all he had to do was put his cart back in his storage room and get topside.

Once the explosions started, he would move for the gate and slip out in the ensuing confusion. He opened the door to his storage room and pulled the cart inside. The windowless room had been his refuge for much of the last year. In the evenings when the facility was mostly empty, he would close the door and drop the façade of Moshen Norwrasteh the Iranian. Slowly, Adam Shoshan the Israeli would assert himself. What Shoshan came to realize was that the two men were not all that different.

Those were the moments when he felt most conflicted. When he worried about the nice people he had met and what would happen to them when the attack came. Shoshan felt a pang of guilt over moving up the timetable. Headquarters had made it clear to him that they wanted the facility to be destroyed in the middle of the day. They wanted not only to obliterate the facility, they wanted to extinguish the scientific power behind Iran's nuclear program. The more people working down in the labs when the bombs went off, the better.

It was not a surprise to Shoshan when he received the order to create maximum damage. He was himself a hard man who had been forced to give orders that to some might seem heartless. Since receiving the directive, though, he had lain awake in bed nearly every night trying to figure out a way around it. He had met some very kind people during his time at the facility. There were a few hate-filled anti-Semites, to be sure, but most of the people were no different from his neighbors and colleagues back in Israel. It seemed wrong to him that they should have to die for following the orders of religious fanatics.

Seeing Imad Mukhtar, though, had caused most of those reservations to simply vanish. There was perhaps no more vile man in the modern history of Israel. Mukhtar was the purveyor of suicide bombers, rocket attacks on civilians, and countless kidnappings. He had the blood of thousands of Israelis on his hands. As one of the founders of Hezbollah, he was hell-bent on the absolute destruction of the state of Israel and nothing less. The mere fact that he was visiting the facility confirmed Israel's worst fears; that Iran would simply hand off one of their new bombs to a stateless terrorist group like Hezbollah. Catching the man at the facility so close to the appointed hour was simply too difficult to resist.

Shoshan took a brief look around the room, pondering if there was anything worth taking. Sanitizing the place was not a concern. What little he had left was well concealed and would be destroyed by the explosion. Shoshan backed out of the room and closed the door behind him. As he headed for the elevator his thoughts turned to his friend Ali Omidifar. He'd come up with a plan to distract his friend and make sure he was out of the building when the bombs went off. He pushed the call button for the elevator and thought that it was the one humane thing he could do to help assuage his guilt over all the other people who would die.

When the doors opened, he found himself standing face-to-face with Ali Farahani, the facility's head of security. He looked frazzled and in a hurry. Shoshan guessed it had to do with the two men who were standing behind him. Shoshan quickly stepped out of the way and murmured a quiet apology. He kept his eyes averted as the three men got out of the elevator and started down the hall toward Farahani's office. Shoshan stepped into the elevator and pushed the button for the ground floor. As the doors began to close, he looked down the hall at the back of Mukhtar's head and his subservient expression gave way to a broad smile.

7

Puerto Golfito, Costa Rica

Rapp kept the cool steel of his knife pressed against Garret's bare skin as a reminder that his mortality was very much in question.

In a voice tinged more with amusement than disdain Rapp whispered, "You thought you'd gotten away with it, didn't you?"

Garret made a lame effort to break free.

"Easy, Stu. If you want to live, you'll do exactly as I say."

Giving Garret hope that he might survive was as important as the obvious threat of force. The right balance had to be struck. Rapp was more than capable of subduing the paunchy political kingmaker, but tonight, brute force would be a last resort. Even the position of the knife had been considered. Rapp held the blade flat against Garret's skin so as to not leave a thin laceration that would be discovered during his autopsy. This was about deception, and to pull it off, he needed Garret to hold on to the idea that he might survive the next few minutes.

With his mouth mere inches from Garret's ear, Rapp said, "I wanted to come down here, slit your throat, and dump your worthless ass in the drink, but my boss, for some reason, thinks you might be useful." Rapp paused to give Garret a moment to realize the false hope. "The only problem for you is, I have a history of disregarding orders."

Rapp moved to his right and cranked Garret's head around so he could look him in the face. Rapp could see Garret's eyelids narrow as he tried to place the face of his assailant. They stayed that way for several seconds and then suddenly grew wide with fear.

Rapp smiled. "That's right, Stu, you know who I am. You tried to screw me over last year by feeding Tom Rich that bullshit story that the *Times* ran. It ended up blowing up in your face, didn't it?"

Garret tried shaking his head.

"I'm only going to say this one time. I want to kill you, and I'm pretty sure if I do, Director Kennedy, despite telling me not to, will find it in her heart to forgive me since you are one of the biggest pieces-of-shit political operators in American history. So if you want to save your own ass, you'll stop lying to me. Are we clear?"

Garret closed his eyes and nodded.

"All right, get down on your knees, and then I'll take my hand off your mouth so we can talk." Without giving him time to think, Rapp started lowering Garret to the teak deck. When he had him kneeling at the edge of the platform, he brought the knife around and placed the dull edge of the blade against Garret's throat. "I'm going to take my hand off your mouth. If you make any noise louder than a whisper, I'll stick this blade straight through your voice box and shove it all the way back to your spine. You'll end up drowning in your own blood, and trust me, it won't be enjoyable." Rapp gave Garret a long moment to consider the agonizing death and then slowly took his hand off Garret's mouth.

The political consultant and former presidential chief of staff took in a deep breath and whispered, "Please, don't kill me. None of it was my idea." His voice grew louder. "It was that idiot Mark Ross."

"Quiet," Rapp hissed.

"Sorry," Garret said, much softer now.

"It may not have been your idea, but you went along with it."

Garret hesitated and then nodded.

"You did more than go along with it. You helped carry it out."

"I was only following orders."

"Bullshit. You weren't some private on the front line

53

following orders. You're a political whore who doesn't give a rat's ass about anything other than seeing your guy win. You ran that campaign, and you wanted to see Jillian Rautbort dead just as bad as Ross did."

"That woman was not without fault."

"Why, because she cheated on her husband?"

"I'm just saying, if she would have kept her legs crossed, none of it would have happened."

Rapp grabbed Garret's hair with his left hand and pulled his head back. "Why don't you join the Taliban? You're going to sit here and tell me because a woman cheated on her husband, she deserved to die?"

"No," Garret struggled, "I'm just saying, if she would have kept her dress on, none of this would have been set into motion."

"And the fourteen other people who died?"

"That was unfortunate."

"Unfortunate," Rapp hissed. "You stole a presidential election by blowing up a motorcade and killing fifteen people, and the only word you can come up with is *unfortunate?*"

Garret could sense the anger in Rapp's voice. "It was bad. It was wrong. I should have stopped him."

"You're damn right you should have, you fucking sociopath." Rapp withdrew the blade from Garret's throat and put it back in its scabbard. With his left hand still holding on to Garret's hair, he said, "And that's why I'm going to kill you."

Before Garret could react, Rapp yanked him to the

left. Garret's reaction was to lurch his body to the right so he wouldn't fall in the water. This was what Rapp wanted. Using Garret's own momentum, Rapp reversed direction and yanked Garret's head back toward the port stern corner of the boat. Garret's temple struck the hard fiberglass with a thud, leaving him dazed and barely conscious, his arms limp at his sides.

Rapp let go of Garret's hair and wrapped his arms around the man's chest in a bear hug. He took a deep breath and propelled himself and Garret over the edge of the swim platform headfirst. When they hit the dark cool water, Rapp began calmly kicking his legs, driving them away from the surface. The water seemed to have shocked Garret back to alertness. He began struggling, but it was no good. Rapp had his fists locked around Garret's chest. As he drove them deeper, Garret tried to claw at Rapp's gloved hands. Not having any luck, he reached for Rapp's face, the only part of his body other than his feet that wasn't covered.

Rapp responded by lowering his fists a few inches to restrict Garret's ability to move his arms. He then gave him a quick Heimlich, forcing more air from his lungs. All the while, Rapp's legs kept them under steady propulsion, moving them farther away from what Garret needed most—oxygen. Garret began twisting his body and moving his legs violently. Rapp kept his eyes shut and drove them deeper. Based on the number of kicks, he guessed they were around twenty-five feet beneath the surface. It was more than enough. Garret's lungs would be on fire. He would feel like his chest was going to explode.

Rapp stopped, allowing them to level out and then exhaled a little air from his lungs. They'd been underwater for less than half a minute, but Rapp knew Garret was near the end. His movements were diminishing in both frequency and force. Rapp loosened his grip a bit to see if Garret was playing possum. His arms stayed limp at his sides. Rapp opened his eyes and looked up toward the ever-so-faint light on the surface. He released his hold on Garret and grabbed him by the hair. If the man was still alive, this was when he would make his break for the surface. He didn't, however. He simply floated in front of Rapp, a dark silhouette against a slightly lighter backdrop. Rapp put his hands on Garret's shoulders, pushed him farther down, and then started for the surface.

Rapp could see the dark underbelly of the boat and headed for the narrow bow, exhaling small amounts of air as he went. Ten seconds later he quietly broke the surface and finished exhaling before taking in a short breath followed by two deeper ones. His heart was moving at a pretty good clip. Between his pounding heart and with the water in his ears it was difficult to hear anything. He hovered quietly, taking deeper and deeper breaths. His head was the only thing out of the water. His heart rate quickly recovered and he shook the water from his ears. He listened for any sign that Garret's wife had woken up, but there was nothing.

After another minute he gathered his swim bag from the anchor line and started for shore. With any luck, he'd be back in Washington by noon.

8

Isfahan, Nuclear Facility

The bickering had gone on for the better part of the morning. For Ashani it was like being on a long car trip with his teenage daughters. Most men were easily intimidated by Imad Mukhtar. With his close ties to the hard-line zealots and his propensity for violence, it was wise to steer well clear of him. Farahani, due to either stupidity or conviction, had decided to concede nothing. While Mukhtar pointed out the facility's shortcomings with the tact of a drill instructor, Farahani defended himself like an insulted artist. The two fed off each other, the rhetoric escalated, and Ashani found himself wishing desperately that his office would call with an emergency that needed his immediate attention.

Ashani leaned against the wall of Farahani's office watching Mukhtar tick off a list of files he wanted to review.

Farahani, in the midst of lighting a cigarette, exhaled a cloud of smoke and shook his head. "I know that man very well. He would never betray the revolution."

Ashani had never seen Farahani so stubborn. Maybe

after all these months he was finally sick of people making the trip from Tehran to second-guess his every move. Even so, Mukhtar was not some mindless bureaucrat trying to cover his backside. At the young age of fourteen the man had joined the Palestinian terrorist group Force 17. By the time he was twenty, he recognized Yasser Arafat for the corrupt megalomaniac that he was and broke from the PLO. He formed a little-known group called Islamic Jihad that eventually spun off another organization called Hezbollah. That next year he changed the landscape of the Middle East by successfully using car and truck bombs to level the U.S. Embassy, the marine barracks, and the French barracks in Beirut. After those three gruesome attacks, Mukhtar and his men went on a kidnapping spree that turned the international political landscape on its ear for the rest of the decade. Mukhtar was a man of action who did not shrink from violence. He did not hesitate to kill those who did not share his all-or-nothing vision of jihad. Even if they were fellow Muslims.

"Three of your top scientists have been poisoned," Mukhtar accused.

"No traces of the poison were found anywhere in this facility," Farahani shot back.

"Who do you think poisoned them?"

"I'm sure the Jewish pigs had something to do with it, but since it did not happen in this facility, the investigation is out of my hands." Farahani turned to look at Ashani. "If you want to know who killed them, you should ask Azad."

"I know who killed them," Mukhtar half shouted. "The point I am trying to get through your thick skull is that the Jews have spies in your country. They have been sniffing around for some time. They specifically targeted those three scientists because they were the backbone of your uranium enrichment program."

"Anyone can make that assumption. I am not arguing with you. Those men were poisoned at the university. Not here in this facility. There are no Jewish spies here. It is impossible."

"I want to talk to this man." Mukhtar held up a personnel file.

Farahani straightened his posture and said, "That man comes from a family whose reputation is beyond reproach."

Ashani watched as Mukhtar's fists clenched and his nostrils flared. It now all fell into place for the man who ran the Ministry of Intelligence. He could not believe he had not seen it earlier. Farahani came from a very proud Persian family. A family who could trace their genealogy back to Persia's dynastic roots. A very pious family who could see the shah was about to lose his throne, and who in a move of self-preservation threw their support behind Ayatollah Khomeini and his revolutionaries. Farahani was very proud of his Persian lineage, and he was not about to take orders from some Palestinian mutt like Mukhtar.

In the blink of an eye Ashani saw how this could turn out. If Mukhtar got a whiff that Farahani was looking down his prominent Persian beak at him, there would be violence, and there would be a better-than-even chance that Farahani would end up dead or permanently injured. Farahani's brother, who sat on the Supreme Council, would be extremely upset. Mukhtar was too valuable to punish, so he would be sent back to the front lines in Lebanon. Powerful people would want to know why Ashani did not step in and stop things before they got out of hand. As tempted as he was to let it play out, Ashani decided that in the long run it would only make his life more difficult.

Ashani pushed himself off the wall. "I know the man you are asking about. He is indeed from a good family, which is exactly why we should talk to him."

Farahani looked at Ashani with a confused, almost hurt expression.

"He will speak honestly," Ashani said. "If there is anything he has seen, or anyone he is suspicious of, he will tell us."

Farahani paused and then gave his consent.

"Good," Mukhtar announced. "Where is he?"

Ashani checked his watch. It was almost noon. "Why don't you send your people to collect him and have them escort him to the café?" Ashani did not give Farahani a chance to argue. He opened the office door. "I will wait for you by the elevator."

Mukhtar joined him in the hall a few seconds later. He pulled up alongside the Intel Minister and said, "This man is an idiot."

Ashani shrugged. "He is a very hard worker."

"If that is all you want then you should hire an ox."

Ashani sighed. "Imad, I do not make personnel decisions outside my ministry."

"Well, you should."

"There are other things at play, and although he is not the shrewdest man in the government, he is incorruptible."

"He likes these people too much. He is too easily fooled."

"I am not sure any of it will matter."

"What is that supposed to mean?"

"We have been too open about this program. The Americans have learned the Natanz facility is a sham. We pumped millions of dollars into a fake facility, so if they ever did attack they would pick the remote location where the reactor was supposedly located. It was a good plan. There is no population in the immediate area. The Americans would have taken the bait and left this facility alone."

"They know Natanz is fake?" It was obvious by Mukhtar's tone that this was news to him.

"Yes, and now they and the Israelis know we have placed all of our eggs in one basket."

"I do not think they will attack. At least not by air. They are already on shaky ground with the international community."

Ashani hesitated to say what was on his mind, but a part of him wanted to take a stand. "A year ago I would have agreed with you."

"What has changed?"

They reached the elevator and faced each other. They were the same height. Ashani was slender where Mukhtar was boxy. In a conspiratorial whisper Ashani said, "Our good friend has been a bit too verbose about his desire to see Israel wiped off the face of the map."

"You don't share his views?" Mukhtar asked with suspicion.

"I said no such thing. I am simply questioning the wisdom of making the threat before you can back it up."

Mukhtar nodded ever so subtly. "There is no undoing the past. The important thing now is to make sure this facility is secure, and I do not think this halfwit is up to the task."

Ashani did not want to be pulled any further into this mess. "I am not as convinced as you that they will not attack by air. A single B-2 bomber could enter our airspace and we would never see it. They fly at fifty thousand feet and can carry a payload in excess of forty thousand pounds. I have no doubt that the Americans have designed a new weapon that is capable of penetrating each and every floor of this facility."

"They would need a nuke." Mukhtar shook his head. "And they would never do that. Besides, the Americans aren't my concern. Their hands are tied with the mess they've created in Iraq. Their European allies would have no patience for such an attack. It is the Jews that worry me, and the Americans aren't about to give them one of their B-2s."

"Then how will the Jews stop us?"

"The obvious answer is that they will continue to harass. They will kill more scientists if they have to, but that will only slow us down. Eventually, they will try to destroy this place. The only question is how."

Ashani did not particularly care for Mukhtar. The man had a violent streak that made him hard to like in a civilized environment, but he was not someone to be dismissed lightly. He had succeeded where nations had failed. The suicide and rocket attacks that he launched at Israel year after year were the reason behind the Jews' decision to finally give up some land. It was not the United Nations and their threats of sanctions. It was not Egypt, Syria, Jordan, and the other Arab neighbors threatening war. That had been tried one too many times, and the Jews had proven themselves extremely difficult to evict from the tiny scab of land. He was a fighter who had the uncanny ability to predict the actions of his adversaries.

Ashani was about to speak when Farahani interrupted them with the news that the scientist in question was already having lunch in the café. The doors opened to the large elevator and Ashani gestured for Mukhtar to enter first. The head of Hezbollah hesitated, made an unconscious grimace, and then stepped into the steel box. Ashani observed the man's behavior with a new interest. He followed him into the elevator and walked to the far wall where Mukhtar had positioned himself like a cornered animal. It occurred to Ashani that the head of Hezbollah did not like confined spaces. As the door shut, he watched Mukhtar close his eyes and mumble something to himself. Ashani filed the information away.

The elevator lurched and began moving very slowly. Ashani looked at the numbers above the door and in a faraway voice said, "Damien Chaussepied."

"Who?" Mukhtar asked in a terse tone.

"Damien Chaussepied. Have you ever heard of him?"

"No."

"He was a French contractor working at the Osirak reactor in Iraq back in nineteen eighty-one."

"And why are you bringing him up?"

"He turned out to be an Israeli spy. He placed homing beacons throughout the facility, so the Israeli pilots knew exactly where to drop their bombs."

"And the Israelis killed him," Farahani scoffed. "That is how they treat the people they recruit."

Ashani ignored the head of security and focused on Mukhtar. "He was supposedly killed in the air strike."

"Supposedly?"

"That is what the Iraqis and the French claim. I have never believed it."

"Why?"

"Over the years there has been certain information that points to the French DGSE working with Mossad on this operation."

Farahani scoffed. "That sounds like typical Zionist propaganda."

Mukhtar ignored the head of security and asked, "You said he died in the raid."

"That is what they claim."

"Did they find his body?"

"They found parts of a body. There was a lot of damage done to the facility."

"So you think the French worked both sides of the deal."

Ashani nodded. "They were paid millions to help build it, and then they helped the Israelis destroy it."

"That is pure speculation," Farahani responded.

"Conjecture," Ashani stressed, "based on certain information that you are not privy to."

Farahani's face formed a disagreeing frown.

"I see you are skeptical, so let me ask you a simple question. Do you trust our Russian friends who are helping us build our nuclear program?"

"Yes."

Mukhtar laughed out loud. "Then you are a fool. The Russians are worse than the Saudis. They would sell their own children if they were offered enough money."

Ashani had just begun to open his mouth. He was going to add his own anecdotal information about the Russians, but the words never got past his lips. Something very wrong happened at that exact moment, and even though Ashani did not yet know what it was, he knew it was not good.

It began as a rumble that appeared to come from beneath them. At first Ashani thought it was remote and somewhat muffled, but any such hope was quickly extinguished by a much louder explosion that grew with intensity. The elevator shook, the lights flickered, and then to Ashani's horror he felt himself being pulled toward the door as the air was sucked from within the elevator compartment. Time froze for the briefest moment as all three men stared at each other in shock and then one by one they began gasping for air. In the midst of dealing with their most immediate need, which was to fill their lungs with oxygen, their relatively tiny space was hit by a much larger secondary explosion. All at once the elevator shot upwards, hung in the air for a second, and then came crashing back down. The safety cable snapped tight and the box lurched to a violent stop, knocking all three men to the floor. The lights again flickered but managed to stay on.

Ashani rolled onto his side and ended up face-to-face with Mukhtar. The terrorist's eyes were wide with fear. Ashani continued holding his breath and looked toward the door. There was a hissing noise as air rushed back into the space. It had a burnt smell to it, but was breathable. Farahani got to his knees and reached for the control buttons.

"We need to get out of here. They target the elevator shafts."

Mukhtar gasped for air and asked, "What?"

"The Americans target the ventilation ducts and elevator shafts."

Ashani rose to one knee. He could feel the elevator moving again. He was well aware of the American bombing strategy of trying to drop their laser guided

66

bunker-buster bombs through air shafts. Knowing this, they had taken special precautions to foil such an attack. Not a single duct or shaft went directly from the surface to the last subfloor where the reactor was located. Additionally, every elevator shaft had extra shielding on the surface.

Farahani was attempting to pry open the door with his fingers while Mukhtar banged his fist against the door-open button.

Ashani stayed on one knee. He was not convinced that leaving the relative security of the elevator was such a good idea. What they had just experienced was undoubtedly the first wave of bombs. There would surely be more. Suddenly, there was a noise that was so ominous it caused Ashani to reflexively cringe. It started as a groan, steadily growing in both volume and pitch. Almost something you would expect from some large mammal about to expire. The groaning was joined by loud popping noises. The elevator shook once again, knocking Farahani off balance and into Mukhtar, pinning him in the corner.

For Ashani, there was something strangely familiar about the noise he had just heard, but he couldn't place it. All of a sudden, the doors began to slide open, and from his position on one knee Ashani was greeted with a sight that made absolutely no sense. Having been underground for the entire morning the last thing he thought he would see was blue sky. They had always assumed the Americans or the Jews would attack at night. In the midst of the explosions he had lost track of time. Almost as an afterthought it occurred to him that something else was wrong. Day or night, he shouldn't have been able to look at the sky. He should have been looking at the ground floor ceiling.

Mukhtar pushed Farahani off him toward the now fully opened doors. Ashani stood and took a tentative step forward. His brain was still telling him that something was wrong. He kept going back to that horrible screeching noise. Like a fog rolling in off the ocean, a cloud of dust floated up from below obscuring everything beyond the door. Alarm bells began sounding in Ashani's brain as he realized what was going on. He had heard that screeching noise once many years before, when he'd participated in a clandestine raid against an Iraqi oil platform. It was the sound of steel twisting and snapping.

Farahani ran out of the elevator and dropped like a rock. His scream floated up from below. Mukhtar was right on his heels. For Ashani what happened next was more a reaction than a decision. His arm shot out and grabbed Mukhtar by the back of his shirt. The master terrorist hung on the edge for a second, one foot safely in the elevator, the other floating above what could have been certain death. Slowly, Ashani pulled Mukhtar back into the elevator. Almost immediately, he knew he had missed a great opportunity. And if Ashani had even a glimpse of the problems that Mukhtar would create for him in the ensuing weeks, he would have shoved him to his death right then and there.

9

R app stared out the window of the Gulfstream 5 as the landing gear thudded into the locked position. Rivera reached out and grabbed his hand, which he took as a good sign, considering the fact that she had been mute for most of the morning. Rapp had never excelled in the relationship department. He was sure if he sat down with a shrink he or she would be able to surmise his problems in a few minutes. Maybe less. His father had died of a heart attack when he was young, his high school sweetheart had perished in the Pan Am Lockerbie tragedy, and his wife had been murdered just two short years ago. Add to that his inherent lack of trust in people, and you were left with a person who was better suited for bachelorhood. Being the realist that he was, Rapp should have found solace in the knowledge that he was better off alone. He didn't, though. There was a gaping hole where he expected his life to be at this point. He was growing tired of the solitude. Not the job so much. He was still extremely passionate about that. It was more what it did to his personal life.

Rivera offered hope, though. Yes, her Latina temper could bare its fangs over the most inconsequential things, but the woman had a sense of proportion when it mattered and even more importantly a sense of duty and sacrifice. That was something Anna had never understood. His wife claimed to know why he did what he did, but she was never entirely on board. How could she have been? She was a reporter, and he was a clandestine operative for the CIA. She fundamentally believed that media had a right to know everything the government was doing. He fundamentally believed there were certain things a civilized society was better off not knowing. If they had taken one of those premarriage tests they would have failed miserably. Even so it wouldn't have deterred them. They were madly in love, and not a day passed where he didn't long to hold her in his arms once more.

"What are you thinking about?"

Rivera's words yanked Rapp back to the here and now like a slap to the face. He slowly turned and looked into the caramel eyes of the woman he had slept with less than a day ago. As bad as he was with relationships, he wasn't so stupid as to tell her he was thinking about his deceased wife.

"I'm just wondering why they need me in Atlanta."

Rapp was referring to his boss, CIA Director Irene Kennedy. She had called and had their plane diverted while it was over the Gulf of Mexico.

"She didn't tell you why?"

"Only that the president needed to talk to me."

Rivera got nervous. "You don't think?"

"No." Rapp shook his head. He knew what she was hinting at. The president knew nothing of Garret's role in the death of his wife.

Rivera looked past Rapp out the window for a moment and then slowly let her gaze fall on him. She squeezed his hand and said, "I want you to know that I think I know why you did what you did last night, and I'm not mad."

Rapp was surprised. "Really?"

Rapp had arrived back at the beach a little before 4:00 in the morning to find Rivera waiting for him. She was sitting at the tree line holding the secure radio looking worried. He walked out of the surf and across the soft sand not knowing what to expect but was fairly certain she was not going to be happy with him. For a brief moment, he even considered lying to her. Since the plan was to kill Garret on the second night, he thought about telling her he was doing some reconnaissance, but the lie wouldn't hold up for long. The wife was sure to report him missing as soon as she awoke. They needed to leave the country before the police started poking around.

Rapp walked up to her and extended his hand. She grabbed it, and he pulled her to her feet.

She looked him in the eye for a long moment and then asked, "You killed him, didn't you?"

Rapp hesitated and then said, "Yes."

After studying him with her discerning eyes, Rivera nodded and in a very casual tone said, "We'd better pack up and get out of here."

Rapp was expecting more of a confrontation. He followed her up to the house, pretty sure the interrogation would ensue later. While Rivera got started sanitizing the place, Rapp called the pilots and told them to get the plane ready. It took them less than an hour to put everything in order. As the Eastern sky was beginning to brighten, he threw their bags into the back of their rented Toyota FJ Cruiser and locked up the house.

They'd flown into Golfito on a rented corporate jet flown by former military pilots who were paid well to keep their mouths shut. Entering the country had given Rapp little concern. He and Rivera had landed at the small Golfito airport where the customs and immigration controls were almost nonexistent. An advance team had already made arrangements for a vehicle and the house. The only downside was all the nosy realtors who trolled the airport looking for potential buyers. The real estate boom had finally reached the remote southern part of Costa Rica. There were a lot of Americans who were living in the area trying to make their fortune. It was not unusual for private jets to land at the small airport, but it was not so common as to not be noticed. There was a chance that some aggressive reporter might try to run down the lead, but it wouldn't get them very far. Rapp and Rivera were traveling with Mexican passports.

They were wheels up and heading north shortly before 7:00 a.m. A few hours later they touched down in Cancun and pulled into a private hangar where they changed planes as well as identities. This time they were Bob and Susan Luther, a married couple from Nashville. The next leg of their journey was to take them to Houston, but shortly after takeoff they received the call from Langley. Not wanting to go into detail over an unsecured line, Rapp's boss explained to him that the president wanted his counsel on an urgent matter. She was with him in Atlanta, and they would be traveling back to Washington shortly after lunch.

Rivera had been quiet for most of the flight. She kept her head buried in a book and for the most part ignored Rapp. The fact that she was now telling him she understood why he had taken care of Garret himself was a good sign.

"You are very good at what you do," Rivera said. "It scares me sometimes, but that's not the point. There was a lot riding on this, and it had to go down perfectly. As much as I wanted to choke the life out of that piece of trash, it was foolish of me to think that I should be the one to do it."

"Thank you. I'm glad you understand."

"Now it's your turn."

"My turn?"

"To apologize." Rivera brushed her shiny black hair back over her shoulder and twisted in her seat. Smiling, she said, "Come on. Let's hear it."

"Hear what?"

"Your apology for not telling me what you were up to."

"I . . ." Rapp stammered.

"You thought you knew best, and you were afraid of how I would react, so you got me drunk, slept with me, and then snuck out of bed and went and took care of the job all by yourself."

"That's not entirely true." Rapp wriggled uncomfortably in his seat. "I never planned on . . ."

"Yes, you did," she cut him off. "You may not want to admit it, but you were thinking it from the moment we began discussing the operation. And I have no problem with your decision."

"You wouldn't have been upset? You wouldn't have argued with me?"

"I might have, but in the end I would have respected your decision."

Rapp laughed in disbelief.

"So your way is better?" Rivera shot him a watch-your-step sideways glance. "I'm your partner. I'm your backup. If things go south I'm supposed to be there to bail your ass out. I can't very well do that if I'm asleep."

"I left the radio turned on. If things got tough I would have called you."

Rivera withdrew her hand and folded her arms across her chest. "Don't tell me you're one of those guys that can't admit he's wrong to a woman."

"That's not it at all."

"Then what is it? I told you that I respect your tactical decision to take the lead on this one. All I'm looking for is for you to admit that you should have kept me in the loop."

"Fine . . . I should have kept you in the loop."

Rivera smiled. "That wasn't very hard, was it?"

"Actually, it was."

Rivera smiled and then leaned over and kissed him on the lips. "I know who you are, Mitch. I'm not going to try and change you. At least not very much. Maybe just smooth out your rough edges a bit."

10

The Atlanta International Airport was one of the busiest in the world, and thanks to a certain 747 parked alone on a remote section of the tarmac, it was about to become the most backed-up airport in the world. The presidential motorcade didn't just stop ground traffic, it stopped air traffic as well. The caravan of cars, limousines, SUVs, vans, and motorcycles raced across the smooth concrete tarmac like they were late to catch a plane. They weren't, but the men and women in charge of moving the president and his entourage knew that minutes meant money. The Secret Service worked very closely with local officials and authorities to make sure things ran smoothly. In this modern era of jet-setting commanders in chief they were acutely aware of the negative economic impact a visiting president could have on an airport. If you shut down a major hub like Atlanta for thirty minutes, it could back up the entire region and beyond, costing millions to air carriers and lost productivity to fliers.

Taking that into consideration, the folks from the 89th Airlift Wing and the Secret Service give it their all to make sure the plane is ready to roll the second the president is on board. The pool reporters had already been bused from the event at Ebenezer Baptist Church where the president had launched his inner-city faith initiative. They'd gone up a second set of stairs closer to the tail of the plane and were now settled and buckled in for takeoff. The Air Force crew had already completed their preflight checklist and had the four General Electric engines humming and ready.

As the motorcade approached the massive white and blue 747-200B, vehicles began to peel off. Normally, a line of dignitaries would have been at the bottom of the stairs but the president was in a hurry so it was canceled. Before the first Cadillac DTS Presidential Limousine stopped at the red carpet, doors began opening. Men in dark suits and a few women began joining those already standing post around the plane. President Alexander stepped from the back of his limousine and moved toward the forward set of stairs. He paused just long enough to take CIA Director Irene Kennedy by the elbow and start up the stairs with her. The president's national security advisor and chief of staff were right on their heels. Three agents from his personal detail followed while more agents hurried up the second set of stairs.

Barely thirty seconds after arrival, the stairs were being pulled away from the craft and the vehicles were off to another part of the airport where they would be loaded onto cargo planes from the 89th Airlift Wing. The Air Force ground crew yanked the bright yellow blocks from the landing gear and gave the signal that everything was clear. A senior airman in an orange vest and headset walked out past the nose of the plane and gave the area one more visual check to make sure it was clear. He held up his signal sticks and started motioning for the plane to follow him. After the wheels began to roll, the airman walked off to the port side and saluted as the big beautiful bird rolled past.

Inside, President Alexander and his closest advisors were filing into the conference room where Rapp was waiting.

Rapp stood and said, "Mr. President, I apologize for my appearance." He was wearing a pair of worn khaki cargo pants, a faded polo shirt, and a suit coat he'd borrowed from one of the Secret Service agents. To make matters worse, he hadn't shaved in five days.

"Don't worry." The president took off his suit coat and threw it on the couch across from the conference table. "By the looks of you, I'm assuming you were off doing something I don't want to know about."

Rapp almost laughed, but thought better of it. He was momentarily at a loss for words.

The president read his discomfort and flashed Rapp one of his Southern grins. "I'm just kidding. Take a seat and buckle up."

All five people settled into the fixed leather chairs. The president sat at the head of the table; his National Security Advisor, Frank Ozark, sat immediately to his right and then Ted Byrne, his chief of staff. Rapp and Kennedy were on the other side of the table with Kennedy sitting closest to the president.

As the plane began to roll, the president looked at an Air Force officer standing in the door and said, "As soon as we reach altitude I want the call placed."

"Yes, sir." The man saluted and closed the door.

With the powerful engines roaring outside, Rapp put his mouth within inches of Kennedy's ear and said, "Would you mind telling me what the hell is going on?"

Kennedy had already grabbed the file in anticipation of this question. She opened it, revealing a satellite image, and slid it between them. "Do you recognize this?"

Rapp studied the picture intently while he scratched the thick black stubble on his face. "It's the Isfahan facility. Isn't it?"

"Yes." Kennedy showed him a second photo that at first glance appeared to be the same as the first.

"What am I looking for?" Rapp asked.

Kennedy tapped her finger on the upper right quadrant of the photo. "Right there."

Rapp's eyes moved back and forth several times to both the before and after shots. "Is that a cloud of smoke?"

"It would appear so." Kennedy removed both photos and laid out two new ones. These were blown-up shots focusing on the immediate area of interest. In the first one you could clearly see the large air-conditioning units on the roof. In the second one everything was obscured by a large debris cloud.

"What the hell happened?" Rapp asked in a hushed voice.

"We're not sure."

"So it wasn't us?"

"No."

"Then it had to be the Israelis."

"One would assume." Kennedy showed him another photo while the plane taxied to the main runway. The debris cloud was clear in this shot.

Rapp studied the shot for a few seconds and then asked the obvious question. "Where the hell is the roof?"

"It appears to have fallen into that large hole."

Rapp was trying to make sense of it all. "Let's back up for a moment. When did this happen?"

"Shortly after noon today. Tehran time."

"We have real-time footage?"

"Partial. The NRO is analyzing it as we speak." Kennedy was referring to the National Reconnaissance Office.

"Have you talked to Ben?" Rapp was referring to Ben Freidman, Kennedy's equal at Mossad.

"He hasn't returned any of my calls."

Rapp shook his head. "That's not a good sign."

"Possibly, but I would imagine he has his hands full."

"Or he's dodging you. How about their ambassador?"

"Nothing so far. State has reached out to him, but he claims he knows even less than we do."

"He's probably telling the truth." Rapp glanced over at the president who was talking to his chief of staff and national security advisor. Moving closer to Kennedy, he asked, "Why am I here? This all seems a bit above my pay grade at this point."

Kennedy pulled her reading glasses to the tip of her nose and said, "I have no idea."

Rapp's brow furrowed in disbelief. "Come on."

"Seriously. I found out about this right before I gave him his morning briefing." Kennedy tapped one of the satellite photos. "That was why he had me come on the trip. Midway between DC and Atlanta he went into his office to make a call. Ten minutes later he emerged and told me he wanted you on the return flight to DC."

Rapp leaned back in his chair, folded his arms, considered the possible implications of the president's sudden interest in him and muttered, "I wonder who in the hell he talked to."

11

In the last year Rapp had sat through more video-conferences than he had in all his previous years of government service combined. The post–9/11 counterterrorism bureaucracy had exploded from a few hundred dedicated men and women at the CIA, FBI, State, and a handful of other agencies to thousands of people with a combined budget of more than a billion dollars a year. In the grand tradition of Capitol Hill, the politicians had thrown vast amounts of money at the problem whether it was needed or not.

New agencies were created like Homeland Security, the National Counterterrorism Center, and the Terrorist Threat Integration Center. Agencies that Rapp didn't even know existed like the National Geospatial Intelligence Agency were elevated in importance and brought into the big tent of counterterrorism. Rapp still wasn't exactly sure what the Geospatial gang did, but he did know they had a shiny new headquarters and a budget big enough to embarrass a lobbyist. Add to this satellite offices in major cities all over the world, the ever-burgeoning counterterrorism operations at Defense, Justice, and State, and you were left with an unwieldy bureaucracy that was about as agile as a ballistic missile submarine in the Potomac River.

One of Rapp's great fears had come to pass. Talented people and countless resources had been sucked into the support side of the business as opposed to the operations side, where it was really needed. And because one of the great lessons of 9/11 was that not enough people were talking to each other, the dictum had come down from Capitol Hill that everyone was to play nice and share information. Hence the boom in videoconferences. It had become a way of life, but not one that Rapp embraced.

A forty-inch plasma screen hung on the far wall of the conference room opposite the president. It was currently split in two, with Secretary of Defense Brad England on the left and Secretary of State Sunny Wicka on the right. President Alexander had been in office a little over a year, and fortunately for the young leader his administration had thus far avoided any major international conflicts. That was all about to change. Rapp had heard good things from Kennedy about the president's national security team, which was reassuring given the seeming gravity of whatever had happened at the Iranian nuclear facility. As with most videoconferences, Rapp's plan was to say as little as possible. He was very suspicious of the claims made by the communications folks that the lines were secure. Whenever you started bouncing communications off satellites Rapp assumed someone was capturing those signals and decrypting them.

"Brad," the president started, "I'm sorry for pulling you off the slopes."

"That's all right, Mr. President, it's part of the job." England had been taking a long weekend at his mountaintop retreat in Beaver Creek, Colorado. He was in his early fifties and despite his gray hair, he had a very boyish way about him. A former big gun for Merrill Lynch, England fit into the president's plan of putting private sector people in his cabinet.

"Hello, Sunny," the president greeted the secretary of state. "Have you heard anything further from the Israeli ambassador?"

"No. At least not anything useful."

Wicka was at her desk in Foggy Bottom. Rapp knew

his boss and Wicka had a good relationship. He took it as a good sign that she didn't have five of her underlings sitting in on the call.

"Has the foreign minister returned your call?" the president asked.

"Yes. I just got off the phone with her."

"And?"

"Officially, the Israeli government has no idea what happened at the Isfahan facility."

"Unofficially?" the president asked.

Wicka twirled a black Mont Blanc pen in her right hand. At seventy-one she looked a decade younger than her age. "There are some rumblings that a certain outfit may have had a hand in it."

The president turned and looked at Kennedy who was immediately to his left.

"Director General Freidman," Kennedy said, "has not returned any of my phone calls."

"Is that unusual behavior for him?" President Alexander asked.

"Not necessarily," Kennedy said in an even tone.

Rapp kept his editorial comments to himself. He had known Ben Freidman for a long time and had worked very closely with the Mossad on at least a half dozen operations. Freidman would do whatever it took to protect his beloved Israel. He was unapologetic in his belief that Israel should be the one that benefited at every juncture of their relationship. Rapp respected the man's abilities and tenacity, but he never lost sight of the fact that Freidman would sell him down the river if it meant giving his country the slightest edge.

"What are we hearing from Iran?" Alexander asked the group.

Wicka was the first to chime in. "Nothing official."

"The National Security Agency is reporting a huge spike in communications," Ozark answered.

"What kind?" Alexander asked.

"Everything. Cell phone traffic, Internet, military, civilian critical response, religious leadership, politicians . . . the whole country is talking."

"What about the media?"

The secretary of state fielded the question. "Twenty minutes ago al-Jazeera broke into their newscast with footage of fire trucks and ambulances entering the base."

The president pondered that thought for a moment and then looked at the plasma screen. "Brad, what are the Joint Chiefs telling you?"

"We had two AWACS on station." The secretary of defense was referring to the Air Force's E-3 Airborne Warning and Control System. "One over Baghdad and the other out over the Northern Gulf. Nothing moved through that airspace this morning that wasn't either ours or the Brits'."

"They're sure?" the president pressed.

"Yes," London hesitated. "There is, however, one extremely remote possibility."

"What's that?"

"If the Israelis have developed a stealth bomber, it is possible that they could have pulled it off, but the entire Joint Chiefs think this is not a realistic scenario."

"Irene?" the president asked the director of the CIA.

"We've heard nothing along those lines. Our own B-2s cost over two billion dollars apiece. Their economy could never support that kind of expenditure, and even if they could, why would they risk flying it in broad daylight?"

"I agree," said England.

"Satellite photos?" the president asked.

"The NRO should have a report for us within the hour." Kennedy took off her reading glasses and set them on her briefing book.

"I have a preliminary report from my bomb damage assessment experts," England announced. "They say they see no evidence of an air strike."

The room went quiet for a full ten seconds and then the president asked, "So we're left with what?"

Kennedy picked up a pen, tapped it on her leather briefing book a few times, and in a soft voice said, "Sabotage or disaster."

"Disaster?"

"The Iranians aren't exactly known for their stringent building codes. They've had structural engineering problems before, usually during earthquakes, but they did have a relatively new apartment complex collapse a few years ago. It turned out the builder was using substandard practices. Almost a hundred people died."

"And you think they would allow substandard

building practices on a project this important?" the president's chief of staff asked.

"One would think not, but I've learned the hard way that the Iranians can be very hard to predict."

President Alexander thought it over. After a few seconds he looked at Rapp and asked, "Any thoughts?"

Rapp briefly considered censoring what he was about to say and then decided it wouldn't matter. "Without having all the facts I'd say there's a ninety-five percent chance the Israelis are behind whatever happened. There's a remote chance the collapse was due to shoddy construction, but I really don't think it's going to matter."

"Why?" the president asked.

"The Persian ego will never admit to such a failure. Even if this thing collapsed on its own they will blame Israel. Either way they will be looking for blood."

"I agree," Secretary of State Wicka jumped in. "The only thing I would add is that they are likely to blame us as well."

"Any chance you can get their foreign minister talking?" the president asked.

"I don't think so. I expect them to close ranks on this one and let Amatullah do the talking. This would be a good time to use our back-door channel."

Alexander looked surprised. "I wasn't aware we had one."

Kennedy cleared her throat. "After 9/11, sir, we opened a line with Iran's Ministry of Intelligence. They are not big fans of al-Qaeda and the other Sunni terrorist groups. They had been keeping tabs on the Taliban and al-Qaeda for some time. They gave us crucial intel that helped us in the early months of the war."

"Who do you talk to?"

"Azad Ashani. My counterpart."

"Do you trust him?"

"Trust might be a bit strong, but I consider him to be pretty levelheaded."

"All right. See what you can find out. What about the Israelis? Is it time for me to give the prime minister a call?"

"I don't think so," said Secretary of State Wicka. "I don't want to put you in a position where he might have to lie to you. The rest of us should see what we can find out first."

"I agree," said Ted Byrne.

"Fine." The president checked his watch. "I need to make a phone call. Let's reconvene in an hour." The president looked to his national security advisor and added, "I want all the key players in the Oval Office once we land."

"Yes, sir."

Alexander stood and looked at Rapp. "Mitch, would you come with me, please? There's something I want to talk to you about."

12

It was dark by the time Azad Ashani arrived at the offices of the Supreme Leader Ali Hoseini-Nassiri. He was tired, and growing more annoyed with each coughing attack. It had been a grueling day that started with a 5:00 a.m. trip to the airport for the flight to Isfahan. He had just completed the return trip on a military flight after spending all afternoon at the nuclear facility trying to discern exactly what had happened.

After he had saved Mukhtar from the fate of falling to his death like Ali Farahani, things went from bleak to dismal. A cloud of dust and debris had come billowing into the elevator and coated every millimeter of Ashani's body. He was forced to cower in the corner and take tight, shallow breaths through his dress shirt that he had pulled up to cover his mouth and nose. More than once he wondered if his survival was in question. With his eyes burning from the dust and each breath growing more difficult than the previous, he thought of his wife and precious daughters and wondered how they would fend for themselves in a country whose future was so uncertain.

When the fine particles finally floated back to the ground, everything was covered with a thick film of gray concrete dust. Ashani rose from his spot in the corner of the elevator feeling as if someone had laid a heavy blanket over him. The dust cascaded off his body in sheets. He walked to the threshold of the elevator and looked out at the carnage. It was as if a long-dormant volcano had awoken and spewed its gray ash down upon the landscape.

Ashani stood at the edge peering through the settling dust at the destruction beneath him and felt a deep sadness for his country. He had not been a supporter of the nuclear program, and he surely wasn't a proponent of taunting the West before they had achieved the weapons to back up their rhetoric, but this was simply too much to take for the fragile Persian ego. An ego that relied on accomplishments that were thousands of years old. Such total and absolute destruction was unthinkable.

It was one thing to see a building with a few relatively small holes where bunker-buster bombs had penetrated. They had discussed this many times. The consensus was that the bombs would not be able to penetrate the first layer of defense, let alone all four. It was conceivable that the upper floors would be ruined. There was even a little-known plan that had been discussed only at the highest level. If the Jews and their handlers were lucky enough to penetrate every level and destroy the reactor, they were going to lie to the world and their own people. They would tell them the facility had survived. True or not, it was deemed the people would need to hold on to the illusion that their engineers could stop anything the Americans and their lapdog could throw at them.

But, this, Ashani thought as he looked over the edge. *The total and complete destruction of the facility will be impossible to hide. Their inferiority was now laid bare for the entire world to see.*

He stood in awe of the Americans and their technology. Israeli pilots or not, it was still the Americans who had developed some new bomb able to defeat the best that the Iranian engineers could construct. How had they so precisely targeted the facility as to get it to implode on itself? Had they known all along that they could totally annihilate the facility at a time of their choosing, and if they did, had they intentionally allowed his country to pour a billion dollars into the project? As someone who had played in the arena of espionage for more than two decades, Ashani was momentarily unnerved by the possibility that his enemies had masterminded such an operation.

Rescue workers snapped him from his literal pit of despair. Using ropes they pulled Ashani and Mukhtar out of the elevator. The two men were given water to clear their eyes and cleanse their mouths. Medical personnel looked him over, and before Ashani knew it he had an entirely new set of problems to worry about. Breathing in concrete dust was bad enough, but if it were radioactive he'd be lucky to live to the end of the month. Ashani and Mukhtar were stripped naked and run through decontamination tents where they were hosed down, scrubbed three separate times, and given blue worker's coveralls to wear. A doctor working in conjunction with one of the scientists who had been lucky enough to be out of the building at the time of the attack told them the levels of radiation were acceptable. Ashani did not find their views reassuring. Understating problems to the populace was just the type of thing for which his government was notorious.

The coughing had started almost immediately. The doctor told him tiny concrete particles had lodged in his throat and lungs. He counseled him that the coughing was his body's natural way of cleansing itself. The quack told Ashani he'd begin to feel better in a day or two. Ashani knew better. He had seen the documentary *Sicko* by Michael Moore. A brilliant piece of anti-American propaganda, the movie followed a handful of rescue workers who had worked at Ground Zero in the massive cleanup effort after 9/11 as they tried to navigate America's crass, profit-driven medical system. Years later those men were still suffering from horrible respiratory problems, and more than a few had died.

It wasn't until mid-afternoon that Ashani began to realize that he might be looking at things the wrong way. Rescue workers in protective gear were lowered into the massive chasm to see if there were any signs of life. Iran was no stranger to earthquakes, so the first responders had been trained to pick through the rubble with dogs and a variety of devices that helped detect potential survivors. After being assured again by an army officer that the radiation levels were acceptable, Ashani returned to the edge to watch. It was then, peering down into the chasm, that he began to recognize that his initial assumptions had been wrong.

The gray dust covered everything, but you could still see cracks and heaved slabs of concrete. Nowhere, though, were there any round holes with twisted and smashed rebar marking the spot where the bombs had penetrated the roof and first floor. Ashani walked the entire perimeter, stepping over debris while he searched for the telltale sign that was always left by a bunker-busting bomb. When he was done encircling the pit, he looked skyward and it occurred to him for the first time that something entirely different may have happened.

It was at that very moment that panic set in among the rescue workers. Several of the men down on the pile were carrying Geiger counters. One of them announced that he'd found a hot spot that hadn't been there minutes before. One by one the other Geiger counters began chirping like canaries in a coal mine. It was as if an unseen and deadly fog had begun to roll across the pile of destruction. This was what the scientists from the Atomic Energy Organization had most feared. The reactor had melted down. Highly radioactive fission products were releasing into the environment from beneath the debris. The scientists had an emergency plan in the event of a reactor failure, and they wasted no time putting it into play. The rescue workers were ordered out of the hole and decontaminated while the calls went out to the local quarries.

Twenty minutes later the first cement truck pulled up

and dumped its load into the billion-dollar pit. Another truck arrived a few minutes after the first. Within an hour twin-axle mixing trucks were lined up two dozen deep, two trucks dumping at a time. The hopes and pride of the Iranian people were unceremoniously buried under a slag heap of radioactive concrete.

A military transport brought Ashani and Mukhtar back just before dinner. President Amatullah had called an evening meeting of the Supreme National Security Council or SNSC. Ashani stopped home just long enough to shower and put on a suit. He kissed his wife and daughters and left for his office, where his deputy ministers were waiting to brief him. With only twenty minutes to spare he listened while each deputy reported on what they were hearing. The quick briefing confirmed Ashani's belief that the entire government was operating under the premise that the Americans or Jews had decimated the facility with a surgical air strike.

Ashani asked if air defenses had picked up any radar contacts before or after the attack. Two deputies gave contradicting reports. A third deputy interjected that he had talked with an Iran Air pilot who told him he saw Israeli jets in the area. By now the story was all over the news. Ashani told his deputy to call the pilot back immediately and make sure the man was not fabricating the story for his own self-aggrandizement. The Persian populace had a unique way of inserting themselves into the periphery of a national crisis like this. Ashani stressed that the deputy tell the pilot he would be thrown in jail and tortured mercilessly if he found out the man was lying to him.

Ashani left for the office of the Supreme Leader at a quarter past eight in the evening. By the time he arrived he had a splitting headache. He knew the upcoming meeting was the cause. The blame game would be in full swing. The peacock president would be intolerable. Ashani normally held his tongue in these meetings, especially when the Supreme Leader was in attendance, but tonight might be different. The realization that he had almost lost his life earlier in the day made him feel less circumspect.

Gripped by another coughing fit, Ashani wondered if a quarter of a century had just been taken from him. If he would spend the next year or two struggling for every breath. And for what? That was the big question. None of this had been his idea. He was the one who had advised against seeking the bomb for this very reason. He had known for some time that Amatullah and his cronies were bad for the future of Iran, but tonight those feelings were suddenly crystallized and pushed to the surface. Ashani decided that he would no longer sit by quietly and allow Amatullah to misstate the facts.

13

Air Force One

The president's office on Air Force One was right next to the conference room, just a few steps away. The proximity left Rapp only a few seconds to ponder the commander in chief's character and why he had taken such a sudden interest in him. At forty-six Alexander ranked as one of the youngest men elected to the top office. He was easy to like, but Rapp had a deep-seated distrust of all politicians. Too often their party and their own political careers took a front seat to national security. Agencies like the CIA were a dumping ground for problems, regularly used as a pawn in the game played by the two parties. If something went right it was the politician who took credit, but if something bad happened they were quick to lay the blame at the feet of Langley. They weren't all that way, of course. Rapp knew of a handful of senators and congressmen who could be counted on. Men and women who knew what was at stake. Men and women who knew how to provide oversight and keep their mouths shut.

Rapp followed the president into his office. At six-two Alexander was an inch taller than Rapp. He was thin, maybe 190 pounds, with a full head of sandy brown hair. His hazel eyes had an alertness that stopped just short of being overly intense. Alexander walked straight across the room between his desk and credenza. He sat in a fixed, high-back leather chair identical to the one in the conference room. The chair could be swiveled and moved as well as locked into position for takeoffs and landings. An identical chair sat across from the desk up against the starboard side of the craft. Rapp eyed the long leather couch and decided it looked less confining. He plopped down, spread his arms out across the back and crossed his left leg over his right.

Alexander eyed a piece of paper on his desk. When he was done reading it, he tore it in half and fed it into a shredder. "You're probably wondering why I asked you to join me on the trip back to Washington."

"When presidents call on me, I assume I've done something to piss them off."

Alexander smiled, producing a set of elongated dimples. "I wouldn't know about that. My immediate predecessor holds you in very high regard."

Rapp nodded. There had been some rough patches, but for the most part he had gotten along very well with President Hayes. "Did he also tell you I can be a real pain in the ass?"

The smile stayed on Alexander's face. "He didn't have to. In that regard your reputation precedes you." Alexander pushed a button on the side of his chair and the back reclined. He spun the chair and put his feet up on the corner of his desk. "You are very good at what you do, Mitch. One of the last things President Hayes told me before leaving office was to use you wisely."

"Use?" Rapp repeated the word, vaguely amused that Alexander had chosen it.

"Maybe *deploy* is a better choice. Maybe *cut loose* is even better. The point is, I'm not foolish enough to think we live in a world where violence is never the answer. There are moments when force will have to be met with force."

Rapp liked what he was hearing. "I couldn't agree more."

"You have many talents, Mitch. What would you say is your greatest asset?"

"I'm the wrong guy to ask, sir."

"So we can add modesty to your long list of strengths. Well, I'm a politician, so I can't really say being humble is part of my job description. Having said that, though, I do think we have something in common."

Rapp raised one of his thick black eyebrows in a manner that said he was intrigued. Internally he wondered what attributes he could possibly share with a refined, calculating politician like Alexander.

"I read the report you prepared last year. The one that outlined how Iran would react if we took out their nuclear program."

Rapp nodded. He had written the report before Alexander had taken office. Due to the sensitivity of the subject matter, the distribution was very limited. Rapp was more than a little surprised that Alexander had both gotten his hands on a copy and that he had taken the time to read it.

"In light of recent events, are you still willing to stand by what you wrote?"

Rapp took a second to recall the specifics of the report. "Since we didn't actually bomb them, it's less clear-cut, but for the most part I think they will react the way I predicted."

"They'll use Hezbollah and its affiliates to launch a series of terrorist attacks and conduct kidnappings of Americans abroad."

"They'll hit Israel first, and then they'll come after us."

"You're sure?"

"Ninety-nine percent. It's not in their character to do nothing."

The president thought about Rapp's comment and then asked, "So you think Israel was behind this?"

"I've known Ben Freidman for a long time, sir. I've worked very closely with the Mossad. They have a track record of conducting extremely audacious operations. Operations that we would never dream of."

"Why is that?"

"Survival. They're a lot closer to it than we are."

"It?" the president asked.

"The heart of radical Islam. They don't have enough real estate to sit back and wait, so short of all-out war, they do what they can to slow the crazy bastards down, like killing those three Iranian scientists last year."

"My greatest fear as president is losing a city," Alexander said in a heavy voice. "I know they're out there . . . these fanatical jihadists. It's what keeps me up at night. Knowing that they are recruiting . . . training . . . planning . . . looking for any opening to strike. That they would love nothing more than to level an entire city, every man, woman, and child."

"You got that right, sir."

Alexander's face showed his frustration. "There are too many people in my party who think that violence is never the answer. It's a very enlightened and alluring argument when made in a civil society that has a relatively efficient justice system. Even more so when unchallenged in the lecture halls of academia, but in the real world," Alexander shook his head, "it's a bunch of bullshit."

"You'll get no argument from me, sir."

"I didn't think so. Back to the attribute that we share . . . it's called vision. Having a sense of how things will play out when certain things are set in motion. I recognized it in your report. I think you understand the mind-set of the Iranian leadership better than anyone I've encountered in my administration."

"Thank you, sir."

Alexander grew tentative for a moment and then lowered his voice. "President Hayes told me about your sausage factory analogy."

Rapp nodded. "The people want to eat it, they just don't want to see how it's made."

"Exactly. Which brings me to the reason why I have asked you to join me." Alexander took his feet down and leaned forward, placing his forearms on the desk.

"I am not going to sit here and play by Queensbury rules while the Iranians send their proxies off to wage a war of terror."

Rapp sat up a little straighter. "I'm listening."

"Did you know I played football at Alabama?"

"I seem to remember hearing something about that during the campaign."

"I was a backup quarterback. Got hurt during spring practice my junior year and never fully recovered. I was there for Bryant's last year and then Perkins. I learned two big lessons. The first, if you plan on running for governor of Georgia someday, you should attend the University of Georgia or Georgia Tech. Not Alabama. I saw a double-digit lead in the polls evaporate the week my alma mater faced off against the Bulldogs. I barely held on to win. Lesson two, blitz."

"Excuse me?"

"Blitz hard and blitz often, and remember, this is coming from an ex-quarterback. You have to have the athletes and the speed to do it, of course, but there is nothing that can screw an offense up quicker than a defense that knows how to blitz. Do you remember Alabama's nineteen-ninety-two National Championship team?"

"No."

"Their offense was average, but their defense may have been the best that college football has ever seen. They put ten guys up on the line almost every play. They came so hard, and so fast, on every snap that opposing offenses were fighting to not lose yards. All they could do was try to react and adjust . . . find some magic way to slow these guys down. Offenses aren't good at that. They're supposed to make defenses react and adjust. Not the other way around.".

"I think I'm with you," Rapp said.

"I want you to put together a game plan," Alexander said eagerly. "A list, really. The who's who of Hezbollah and anyone else that might give us a problem. It stays between the two of us and Irene. We review it, and then it gets shredded. I don't want any copies. I don't want any paper trails."

"I can do that."

"Good. If we get even the slightest whiff that Iran is going to use Hezbollah to do its dirty work I want ten guys up on the line of scrimmage. And I'm not just talking about targeted air strikes. I want you to be creative. I want you to put them back on their heels. I want you to make them fear for their lives."

Rapp smiled and slowly nodded. "I would be more than happy to do that, sir."

14

TEHRAN, IRAN

Ashani followed one of the Supreme Leader's bodyguards into the meeting chamber and took a seat on one of the long couches. The minister of intelligence found the room depressing. The clerics who considered themselves the guardians of the revolution had gone overboard in their effort to purge the opulence of the shah. The room had been stripped of all paintings and decorative adornments. The walls were white, and the two large windows were covered with a cheap gray fabric that qualified as a curtain only in the sense that it helped block the sun. The carpeting was brown, relatively new, and cheap. The wood-frame couches were embarrassing. Covered in an inexpensive floral pattern, they looked as if they could be found in any remnant store the world over.

Ashani was reminded of a recent state visit by the king of Saudi Arabia. Not a single hotel in the capital met the monarch's standards, so a team of decorators flew in the week before on a 747 loaded with furniture, art, rugs, and all sorts of amenities to make the king's stay more bearable. The monarch had come to this exact room for an audience with the Supreme Leader. The entire Saudi delegation was mortified that a leader of a country with the resources of Iran would have such little regard for the trappings of international diplomacy.

Ashani knew it was all part of a great effort by the clerics who ran his country to show their Arab brothers that they were better Muslims. The Saudis and their Sunni sect of Islam may have been the custodians of Mecca and Medina, but the Shia held true to the prophet. Unlike the Saudis, they heeded the call of Muhammad and rejected a life of possessions and opulence. Ashani, however, knew this to be an act. Many of these same clerics who publicly abhorred modernity, were surrounded by luxuries in their homes. They spent thousands of dollars having their robes and vests custom made for them. There were a few exceptions of course, and one of them had just entered the room.

Ashani looked up and saw Ayatollah Ahmad Najar, the head of the Guardian Council. In many ways he was the second most powerful man in Iran. After he had run the Ministry of Intelligence and Security for nearly a decade, the Supreme Leader had picked him to head the council that was the behind-the-scenes arbiter and advisor to the Supreme Leader. The move had been welcomed by many at first. Najar was a hard-liner, and as minister of intelligence and information he had made life very difficult for the media and anyone who chose to disagree with the Supreme Leader. Ashani had worked for Najar for years and despite his grumpy disposition he liked him for the simple reason that there wasn't a single hypocritical bone in the man's body. If you were straightforward and respectful in your dealings with him things went smoothly. If you weren't, you ran the risk of suffering his monumental temper.

Part of their job was to make sure the media was reporting only the news that was fit to print. The Ministries of Intelligence and Information were the official censors of the revolution. Ashani could think of no better example of Najar's temper than an incident with a newspaper editor several years earlier. The paper was running a series of articles about young Muslim men and women dating. The day before they had run a photo of a young couple holding hands. Najar's fervent religious sensibilities were inflamed, and the editor was hauled in for a stern reprimand. Ashani watched with amusement as the smarmy journalist began to explain to Najar that they could not live in the past forever. The debate grew heated with the editor refusing to admit he had made a poor decision. Najar became so enraged that he threw a teapot at the man.

Ashani remembered that he was grateful that it was only a teapot. Najar carried a gun with him at all times and had been known to wave it around and point it at people when he became really upset. In this instance Najar decided that rather than draw his gun he would throw himself at the editor. Najar wrestled the man to the ground and began chewing on his arm like a dog. The editor was taken to the hospital where he received more than a dozen stitches. The incident galvanized Najar's enemies and within months he was removed from his position as minister of intelligence and information.

Any hope that Najar would be content sitting on the council of old men and simply fading away quickly vanished. In a matter of months he reformed the council and began to comment publicly and harshly about anything that led the people away from the roots of the revolution. Less known to the people, and the world at large, was the fact that Najar had been locking horns with President Amatullah with increasing frequency.

Looking back on it now Ashani could see that the Supreme Leader had elevated Najar to the council so he could act as a bulwark against the increasingly bellicose and popular Amatullah. The one steadfast rule of modern Iranian politics was that the Supreme Leader did not get his hands dirty. As the religious leader of Iran, he had a duty to stay above the fray.

Najar moved quickly across the room to where Ashani was sitting. He was wearing a long, black qabba and a white turban. His beard was mostly ashen with patches of dark gray along each side of his mouth. He looked down at Ashani, who was trying to get up, and said, "Don't you dare move. I can't believe you are here."

"I am fine," Ashani responded.

Najar reached out and clasped Ashani's right hand in both of his. "You should be in the hospital."

"It won't hurt me to sit and listen."

"I will do the talking for both of us. You don't need to worry about that."

Ashani smiled. "Thank you."

The minister of foreign affairs and the chief of the Supreme Command Council of the Armed Forces entered the room with the vice president of Atomic Energy on their heels. All three men looked sullen, none more so than the vice president of Atomic Energy. The full council had eighteen members plus the Supreme Leader, but this evening only the executive council had been asked to attend the high level meeting. All of them had heard of Ashani's near-death experience. Some expressed genuine relief that he had been saved. Others feigned concern. The problem for Ashani was that they were all such practiced liars he couldn't tell who was sincere, and who was merely politicking.

President Amatullah entered the room five minutes late, as usual. Trailing on his right was Major General Zarif of the Islamic Republican Guards Corps, and on his left was Brigadier General Suleimani of the Quds Force. Ashani would have liked to think it was merely coincidence that Amatullah had entered the room with the two military men who would be in charge of making Iran's enemies pay for the attack, but he knew the diminutive politician too well.

Amatullah was barely over the threshold when he announced, "Well, gentlemen, we finally have our excuse to push the Zionist dogs into the ocean."

Ashani stared at the vertically challenged president in his boxy, ill-fitting suit. It was one thing to lie to the press and the people; it was an entirely different matter to have the audacity to do so to men who knew better. Everyone was now seated except Amatullah, the two generals, and the head of the Guardian Council. Ashani slowly turned to witness Najar's reaction.

The fiery cleric looked through his tinted glasses at Amatullah and said, "And with what do you propose we push them into the sea?"

Amatullah remained unflinching. "General Zarif has assured me that the Republican Guard is ready and willing to fight. Over five hundred thousand men. The Jews will be lucky to field an army of a hundred thousand."

"And how will we get them there?" Najar asked with unbridled contempt. "Should we ask the Americans if we can march them across Iraq? Or should we put them on magical troop transports and float them through the Suez Canal? Do you think the Jews would allow us to put all of our men ashore, or do you think they might sink the transports while they are at sea?"

Amatullah gathered himself and in a reasonable tone said, "I was not implying that we could begin military action tomorrow or even next week. I am simply saying that the Jews and the Americans have committed an act of war and we must make them pay for it."

"I am in complete agreement, but let's not delude ourselves into thinking that we are going to push the Jews into the ocean. It was that kind of thinking that led us down this path to begin with." Najar had been an early, outspoken critic of the nuclear program.

Amatullah feigned shock. "What are you implying?"

"I am implying nothing. I am stating a fact. I was against developing this program for this very reason. I told you years ago that this was how it would end. Countless dollars and irreplaceable scientists, all gone!"

"We have a right to defend ourselves," Amatullah shouted.

"And we have a duty to the Iranian people to do so wisely!" Najar countered forcefully.

"You are both right," a calm voice announced from the doorway.

Ashani turned to see the Supreme Leader standing tall in his finest robes. The look on his face was one of intense interest. He was a thoughtful man, not known to be ruled by his emotions, and Ashani couldn't help getting the impression that Ayatollah Ali Nassiri often viewed his president and closest advisor as two bickering children.

15

AIR FORCE ONE

Rapp's preference would have been to have this conversation in person, but there was only a brief window of opportunity. He figured at a bare minimum China and Russia were tracking Air Force One with spy satellites, looking to pluck any signals that were beamed to and from the plane. The techies at the Pentagon and the National Security Agency swore that the communication links with Washington were secure, but Rapp had his doubts. Having read enough history to understand that previous scientists had given those same assurances only to be proven drastically wrong, Rapp operated under the premise that there was no such thing as a totally secure line. Even so, his business was often time sensitive, and one could not always wait to speak in person.

The president had got him thinking. Rapp had always begrudgingly admired the Iranians and the way they churned out propaganda. Their leaders understood the key to survival was to get the people to blame America and the West for all of the ills in their lives. It didn't matter if there was no substance to their accusations, it only mattered that they enflamed their people's national pride. There would be a lot of that going on in the coming weeks. America would be blamed, evidence or not. All they had to do was make the accusation and it would stick. It wouldn't matter a bit to the Iranian people that America had no hand in the destruction of their facility. So ingrained was their hatred for America that they would believe without asking their leaders for proof.

It was this realization, and the president's gloves-off attitude, that steered Rapp's thinking toward a classic clandestine operation. If Iran wanted to play fast and loose with the facts, they were automatically opening themselves up to a counterattack. One that could prove very embarrassing for their loud-mouthed president. The absence of any plane, American, Israeli, or other, over the facility at the time of its destruction left only two options. The first Rapp dismissed because he knew his Israeli counterparts all too well and because he believed the odds of an accident destroying the facility so completely were simply too large. The second option was that the Israelis did it. Again, knowing them as well as he did, he had no doubt that they had somehow managed to destroy the place.

Rapp would find out soon enough. Kennedy had called ahead and made arrangements. One of the Agency's G-5s was waiting for him at Andrews Air Force Base to take him to Tel Aviv as soon as they landed. She had also left word with her Israeli counterpart that Rapp was on the way and that until he got there it would be prudent to stay mute on the current crisis in Iran.

To put his plan into motion Rapp needed the help of someone back at Langley. He could make the call on his own satellite phone, but there was a good chance the Air Force crew on board would detect the call and go apeshit. His second option was to elicit their help and ask for the most secure line they had to Langley. More than likely this would work, but it would also alert the Russians and the Chinese that it was an important call. In the end he decided to make the call on an unsecured line. It would be flagged as routine traffic and if he stayed vague enough no one listening in would have any idea what they were talking about. Past the president's office and conference room were a section of seats for his advisors. Similar to first class on international travel, the seats were big with plenty of room. Rapp spotted an open one and grabbed it.

Some junior staffer in his mid-twenties was in the next seat. The guy tore his eyes away from his laptop and looked at Rapp with an expression that said, *Who in the hell are you?* Instead he said, "I'm sorry, but that seat is taken."

Rapp remembered his appearance was far from White House standards. He smiled and said, "That's all right. I just need to make a quick call." Rapp grabbed the phone from its cradle and started punching the number for an office in Langley, Virginia. He could tell that the guy was still looking at him.

"Are you with the press?"

Rapp glanced over. "That's a good one, junior."

"I don't see your badge," the guy said more firmly, "and the press is not allowed up here."

"Badges," Rapp said with a Mexican accent, "we don't need no stinking badges."

The staffer looked back at him with a blank expression.

"*Blazing Saddles.* You've never seen it?" Rapp could hear the phone starting to ring on the other end.

"No." The guy was not amused. "Why aren't you wearing your credentials?"

A woman's voice answered on the other end of the phone. "Rob Ridley's office. Penny speaking."

"Penny, Mitch here. Is Rob around?"

"Where are your credentials?" the staffer persisted.

"Hold on a second, Penny." Rapp covered the phone and looked the man in the eye for the first time. "Let me guess . . . law school? Ivy League, University of Michigan something like that . . . someplace that taught you to be assertive and persistent."

"Dartmouth."

"Good for you. Great school. Now get lost." Rapp stuck his thumb out and pointed toward the aisle. "I have an important call. Now would be a good time for you to hit the head."

"I do not appreciate . . ."

Rapp cut him off. "Go find Ted Byrne, and ask him who I am."

The young man reluctantly closed his laptop and left.

Rapp put the phone back to his ear and said, "Rob."

"Well, if it isn't Mr. Big Shot. I hear POTUS asked you to catch a ride with him."

"I would think that today of all days, you would have more to do than gossip."

POTUS was the acronym for president of the United States. Ridley was Deputy Director Operations, Near East Division. His division was at the center of the brewing storm. He was a former marine, a major league smartass, and one of the most capable people Rapp had ever worked with.

"You never call anymore. It's the only way I can keep tabs on you."

"What are you hearing?"

"Well . . . practically every politician in town is demanding a briefing so that they can go on TV and claim they know what they are talking about, my counterpart in Israel won't return my calls, and the phone lines between Tehran and Beirut are so hot they're melting."

"Have you been able to get a hold of a single person at Mossad?"

"Nope, and I've tried a couple end-arounds. Some

old buddies I used to tip a few with. No one is answering their phone over there."

"So you've got nothing."

"From them, but I wouldn't say nothing in general. Just nothing concrete. There are a lot of rumors flying around out there."

"How do you feel about starting another one?"

There was a pause and then, "I'm listening."

"Remember that character we met with in the Sand Box last year?" Rapp was referring to Iraq.

"I meet a lot of characters over there. You'll have to be more specific."

"The guy from PMOI."

"PMOI?"

Rapp was talking about the People's Mujahedin of Iran, but he didn't want to say it out loud. "Remember, we were at the palace and we stayed up until four in the morning drinking brandy and smoking cigars. He told us how a certain leader over there is referred to as the peacock president."

"Oh, yeah," Ridley replied. "I'm with you."

"Do you know where he is?"

"Last time I checked, he moves back and forth between Mosul and Baghdad. He's got a car parts business, if you can believe it. I hear it's booming."

"Track him down and set up a meeting."

"For when?"

"First thing tomorrow," Rapp said. "And find someone else to brief the president. You're coming with me."

"Are you going to fill me in?"

"I'll explain it all on the plane. Meet me at Andrews in two hours."

"You got it."

16

TEHRAN, IRAN

Ashani found if he took controlled, shallow breaths it helped minimize the coughing attacks. He sat hugging the arm of the couch, with the Chief of the Armed Forces to his right and the Foreign Minister next to him. The Supreme Leader sat alone in a simple chair almost directly across from Ashani. His meeting chamber was void of all technological advances. There were no computers or plasma TVs. No projectors or drop-down screens. There wasn't even a conference table for them to sit around. It was the century-old setting of kings and religious leaders. Supplicants and advisors came to plead their cases, and the monarch would lay down his edict. He was not to be bothered with details or execution. The advisors would sort things out later. The system also conveniently gave the Supreme Leader the ability to take credit for what worked and distance himself from what didn't.

The walls were bare, with one exception. A framed photograph of the Supreme Leader hung on the wall above his right shoulder. Between the Supreme

Leader's chair and the love seat where Najar and Amatullah were seated the Iranian flag stood upright in an effort to give the dull room an air of official state business. The president and head of the Guardian Council had dropped any pretense of liking each other. They were adversaries, and everyone in the room knew it. Both men sat stiffly and leaned away from one other, Najar toward the Supreme Leader and Amatullah toward Ashani.

Ashani had hesitated for only a second when his doctor told him he would like him to come straight to the hospital so he could check him out. Ashani knew it was essential that he be at this meeting, if for no other reason than to make sure Amatullah did not try to blame him for what had gone wrong, or somehow convince the Supreme Leader to rush into some foolish act of reprisal. There was one other reason, though, that continued to nag him. He was deeply worried by what he had seen when he looked down into the pit of what was not so long ago his country's epicenter of scientific advancement and national pride. More to the point, he was worried about what he didn't see.

Persian pride would demand that they hit back. Ashani and his ministry would play a crucial role in whatever they decided to do. A straight-out military counterstrike was foolish, but that wouldn't stop several key members of the council from advocating all-out war with Israel. There would be a lot of saber rattling in the coming weeks, but in the end they would find surrogates to do their dirty work. That part would not be difficult. There were plenty of impoverished Palestinians who would jump at the chance to martyr themselves.

Ashani's more immediate concern was in protecting himself and his people. Someone was going to be blamed for what had happened. One would think that the Ministry of Intelligence would be safe, but with Amatullah one never knew. The man never let the facts get in the way of his version of events. Things were going to get ugly. Alliances on the council were sure to shift as the inevitable blame game ensued. Who would try to rewrite history? Who would try to deflect? Who would stab whom in the back? Anything was possible and Ashani could not afford to be laid up in a hospital with doctors poking and prodding him.

The Supreme Leader finished leading the group in prayer and then gave his friend Najar the signal to begin.

Najar looked at Major General Dadress and said, "General, your report."

Like every man in the room Dadress had a full beard. His was thicker than the others and dyed an oily black. He had a broad forehead and a receding hairline. He was in his olive green army uniform, and he looked decidedly uncomfortable. Leaning forward, he said, "By our best estimates the attack took place shortly after noon. We had no radar contact with the bombers, so we are assuming they used the B-2 stealth bomber. We estimate that they flew near the operational ceiling of the B-2, which is fifty thousand feet."

"I seem to remember the Russians telling us their new missile system would be able to detect the Americans' stealth aircraft," Najar said in an unhappy tone.

"They claimed that the bombers would be vulnerable when they opened their bomb doors."

"And our air force detected nothing."

"Correct."

"Wonderful," Najar said in a sour tone. "Twenty-seven million dollars for a missile system that doesn't work."

Ashani's doubts were beginning to grow. He knew the science behind the stealth bombers, and they should have in fact left themselves open to detection for five to ten seconds while they dropped their payload. More worrisome, though, was the time of the bombing. Ashani had no knowledge of the Americans ever using one of the valuable stealth bombers in a daylight operation. Why would the Americans expose their billion-dollar planes during a daylight bombing run? The answer for Ashani was that they wouldn't.

"There is a pilot," Amatullah announced, "who made a positive identification of an Israeli plane in the area. My people are debriefing him at this very moment."

Najar slowly turned his head and looked at the president. "I heard your comments on TV earlier this evening, and I saw your pilot interviewed. I am not sure I believe him."

"You are a born skeptic," Amatullah countered.

"Have you not listened to anything General Dadress has told us? The Air Force detected nothing. They think the stealth bombers flew at their operational ceiling of fifty thousand feet. Commercial air traffic flies at thirty to thirty-five thousand feet. Your pilot must have very good eyes to see a plane from such a distance."

"Fifty thousand feet is an estimate by radar operators who failed to do their jobs. At this point I am more than happy to take the eyewitness account of a veteran pilot."

"Really." Najar turned to Dadress. "General, how many stealth bombers do the Israelis have?"

"None that we know of."

"And if the Americans had given them some, do you think they would paint big white and blue Stars of David on the wings?"

"No."

Najar nodded and waited to see if Amatullah had anything further to add.

"You may quibble over the specifics of how it hap-pened, but it is obvious to everyone that it was the Jews and the Americans who were behind this."

"Even so, this council would appreciate it if during a national crisis you would consult us before you rushed to get in front of the cameras."

Amatullah looked past Najar to the Supreme Leader. "My apologies."

Ayatollah Nassiri acknowledged the apology with the faintest of nods. In a soft voice he asked Najar, "How many perished?"

Najar turned to Golam Mosheni, the man in charge of the country's nuclear program, and in a much louder voice asked, "How many?"

Mosheni was a large man, probably only a few pounds shy of 300. His forehead was glistening with sweat. "Sixty-seven scientists and technicians. We were fortunate that they struck during lunch. Twenty-three scientists and technicians were on their break when the bombs fell."

"Fortunate." Amatullah repeated in a whimsical tone. "I'm not sure I would use that word to describe anything that you are associated with."

There it was, Ashani thought. Amatullah had chosen his scapegoat. He had been a champion of Mosheni for years, touting him as the man who held the hopes of the future of Iran. In addition to running the nuclear program, it appeared that the diminutive president expected him to stop foreign incursions into their airspace.

"It could have been worse," Mosheni replied in a weak effort to defend himself.

Amatullah clasped his hands in his lap. His short legs barely touched the floor. "Our nuclear program has been destroyed, we have a toxic hole in the middle of our second largest city, and the West is laughing at us. Please tell us how it could have been worse?" He unclasped his hands and threw them up in the air. "I would love for you to explain to us how it could have been worse."

Mosheni's face grew flushed. He kept his mouth closed and refused to speak. His discomfort and embarrassment was obvious.

"Has the radioactive fallout been contained?" Najar asked.

"Yes."

"The rest of the facility?"

"The equipment can be salvaged, but it will have to be moved to a different location."

"Natanz?" Najar asked.

"That would be my recommendation."

Najar swiveled his head to look at Amatullah. "I seem to remember you advocating Isfahan to be the main nuclear site over Natanz. Something to do with the fact that the Americans would never attack a site in the middle of a city."

The head of the Guardian Council was referring to the country's two main nuclear sites. Natanz was buried in a mountain hundreds of miles away from Isfahan in a remote location. There had been a heated debate years earlier over where to put the most crucial parts of the program. Isfahan was pushed by Amatullah for the reason already stated and because the country's scientists lobbied hard for the site. They did not want to have to relocate their families to the remote region of Natanz.

Amatullah bought time with one of his sly grins. "I did no such thing. I merely passed along the recommendations of others." The president glanced at the vice president for atomic energy.

"I seem to remember you guaranteeing this council that Isfahan could survive anything the Americans could throw at it?"

"If I made such a guarantee it was based on the advice of those who know about such things."

"You made the guarantee. I remember it very well."

Amatullah exhaled in frustration. "Experts who do not work for me stated that the facility could withstand anything short of a nuclear strike. Obviously, the Americans have come up with a new weapon. I am a politician, not a scientist, my friend. I am not a military expert nor am I an oracle who can see the future."

"Maybe we will have to be less trusting of your word from now on."

Amatullah looked deeply offended. "If you want to blame me for what happened today, I am truly insulted. I did not come here to discuss the past. I am here because I want to know how we are going to make the Jews and Americans pay for this." The president took a moment to glance around the room and make eye contact with each man. "It is understandable that some of us are upset, but we must put that anger aside and focus on striking back at our enemies. Who in this room was not behind our nuclear program?"

"We will strike back at our enemies," Najar said in a measured tone, "but there must be accountability. Not everyone on this council was as behind this program as you were. Several of us feared this was exactly where we would end up. Pouring countless treasure into a program that would one day be destroyed by our enemies. If I had known that you were going to speak so freely to the press about our right to develop nuclear weapons and your desire to see Israel wiped off the face of the map, I would have never supported this."

"I . . ." Amatullah started to speak.

"Do not interrupt me," Najar said sharply. "I think you should be removed from office." The cleric paused to let Amatullah know just how serious he was. "But unfortunately, we can't do that right now. Do you know why?"

Amatullah shook his head.

"We can't do it because the Jews would be dancing in the street. It would be a dual victory for them. Whether I like it or not, you are exactly who we need to galvanize our people and get them focused on the retribution that must be meted out."

Amatullah's face transformed from worry to pride and then elation. "The people will be behind us, I can promise you that. We will strike back at the Jews and the Americans like never before, and I know exactly where to hit them. We will make them pay for their arrogance. We will destroy them."

17

AIR FORCE ONE

Rapp approached the president's office door and knocked. He waited a second and then entered. Alexander was behind his desk, and Kennedy was sitting across from him in a chair. Rapp closed the door and sat on the arm of the couch immediately to his right.

Kennedy looked at him and said, "We're discussing what I should say to Azad."

Rapp thought of the Iranian intelligence minister and shrugged his shoulders. "I heard about your little accident. I'd like to say sorry, but the truth is we've been quietly hoping the Israelis would take care of this for some time."

"I don't think that will work."

"It's the truth."

"What did you find out?" the president asked.

"The Israelis aren't talking to anyone. From the top down to the mid-level guys, no one is answering their phones."

"Your assessment?"

"They did it," Rapp said plainly.

"You're sure?"

"One Hundred Percent."

"Mitch," Kennedy said cautiously, "you can't give that kind of guarantee."

"All right . . . ninety-nine point nine, nine, nine."

"Explain." The president leaned back and crossed his legs.

"The Israelis are very insular. They can close ranks like no other outfit I've ever worked with. They're trying to get their story straight. Figure out if they can weather this and lie to the world that they had no involvement in it."

"But why wouldn't they have given us some signal that this was coming?" Alexander asked.

"Easier to ask for forgiveness than permission," Kennedy answered.

"Exactly," said Rapp.

The president thought about it for second and then asked, "What if it was an accident?"

"This was no accident, sir. Israel was behind it, and their silence is all the proof we need. If they honestly had nothing to do with this they would be calling us asking why we didn't give them a heads-up. My guess is that this was a very tight operation run by a very limited team within Mossad, possibly including a few people from the military, the prime minister, and one or two cabinet ministers. I don't know how they did it, but they caught the Iranians flatfooted. The analysts back at Langley reviewed the satellite footage, and there is absolutely no sign of any activity prior to the place collapsing. No response from the guard barracks on site, no rush of people fleeing any of the buildings. No sign of anything unusual."

"And why is that significant?"

"There were no gunshots. If this thing were a full-blown commando raid, you would have seen a reaction from the base security. This is part of why the Iranians think it was an air strike. No one alerted them that anything was wrong. One minute the place was there, the next minute it wasn't. The logical assumption for them is that it was stealth bombers even though to the best of my knowledge we've never conducted a daylight bombing run with ours."

The president looked over at Kennedy. "I know I've asked this, but is it possible that the Israelis have developed their own stealth plane?"

"Highly unlikely."

"But possible."

Rapp waved his hands in front of him, signifying not to go down that road. "The Israelis don't have the money to develop a plane like that, and even if they did, there's still one other piece of evidence that points to an inside job. When you get back to Washington, Secretary England is going to give you a bomb damage assessment report from the Pentagon. I haven't seen it, but I know what it's going to say."

"How?"

"Because I've been there. I've been in the field marking targets for these flyboys when they drop their bunker-busters. I've crawled down into a few of those command and control centers after they've been hit, and they don't look like the satellite photos we've seen of this place. Holes are made, parts of floors and ceilings collapse, and everything inside is charred, but it doesn't look like the earth opened up and swallowed the whole damn building."

"Then what was it?"

"They had some people on the inside and they've probably had them there for some time. They were able to move unnoticed, place the charges, and blow the building. It's the only thing that makes sense."

The president swiveled his chair and thought about what he'd heard. After a long moment he looked up and said, "What does it really matter if the Israelis destroyed it by air or by any other means? In the end they are still the ones who destroyed it."

Rapp smiled. "It matters because it gives us an

opportunity to create an alternative truth and make the Iranians look like they are lying to their own people and the world."

The president was speechless for a second. He looked at Kennedy briefly and then back at Rapp. "I have no idea what you're talking about."

"Neither do I," Kennedy added.

"Have you ever heard of a group called the People's Mujahedin of Iran? The PMOI? They're a group that falls loosely under the control of the National Council of Resistance of Iran. It's made up of dissidents of all different stripes. They live mostly in Europe. They're scientists, teachers, artists . . . pretty much anyone who felt repressed by the clerics and decided to leave. They were around during the revolution back in seventy-nine and then found out they weren't welcome at the table after the shah fled. In 1981 hundreds of their top members were rounded up and taken to Evin Prison, where Khomeini had them shot. The PMOI is also referred to as the MEK. These guys have been our saving grace in Northern Iraq. Every time the Sunnis get out of line or the Iranians send one of their Badr Brigades into the area to cause trouble, we call in the MEK and they make the problem go away."

"Aren't they on a terrorist list?" the president asked.

"Bad move by the previous administration. They thought they could get some brownie points with Iran, which was foolish, but now's not the time to get into it. The important thing is that the MEK has become a force to be reckoned with. There are a few reasons why Mosul is far more peaceful than Baghdad or Basra, and one of the biggest ones is the MEK. The Iranian government hates these guys with a passion, and MEK suffers no lost love for the hard-line clerics."

"So how do they figure into the current crisis?"

"They don't," Rapp said with a grin, "but we're going to make them part of it."

18

TEHRAN, IRAN

A shani felt as if he had been sucked into some alternate universe where up was down and down was up. It was one thing to put on a brave face and plot a proper course of retribution, but this was simply nonsense. The man who had put them in this tenuous position was yet again going to be the chief propagandist in the next phase of the conflict. The last thing they needed was more inflamed rhetoric and promises of grand retribution. The council needed a reality check. Under normal circumstances Ashani would have never thought of confronting Amatullah in front of the Supreme Leader, but it was different now. Something had changed within him, and he had no doubt it was precipitated by his close brush with death earlier in the day.

He had always known Amatullah was perhaps the most reckless and arrogant man in the government.

His inflammatory words more than anything else were what had gotten them into this national crisis. There was no limit to the man's ability to delude himself and others. He was incapable of understanding the obvious. Iran's nuclear program was in shambles. Literally, not a speck of equipment was salvageable. All of their intelligence estimates told them that Israel had in excess of one hundred nuclear devices and America had so many they spent hundreds of millions of dollars decommissioning old ones. The idea that they could bring utter devastation to either country was simply ludicrous.

Emboldened by his near-death experience, Ashani looked at the diminutive leader and asked, "And just how are we going to destroy them?"

"What?" Amatullah was caught off guard by the question.

"I said, how are going to destroy them?" he asked with a slight edge.

"We will launch wave after wave of martyrs. We will target their infrastructure. We will bring their economy to its knees." Amatullah dismissed his intelligence boss with an irritating frown.

Ashani was not to be deterred. "The 9/11 attacks were nothing more than a twenty-four-hour flu for their economy. They bounced back even stronger than before."

"We will make 9/11 seem like it was nothing."

Ashani gave Amatullah a doubtful look. "And you think the Americans will sit there and take it?"

"Yes. They cannot afford to go to war with us. They have learned their lesson in Iraq."

"What if you're wrong? Suppose they *are* willing to go to war with us. According to you, they are behind this attack which by de facto means they are willing to risk open war."

"Never." Amatullah shook his head vigorously. "That is why they had Israel drop the bombs. They themselves did not have the courage to confront us."

The man's absolute confidence in his ability to predict what the Americans would do was unnerving. Ashani turned and looked at the Supreme Leader. "Mark my words. If we push the Americans too far, they will strike back."

"They will never invade," Amatullah said dismissively.

"I did not say they would invade. They will drop bombs, and plenty of them."

Amatullah scoffed at the threat. "And we will hit them everywhere. Not just in America, but all over the world. We will bring their aviation industry to its knees. We will disrupt oil flow and their economy will collapse."

Ashani shook his head sadly. "Escalation will lead to escalation. They will rain bombs down on us like nothing we have ever seen. Mark my words, they will destroy our entire air force on the first day, and then they will turn their sights on us." Ashani paused to look around the room, letting each man know that this time their own hides might be on the line. "It will take time for our martyrs to strike, and their success is not guaranteed. The Americans, on the other hand, have us surrounded. They have bases in Iraq and Afghanistan, and they have two aircraft carriers in the gulf. If war starts, they will send a third and maybe even a fourth and fifth carrier."

"Good," Amatullah proclaimed. "Let them pack all of their vaunted carriers into the gulf, where they will be that much easier to sink." He leaned forward and pointed at himself. "We control the Strait of Hormuz. Not them."

"You underestimate the Americans if you think they are dumb enough to put five carriers in the gulf. They will move their marine and navy air units to Qatar, the UAE, or Bahrain. They will have us surrounded on three sides."

"Never!" Amatullah shook his head vigorously. "Our Arab brothers would never commit such a treacherous act."

"Our Arab brothers are not exactly enthralled with our growing influence in Iraq. Don't be so sure of their support, and even if they do as you say, the Americans can operate from the Arabian Sea. They will decimate our entire infrastructure within one week. Every refinery, every pipeline and rail line will be severed. All telecommunications facilities and power plants will be demolished. Except in the north, of course, where they will leave everything in place and begin arming the Kurds. It will take years for our already fragile economy to recover, and we will have to deal with an insurrection in the north."

"You underestimate the strength of our people," Amatullah said dismissively. "Unlike the Americans, who are fat and lazy, our people know how to sacrifice and make do."

"And you," Ashani shot back, "overestimate your popularity with the people. Don't be so sure they won't turn on you when their power is out and they have no food on the table."

"You traitor!" Amatullah yelled. "How dare you!"

Ayatollah Najar reached over and grabbed Amatullah's arm. "Both of you," he said firmly, "need to remember who you are in the presence of."

Both Ashani and Amatullah looked at the Supreme Leader and then averted their eyes in either a sign of compliance or humiliation. The Supreme Leader sat stoically in his chair, his arms at his sides and his long fingers draped over his knees. By design or nature the man gave off an air of tranquility.

In a measured, confident voice he said, "We have been attacked." He took the time to look each man in the eye before moving on. "It is our just right to demand retribution in both blood and treasure." He glanced at his minister of Foreign Affairs. "You will take our case to the United Nations. Those responsible will have to pay." His gazed shifted to Ashani and Amatullah. "We must move carefully. It would appear that the United States has yet again used Israel to do the work of the devil."

Every man in the room save Ashani nodded in agreement.

"There is a chance," Ashani started, "that the United States did not have knowledge of this act."

"Do you think they are mourning our loss?"

"No, but I would like to remind the council that the Americans have rid us of both Saddam and the Taliban. We have a back channel with their government. I would like to see what I can find out before we take action."

"Lies," Amatullah bellowed. "That is what you will find out."

Ashani ignored Amatullah. "I do not see what harm it could do to hear what they have to say."

Amatullah tried to speak, but the Supreme Leader silenced him with a disapproving look. He took a moment to straighten his robes and then said, "The right hand does not always need to know what the left hand is doing."

Ashani had grown used to these imprecise proclamations from the Supreme Leader. It allowed him to keep his hands clean. The problem, as Ashani knew all too well, was that his edicts left too much room for interpretation.

"There is nothing wrong in finding out what the Americans have to say, but do not trust them. I will leave the details to all of you, but I want to be clear about one thing. This attack cannot go unpunished."

The members of the council nodded enthusiastically, and a few broke into applause. Ashani had the sinking feeling that they were going down a dangerous road paved with emotion and national pride. The thought of where it might lead them brought on a violent coughing fit. Ashani doubled over in pain. The other members of the council grew concerned until at last it stopped.

"Excuse me," Ashani said sheepishly. He felt a wetness on his chin and drew the back of his hand across his mouth. He looked down with embarrassment to see it was covered in blood.

The Supreme Leader looked at him with grave concern and said, "My son, you should be in the hospital."

"My apologies. I will go at once." Ashani stood and bowed. He felt a sudden shortness of breath. He took two steps toward the door, wavered, and collapsed.

19

WHITE HOUSE

On a slow day Washington, DC, was an electric city. People flocked to the capital from all over the world to conduct business, espionage, and a myriad of other activities legal and illegal. The city was home to countless nonprofits, trade organizations, and financial institutions, and the second-largest hub of journalists outside of New York City. Counting Baltimore, there were six major pro sports teams and another dozen college teams to cheer for. Everything, however, took a backseat to politics. A potential showdown with Iran had the town running on adrenaline. The city had awakened to find the papers plastered with photos of an angry Iranian president and aerial shots of Iran's destroyed nuclear facility. Every TV and radio channel was buzzing with the story. Iran was blaming the United States and Israel. Thus far Israel had remained silent, but the administration had released a statement through Sue Glusman, the White House press secretary, saying they had absolutely no involvement whatsoever in the accident.

Kennedy had stressed to Glusman and the president that they should refer to the incident as an accident until Iran could prove otherwise. Kennedy was running on a few hours' sleep. After landing at Andrews Air Force base the day before, she had hopped a helicopter out to Langley, where she worked until 11:00. Her driver took her home. She thanked her mother for watching her son, Tommy, kissed the sleeping boy on the forehead, and then grabbed five hours of sleep, before waking up, kissing her still-sleeping son on the forehead again, and then heading back to the office, all before the sun was up. This was, unfortunately, more common than she would have liked. The director of the CIA didn't mind the work, but she did mind being away from her son.

Kennedy's armor-plated Suburban pulled through the Secret Service checkpoint at the Southwest Gate and rolled up to the ground floor entrance. As requested by the president, she was early. An 8:00 a.m. meeting of the National Security Council was scheduled, and Alexander wanted Kennedy to bring him up to speed on any overnight developments beforehand. The director of the CIA said good morning to the Secret Service uniformed officer who was sitting just inside the door. She continued down the hall and took the stairs up one level. When she entered the president's private dining room, she was momentarily surprised to find both Secretary of State Wicka and Secretary of Defense England.

The silver-haired secretary of defense was about to stick a spoonful of oatmeal in his mouth when he saw Kennedy. In his typical cut-to-the-chase mode he said, "I love Rapp's idea. The president was just filling us in. These guys never let the truth get in the way of their message. I say it's time we give them a little taste of their own medicine."

Kennedy smiled uncomfortably, which caused the gregarious England to laugh.

He pointed across the table to the president and said, "I told you she wouldn't like it that you told us."

Secretary of State Wicka was sitting directly across the table from Kennedy. She frowned at England and said, "That's because she is one of the few people in this town who can keep a secret."

"Don't worry, Irene," England said. "You don't survive in investment banking by running around shooting your mouth off. At least not for very long." England was referring to his tenure at Merrill Lynch and Piper Jaffray. The president had brought him on board because he wanted an analytical businessman to help him drag the Pentagon into the new millennium.

Alexander gestured at the one remaining chair and said, "Please sit."

Kennedy set her briefcase next to the chair and handed her coat to a navy steward.

"What would you like this morning, Dr. Kennedy?"

"The usual, José. Thank you."

The president pushed his plate of half-eaten eggs and sausage to the side and wiped the corners of his mouth with a white napkin. "Mitch was right about the bomb damage assessment report?"

"My experts," England said, "concur, with one exception."

Kennedy sat and asked, "What is that?"

"One analyst thinks the Israelis dropped a low-yield tactical nuke into the place."

"Interesting. One of my people brought up a similar scenario last night. What led your analyst to decide it was a nuke?"

"Not so much evidence as plausibility. He says the other way is too complicated. Too many variables."

Kennedy thought about it for a moment and asked, "How does he say the weapon was delivered?"

"That's where his argument gets a little thin. Possibly a cruise missile."

"Our satellites would have picked up a missile launch."

"More than likely. He also thinks there is a good chance the Israelis must have developed a stealth bomber."

Kennedy glanced at the president and then looked back at England. "Your people probably have a better handle on this than my people do. Do *they* think it's that Israel developed a stealth bomber?"

"No," England said emphatically. "I put the question out last night and all my experts are in agreement that they just don't have the money."

"They might not need as much money as you think," Wicka said.

"How so?" the president asked.

"They have a history of stealing what they need. That's how they developed their own nuclear weapons program. We did all the research, development, and testing and they came in and stole all of our data. They even stole nuclear materials from us to make their first bomb."

The president looked at Kennedy. "Is this true?"

"I'm afraid so. It happened in the sixties. They stole approximately two hundred pounds of highly enriched uranium."

"I agree it's possible," England said, "but it is still highly unlikely. Remember this attack happened in broad daylight. My imaging people went back and reviewed every airfield in the country. They paid special attention to the bases in the Negev. They came up with nothing. Every takeoff they discovered was corroborated by other tracking assets. It's too big of a leap of faith to buy into the idea that Israel secretly developed a multibillion-dollar plane and then flew it during the day."

"So you agree with Mitch's theory," Kennedy said.
"Yes."

The president took a sip of coffee and then said,

"And we're all in agreement that Mitch's plan could work?"

One by one the president's three advisors agreed.

The president looked at Secretary of State Wicka. "You have any problem lying to the United Nations?"

Wicka beamed with amusement and then laughed. "If I was afraid of skirting the truth in that den of pathological liars, I would not be a very good secretary of state. What did you say Mitch called it? Creating an alternative truth."

"Yes."

"I like that. The UN runs on alternative truths. All of them self-serving, of course."

"Wonderful." The president turned to Kennedy. "What about your meeting with the Iranian intel chief?"

"It has been agreed to in principle. The details are being worked out."

"Where will it take place?"

"Mosul. That is where we have met in the past."

The president glanced at Wicka. "Do you have any problems with this?"

"The State Department has no official and very few unofficial ties with Iran. I think this is the right move."

Glancing at Kennedy he asked, "Have you heard from Mitch?"

Kennedy checked her watch. "He should be landing in Tel Aviv shortly."

"You think they'll give him a straight answer?" Wicka asked.

Kennedy thought it over for a second. "I'm not sure it will matter. They'll love Mitch's idea for the simple reason it will give them diplomatic cover. It'll muddy the waters enough to give countries on the UN Security Council a reason to vote against whatever sanctions Iran asks for."

"You honestly don't think they'll tell him?" Alexander asked in a surprised tone.

"Mr. President, they are a tough bunch. If anyone can get them to talk, though, it would be Mitch."

20

TEL AVIV, ISRAEL

The Gulfstream 5 landed at Ben Gurion International Airport, where it was met by a refueling truck. After the tanks were topped off, the pilots were directed to a dilapidated hangar far away from the commercial terminal. The CIA pilots eased the plane's ninety-three-and-a-half-foot wingspan through the hundred-foot opening with great care and then shut the engines down. Mitch Rapp looked out the port side window and checked out the men who were assembled to greet him. They looked like misfits from some Cold War–era film about to handle a prisoner exchange at Checkpoint Charlie.

Rapp unbuckled his seat belt and stood. He looked over at Rob Ridley, who was about to get up. "Stay put."

"Yeah, right." The chief of the CIA's Near East Division began to stand up.

Rapp put a firm hand on his friend's shoulder and pushed him back down. "I'm serious."

"We just finished a twelve-hour flight," Ridley complained. "Are you out of your mind? I need to stretch my legs."

"Yeah . . . well, if you get off this plane, I might have to break your legs. So stay put until I tell you otherwise."

"I swear you were raised by a pack of wolves. Why do you always have to threaten violence?"

"Just sit tight. You know how secretive Ben is." Rapp moved past Ridley and stopped next to Marcus Dumond, Langley's resident computer genius and hacker extraordinaire.

Dumond looked up at Rapp and asked, "What's up?"

"Sit tight until I've had a chance to talk to Ben. He doesn't like strange faces."

Rapp proceeded forward and lowered the stairs. He tilted his head to the right to get through the opening and moved stiffly down the short run of steps. Rapp was dressed in black dress pants and a loose-fitting, untucked Bugatchi short-sleeve shirt. His black Italian loafers hit the smooth concrete floor, and he started toward the director general of Mossad. With his thick stubble and shaggy black hair he looked more native to the region than the men he was walking toward. This was not his normal attire, but it allowed him to fit in. Too many security contractors flew into the region wearing 5.11 tan, tactical clothing, and SWAT boots. They stood out like a sore thumb among the locals, which in a way served as a deterrent. A kind of don't-mess-with-me sign. I carry a gun, and I have the permission to shoot anyone who messes with me. The flip side of that was that it also marked them. Rapp didn't want that. Where he was headed, he needed to blend in.

Rapp proceeded across the hangar toward Freidman, who was flanked by two huge men who looked as if they were waiting for Freidman to give them the okay to snap Rapp in half. Freidman himself was no wilting flower. He stood five feet ten inches tall and weighed at least 250 pounds. Set atop his bull-like shoulders and neck was a bald shiny head with heavy jowls. In his day he'd been known to do a lot of the heavy lifting himself. Now in his late sixties, he left that to men like the two standing next to him.

As Rapp neared, he said, "Ben, good of you to come out here and meet me."

Freidman's acerbic expression remained unchanged. "I think of you every day when I get out of bed."

"You can still get a hard-on after all these years?" Rapp asked. "Good for you, you old dog."

The bone crusher on Freidman's right took a half step forward.

"Easy, killer," Rapp said. "I don't want to have to kick your ass in front of your boss and your twin brother here."

"I am referring to the bullet hole you put in my leg," Freidman continued.

"Well, Ben," Rapp said, "I hate to think what you would have done to *me* if I had been dumb enough to assassinate an Israeli citizen and got caught trying to interfere in your country's political process."

Freidman raised his chin in defiance and ignored his two bodyguards, who were now looking at him.

"What . . . you didn't tell Mongo and Loid here?" Rapp asked with feigned shock. "I'd be happy to fill them in on the little operation you were running against your country's most loyal ally. It went like this, boys . . ."

"Enough!" Freidman shouted. "Wait for me outside," he snapped at the two men. Like obedient Rottweilers following the command of an owner, they turned and left without having to be told a second time. As soon as they were out of listening range, Israel's chief spy snarled, "What do you want?"

"You look a little haggard, Ben. Not enough sleep lately?"

"The only reason I am here is because your president requested that I meet you. What do you want?"

"I don't want anything, Ben."

Freidman scoffed. "I suppose you flew all this way because you missed my pretty face."

"No, I flew all this way to thank you."

The Israeli spy chief rolled his eyes. "For what?"

"For doing us all a favor and destroying Iran's nuclear program."

Freidman stared Rapp straight in the eye and said, "I have no idea what you are talking about."

Rapp put one foot in front of the other, crossed his arms, and admiringly said, "I think you're the best liar I've ever met, Ben."

"That means a lot, coming from someone as accomplished as you."

"Thank you. Now let's get serious. I know you destroyed that facility, and you know you destroyed that facility. I'm on your side. I told President Alexander you guys did us a huge favor."

"We did not drop bombs on that facility. I don't care what that crazy little man has said. . . . No Israeli planes were anywhere near his country when this attack occurred, which leaves me with only one conclusion."

Rapp smiled. "This should be good." He waved his hand toward himself. "Let's hear it."

"I think maybe it was American planes that were spotted over Isfahan."

"Yeah, right. One of our pilots decided enough was enough and he just went and bombed the hell out of that place without getting approval from the Pentagon or the president."

"All I'm saying is that this plane that was reportedly seen over Isfahan was not one of ours, which means it was more than likely one of yours."

"You're unbelievable. I fly almost six thousand miles to save your ass and you think I'm dumb enough to buy some load of crap like that?"

"I don't remember asking you to save my ass."

"You didn't, but I'm going to anyway."

"I don't need your help."

"The hell you don't," Rapp said with frustration building. He took a step back and then admitted, "Maybe I was the wrong guy for the president to send, considering our history, but here it is. I am sincerely grateful that you guys had the balls to do what needed to be done. The president, while he can never say so publicly, feels the same way. I have permission from him to launch an operation that will take the blame off you guys, and expose the Iranian leadership for the lying bastards that they are."

"I don't . . ."

Rapp cut him off. "Ben, please let me finish. I know you did it, and I know how you did it. There was no plane or planes. No missiles. Nothing like that. You had someone on the inside. You guys blew that damn thing up and it collapsed into a nice little pile right on top of itself. I admire you for it, and if you weren't such a pain in the ass I'd probably give you a hug right now."

Freidman's already sour face twisted into a deeper frown. "How many people have you discussed this with?"

"Only Irene and the president."

Freidman exhaled and took a look around the hangar. The pained look on his face said it all. He was deeply troubled that Rapp knew one of his government's most closely kept secrets. "What are your sources?"

Rapp smiled. For Freidman to ask such a question

was as close to an admission as he was ever going to get. "I've got a friend in your building." Rapp knew the lie would drive Freidman nuts. Changing gears, he said, "I need you to get your government on the same page. Stay silent. Keep denying. Whatever you need to do. I don't care what kind of evidence the Iranians say they have, just don't admit you were behind this thing. They're going to show up at the UN on Friday and try to pin this whole thing on you. After they've presented their case, we're going to pull the rug right out from underneath them and leave them looking like lying fools."

Freidman was intrigued. "What do you have planned?"

"Don't worry. You'll see soon enough. Again the president sends his thanks. I don't like you, Ben, but I sure as hell admire your audacity." Rapp turned and started walking away.

"Where are you going?" Freidman yelled.

"To Northern Iraq," Rapp shouted over his shoulder. "To bail your ass out."

21

TEHRAN, IRAN

Ashani had spent the night in the hospital under sedation. He woke up in the morning with a screaming headache and a vague memory of the meeting he had attended the evening before. His wife and daughters were there to explain what had happened and offer comfort. They made a great joke out of the fact the doctor wanted him to abstain from work and talking for at least two days. His lungs were operating at ten percent of their normal capacity due to the amount of dust he had inhaled. The doctors tried to remain positive. They told him that with rest, and antibiotics to ward off an infection, he should be back to himself in a week or so. Ashani got the distinct impression they were lying to him.

Deputies from the Ministry of Intelligence began showing up at his bedside by mid morning to deliver briefings and keep him apprised of what was going on. At first these were nothing more than routine reports, although in the wake of the attack on Isfahan there was a new sense of importance to everything. His wife hovered nearby and twice she tried to stop people from getting into the room. While Ashani appreciated her trying to protect him, it was not realistic. He needed to know what was going on.

It was shortly after noon when Ashani started to get the feeling that trouble was brewing. There were little signs here and there that Amatullah was putting the country on a full-blown war footing. To a certain degree this was fine. It would force the Americans and the Israelis to react. Putting bases on high alert and organizing protests was one thing, but ordering the entire Iranian Submarine Fleet to sea was an entirely different matter. The Americans were very skittish about the Kilo-class submarines his country had purchased from Russia. Putting all of them to sea as well as the minisubs and the noisy Iranian-made subs would make the Americans even more skittish.

Ashani was sipping his lunch through a straw when his number two entered the room with a box of chocolates and a worried expression. The man leaned over him so that no one else in the room could hear and he whispered, "We have problems."

Ashani had known Firouz Mehrala Jalali for sixteen years. He was not prone to exaggeration. The worried look on his face told him the problem was internal. Ashani lifted his hands from his lap and made a shooing motion. Four people filed out of the room, but his wife held her ground. Ashani's jaw line tightened and he jerked his head toward the door. His wife shook her head in disappointment and left.

Jalali pulled up a chair and sat at the edge of the bed. "Has your room been inspected?"

Ashani nodded. The sad truth was that he was more concerned with espionage from within his own government than from a foreign agency.

"The mutt," Jalali said with a look of disgust, "is prancing around demanding this and that. He acts like he is running things."

Ashani nodded. His friend was talking about the abrasive Mukhtar. The man's non-Persian roots did not endear him to Jalali and many others.

"Amatullah has told us to give him whatever assistance he wishes. The man is planning attacks on a scale that will provoke the Israelis and the Americans to strike back. And that isn't even the worst of it. Our fearless president has come up with another one of his ideas." Jalali held his index finger next to his right temple and rolled it over and over in a circular motion, the universal sign for crazy. "He wants us to put together a plan to sink one of our own tankers in the Strait of Hormuz."

Ashani's eyes grew wide.

"I know," Jalali shook his head. "He wants to frame the Americans. He says everyone will believe us and it will further isolate the U.S."

Ashani checked the door and then in a quiet voice croaked out the words, "You can't be serious."

"I am. He says it will put oil prices through the roof, which will give the treasury a much needed boost, but mostly he says it will cement the fact that the Americans are waging war against us."

Ashani could feel his blood rising. He thought of Amatullah's stupid plan to kidnap the British sailors and marines the previous spring. It had been his crazy idea to create an incident after several high-ranking Iranian officials had defected to the West. While Amatullah thought the entire thing played very well with his countrymen, he had never realized the damage it had done to them internationally. It showed him to be a thug and a man who lied with great ease. The British, with the aid of the Americans, had presented rock-solid satellite images that the sailors had been plucked from Iraqi water, not Iranian. Amatullah had declared the evidence fabricated and was willing to put his fate in the hands of the UN Security Council, but Ayatollah Najar intervened at the last minute and convinced Amatullah to release the hostages. The propagandist then had the gall to hold a staged ceremony where he announced the release as a gift to the British people.

Ashani knew he had to get hold of Najar and try to talk some sense into someone before these reprisals began. Glancing toward the door, he whispered to Jalali, "You need to get me out of here."

22

WASHINGTON, DC

CIA Director Kennedy looked out the heavily tinted side window of her armored Chevy Suburban with a dazed expression. The buildings, pedestrians, and naked trees zoomed by like a reel of film in fast forward. She was running on fumes, and it was only 4:00 in the afternoon. Her expanded security detail was plowing its way through early rush hour traffic trying to get her to the State Department. Secretary Wicka had requested an informal meeting to help her prepare for her presentation at the UN. This was all a new experience for Kennedy. To say that the previous secretary of state disliked the CIA would have been too strong. It was probably more accurate that he was guarded. Which was not unusual. Association with the CIA had a way of making most people nervous. Kind of like being around someone with a communicable disease. An ominous and even nefarious label was often attached to America's top spy agency. She had dealt with people who openly despised the agency, some going as far as to tell her the place should be shuttered and its employees thrown into jail. Kennedy wrote these confrontations off as vitriol launched by left wing extremists who deluded themselves into thinking everyone would get along if America simply played nice.

Secretary of State Wicka, fortunately, did not hold those opinions. Liberal in her politics, she was a woman who had traveled the world and understood both human nature and the complexities of individual cultures. A widow and the mother of five boys and a girl, she had been hammering the president on sexism since the day she had been confirmed. Not sexism in his administration or even the country. Wicka held the belief that the long-term key to winning the war on terror was to get the women involved. As long as the Muslim extremist culture was dominated by bigoted men stuck in the Middle Ages, there could be little hope of finding peace. Kennedy had joined ranks with her in pushing this as a key policy for the president.

The vehicle came to an unexpected stop a mile from Foggy Bottom. She was about to ask her driver what was going on when she saw the intersection was blocked by another motorcade of sedans and SUVs. With Iran making noise and threatening reprisals, the Department of Homeland Security had recommended that personal protection details for all key administration figures be stepped up. Kennedy's security chief had already made the adjustment even though she voiced her opinion that the decision was premature. DC traffic was some of the worst in the country, and all of these motorcades only made things worse.

Just as the intersection cleared, Kennedy's mobile Secure Telephone Unit began buzzing. She looked at the readout and saw it was her office. She pulled the black handset from its cradle and said, "Hello?"

"I have Mitch on the line." It was the voice of one of Kennedy's three assistants.

"Patch him through, please."

There was clicking noise and then Rapp came on. "Irene?"

"Yes."

"I just finished the first leg of my journey."

"Are you back in the air?"

"I wouldn't be talking to you if I was still on the ground."

"How did it go?"

"The guy is unbelievable. He actually tried to blame it on us at one point."

Kennedy sighed. Moments like this made her wonder if Ben Freidman was actually an ally. "What did he say?"

"He tried to say it was our planes that were seen in the air."

"How did you respond?"

"I told him there weren't any planes in the air. Theirs

or ours. That was when I saw the chink in that ugly mug of his. He started to get real evasive and nervous. Especially when I laid out for him exactly how the place had been destroyed."

"How did he react?"

"Worried . . . he wanted to know who I had talked to."

"And?"

"I told him I had a source inside his government."

Kennedy smiled and said, "You didn't."

"Damn right. That prick. He's got more spies in America than practically every other country combined, and what'd we give them last year? Five billion dollars in aid?"

"Roughly." The motorcade was now pulling up to the first checkpoint a block away from the State Department. The CIA security people had called ahead, so the crash gate was down and they were being waved through. "You do know he's going to launch an investigation to find out who talked to you?"

"Good. It might keep him out of my hair for a while. I told him to stay silent and tell his government to keep denying."

"You didn't tell him what you were up to, did you?"

"No."

"Good." The motorcade breezed through the checkpoint and pulled up in front of the main entrance. "Anything else?"

"No. Our guy in Mosul has everything set up. I'll call you as soon as I finish the meeting."

"Thanks." Kennedy placed the phone its cradle and waited for the door to be opened. It seemed like overkill, but it was the policy of her protective detail. They wanted to sweep the area to make sure there were no threats before she left the cover of the Suburban. Five seconds later the door was opened. Kennedy left the vehicle and was flanked by men as she headed up the stairs and into the building. They were greeted by a State Department official who escorted them past the metal detectors and into a waiting elevator.

Wicka was waiting for Kennedy in her expansive office. While the outside of the Harry S. Truman Building would not ever be chronicled in the annals of great American architecture, the secretary's office was impressive. It looked as if it had been transported from an eighteenth-century French villa. The furniture, carpeting, gilded ceiling, and alabaster fireplace radiated wealth and prestige.

The secretary of state looked over the top of a pair of horn-rimmed spectacles perched on the end of her nose. Her short frosted hair was cut in layers. She pushed her chair back and stood.

"Thank you for coming, Irene."

"My pleasure, Sunny."

"Can I get you anything to drink?"

"No thank you. I'm fine."

Wicka walked over to a small wet bar and grabbed two coffee mugs. She set them down and pulled a bottle of Hennessy brandy out of the cupboard. She poured some brandy into each mug and then carried them over to where Kennedy was standing.

"You look like you could use some." Wicka handed Kennedy one of the mugs.

Kennedy smiled. "Nice choice of stemware."

"This place is filled with prudes and teetotalers. It's not like the old days, I'll tell you that."

Kennedy held up her mug. "To the old days."

Wicka raised her mug and clanged it against Kennedy's. "Although, I suppose in the old days they would have never let us out of the secretarial pool."

"That's right."

"Well, screw the old days." Wicka pointed toward the fireplace and two waiting chairs. "I saw in the paper today Stu Garret drowned while vacationing in Central America."

"Costa Rica," Kennedy offered.

Wicka took the chair on the right and studied Kennedy for a moment. Finally, she offered, "The man was a real jerk."

Kennedy pursed her lips while she thought of an appropriate response. She got the sense Wicka might know more than she was letting on. "He had a knack for getting under people's skin."

"He sure did." Wicka took a drink and said, "I hear you're leaving for Iraq in the morning?"

"Yes."

"Be careful."

"I always am."

"I mean extra careful. I don't trust the Iranians."

Kennedy brought the mug up to her lips but didn't take a drink. "I've found Ashani to be a pretty reasonable person to deal with."

"I don't know him, but he's not the one I'm worried about. It's that little Amatullah who scares the heck out of me." Wicka took a drink of brandy. "Why is it that these wacky dictators are all short?"

"Coincidence." Kennedy took a sip. "Saddam was over six feet tall."

"What about Hitler? He couldn't have been more than five ten."

"Yeah, you're probably right."

"Pol Pot, Kim Jong Il, Chairman Mao."

"What about Stalin? I don't think he was short."

"Well . . . whatever it is, I don't trust Amatullah. Just be very careful while you're over there. Especially after I put on my little performance in New York tomorrow. They are not going to like being embarrassed like that."

"No, they won't, but that's why I'm going over there to offer them the olive branch."

"Don't forget that men like Amatullah don't want peace. They need us as an enemy to stay in power."

"True, and that's why I'm the one making the trip and not you. There's nothing official about this. Not until they agree to keep a leash on Hezbollah."

"I'm not saying I don't agree with the plan. I do. I'm saying be careful."

Kennedy smiled. "I will. So what can I help you with for tomorrow?"

23

MOSUL, IRAQ

The sun was dropping beyond the horizon as the G-5 descended out of a patch of wispy clouds. The city of Mosul spread out beneath them, the Tigris River slicing along the eastern edge of the metropolitan area of two million. Five main bridges connected the old city to its sprawling suburbs. The city's roots were steeped in trade. For centuries it had been an extremely ethnically and religiously diverse place. In the late eighties Saddam Hussein put an end to that. He drove out the Jews, the Christians, and most tragically the Kurds.

Saddam replaced them wholesale with Sunni families who had sworn allegiance to him or were from his hometown of Tikrit. The Kurds were forced out of the city and took refuge in the foothills along the Turkish border, where they continued to build a guerrilla force and live in defiance of Saddam. Since the fall of Saddam, the city had been in flux. The CIA had formed a very effective relationship with the Kurds. Whenever things got ugly in Mosul, the CIA would call their Kurdish friends who were garrisoned to the north. They would roll back into the city and slap down whichever faction was causing trouble. The Shia population this far north was nothing like it was in the south, but that didn't stop Iran from sending in its Badr Brigades to stir up trouble, or al-Qaeda in Iraq from trying to foment violence between the Sunnis and the Kurds.

Rapp looked past the port-side wing and counted the bridges. He couldn't understand why the damn country just wasn't split in three. It didn't even exist in its current state until the aftermath of WWI. For five centuries the Turks, the Kurds, the Persians, and the Safavids had all fought over a piece of land made fertile by the Tigris and Euphrates rivers. Then the British and the French came along and decided to redraw the map of the Middle East and everything went to hell. Mosul, thanks to the Kurds, however, was showing real stability. So much so that the pilots felt safe enough to take a straight approach over the heart of the city. If it had been Basra or Baghdad they would have corkscrewed their way down onto the strip. Not an enjoyable way to land.

The plane set down gently and proceeded to the CIA's sector within the base, where the sixty-million-dollar Gulfstream 5 was placed inside a hardened hangar. One by one they filed off the plane and opened the cargo hold. Rapp grabbed his oversized backpack along with two black rectangular cases. He walked to the door of the hangar in time to see two sedans approaching. The first was a Ford Crown Victoria, and the second was a Chevy Caprice Classic. The vehicles were dusty and dented and approaching at a speed that made Rapp a little nervous.

The driver of the first car began waving through the open window. Rapp could barely make out the face of the person on the other side of the tinted windscreen. It was Stan Stilwell, the CIA's chief of base in Mosul. The car came to an abrupt halt and the door sprang open. In the tradition of T. E. Lawrence, Stilwell had gone native. He was dressed in a loose-fitting pair of black dress pants and a gray and black check-patterned dress shirt. His face was a dark shade of bronze, and his black mustache was so thick it looked as if he'd been growing it since puberty.

"Brother Mitch," Stilwell announced as he transferred his cigarette from his right to his left hand. "It's good to see you."

Rapp took Stilwell's hand and met him with a half hug. "How the hell have you been, buddy?" Rapp had known Stilwell for more than a decade. A few years his senior, Rapp had been a mentor of sorts for Stilwell on his first overseas assignment.

"I'm great. Things are good here in Kurdistan."

"I bet. How many girlfriends?"

"A few." Stilwell smiled, revealing a thin gap between his top front teeth.

"You know one of these days you're going to end up with a very angry father on your hands, and he's going to make you choose between castration and the altar."

"No one's caught me yet."

Rapp thought about reminding him of the time he'd had to talk Kennedy out of reprimanding him for one of his unreported dalliances but didn't want to bring it up in front of Ridley. "Famous last words."

"Don't say that."

"I'm just saying sooner or later your luck is going to run out."

Stilwell took a drag from his cigarette. "You're probably right."

"Is everything ready to go?"

"Yep. He's waiting for us back at my place. Give me those bags." Stilwell looked over Rapp's shoulder and saw Ridley. "Hey, boss. How you doing?"

"Stiff," Ridley said in a grumpy voice.

"Good to see you too." Stilwell picked up Rapp's two cases and stuffed them in the sedan's big trunk. "Boss," he said to Ridley, "why don't you ride with Mike in the second car? I don't expect any problems, but there's no sense in making it easy for them."

"Stan," Rapp said as he pointed to Dumond, "meet Marcus."

"Hey, Marcus, let me take those bags from you." Stilwell grabbed the first black case and almost dropped it. "Jesus, what in the hell do you have in here?"

"Equipment."

"No shit."

Rapp walked to the rear of the car where everyone had congregated. Looking at Stilwell he asked, "Did Rob brief you on everything?"

"Not all the details, but I can see where you're going."

"And?"

"I love it."

"What about Massoud?" Massoud Mahabad was MEK's main guy in Mosul.

"He thinks it's great."

"Can we depend on him?"

Stilwell tossed his cigarette to the ground and fished a new one from a crumpled pack. "Massoud is probably the most trustworthy person I've met since I've been here."

"Good. Do we need any extra hardware for the drive?" Rapp was referring to guns.

"No. We won't be stopping."

"Are you sure?" Rapp asked in a doubtful tone.

"If it'll make you feel better, go ahead." Stilwell lifted up the right tail of his dress shirt to reveal a Glock pistol and two extra magazines. "There's a twelve-gauge mounted on the ceiling and a P-Ninety under the dash."

"Good enough for me. Let's roll."

Ridley and Dumond got in the second car and Rapp got in the first car with Stilwell. The first thing Rapp did when he got in the front seat was reach under the dash and yank the P-90 from its spring-loaded grips. The small bullpup submachine gun was extremely accurate and great for tight fights. Rapp slid the breach back to see if a round was chambered and then put the weapon back.

As they rolled toward the main gate Rapp asked, "You been hit since you've been over here?"

"A few times, back when we were driving the Suburbans around." Stilwell shook his head. "It was really stupid of us. Those things just turned us into a big fat target." He glanced over at Rapp. "I won't get in one now."

"Smart move. This door seemed pretty heavy. You put some armor plating in it?"

"Yep. In fact Massoud did it for me. He's making a killing on his auto parts business in addition to armoring old cars like this."

They were waved through the main gate and then zigzagged their way through the big concrete Jersey barriers before they made it to the main road. Stilwell turned north and stubbed out his cigarette in the ashtray. He grabbed a clear plastic mouth guard from the dashboard and held it up for Rapp to see. He put it in his mouth and then punched the accelerator. The big Detroit V8 engine roared to life.

"This is the worst part of the trip, right here. It's like the Indy five hundred, but with bombs."

Rapp hurried to put on his seat belt. "What's with the mouth guard?"

"These people are some of the shittiest drivers in the world. One of our guys got in a collision a few months ago. He got hit so hard he bit off his tongue."

Rapp looked over at Stilwell to see if the man was pulling his leg. He noticed him white-knuckling the steering wheel and decided it was no act. Rapp gripped the door handle tightly and swore to himself.

24

I mad Mukhtar was in a foul mood. He looked around the rectangular table with contempt. As a man of action nothing bothered him more than having to listen to soft men spout platitudes. It was the same thing with these pretenders every time. *We will push Israel into the sea. We will vaporize their entire country. We will wipe them from the map. We will make the Americans beg for forgiveness. We will, we will,* it went on and on and they never lifted a finger to do one hundredth of what it was that they talked so boisterously about.

Mukhtar wanted desperately to move beyond Israel. The stubborn little country bored him. They were showing signs of weakness. The old guard was dying off. The ones who remembered all the broken promises. They were slowly being replaced by younger Jews who were sick of the attacks. Sick of the murders and carnage. So sick, they were willing to grasp at the illusion of peace. Mukhtar had no respect for them. He may have hated their parents and grand-parents, but he respected and feared the stubborn old bastards. This young crop in both Beirut and Tel Aviv, with their iPods and cell phones, were losing their identities.

Mukhtar was in a race against time and technology.

None of the other men sitting in Amatullah's conference room understood the change that was occurring beyond their borders. They had so thoroughly bought in to their Islamic revolution that they now believed their own propaganda. They actually thought they were carrying the day in the battle between East and West, but Mukhtar knew different. The number of dead American soldiers was laughably small compared to other conflicts. A million people had died the last time Iran went to war with Iraq. Even so, they needed to get the Americans to pull out as soon as possible. The effects of their occupation were far-reaching.

The Internet, TV, radio, cell phones, and travel were all blurring the lines of race and ethnicity, and every day the American war machine stayed in the region more youths were lost to the seduction of capitalism and commercialism. Economic prosperity was spreading, as were the effects of decades of immigration from Lebanon and Palestine to Europe, America, and Canada. This new prosperity was bleeding them of the angry young men they needed to sustain the fight. A contented youth was not about to offer himself up as a suicide bomber. Fortunately in Iraq the Saudis and Pakistanis had been able to provide a steady supply of youths who had been brainwashed in Saudi-sponsored madrasas. This slow yet persistent trickle of suicide bombers was the only thing that was preventing the Americans from peace and stability. They needed to open a new front. They needed to hit the

Americans in their nose and make them withdraw. If they didn't, they risked the spreading malaise of economic prosperity. Once that happened, the people would no longer have the stomach to fight.

The yammering continued, with each advisor to Amatullah trying to outdo the next in the arena of tough talk. Mukhtar's patience was threadbare. Allah surely had important plans for him. Why else would He have allowed him to survive the horrible attack at the nuclear facility? He'd spent the first day in the hospital heavily sedated. His lungs ached from all the coughing. When Amatullah sent for him, he was eager for the chance to get away from the poking and prodding of the nurses and doctors. If he had known the meeting was going to be like this, however, he would have stayed in his bed.

Major General Dadress, the chief of the armed forces, was backtracking from his earlier statements that his shore batteries could sink every U.S. ship in the gulf if given the word. He was now saying that while he could inflict heavy casualties on the United States, such an aggressive move would undoubtedly be seen as an act of war and would invite heavy reprisals.

"And what do you call what they did to us?" Amatullah asked with his signature half grin. "Was it not an act of war? Can we sit here and let it go unpunished?"

"I agree," said General Dadress, trying to sound reasonable, "but we must carefully consider what is proportional."

Mukhtar tilted his head back and let out a contemptuous groan. Amatullah and all of his advisors turned to see what had upset the uncouth leader of Hezbollah.

"What is wrong?" Amatullah asked, showing only amusement.

"I can't believe I am hearing this," Mukhtar said with no attempt whatsoever to conceal his disgust. "Proportional. War is not about equal portions. You have been attacked by Israel and America without provocation. You were doing exactly what Israel did thirty years ago when they developed nuclear weapons in defiance of the United Nations and the International Atomic Energy Agency. They, more than any country, had no right to do this to us."

There was a knock on the door, and then it opened to reveal Azad Ashani. The minister of intelligence looked down the length of the table at Amatullah and said, "I am sorry I wasn't here on time."

"I was told you were in the hospital."

Ashani grabbed one of the few remaining chairs. "Doctors like to err on the side of caution."

Amatullah squinted at Ashani with suspicious eyes and then turned to General Dadress. "Where were we?"

"I think our *Lebanese* friend was about to tell us what we should do."

Mukhtar noted the way the general chose to use the name of his adopted country. He was tempted to ask him how many of his men he had lost in their battle against Israel and America, but he decided to let it pass. "You hit them," he said in a slow, steady voice. "I like your idea," he said to Amatullah, "of sinking one of your own tankers and blaming it on the Americans, but I think you should take it one step further. You should sink your tanker and then let those new Russian subs of yours hunt their carriers and sink them."

"If we touch one of their carriers," Dadress said in shock, "they will send our entire navy to the bottom of the ocean."

"Then let them. It's not much of a navy to begin with," Mukhtar retorted.

Dadress turned away from Mukhtar and addressed Amatullah. "I am advocating taking decisive action, but one would be a *fool* to not take into account the American ability to strike back."

It wasn't in Mukhtar's nature to sit still while an overfed, over-the-hill general called him a fool. "Do you know how many of my people have died in the fight against America and Israel?" He didn't wait for the general to answer. "Thousands. How many of your men have died, General?"

Dadress's face flushed with anger. He pounded his balled fist down on the table and barked, "I will not allow you to insult my men."

"Good!" Mukhtar stood. "Then it is settled. You will send them into battle as I have been doing with my men for three decades."

"How dare you?" The general stood.

"All I have been doing my whole life, General, is

daring. Daring myself to go into battle. Daring my men into battle. Daring the Israelis to kill me. The French. The Americans. The list goes on and on. Let them drop their bombs. Let them sink your navy. They will never invade your country."

"Even if we sink one of their carriers?"

"Especially if you sink one of their carriers. The American people are growing tired of war, and they are growing tired of defending the criminal Jews. Now is the time to be bold." Mukhtar started for the door.

"Where are you going?" asked Amatullah.

"Back to Lebanon and then to America, where I am going to avenge the attack against your country." Mukhtar yanked open the door and then slammed it behind him as he left.

Ashani slowly looked away from the door. One by one he looked at the men arrayed around the table. Every single man had his eyes cast down in shame, save one. Amatullah had that crooked grin on his face and a faraway look in his eye. Ashani watched as the corners of his mouth turned upwards to form a smile of satisfaction. He was already troubled by what he had heard, but now the minister of intelligence got a new sinking feeling in his stomach. Something told him Amatullah had recruited Mukhtar to goad these men into taking reckless action.

Ashani had no doubt what the Americans would do if one of their carriers were hit. Especially if they could claim they had no hand in the attack that destroyed Isfahan. Ashani knew his colleagues well. If their honor were called into question by a half-breed like Mukhtar, they would take action. He needed to give them time to cool down.

Ashani cleared his throat loudly and said, "Minister Salehi will be addressing the UN Security Council in a few hours. I have been informed that the U.S. secretary of state has flown to New York and would also like to address the council. The director of their CIA has reached out to me and would like to sit down and discuss what happened."

"And your point is?" Amatullah asked.

"Before we do something that could place this government and its people in harm's way, I think we should talk to the Americans and find out what they might be willing to offer us to avoid further conflict."

One by one the advisors slowly nodded their heads in agreement.

Amatullah looked at the men and said, "I can wait another day or two at the most before we take action, but I want plans drawn up. When I give the order I want them implemented immediately. Have I made myself clear?"

One by one each man at the table said they understood. Even Ashani. Despite his health he would be heading to Mosul in the morning. If he didn't speak to Kennedy soon, things might spin out of control.

25

MOSUL, IRAQ

As the chief of base in Mosul, Stilwell could move far more easily around the city than both the chief of base in Basra and the chief of station in Baghdad. His counterpart in Basra lived on the base at the airport and was in constant fear of being kidnapped or assassinated. The chief of station in Baghdad rarely left the Americanized Green Zone, and when he did it was usually in a helicopter.

Stilwell liked to keep three safe houses in rotation at any given time. Every couple of months he'd rent a new one and close up one of the old ones. They were all fairly nondescript, two-story brick or stucco homes with high walls and a strong gate. He staffed them with private contractors and never stayed in one more than two nights in a row. He was constantly changing his routine so as to confuse anyone who might attempt to kidnap him. Dozens of contractors and private citizens in Mosul had been ambushed and held for ransom. About half of them made it back alive. The other half ended up floating downstream in the river. Massoud would from time to time provide a shadow for Stilwell to see if anyone was following him. Massoud's men caught a local thug getting a little too close a few months earlier and put him in the hospital with a broken jaw and two broken legs.

As they crossed over the Tigris, Stilwell brought Rapp up to speed on Massoud.

"He's been trying to get this house for three years."

"Why this house in particular?" Rapp asked.

"It's on the east side of the river. There's more land and it tends to be less violent. It also puts him that much closer to the Iranian border which for some reason means a lot to him."

As they crossed over the river, Stilwell pointed north. "You see that patch of land past that other bridge with all the trees. It looks like a park?"

"Yeah."

"That's his new place. It used to belong to one of Saddam's cousins. The guy had a monopoly on the textile industry in northern Iraq. With Saddam's help he used forced labor to run his factories. I guess the guy made a killing."

"Did we get lucky and drop a bomb on his head?"

"Nope. He took off to Jordan the week before the war started. The guy has been holding out hope that he would be able to return. A few months ago he finally saw the light and sold to Massoud."

They made it across the bridge and turned north. A mile later they turned on to a quiet road and then a few hundred yards after that they approached a massive steel gate with guards milling about. The men recognized Stilwell and greeted him with smiles and waves. A signal was given and a twelve-foot-high steel gate began rolling back.

"They're not going to search us?" Rapp asked.

"Massoud and I are tight. They trust me."

As they drove up the tree-lined drive, Rapp got his first glimpse of the house. It was massive. "I don't remember him being this wealthy when I was here last year. Is this guy into anything other than used car parts?" Rapp asked with suspicion.

"He might be into a few other things."

"Like what?"

"Guns."

"He's an arms dealer?"

"More of a financier. He helps put the deals together."

"Anything else I should know about?"

"Saddam's cousin . . . the one he bought this place from?"

"Yeah."

"He also bought his business."

"At a steeply discounted price, I'm sure."

Stilwell stopped in front of the massive portico. "These Sunnis have been screwing people for years. You're not going to get any sympathy out of me."

Rapp opened his car door and stood, taking in the full scope of the front of the house and the motor court. Massoud Mahabad had done very well for himself.

"Mitch."

Rapp turned to see Massoud coming toward him down a walking path covered with crushed rock that looked as if it led to an orchard of some sort. The man stood five feet eight inches tall and Rapp figured he weighed over 200 pounds. He had mostly gray hair and was probably in his late sixties. He was wearing a short-sleeve Tommy Bahama shirt. Rapp began walking toward the man.

"Thank you for traveling all this way to see me," Massoud said in perfect English as he extended his hand.

"If I had known you'd moved into this beautiful place, I would have planned on staying longer."

"You are welcome to stay as long as you like." Massoud took Rapp's hand with both of his and smiled warmly. "I can't thank you enough for what your country has done for the Kurdish peoples."

"And I can't thank you enough for your loyalty and support."

"You are welcome." Massoud looked over Rapp's shoulder and said, "Hello, Rob. How are you, my friend?"

"I am good, Massoud. And how is your family?"

"Good. Thank you for asking. Although every time this one comes around I have to lock up my daughters." Massoud looked at Stilwell. "They all swoon over him."

Ridley shook Massoud's hand. "I can have him castrated if you would like."

"Yes, castration." Massoud laughed heartily. "That would be very nice."

After the laughing died down, Rapp introduced Dumond, and then Massoud led them through the house. He stopped several times to discuss artwork that he had purchased and pieces he was hoping to get his hands on. The place looked more like a small palace than a house. The interior walls were constructed of limestone blocks. The main staircase with its black iron banister dominated the left side of the entry hall. Antique tapestries and oil paintings covered the walls. They made it out onto the veranda just in time to see the sun floating on the western horizon. The entire city of Mosul lay before them with the long shadows of evening stretching toward them.

Indoor furniture and rugs had been moved outside and were waiting for them along with two butlers. Drinks were served and then appetizers. They all sat and Massoud worked his way around the group offering each guest a cigar from his humidor. As the sun went down, heat lamps were set up and ignited. After everyone had lit up, Massoud settled into his oversized chair and looked at Rapp with a devilish smile.

"You are aware of my hatred and disdain for that little peacock Amatullah."

"Yes, I am," Rapp replied.

"And you know I would love nothing more than to see him embarrassed."

"That makes two of us."

"Then I'll do whatever I can to help you. Tell me more about your plans."

Rapp set down his scotch and took a long pull off his Montecristo cigar. "I want you to think this through because there could be reprisals."

Massoud grunted with disdain as he shook his head. "I am not afraid of the Iranian government or their cowardly Badr Brigades."

"You know their history as well as anyone. They are not afraid to assassinate their enemies."

"And I am not afraid to strike back. If what Stan has told me is true," Massoud gestured at Stilwell, "and you have a chance to really embarrass that little bastard, to catch him in one of his lies, then I want to be involved."

"What about the MEK and PMOI? Do you need to speak to them before you agree to this?"

"I could speak for the PMOI, but I won't. The MEK I can and will speak for, and if I am right about what you would like to accomplish, the MEK is more believable."

"I agree."

"We will support any attempt to create instability within Amatullah's administration."

"Compensation?" Rapp queried.

Massoud adopted an uncomfortable expression and shifted in his oversized chair. "You have been very good to us."

"And you to us," Rapp replied.

"There might be some dealings you could help me with, but I don't want to make this about that. We are allies. We will both benefit from this."

"True."

"Now tell me of your plan. I am very interested to hear more details."

Rapp held up his glass to toast Massoud. "Here's what we're going to do."

26

Ashani checked his watch. If his driver made good time, they would avoid being late. The minister of intelligence popped the top off a small container of sedatives his doctor had given him and downed a few. Between meetings he had gone back to his office at the Ministry of Intelligence and checked in with his deputies. The get-together with Kennedy was set for the following afternoon in Mosul, where they had met the last time. Everyone was on edge except Ashani, which made him wonder if it was the pills. Ashani's head of security was not happy about the rushed nature of the meeting. He wanted more time to do an advance review of the site. This did not come as a surprise to Ashani, since his security people by necessity were paranoid. He had to calmly tell them to stop sweating the details. The last thing the Americans would want right now would be to make matters worse.

Ashani's security chief, Rahad Tehrani, told him it wasn't the Americans he was worried about. It was the Mujahedin-e-Khalq. Tehrani explained that there had been a spike in MEK communications in just the last day and there were reports of civil disobedience in the northern provinces. Ashani wrote it off as the Kurds picking an opportune time to stir up trouble. Ashani assured Tehrani that he could relax, but inside he held some doubt. With every crisis the northern provinces were becoming increasingly bold in their defiance. The last thing they needed at the moment was to have to put down an insurrection.

As they neared the presidential palace the streets became choked with pedestrians and buses. Amatullah had sent his propagandists out into the city to foment an anti-American demonstration. Classes were canceled at the universities and free buses were provided. They were all headed for the old American embassy. Even though the Americans had been gone for more than a quarter century, Amatullah and the other revolutionary faithful still used the compound as a rallying point to preach against the Great Satan. They reached the gates of the Presidential Palace and entered the lush grounds. Ashani had no desire to see Amatullah for a second time in what was becoming a very long day, but he had learned in the past that a request from Amatullah was really a command.

Ashani was shown into a comfortable room next to Amatullah's office for the viewing of Minister Salehi's presentation to the United Nations Security Council. Brigadier General Sulaimani of the Quds Force was already there, as well as Golam Mosheni, the Vice President for Atomic Energy, and Major General Zarif, the head of the Republican Guards. Tea was offered to each man. Ashani said hello to everyone and took a seat next to Sulaimani on one of the leather couches. The big-screen TV was tuned to CNN. A man and woman were on the screen talking about the tension in the chamber between the Iranian foreign minister and the U.S. secretary of state.

Amatullah entered the room holding a glass of water. He was smiling from ear to ear. "I just spoke with Salehi. France, Russia, and China have all agreed to back our resolution. He said if we withdraw our language about the U.S., he thinks England will back it as well."

"What about the other members?" Ashani asked.

"South Africa and Italy are on the fence. Everyone else is behind us. He said the Israeli ambassador looks very uncomfortable."

"They didn't send their foreign minister?" Mosheni asked in a surprised tone.

"No," Amatullah answered. "They obviously don't want to embarrass him."

Amatullah sat down seconds before Salehi began to talk. The Iranian foreign minister was sitting at the large semicircular shaped desk that looked down into the well where the fifteen members of the Security Council sat at a long rectangular table.

Ashani had received a copy of the speech and skimmed it in advance. It was less than five minutes long. The first third dealt with a sovereign country's right to seek energy independence and be safe from the aggression of other nations. Everyone on the Security Council knew the facility at Isfahan had nothing to do with energy independence and everything to do with nuclear weapons, but that didn't deter Minister

Salehi from playing his part. The middle third of the speech outlined the damage done by the attack.

Salehi pounded his fist on the desk as he gave the number of dead—328 scientists, technicians, and laborers. Ashani knew that the actual number was roughly a third of that, but Amatullah wanted it tripled for effect. On the screen behind Salehi flashed the photos of some of Iran's best and brightest scientists. Salehi listed the price of the facility at three billion dollars, again roughly triple the actual cost. Most egregious of all, however, was the mess that had been created. The beautiful city of Isfahan now contained a nuclear disaster second only to Chernobyl. The damage to the citizenry was incalculable.

The last third of the speech spelled out the recourse Iran was seeking. There was no debate over who had carried out the attack. No offer of evidence that could pinpoint the rogue country that was behind this savage breach of international diplomacy. Salehi for the first time mentioned Israel. He ran off a litany of historic events where Israel had attacked her Muslim neighbors, while conveniently leaving out the times Israel's Muslim neighbors had attacked her. He pointed out that Iran had done nothing to provoke this attack, and finally he listed his country's demands. The price was steep. Ten billion dollars in reparations plus whatever the cost would be to clean up the Isfahan site.

Ashani knew about these points and had helped craft them. In light of the destruction of the facility he felt they were reasonable, and in fact he thought the

Americans might even pay. The next demand was intended to make Israel squirm. Ashani didn't think they would get it passed, but it was worth a shot. Salehi demanded that Israel admit that they had a nuclear arsenal and allow UN inspectors full access to their facilities. The Israeli ambassador actually appeared to squirm when this point was made.

Ashani thought Salehi was done, but the man took a drink of water and announced that he had one more point. He began by recounting the horrible downing of Iran Air Flight 655 by the U.S. warship *Vincennes* which had resulted in the deaths of 290 people, 66 of whom were children. He listed another half dozen merchant ships and Iranian naval vessels that had been sunk. He decried America's continued support of Israel and their abominable persecution of the Palestinian people. He said his country would no longer tolerate the bullying of the world's lone superpower.

Ashani got the sense Salehi was building toward something very dramatic.

"This organization," Salehi said, "has failed to protect us in the past. We have been attacked by the two greatest antagonists in the world today, and we will not allow these crimes against our sovereign nation to go unpunished. In forty-eight hours' time we will suspend the right of innocent passage for all U.S. and Israeli ships through the Strait of Hormuz. We will consider the attempted transit of any ship sailing under the American or Israeli flag an act of war, and we will take decisive action."

The chamber exploded in an uproar of discussion. Salehi paused for a moment and then began talking over the clamor. "When the United States and Israel have admitted to this cowardly attack against the sovereign state of Iran, and has made assurances that recompense will be paid, we will reopen the strait."

The reality of what had just been said took a moment to sink in. Amatullah had intentionally kept this last demand from him, knowing full well he would have said it was too inflammatory. The Security Council would undoubtedly make a move to separate each demand before voting, and there would be calls for investigations that would take months, but the closing of the strait could short-circuit all of that and lead to a speedy resolution. Or it could lead to an escalation that Ashani was afraid would not benefit his country. Ashani glanced over at his president and wasn't the least bit surprised to find him nodding at the TV and looking very full of himself. Ashani had the sinking feeling that Amatullah actually wanted a confrontation in the gulf.

27

MOSUL, IRAQ

Rapp was sitting in Massoud's theater room with Ridley, Stilwell, Massoud, and one of Massoud's nephews. They too were watching the proceedings at the United Nations, but instead of drinking tea and water they were drinking beer and smoking cigars. Rapp had learned to expect strange behavior from the Iranians. Especially their president. In a way, they were a cross between the Cold War diplomats of the Soviet Union and the South American thug Hugo Chávez. Never afraid, for example, to take an issue like freedom of the press and decry restrictions by the United States while touting their own supposed openness. Closing the Strait of Hormuz to U.S. traffic, however, Rapp did not see coming. It was difficult for the press to prove the lie when people were talking about human rights and freedom of speech. There was all kinds of wiggle room, but in this case the line had just been drawn in a very clear way. An aircraft carrier sailing through the twenty-mile strait was impossible to miss.

International waters were simply that—international waters. Anyone was allowed to be there. Iran owned the water twelve miles from the beach and not an inch further. As long as the United States stayed far enough away there was nothing the Iranians could do. At least that's what a logical person would conclude, but Rapp knew better. Iran liked to write their own rules and then rewrite them. They exemplified the adage, don't let the facts get in the way of a good piece of propaganda.

Secretary of State Wicka appeared on the screen. Rapp noted that the usually calm and classy Wicka looked to be barely containing her anger. She was wearing her reading glasses and looking sideways in the direction of the Iranian foreign minister while one of her aides was whispering in her ear. Wicka nodded and then the aide sat back down. She opened her leather briefing book with the flick of a wrist, took a moment to review her notes, then closed the book and took off her glasses. Looking into the well at the ambassadors who represented the fifteen countries holding seats on the council, she slowly began shaking her head in the manner of a disapproving mother.

"I would like to start out by assuring this body that the United States had no hand whatsoever in the events that took place at the Isfahan nuclear facility earlier in the week. What you just witnessed is the same old tired tactic used by the Iranian government every time they have a problem. Blame the U.S. Blame Israel. It is the great Satan's fault." Wicka glared at Salehi. "Every time there is a catastrophe in Iran, the leadership trots out the Stars and Stripes and the Star of David to distract the people from the failed policies of their own government. We have been your convenient whipping boy for far too long."

Wicka glanced over her shoulder and pointed at the screen. "First slide, please."

A satellite image of the Isfahan facility appeared on the large drop-down screen. "These photos were taken in the moments preceding the destruction of Iran's nuclear facility. A facility that I would like to remind the council was in violation of both Security Council Resolution sixteen ninety-six and seventeen forty-seven." Wicka paused for effect. "This next series of photos will show you the actual destruction of the facility."

Images played out across the screen in a succession of time-delayed, high-resolution photographs. Wicka narrated. "Note the absence of any flashes, explosions, or debris plumes." Wicka again looked over her shoulder. "Next slide, please."

Highly magnified photos of the building's roof appeared. It was split into four sections. Air-conditioning units could be clearly seen, as well as the textured gravel of the massive asphalt roof. The slides cascaded across the screen, progressing from an undamaged roof to shots displaying the early signs of trouble, fissures that from space looked like nothing more than hairline fractures. Red arrows pointed to each crack, and a side-by-side comparison of the before and after photos was shown. The next series of slides showed cracks emanating from the center of the roof outward like a jagged spiderweb. The lines were now clearly visible, and there was no need for the red arrows.

"Notice," Wicka said, "at no point can you find the telltale sign of a bomb breaching the roof. Our experts have gone over these photos in great detail, and we encourage the other permanent members of the council to do the same with your own satellite imagery."

The next series of photos showed the structural failure of the roof as a large portion in the center gave way and collapsed. Other sections followed in quick succession. It literally looked as if the earth were swallowing the building en masse. The last image showed the beginnings of the debris cloud billowing up from the center of the massive rectangular hole.

"Not only is the roof not breached by a bomb, there are none of the telltale explosions one would expect to see from an aerial bombardment. We have shown these photos to dozens of experts, both civilian and military, and they all agree that what happened at Isfahan was a complete structural failure from the inside of the building. There was no external attack. No bombs dropped from planes as the Iranian government claims." Wicka looked directly at the Iranian foreign minister and said, "At first we thought the collapse was possibly due to faulty construction, but we began to rule that out yesterday as new information became available."

Wicka looked over her right shoulder and gave a slight nod to her deputy. "The Iranian government would like the world to believe they enjoy the full support of the Iranian people when in fact the opposite is true. The People's Mujahedin of Iran, the National Council of Resistance of Iran, and the Mujahedin-e-Khalq are just a few of the many groups who stand in opposition to the dictatorial Iranian government." The names of the groups played across the screen. "For over twenty-five years the hard-line clerics have attempted to thwart these groups by assassinating their leaders and imprisoning their members for daring to speak out against their harsh policies. By strictly controlling the press, the Iranian government has managed to, for the most part, hide this growing insurgency from the rest of the world. That is, until now. With the Internet it has become increasingly difficult for dictatorial regimes like the one in Tehran to control the flow of information.

"The following is a statement released by the Mujahedin-e-Khalq, or MEK as they are more commonly known. I would like to stipulate that this video is available on the Internet, for anyone who is willing to look. Al-Jazeera, I have been told, has also started airing it in the past hour."

Rapp watched as the video that was shot in Massoud's house the day before appeared on the screen. There was a man sitting on the ground with his legs folded in front of him. He was wearing green military fatigues and a black hood with slits for his eyes. A Russian-made AK-74 rested on his lap. Behind him a blue banner covered the wall. In both Persian and English were the words Free Iran and Mujahedin-e-Khalq. The man under the hood was Massoud's nephew, who was fluent in both Farsi and English. He started out speaking Farsi and then switched to English.

"The people of Iran have suffered for far too long while their leaders have enjoyed the spoils of the late Shah Mohammad Reza Pahlavi. The brave Iranian people stood up and threw off the oppressive bonds of the shah only to have their revolution stolen by a group of selfish men who have lined their pockets while the rest of us have struggled to feed our families. They have held on to their power by strangling all dissent. There is no free thought, no free speech, and no freedom of faith in Islam. Only the harsh edicts that are thrown down by selfish men who live in the shah's palaces where they drink his wine and watch pornography on their satellite TVs."

Rapp smiled as he listened to the words he had written. He had hesitated to use the line about pornography due to certain sensibilities. To those living in the West, the accusation would sound ridiculous, but to the people living under harsh Islamic law the accusation had the potential to stir up a deep-seated suspicion that those who made the laws lived above them. Such an accusation in this part of the world had the potential to incite a riot.

"They are protected by a secret police," the masked man continued, "that is far more ruthless than the dreaded SAVAK of the late shah. They have beaten, tortured, and assassinated anyone who dares open their mouth in disagreement. They have spent billions in the pursuit of nuclear weapons while the average citizen struggles to heat his home and feed his family. What have we as a people gained in this pursuit of nuclear weapons that we do not need, and the world does not want us to have? The answer is nothing. They have turned our once great nation into a pariah of the free world. I ask my fellow Iranians, how is this life any better than the one we had under the shah? The sad truth is that it isn't. And that is why we destroyed the nuclear facility at Isfahan. We have infiltrated the ranks of the Guardians of the Revolution and virtually every entity within the government. The Isfahan facility stood as an example of everything that is wrong with our leaders. Do they care about our economic and spiritual well-being? No. They only care about the power they have so hungrily hoarded for themselves. We allowed these selfish old men to steal our revolution, and we have paid a heavy price. Many of our fellow countrymen are dead because we did not act sooner. Well, it is time for a second revolution. It is time to throw off the repressive bonds of the hard-line clerics and their little puppet dictator. With the destruction of the Isfahan facility we have marked the beginning of the end of these tyrants, and the start of the fight for a true Islamic and democratic Iran."

28

TEHRAN, IRAN

Secretary of State Wicka's remarks were met with extreme prejudice. Even Ashani, who considered himself to be far more rational than the other men gathered in Amatullah's office, listened with the long-held belief that candor was an extremely rare commodity at the United Nations. Wicka's first point, however, couldn't have been more accurate. Every time Amatullah ran into trouble with the people or the

Supreme Leader, he would run to the nearest microphone and deliver a speech bemoaning the evil nature of the United States. Then for good measure he would warn of Israel's impending destruction. It was classic propaganda through deflection.

The satellite photos showing the destruction of the Isfahan facility were met with snorts of derision by the others, but for Ashani they struck a chord. He began listening with far greater intensity as the woman laid out the facts. Facts that dovetailed with his own suspicions. The first sign that something very serious was about to be levied came when Wicka began listing the various dissident groups within Iran. Ashani's mathematical mind was geared to make quick linear progressions. He saw, in the naming of those three groups, exactly where Wicka was going with her presentation. He almost said something to Amatullah. A quick phone call to the Ministry of Communications could have shut the broadcast down, but something had changed in Ashani since the attack. His normal patience of playing along with all of the posturing and chest thumping was gone. It was as if a part of him now wanted to see Amatullah suffer, so he sat there and said nothing.

When Wicka announced the video by the Mujahedin-e-Khalq, the entire mood in Amatullah's office changed in an instant. Smirks were replaced with frowns and flapping mouths grew silent. Ashani watched as Amatullah leaned forward.

The Iranian president said, "What trick is this?"

Ashani watched the first words of the MEK spokesman with guarded interest. He knew firsthand how terrorist groups loved to take recognition for the dirty work done by others, because he had helped orchestrate such statements before. Many of Hezbollah's operations were deemed too controversial for them to take credit, so they allowed fringe groups to bask in the glory instead. The MEK was no fringe group, however. They had grown significantly in influence and numbers in the northern provinces. So much so that government units could not operate without fear of attack.

The words that came out of the TV were without a doubt the most subversive to be spoken in Iran since 1979. Ashani both feared and hoped that they would strike a chord with the general public. His fear was born out of the knowledge that revolutions were messy things with lots of innocent people caught in the crossfire. His hope was for his daughters. If only they could live in an Iran that was rescued from the bigoted, chauvinistic hardliners. A third emotion entered his brain. It was amusement. Amusement at watching Amatullah's reaction.

By the fifth line of the man's speech, Amatullah was on his feet racing for his desk. He grabbed the phone and pressed a single button. Ashani could not see the number that was being dialed but he did not need to. He knew whom Amatullah would be calling. The Ministry of Communications. The state-run television had been told to broadcast Minister Saleh's address to the UN. They had been advertising it all day and were planning to air the lie-filled response of the American secretary of state. The viewing numbers would be huge, and the accusation that Amatullah and the other leaders watched pornography would not be received well. Ashani thought it was a stroke of genius. True or not, it didn't matter. In a society as sexually repressed as Iran's, the accusation merely needed to be leveled and the damage would be done.

Amatullah began yelling into the phone, and he kept yelling as his eyes stayed glued to his big-screen TV. As each excruciating second ticked past, he became visibly more volatile. Finally, he picked up a paper-weight and chucked it at the screen. It hit the protective sheet of Plexiglas and bounced with a thud to the floor, barely leaving a smudge. The intended result not achieved, Amatullah began cursing into the phone with renewed vigor.

Ashani looked back and forth between Amatullah and the screen as if he were at a sporting event. He had secretly wondered when this moment would come. With the war next door in Iraq the MEK had grown in both strength and audacity. For years it was his ministry that hunted down the dissidents and revolutionaries and assassinated them. In recent years it was his own people who lived in fear. The incidents were isolated to the northern provinces, but the tide was nonetheless turning. He had been warning Amatullah and the rest of the council that they were in real danger of the insurgency spreading to other provinces.

But Amatullah and his core advisors were so blinded by their own plans to sow insurrection in neighboring Afghanistan and Iraq that they refused to heed his warnings.

Almost as if it had been cued by a producer, the screen in Amatullah's office turned to fuzz just as the masked MEK spokesman finished saying, "With the destruction of the Isfahan facility we have marked the beginning of the end of these tyrants, and the start of the fight for a true Islamic and democratic Iran."

29

MOSUL, IRAQ

The beat-up Cutlass rolled down the mostly empty street. The extra weight of its armor plating made for a sluggish ride. The sun was not up yet, and a gray haze hung over the entire city. Rapp had been in Mosul for just two days, and Stilwell had already changed cars four times. This particular vehicle reeked of cigarettes and some other sour odor Rapp couldn't quite place and wasn't sure he wanted to. Crumpled pop cans, Styrofoam cups, and sandwich wrappers were strewn about the floor, and the ashtray was overflowing with smashed butts that had been smoked all the way to the nub. It was a ruse Rapp himself had used many times. A play on the Scarlet Pimpernel. Create the illusion that you are a witless slob and people pay you little, if any, attention.

Being the CIA's man in Mosul required a very delicate balancing act. You had to work the street so you could get information and build up your resources, but you needed to be constantly vigilant about your personal security. The other option was to sit behind the relatively safe walls of the nearest American base and let locals come to you. But it was hard to get a sense of what was really going on unless you got out and mixed with the population. Stilwell understood that you needed to put yourself in a position where you could stumble across the lucky find that made the careers of many a foreign intelligence officer—the lucky walk-in. These people typically fell into three categories. The first was the person who was fed up with the power structure. In Iraq, that meant someone who was sick of the corruption and the violence. These were usually the best. Good people who could no longer sit by while terrorists, thugs, and criminals ran their neighborhood. The second type was the person seeking to exchange information for a new life in America or cash. They could be problematic only in the sense that they often told you whatever you wanted to hear. The third, and by far trickiest, was the person seeking vengeance. Unable to settle a business disagreement with a competitor or partner, or a conflict with a neighbor, these people would turn to the CIA and level wild accusations against their foe. More often than not, the person making the accusation was no better, if not worse, than whoever they were trying to turn in. Stilwell had stopped talking to these people.

The most risky part for Stilwell was that he had to basically open up shop so people knew where to find him. The problem with hanging a shingle was that it also put a bull's-eye on his back, and in a city like Mosul, with all of its vying factions any American, let alone a CIA officer, was a ripe target. Stilwell went to great efforts to protect himself. He never slept in the same place more than two nights in a row, he changed cars frequently, and he played himself off as a low-level CIA officer who had almost no authority. He created a fictional boss named Lady Di who was more like Margaret Thatcher than the deceased princess. She called all the shots and had all the power. Stilwell was merely a conduit. His meets usually took place at one of the city's plentiful Internet cafés or one of the open-air markets. He had half a dozen Kurdish body-guards who were seasoned fighters and were extremely loyal to the CIA.

The car rolled up to an intersection and stopped at the red light. They were headed south toward the air-port to meet Kennedy and her entourage. There were signs that the morning hustle and bustle was starting. A few street vendors were setting up their stands, and traffic was beginning to pick up. Rapp watched as Stilwell looked both ways. He was about to run the light until a woman covered from head to ankle in a black Naqab stepped off the curb with a child on each hand. The little boy was in jeans and a sweater, and the girl was wearing the hijab or Muslim scarf. The mother looked straight ahead through the slits in her hood. The boy of about five and his older sister of a few years looked at Rapp and smiled. Rapp grinned, gave them a little wave and said a silent prayer that they would make it through the day without being maimed or killed. The complete lack of respect for life by the insurgents was heartbreaking.

During a recent session with one of Langley's shrinks Rapp had been asked if he thought killing was too easy for him. He'd been through enough of these evaluations to know that accusations were made in the form of a question. If they were asking it, it was being written down in his file as an opinion or fact. For starters, Rapp had a hard time with people who had no practical field experience. He had no patience with anyone who second-guessed his work from the comfort of a predictable, climate-controlled office while making decisions with a warm cup of coffee at hand and no fear whatsoever of getting killed in the next five minutes.

Rapp would never tell one of the shrinks this, but he had found almost nothing more satisfying than tracking down a man who had the blood of innocent people on his hands and punching his ticket. If it had to be a head shot from a half a mile, so be it. If it meant painting a target with a laser so an American jet could drop a 500-pound bomb on the idiot's head, fine, but if he had his choice he preferred close proximity. Rapp wanted to look them in the eye while it dawned on them that their pathetic life was coming to a painful conclusion. His victims were thugs and bullies who thought of themselves as brave because they loaded a car with explosives and then conned some delusional teenager with a death wish into driving it into a building or crowded market. What was their endgame? How could any moral person think such an action could be sanctioned by a supposedly compassionate deity?

The answer was less complicated than many believed. These were men, and make no mistake about it, they were always chauvinistic, bigoted men, devoted to a perverted interpretation of Islam. Men who had bought into violence and division in their youth and refused to let go. Men who had invested so much of their life in hate and blaming others for their troubles that they were too afraid to step back and really think about what they were doing. Men who were frightened to read the entire Koran because they knew they would be confronted with the words of a prophet who would never condone their actions.

These were the animals Rapp hunted. Men who had no respect for human life and consequently would be afforded none in return. There were only a handful of people who really understood the discipline that Rapp practiced. The satisfaction of tracking them, sometimes for months. Knowing when to strike and when to hold your fire. Looking for the perfect opportunity to get close enough to stick a knife through their brain stem and watch every bodily function below the neck shut down. Knowing that you had delivered justice for all the people whose innocent lives had been cut short by the fanatic and his organization. Knowing that never again would the predator take another human life.

Over the years, the mission had taken Rapp to some very forbidding places. He'd spent nights in the humid jungles of the Philippines and Southeast Asia with mosquitoes as big as hummingbirds dive-bombing him. He'd been forced to cross the northern edge of the Sahara Desert on foot to evade Libyan security forces. He'd nearly frozen to death in the Swiss Alps, and in Afghanistan once he was hit with such violent dysentery that he lost seventeen pounds in one week. Most of it while curled up in a ball on the floor of a dank, depressing apartment.

As he rode through the dusty, ancient city of Mosul, Rapp came to the conclusion that he would take his chances in those other places any day. The city of almost two million people gave him a nagging sense of just how divided this part of the world still was. Last night Ridley had gone back to the base so he could be in secure communication with Langley and help prepare for Kennedy's arrival while Rapp and Stilwell went to check out the safe house and the neighborhood where Kennedy would be meeting her counterpart. He and Stilwell had walked down Ninawa Street to the Tigris and then turned south to Amir Zayo Street, where the safe house was located. Four of the bodyguards were with them, two in front and two trailing who stayed within a block at all times. The reconnaissance took an hour, and while Rapp saw no actual violence, there were signs of it everywhere.

Buildings were pocked from gunfire and shrapnel. A handful were scorched from explosions and a few were half destroyed. The police presence around the courthouse was heavy, even in the evening after it was closed. The main roads were clogged with orange and white taxis and old Japanese-made cars.

At one point a U.S. Army column of Stryker vehicles rolled by. The eight-wheeled armored combat vehicles stopped traffic and rattled windows. Rapp observed as some people stood and watched while others melted away down alleys and inside shops. The tension was obvious. Half of these people wanted the conquering army gone, while the other half desperately wanted them to stay and keep the country from sliding into a full-blown civil war. It was this tension that gave Rapp a sense of foreboding. Like a big storm was coming and there was nothing he could do to stop it. The inability to clearly assess who was a threat and who wasn't complicated the situation in ways that caused immeasurable stress. It was nearly impossible to keep all the players straight, and even if you could, there was no guarantee that some of them wouldn't switch sides in the heat of battle.

Stilwell was the one reassuring factor. The man had done his job to near perfection. The safe house was located directly across the street from where the meeting would take place. It was at one of Stilwell's Internet cafés where he would meet his contacts. The owner was the cousin of one of Stilwell's bodyguards. Stilwell slid him an extra thousand dollars a month in cash just to use the place. The second-story apartment across the street was stocked with provisions. It was a classic no-frills operation. They had military cots, military rations, and lots of military hardware in case the place came under siege. There was a grenade launcher, a half dozen M-4 rifles and Glock .45-caliber pistols, a big Barrett .50-caliber sniping rifle, two M249 SAWs, and a case of M67 fragmentation hand grenades. There was also body armor, a triage kit, a communications/surveillance package, and a stack of old magazines and paperbacks. All of this was protected by a reinforced steel door with three heavy-duty dead bolts. The windows were covered with bars, and tiny security cameras covered the stairwell, street, and the inside of the apartment. Stilwell had all four safe houses set up in the same manner and was able to monitor the cameras over the Internet.

Rapp had fallen asleep around 11:00 p.m. with the door barred and his loaded .45-caliber Glock next to him. Shortly before 2:00 a.m. he was pulled from a dream by the sound of gunshots. He lay awake for more than an hour, and then just as he was falling back asleep, there were more gunshots. This time closer. Stilwell began snoring like a drunk and all Rapp could do was lie there, rest his eyes, and think of all the things he needed to check on in the morning. He finally fell back to sleep as morning approached only to be jolted off his cot by a massive explosion. Rapp flipped on a light and looked over at Stilwell who cracked an eye.

"That was close," Rapp said.

"Don't worry," Stilwell mumbled. "That was one of ours." He then rolled over and was back to snoring in less than a minute.

Rapp looked at the scenery as they hit the main thoroughfare for the airport. He asked himself for at least the tenth time if it was wise to bring Kennedy into this environment. The Iranians refused to meet at the airport, so a neutral spot within the city was agreed upon. They passed the bombed-out carcass of a car, and Rapp let out a yawn.

Stilwell looked over with his toothy grin and asked, "What's the matter? You didn't get a good night's sleep?"

Rapp looked straight ahead and frowned. "I don't know what was worse, the gunfire or your snoring."

"My snoring. You spend enough nights here, you get used to the gunfire."

"I'll bet." Rapp nodded thoughtfully and made a mental note to have Kennedy give Stilwell a commendation and a big fat raise. These guys in the field were never paid enough.

30

The Russian-made Hind Mi-24 helicopter came in fast and looped around the ruins of the ancient city of Nineveh. Ashani looked down at the crumbling Assyrian ruins and thought of his own country's place in history. He didn't remember all the facts, but he knew the capital of the Assyrian Empire had fallen approximately a thousand years before the prophet's arrival. The Medians and the Babylonians had crushed the city and then in turn were conquered by Cyrus the Great. The days when the Persians controlled everything from the Mediterranean to modern-day India were long gone. Any hopes of ever attaining the prominence of his predecessors seemed impossible. Based on recent developments, they would be lucky if the once former empire didn't contract further.

Ashani had felt for some time that the government was in a far more tenuous position than anyone would acknowledge. His fellow members on the Supreme Security Council were either too disconnected from what was going on or had surrounded themselves with sycophants who only told them what they wanted to hear. That was definitely the case with Amatullah. He had grown to believe his own propaganda and his ability to get others to believe it as well.

The debacle at the United Nations had stung. In addition to the entire issue being tabled by the Security Council, America's accusation that Iran was trying to cover up an internal revolt had gained some real traction. Foreign Minster Salehi's weak counter-accusation that America had fabricated the information only seemed to worsen things. Salehi's protest in the face of Secretary of State Wicka's avalanche of information looked lame even to Ashani. The international press was running stories that for the first time since the revolution, questioned the ability of the government in Tehran to hold on to power. Protests were springing up in the northern provinces, and in Tehran his people were telling him the mood on the street was combustible.

The Supreme Leader was characteristically absent, choosing to focus instead on the religious well-being of the country. Ashani had his suspicions that the Supreme Leader was distancing himself from a sinking ship, giving Amatullah all the rope he needed to either save or hang himself. Ashani thought the Supreme Leader was trying to elevate his position of spiritual leader to such heights that he would be safe should Amatullah fail in rallying support from the international community and regaining control of his fellow Iranians. Several banks had been firebombed overnight. Amatullah put the security services on full alert and ordered them to arrest anyone at even the whiff of trouble.

The helicopter leveled out and began a slow descent toward a parking lot near the river. Ashani glanced to his right and looked at the back of Imad Mukhtar, who was looking out the starboard side window and talking on a cell phone. As if things weren't bad enough, Amatullah was now taking counsel from Mukhtar. The head of Hezbollah's paramilitary wing was a useful tool for certain things, but advising the Iranian president during this heightened crisis was not one of them. He was far too obtuse to be offering advice on such complicated matters. Even in the face of what had happened at the United Nations, Mukhtar had lobbied to launch attacks against Israel and America. When pressed by Ashani as to why, he proclaimed that guilty or not the two nations had benefited by the act and should be punished. Not getting anywhere with Ashani, Mukhtar directed his words at Amatullah, telling him that by striking back at the Jews and the Americans the Iranian people would see them as guilty.

"And if they decide to strike back?" Ashani asked yet again.

Mukhtar looked at him smugly and shook his head. "They do not want to fight us. Trust me."

As Ashani thought back to the meeting late last night, he couldn't shake the nagging sense that America would push back. Not a single member of the Supreme Council had any idea just how shaky their footing was. Ashani could feel the trouble in the wind. Civil disobedience was up. Greater numbers of women were wearing makeup and designer clothes that showed more skin than the clerics would ever tolerate. A crackdown was looming, and this time Ashani had a growing suspicion that it would send the people into a real revolt against the harsh policies of their government. Amatullah would do whatever it took to keep his blessed revolution rolling on. It was all he had. All he knew. He had invested too much time and effort to let it fail. Even if it was beyond saving.

Ordering him to bring Mukhtar on such a delicate mission was proof that Amatullah was desperate. The two men were up to something, and Ashani was sure that whatever it was, it would only make matters worse. Ashani was informed of this strange addition to his entourage only this morning. He immediately put a call in to the Presidential Palace to ask why. When Amatullah finally got on the line, he told Ashani that Mukhtar needed to talk to Hezbollah's commander in Mosul. The man had very important information that the Americans had backed the entire MEK operation to sabotage the Isfahan facility. Ashani wondered what could have possibly developed after he had left the Presidential Palace at half past midnight. All night Amatullah had been holding firm that America had fabricated the evidence at the UN, which in his mind proved they had been the ones who had destroyed the facility with their stealth planes. Now, he was suddenly reversing course and claiming the facility was in fact destroyed by sabotage. None of it made any sense.

The helicopter set down in a nearly empty parking lot.

Mukhtar extended his hand to Ashani and said, "Remember. Allah favors the bold. He has great plans for us. That is why we survived the attack in Isfahan."

"Allah is great." Ashani exited the helicopter and approached his security chief, who had flown in the night before to coordinate protection with their people from Department 9000—the group that recruited, trained, and funded Shia insurgents in Iraq. Men from the local Shia militia were providing transportation and security to and from the meeting. All of them were wearing black hoods. Ashani greeted his security chief and then turned to an American whom he had met twice before.

The man from the CIA stepped forward and extended his hand. "Minister Ashani, thank you for coming all this way."

"Mr. Ridley," Azad said in perfect English, "you have traveled much further than I." He shook the man's hand.

"That's true," Ridley replied, "but we still appreciate you making the effort."

"I appreciate Director Kennedy reaching out. Not talking only leads to further misunderstandings." Ashani noticed Ridley looking over his shoulder. He turned and saw the back of Mukhtar. The terrorist was holding a large briefcase and walking hurriedly to the other side of the parking lot. Mukhtar stepped into a blue-and-white police SUV that was sandwiched on each end by police pickup trucks with heavy machine guns mounted in the beds. Policemen wearing black hoods were loaded into the back of the trucks.

"Who's that?" Ridley asked.

For a moment Ashani toyed with the idea of telling the American spy the truth. Mukhtar was on the FBI's list of most-wanted terrorists. The man from the CIA probably had the ability to call in an air strike on very short notice. It would have simplified his life greatly if the man were dead, but he couldn't bring himself to do it. Ashani instead chose to ask a question of his own.

"I trust Director Kennedy is waiting?"

Ridley kept his eye on the other man and watched as the police vehicles began to move. He hoped whoever Stilwell had hired was getting shots of the man. "Yes. As soon as I tell her we are on the way she will move."

"Good. I'm looking forward to speaking with her."

31

Director Kennedy's plane landed just before sunrise. Ridley and General Tom Gifford, the base commander, met her. She was then escorted by Gifford to the officers' quarters, where she was given a room. After a hot shower and a change of clothes she grabbed some breakfast and went over to the CIA's station located within a sector of the base that was highly secure. It consisted of four trailers that formed a square with an open courtyard in the middle. The courtyard was filled with satellite dishes and arrayed antennas. Double layers of sandbags were stacked along the walls of the trailers, as well as the roofs, where the bags sat atop reinforced plywood planks. Random mortar attacks on the base were not uncommon. One trailer was devoted entirely to the sensitive communication equipment. Another was split into four offices and a reception area; a third trailer doubled as a lounge and conference room, and the fourth trailer served as a bunkhouse and storage area. On the far side of the compound four empty cargo containers had been strung together to form a makeshift jail and interrogation facility. The entire area was ringed with a heavy-gauge fence and razor wire.

Stilwell escorted Rapp through the security checkpoint and they found Kennedy in the communications shack. She was receiving a briefing from the deputy director of the CIA's Global Ops Center back in Langley. While Rapp waited for her to finish the videoconference, he took the opportunity to sit down with the head of Kennedy's security detail and go over the plan. Rapp had known Tom McDonald for five years. He had the perfect mentality for his job. He was steady, alert, and typically unflappable. The first thing Rapp noticed was that McDonald seemed unusually edgy this morning. Rapp soon found out why.

McDonald had flown in with Kennedy just a few hours earlier, but he'd sent an advance team out the day before. Six men accompanied three armored Suburbans in the belly of a C-17 Starlifter. They unloaded the equipment and decided to take two of the Suburbans off base and do a dry run to the meeting place and back to the airport. The men got momentarily lost in a bad part of town and came under fire. Both vehicles made it back to the base, but one of them was pretty shot up. McDonald had taken a look at the vehicle right before Rapp arrived. They counted over forty hits from small arms and rifle fire. The armor had performed as advertised, but the vehicle was out of commission. McDonald didn't even want to tell Kennedy about the incident and Rapp agreed.

McDonald wanted to arrange transportation through General Gifford and one of his Stryker brigades, but one of the negotiating points for the Iranians involved military units. If they saw any American military personnel at the site of the meeting they would walk away. Down one vehicle and limited in his options, McDonald was now going to have to borrow an unarmored SUV from the private security contractor who was going to augment his protective detail.

Rapp was tempted to scrap the entire plan, and put her in the backseat of one of Stilwell's beat-up sedans, but it wasn't his call. In an effort to reassure McDonald he explained that he and Stilwell would be directly across the street during the entire meeting. He went over the arsenal that Stilwell had assembled and told him if anything went wrong they would be able to bring a significant amount of firepower to the fight.

"All you have to do, Mac, is get her to the meeting and back to the base. I checked out the entire neighborhood with Stilwell last night. He's got the thing wired. He's had lookouts posted since seven this morning. Four of them. Two blocks away in every direction. He knows the owner of the café, and he's got a half dozen Kurds on standby. These guys know the neighborhood. Who belongs there and who doesn't. If anything doesn't seem right they'll let us know."

"What do you think of the route?" McDonald asked as he pointed at a map with a red line showing the roads they would take.

Rapp studied the options. On the bright side, they were only five miles from the airport. The only worry was the directness of the route. "I think you made the right call. You could take her north and across one of the bridges but it would double if not triple the length of time you'll have her on the road, and you still have to get her back to this main road, which, Stilwell told me, is like the Indy five hundred with bombs."

"I know. I was already briefed by the base commander. He put sniper teams out last night and has a bomb unit on standby."

Rapp looked at the map again. "I think you've got the right idea here. Limit her exposure. Get her from point A to point B as quick as you can."

"All right." McDonald studied the map. "This isn't like Washington."

"No," Rapp said, "it sure as hell isn't."

The door to the communications trailer opened, and Kennedy entered the room. "Mitchell," she said as she walked toward Rapp.

"Good morning, boss." Rapp checked out her outfit. She was wearing a pair of black hiking boots, a pair of jeans, and a formfitting black jacket called a manteau. A black hijab was draped around her neck and shoulders. Kennedy had spent a significant amount of her youth in the Middle East. Rapp was happy to see she still remembered how to blend in.

Kennedy offered her cheek to Rapp. He leaned in and kissed her.

"How are you feeling?" she asked.

"Fine."

"You look tired." She studied him with a frown.

Rapp pointed at her and looked at McDonald. "She's like my big sister. Does she ever tell you that you look like crap?"

McDonald smiled. "Nope."

"I didn't say crap. I said tired."

"You meant to say crap . . . you're just too polite."

"Well . . . you look really tired. You have dark circles under your eyes and you . . ." Kennedy leaned in and sniffed the air. "You've been smoking," she said disapprovingly.

"Yes, I've been smoking. That's what people do over here. Everyone smokes. That's how you fit in. Otherwise you look like a politically correct American and then they either shoot you or kidnap you, which is a hell of a lot more hazardous to your health than a few smokes."

"Good point," Kennedy conceded.

"What's gone on since last night?"

"The resolutions that were brought on behalf of the Iranians have been tabled, but they are holding firm that they are suspending our right to innocent passage through the Strait of Hormuz."

"Yeah . . . let's see them try to enforce that one."

"My fear is that they will."

"You can't be serious. It would be the most lopsided naval engagement in history."

"That's my point. They might try to provoke something and make themselves look like the victims.

209

They're desperate, Mitch. This operation that you started is having a real effect. The Brits informed us that two banks and several gas stations were fire-bombed in Tehran last night. They say anti-Amatullah graffiti is suddenly popping up around the city."

"Good. Maybe they'll storm the Presidential Palace."

"If only we could be so lucky."

Stilwell entered the room and said, "Good morning, Director."

"Morning, Stan."

"I just got a call from Rob. He says Ashani has landed and is on his way. It's time to go."

Rapp looked at McDonald and said, "Give me a five minute head start and then don't stop for anything."

"I won't."

He turned to Kennedy and with a reassuring smile said, "Good luck. I'll be close by in case anything goes wrong."

32

The street was blocked at each end by police cruisers. One of the blue-and-white cruisers backed onto the curb to allow Ashani's motorcade to pass. The three vehicles stopped directly in front of the café. Ashani opened his door and stepped onto the curb as the masked men in his security detail spread out. Ashani thought the whole thing a bit overdone. He proceeded into the café with his security chief and the man from the CIA. The place was small. Fifteen feet wide by about forty feet deep. The floor was covered with beige, rectangular tiles. The grout had turned from gray to black in the high-traffic areas, and the entire floor seemed to have a coating of grime on it. Ashani looked around. The white walls had taken on a yellowish tinge from all the smoking. It made him think of his lungs, which thankfully were feeling much better. Hopefully the doctor was right, and there would be no lasting effects.

"Minister," Ridley said, "may I get you anything to drink? Director Kennedy should be here in a little bit."

"I would like some tea, please."

Ridley looked at Ashani's security chief, and the man shook his head.

Ashani approached one of the tables halfway back and took a seat in one of the blue fiberglass chairs. He was about to start looking for listening devices and thought better of it. The Americans had such good technology it would be a waste of time. It was more than likely that they would be using lasers or directional microphones to capture the conversation. Ridley came over with his tea and a jar of honey. Ashani was amused that the man from the CIA knew he liked his tea with honey, but didn't show it. He thanked him and was about to mix in the honey when he saw his counterpart's entourage show up.

Ashani set the honey down and stood. He watched as a large man carrying a machine gun entered the room in front of Kennedy. He surveyed the entire place and then stepped out of the way and gestured for the director of the CIA to enter. Kennedy stepped over the threshold and took off her oversized black sunglasses.

Ashani had met face-to-face with the director of the CIA on two previous occasions. According to his dossier on her she was forty-six years old. She also happened to be the youngest person to ever run the American spy agency and the first woman. She had a Ph.D. in Arabic studies and was the divorced mother of a boy approximately the age of ten. Ashani knew that obscure fact because several years ago Mukhtar and his animals at Hezbollah had come to him with a proposal to kidnap the boy. Ashani gave the paramilitary leader of Hezbollah a stern rebuke for even considering such an operation.

"Director Kennedy," Ashani said as he extended his right hand, "it is good to see you again."

Kennedy smiled. "I wish it was under better circumstances, Minister Ashani."

"Please call me Azad."

"Only if you'll call me Irene."

"Of course. Sit." He motioned to the chair across from his. "May I get you something to drink?"

"Tea would be nice." Kennedy pulled out her chair and sat.

Ashani looked to his security chief and nodded toward the barista behind the counter. He then joined Kennedy at the table. He studied her face for a moment and thought she looked at ease. Either she was very good at dealing with stress or she was a good actress. He guessed by the lack of worry lines around her eyes that she handled stress well.

Gesturing toward her face, Ashani said, "You did not have to wear the hijab on my account."

Kennedy touched the black scarf she had draped over her head and shoulders. "I don't mind it. I wore one as a girl."

"You lived abroad?" Ashani was playing dumb, as he knew that she had.

"Yes. Cairo, Damascus, and then Beirut."

Ashani nodded and acted surprised.

"But then again . . . I'm sure you knew about Beirut."

"What about Beirut?" he said with a straight face.

"I did not come here to open old wounds, but I think it's very important that we be honest with each other if we are going to find a way out of this mess."

Ashani hesitated and then said, "I would agree."

"Then I find it hard to believe that as Iran's minister of intelligence, you didn't already know that my father was killed in the U.S. Embassy bombing in Beirut back in nineteen eighty-three." Kennedy would have liked to have added that the bombing had been carried out by Hezbollah and sponsored by Iran, but there was no need to state the obvious. Ashani knew who was behind the carnage, and he knew Kennedy knew as well.

Ashani took a sip of tea and then delicately said, "I'm sorry about your father. I do not like all this violence. Too many innocent people have been killed."

Ashani's man placed a cup of steaming tea in front of Kennedy and backed away. Kennedy picked up the cup with both hands and said, "Far too many."

"There are many in my country," Ashani said while putting both arms on the table and leaning closer to Kennedy, "who question how evil the U.S. really is. You have rid us of both Saddam and the Taliban. As you well know, we Shia and Sunni do not like each other. The only time we stop fighting is when someone like you gets in the middle."

"Sad but true."

There was a moment of uncomfortable silence, and then Ashani said, "We have a situation here that I am afraid could spin out of control. There are many people in my government who want blood for the destruction of the Isfahan facility. Our Persian pride demands it."

"Pride can be a very destructive thing."

Ashani snorted. "Yes. You are right, but I'm afraid there are few people in my government who see it that way. They want someone to pay for this offense."

"Then they should crack down on the insurgents and leave us and Israel out of it. Or are they too afraid to admit they have an internal problem?"

"I did not come here to discuss the inner workings of my government," Ashani said a bit more seriously. "I was invited to listen to you and find a mutually agreeable solution to this mess."

Kennedy sipped her tea and then said, "President

Alexander is flirting with the idea of opening limited diplomatic relations."

"Interesting. What is the incentive for my government?"

"You have twenty to thirty percent inflation; you import forty percent of your oil, even though you have the second-highest oil reserves of any country behind Saudi Arabia; and your economy is about to collapse. You have an internal revolt brewing that like before will be met with a crackdown from the religious extremists. Although this time it is less certain they will succeed." Kennedy stopped to see if Ashani wanted to argue any of these points. He didn't, so she continued.

"If you were to meet us halfway and agree that it is time for our two nations to bury old wounds and forge a lasting peace that respects both Islam and freedom, we would restore relations on a level that would encourage American investment in your country."

"There are many in my country," Ashani said, "who think you were behind the destruction of the Isfahan facility."

Kennedy looked him straight in the eye and said, "I can promise you, we had nothing to do with the attack."

"That may well be the case. I am just telling you, the hardliners will want something more concrete than the possibility that American banks might invest in our country."

"American financial institutions will follow the U.S.

government. That is why the president is prepared to offer you a billion dollars in guaranteed loans."

Ashani was surprised. "What is the catch?"

"The money must go toward building new refineries. The loans will be interest-free for the first three years, and after that they will be locked in at five percent."

"The money has to be used to build refineries?"

"The president feels it is the only way he can get a majority of the Congress to back it."

"You want us to renounce our nuclear program?"

"No." She shook her head. "Not publicly."

"But privately."

"It would help."

Ashani winced. "There are those in my country who are obsessed with becoming a nuclear power."

Kennedy leaned in and whispered, "Your economy is close to collapsing. You are on the verge of another revolution, only this time, you guys are going to be the ones thrown out of power. This is a chance for you to stave off disaster."

Ashani scratched his beard, looked past Kennedy and the dusty front door. With just his limited view he counted five men in urban combat gear holding their weapons at the ready. This could be Tehran in a year or two if economic stability wasn't reached. One thing bothered him, though. Ashani looked carefully into Kennedy's eyes and asked, "Why?"

"Why what?"

"Why are you offering to help us?"

Kennedy nodded. Despite Ashani's relatively open mind, there was no getting over the fact the he had spent all of his adult life in a country that blamed America for virtually every woe. "Because we feel," Kennedy started out slowly, "that there are enough people like you, Azad, decent people who want to put an end to the hatred and violence. Who knows what type of government might take over after a second revolution? Who's to say it won't be more fundamentalist and anti-Western than the current government?" Kennedy shook her head. "We have learned the hard way that economic instability in Middle East is not in the best interest of the United States. The lack of opportunity makes it all too easy for the clerics to preach their hatred. We want to see a resurgence in Persian pride. We want you to take control of your own destiny. We want to see you make advances in science and health. We want to see you succeed, if for no other reason than we stop getting blamed for your failures."

Ashani had a look of intense concentration on his face. Everything she had just said was true, but selling it to men whose entire power base was dependent on a hatred of America would be exceedingly difficult.

Kennedy knew what he was thinking. "I know this is risky. That is why I am here and not Secretary of State Wicka. My president sent me because he knows you and I have proven that our two countries can work together."

"That is true, but this is a big step."

217

"What is your alternative, Azad?" Kennedy put her arms out and motioned in each direction. "Is this what you want? Car bombs and sectarian violence, kidnappings and bloodletting? We both know your country is closer to this than the mullahs would ever admit."

With downcast eyes, Ashani slowly nodded.

"Then what is your answer?"

In Ashani's mind there was no doubt this was the right thing to do, but selling it to the Supreme Council would be extremely difficult. His mind kept returning to Amatullah. The Peacock President would hate this with every fiber of his body. Still, there was a chance that the Supreme Leader would see it as an opportunity for his people to avoid years of pain and suffering. Finally, Ashani looked at Kennedy and said, "It is my sincere hope that this will be recorded as the moment our two countries forged a new and lasting friendship. I must warn you, though, that this is going to be very hard for me to sell to the Supreme Council."

"I know it will, but I hope for the sake of both our countries you succeed."

33

U.S.S. VIRGINA, GULF OF OMAN

Captain Pete Halberg was a prime candidate for an ulcer. The forty-five-year-old graduate of Annapolis never lost his temper. Not with his wife, not with his six kids, and never with his crew. He internalized stress by shoving it down into the pit of his stomach, where he fed it with black coffee. Usually ten cups a day or more. His only saving grace was the twenty minutes he put in on the heavy bag in the bowels of his sub's engine room. That and the bottle of Tums antacid tablets that he went through every week. On this particular morning the pucker factor on the bridge was running high.

Command of any submarine was an intensely stressful, yet rewarding job. Commanding one of America's newest fast attack submarines was in a league all by itself. The United States Navy had entrusted Halberg with the two-billion-dollar technological marvel and given him 134 submariners to lead. The cruise had been fairly routine up until two days prior when they'd received a flash message from Submarine Task Force Commander or CTF 54. Their orders were to leave the Dwight D. Eisenhower Strike Group, which was on patrol in the Persian Gulf, and proceed to the Gulf of Oman, where Halberg and his crew were to locate and track one of Iran's three Kilo-class subs that had left port in a hurry.

Shortly after midnight they'd followed a Liberian supertanker filled with crude through the Strait of Hormuz and entered the deeper waters of the Gulf of Oman. At 377 feet the U.S.S. *Virginia* was seventeen feet longer than the depth of the main shipping channel. There wasn't a sub in the world, other than her sister ships, that could come even close to her capabilities, but she had her limits. Halberg and his entire crew had breathed a collective sigh of relief when they reached the deeper water of the Gulf of Oman. The *Virginia*'s strength lay in her stealth, firepower, and speed. To use those, however, she needed room to maneuver. If the Persian Gulf was a six-lane divided highway on a dry sunny day, the Strait of Hormuz was a narrow dark alley on a dark rainy night. Twenty-seven miles at the narrowest point, it was dotted with islands and packed with shipping traffic. Most of its supertankers were nearly 1,000 feet long. The currents were quick and once outside the main shipping channel there were countless uncharted wrecks.

Based on the information provided by CTF 54, Halberg and his executive officer, Dennis Strilzuk, agreed on the most likely location of the Kilo. They set up a patrol grid and then Halberg turned over the command duty officer watch to the exec so he could grab a few hours of sleep. Four hours later he woke up refreshed and returned to the bridge. Traveling at five knots on an easterly heading, the lightweight wide-aperture array picked up the Kilo running at the same speed in the opposite direction, parallel to the Iranian coast.

It was a predictable maneuver that they had seen the Iranians use dozens of times. They would run their subs out of their base in Bandar Abbas in broad daylight for all the world to see and then transit through the strait on the surface. Once clear of the shipping channel they'd dive and then put the pedal to the metal. Usually, just north of Muscat, Oman, they would decrease speed to five knots and begin a series of lazy figure eights to make sure no American subs were trailing them. Then they would slowly work their way north and skirt the Iranian coastline just inside territorial waters, looking for an American warship they could fall in behind and tail back through the strait.

When Halberg arrived in control, Strilzuk explained what was going on.

"About thirty minutes ago, he broke for international water and started running the race track right here on the shelf." Strilzuk pointed to a location on the chart that showed where the Gulf of Oman stepped its way up from a depth of 1,000 meters to 100 meters. The location was right on the doorstep of the Strait of Hormuz.

Halberg sipped his coffee. "That doesn't make any sense."

"No, it doesn't. Why go to all that effort to disappear and then start beating your chest?"

"Unless you want to be found," Halberg mused.

"That's what I was thinking." Strilzuk handed the skipper a printed message from CTF 54. "This came in about an hour ago."

Halberg scanned the message without the aid of glasses. With his oldest child already in college, he was very proud of the fact that he didn't need reading specs. According to the message the Iranian naval base at Bandar Abbas was a beehive of activity. Her two remaining Kilo subs, the *Tareq* and *Noor*, had rushed out of port in the middle of the night along with four of their minisubs.

Strilzuk pointed to the nearest color monitor and said, "These satellite photos were taken at zero four hundred. Every frigate in the harbor is glowing. They're getting ready to put their entire navy to sea."

Halberg looked down at the plotting table. The old paper charts had been replaced by a flat computer screen that provided real-time tactical information. With the aid of a complex navigation system, the display showed the exact location of the *Virginia*, the Iranian Kilo they were shadowing, and virtually every other ship in the Gulf of Oman. Halberg pressed a button and the screen changed magnification to show the tactical situation in the Persian Gulf. Two of the six Iranian subs were already missing. The other four were all headed northwest toward the Eisenhower strike group. Halberg assumed the missing subs were also headed in that direction. He'd been patrolling these waters on and off for nearly twenty years, and this was as aggressive as he'd ever seen the Iranians.

Halberg changed the plotting screen back to his immediate area of responsibility. He looked at the location of the Iranian Kilo that they had identified as the Yunes, the most modern of their subs. She appeared to be guarding the entrance to the Strait of Hormuz.

"Why don't you grab some sleep," Halberg said to Strilzuk. "I'll start the next watch early."

"You sure?"

"Positive." Halberg settled into his chair in the Command and Control Center and asked for a cup of coffee. As he studied the battlefield layout on the array of screens in the CACC, he got the feeling that this was not going to be another boring day at sea.

34

MOSUL, IRAQ

Rapp was wearing a loose-fitting pair of pleated black dress pants and a gray dress shirt that was untucked. He stood behind Stilwell looking down at one of the flat-panel monitors. The screen was split in two. The left half showed Kennedy. The right half showed Ashani. Their conversation was relayed via a pair of desktop speakers with reasonable clarity. As Kennedy had predicted, the dialogue was progressing without conflict. This should have reassured Rapp, but it didn't.

Something didn't seem right. He ran a hand through his thick, black hair and then scratched his beard. His eyes moved to a second monitor showing four separate shots of the street. The policemen at the north barricade looked tense and a bit jumpy. It was decided that they would not be told any specifics about the meeting. Especially that the director of the CIA was one of the two principles. The Iranian demand that no U.S. military personnel be involved with the security complicated things a bit.

The local police were the next best choice for crowd control. At least that's what Ridley thought. Rapp was having second thoughts. The police seemed to be more concerned with what was going on inside the security perimeter than what was going on outside. Their job was to screen pedestrians and make sure no vehicles gained access to the block.

Fortunately, pedestrian traffic was sparse. The natives knew to stay away from the police checkpoints for the simple fact that they provided ripe targets for the fundamentalist suicide bombers. As Rapp was trying to get a read on the situation, two more police vehicles pulled up. They were pickup trucks, each with a .50-caliber machine gun mounted to the roof of the cab. Two .50-caliber heavy machine guns was a lot of firepower. The gunners were wearing flak jackets and black hoods, but beyond that they were standing fully exposed in the back of the pickups. It was the perfect job for a young recruit who would think himself invincible behind the heavy gun. In reality, though, they were ripe targets. In a gunfight they wouldn't last long, standing and exposed like that. Any decent marksman could pick them off. Rapp noticed that the men handling the big guns also appeared more concerned about what was happening inside the security cordon than what was going on outside.

Rapp shifted his gaze to a picture of the men who were providing transport for Minister Ashani. They were parked directly across the street from the café and their American counterparts. As they were dressed in street clothes and wearing black hoods to conceal their faces, Rapp guessed they were either Quds Force or members of a local Shia militia. They were all holding AK-74s. He understood why the militants had to conceal their faces, but the fact that the police did as well spoke volumes about the lawlessness of the city.

Rapp tapped Stilwell on the shoulder and said, "Am I just imagining it, or does it look like the police and these guys in the hoods are itching to get in a gunfight with each other?"

"Nope," Stilwell kept his eyes on screen, "you're not imagining anything. It's the same old story. Most of the cops are Sunni, and these guys in the hoods are Shia. They're like Yankees and Red Sox fans, except they've hated each other for a lot longer."

"Yankees and Red Sox fans don't kill each other."

"They might . . . if they had to live in the same city."

Rapp didn't like any of this. The last thing they needed was Kennedy getting caught in the crossfire between the Hatfields and the McCoys. "Can we trust these militia guys?"

"How do you mean?"

"How do we know they're not going to start a fight?"

"We don't."

"Wonderful."

"Mitch, the only people I trust in this town are my Kurds."

Rapp looked down at all the cops. "Not even the police?"

"Least of all the police."

"You can't be serious."

"I sure the hell am. They're one of the most corrupt groups in the damn city. If a fight starts there's a better than fifty percent chance they'll just run."

"Then why are we using them?"

"Because we don't have a lot of options."

"Shit."

"Mitch, it's not as bad as you think. These guys have no idea who they're protecting. All they know is they're going to get a nice big cash bonus from us if this thing goes off without any problems."

Rapp looked at the security monitor with renewed concern. He pointed at the screen and said, "Look at these two idiots. They've got those fifties pointed in the wrong direction."

Stilwell checked out the screen and shook his head. "There is no such thing as muzzle discipline over here. There isn't a day that goes by where I don't have to tell some idiot to lower his gun. And they're all walking around with the damn things chambered, safeties off, and their fingers on the trigger. Accidental discharges are as common as car wrecks . . . and they aren't good drivers."

Rapp swore to himself. An accidental discharge in a situation like this would likely result in a thousand plus rounds flying through the air in every direction. He walked over to the window and looked through a slit in the curtain down at the street. Rapp had a secure radio clipped to his belt and a wireless earpiece in his left ear. He touched the transmit button and said, "Mac, how are you feeling?" Rapp looked directly at Kennedy's security chief who was blocking the entrance to the café.

"Just great," he said sarcastically. "I'm surrounded by men in masks carrying bigger guns than mine who would love nothing more than to kill our boss. Other than that it's a wonderful morning. The sun is out, the temp's in the mid-sixties. I feel like I'm on vacation."

"I know. It sounds like they're wrapping it up. Irene's gotten through all her main points. It shouldn't be much longer, and then you guys can get the hell out of here and back to the airport."

"I'm counting the seconds."

"Hang in there."

Rapp clicked the secure radio out of the two-way mode and looked to the far end of the street. Several of the cops were now milling about with Russian-made rocket-propelled grenade launchers resting on their hips.

"This place is fucking crazy," Rapp mumbled to himself.

There was way too much unsecured firepower. Sub-consciously, he brought his left hand up and touched the .45-caliber Glock 21 pistol on his left hip. Under-neath his oversized gray shirt, Rapp was wearing level-three body armor with a ceramic chicken plate over his heart. The Glock was in a paddle holster with two spare magazines clipped to his belt. Rapp turned his attention away from the street for a moment and eyed the small arsenal Stilwell had assembled on the other side of the room. On the floor was a black composite case with two locking clasps.

Rapp walked over, knelt, and popped the two clasps. He lifted the lid and revealed his personal arsenal: a 5.56 mm rifle with a suppressor, a spare .45, and a Glock 17 with a suppressor, all sitting in foam cutouts. The M-4 was made by Sabre Defense. It was a Massad Ayoob special broken down into a lower and upper receiver. Rapp assembled the weapon in a few seconds, screwed the silencer onto the end, and loaded it with a thirty-round magazine. He checked to make sure the safety was on, then chambered one of the .233 rounds, grabbed two spare magazines, and walked back to the window.

"Call the base," he said to Stilwell, "and make sure the quick-reaction force is at the gate ready to move, and I mean locked and loaded, engines running."

"Will do."

Rapp clutched the grip of the M-4 and checked his watch. It was 11:17. He looked down at all the firepower on the street and couldn't shake the feeling that something wasn't right. One misstep, by either group, and Kennedy and her detail would be caught in the crossfire. Rapp could hear Kennedy's voice coming from the speaker behind him. His eyes narrowed as another police pickup truck joined the other two at the far end of the street. This one was carrying eight men, all in uniforms and black hoods. They piled out of the truck and moved off in pairs toward each corner of the intersection. Rapp swore under his breath and decided enough was enough.

"Mac," Rapp said as he keyed the transmit button on his radio. "I think it's time to wrap this thing up and get her back to the base."

"I agree."

"All right, get your guys ready to move. Minister Ashani goes first and then once he's gone bring her out and hightail it straight back."

"You want me to tell her it's time to go?"

"That's right. Just whisper in her ear that something urgent has come up. They broke the ice. Next time they can meet in Geneva where we won't have to deal with all these crazy bastards."

"Roger."

Rapp moved his eyes from the front door of the café to the militia men and then the cops at the far end. The sliding glass door was already open. He took a step back so the muzzle wouldn't stick out beyond the curtain and raised his rifle. With both eyes opened, he looked through the L-3 EOTech sight and centered the red dot on the head of the .50-caliber gunner on the far right. He guessed the distance to be about 140 feet. An easy shot. Rapp moved the sight from one gunner to the next and quietly said, "Just stay calm, boys. This will all be over in a few minutes."

Someone who must have been an officer walked up to the two men manning the .50-caliber machine guns and started yelling and pointing in different directions. After a moment the men retrained their guns in the opposite direction. Rapp lowered his rifle and relaxed a bit.

35

Irene Kennedy stood inside the café and watched Ridley and Minister Ashani cross the street. Both men looked back as they were about to climb in their vehicle. The meeting had furthered Kennedy's belief that the Iranian intelligence minister was someone she could work with. Someone she could possibly trust. She smiled warmly at Ashani as he waved at her. Kennedy held her black sunglasses in her right hand and waved back. She could have talked with the man for hours. There was so much they could work on. The relatively short meeting had reconfirmed for her that it was time to bury the hatchet with Iran. Especially if more men like Ashani were in power.

The rest of the men piled into the other two sedans and the motorcade sped off. Kennedy put on her sunglasses and wondered what she was going to do with Rapp. She'd known Mitch since he was a twenty-one-year-old lacrosse star at Syracuse University. She had recruited him, she'd helped train him, and she'd been his handler for most of his storied career. He'd been good from day one. A natural at picking up languages and mannerisms and customs that were unique to every city on the planet. His ability to immerse himself for extended periods of time on overseas assignments, with almost no contact from the Agency, was unique. There'd been plenty of times where the months had ticked away and Kennedy was left wondering if Rapp was still alive.

Somehow, though, he always made it back. And with each successful mission, he became less patient with his handlers. Less comfortable with the suit-and-tie culture of CIA headquarters. Over the years the insubordination worsened. Kennedy's mentor, Thomas Stansfield, told her the good ones were always a bit rebellious. They didn't fit into the bureaucratic structure of Langley. Their missions were too fluid to have real structure. Add to that the reality that they knew everything they did would be picked apart by people who had never been on an overseas assignment in their entire career, and you had a problem.

His marriage had seemed to help a bit. At least Anna had made him see the other side of things. After she was murdered, though, he retrenched and the circle of people he trusted contracted further. Any semblance of patience was now gone. Sitting down with Ashani was a rare opportunity. To have it cut short simply because Rapp thought it was dragging on was infuriating.

Kennedy turned to McDonald and asked, "Why did Mitch think it so imperative that he had to end my meeting?"

"There was a lot of tension out here between the minister's people and the police. It looked like a gunfight was about to break out."

"You can't be serious."

"Boss, I don't joke about stuff like this. Now can we please get you back to the base?"

Kennedy folded her arms and looked across the street at the second-story apartment. She couldn't see Rapp, but she knew he was up there. Kennedy shook her head and said, "Fine. Let's go."

McDonald signaled for three more of his men to come over. A fourth stayed by the rear passenger door of the Suburban. The four men moved in unison, with Kennedy in the middle. The director climbed into the backseat. One of the men followed her and closed the door. Another bodyguard entered from the other side so Kennedy was sandwiched in the middle. McDonald stood by the front passenger door and gave the hand signal for all the other men to load up. When everyone was in their vehicle, he jumped in the front seat of Kennedy's Suburban and gave the order to move out. The five vehicles rolled single file down the block and idled for a second as the police cars moved to allow them through.

Kennedy looked through the front window as they followed the other Suburban past the two police cruisers and turned left. She noted the dozens of masked police officers standing on the other side of the street. They were all in black hoods, holding either machine guns or RPGs. Kennedy reached for her BlackBerry. She pressed several buttons to take it out of silent mode and then, just as she was about to open an e-mail, there was a thunderous explosion. The Suburban lurched to a stop. Kennedy looked through the front window, eyes wide, and mouth agape at the sight of a fireball engulfing the vehicle in front of them.

36

Rapp watched Ashani's entourage move out in a hurry. These militia guys didn't mess around. He moved to a second set of windows to get a better view as they accelerated toward the police checkpoint. This was the moment he'd feared. He half expected the cops to unload on the three vehicles in a modern-day Iraqi version of the climactic scene in *Bonnie and Clyde* where their getaway car gets shredded by a fusillade of bullets. To his relief, the cops cleared the way and the three sedans sped down the open street, toward the Tigris River and their waiting helicopter.

Rapp returned to the other window. "The hard part should be over now that the Hatfields have left town."

"I agree." Stilwell tapped a few keys and changed the camera angles on the main monitor. "This was a hell of an idea you had, Mitch. Could be one for the history books."

"You're getting a little ahead of yourself there, Don Juan. There're plenty of crazy-ass mullahs back in Tehran who are going to hate this."

"Even if they don't take us up on the aid package, you've managed to deflect attention away from us and Israel."

"We'll see." Rapp watched Kennedy climb into her

armored Suburban. The security guys all hustled back to their vehicles and mounted up. The lead Toyota 4Runner started to move. It was all much slower than Ashani's motorcade. One by one the other vehicles followed leisurely down the street. The two police cruisers slid into reverse and provided a gap. The lead vehicle entered the intersection and took a hard left. Next came the first armored Suburban. Rapp had seen Kennedy get in the second Suburban. The other three vehicles were all white Toyota 4Runners that looked like they were on loan from a United Nations convoy. As Kennedy's Suburban started its turn, Rapp noticed something strange. The police on the left side of the street started running in Rapp's direction. Rapp pushed the sliding glass door open and stepped out onto the balcony. He looked to the sidewalk beneath to find out what was going on. There was nothing. No pedestrians. No vehicles. Nothing. He looked back at the running officers and noted that several were looking back over their shoulders. They weren't running toward something, they were running *away* from something. Rapp redirected his gaze to the intersection just as the last vehicle was making its turn.

A flurry of motion just beyond the white SUV caught his attention. Rapp watched as the two police officers manning the .50-caliber machine guns swung them around. Other officers began jumping behind vehicles and taking cover behind buildings. Rapp's body started to tense, his eyes narrowed, and his right hand reached for the safety on his M-4 rifle. Every survival instinct in his body was suddenly screaming that something was wrong. He leaned over the balcony to see if there was some hidden threat that he had yet to identify. As he was doing so, he reached under his shirt and keyed his secure radio so he could hear Kennedy's security detail.

The thunderous report of one of the .50-caliber machine guns caused Rapp to flinch. In this urban setting of hard asphalt and concrete surfaces the concussion of the weapon boomed like a cannon. Rapp watched in horror as two of the big fifties opened up with sustained bursts. The last white SUV was torn to shreds.

There was a loud explosion and then Rapp heard McDonald's voice in his ear. "Shit! We're under attack. Don't stop! Move, move, move!"

The first explosion was followed by two more. Rapp's weapon snapped into the firing position and he screamed back into the apartment, "Get that quick reaction force here ASAP!"

Rapp saw the rear driver's side door of the last SUV open. An obviously wounded security contractor fell out of the vehicle and attempted to seek cover behind the rear wheel. A group of cops hiding behind the trunk of their cruiser opened fire on the man, mercilessly pounding him with dozens of rounds. Rapp took in a deep breath and denied himself the immediate gratification of killing policemen first. They could wait.

The dull, black suppressor on the end of his weapon

only added to its accuracy. The L-3 EOTech sight consisted of a squarish viewfinder with a red dot in the middle. It was an amazing advance in battlefield technology that allowed the shooter to keep both eyes open while zeroing in on a target. Rapp centered the red dot on the head of the .50-caliber gunner on the far right, leaned forward ever so slightly, and squeezed the trigger. The light kick of the M-4 rifle threw the muzzle skyward less than an inch. Rapp's countless hours of training kicked in. He brought the muzzle back on line and swept it to the left in search of the next target. He placed the dot on the open mouth of the gunner who was screaming while he unloaded his heavy-bore weapon on the other vehicles. Rapp squeezed his trigger, the sight jumped and then fell back into place in time to show a cloud of blood silhouetted against the man's black hood as the .223 round blew out a large chunk of his skull. The masked cop continued to clutch the handles of the .50-caliber machine gun for another second, and then his entire body fell backwards over the side of the truck.

"Grab a gun and get out here," Rapp yelled to Stilwell. He was tracking his weapon in search of the other .50-caliber gun, when he saw one of the police officers taking aim with an RPG. Rapp brought the red dot back, centered it on the man's head and fired. The bullet struck the cop in the side of the head just as he was firing his grenade launcher. The force of the bullet sent the grenade off course and into a building where it exploded, taking out three cops. Rapp found the third .50-caliber gun and missed the man on his first shot. He quickly reacquired the target and sent him spiraling out of the truck bed. Rapp began moving from one target to the next in a steady, methodical, unrushed pace, counting each expelled cartridge as he went.

"Mac," Rapp said as calmly as he could. "Give me a status report." He continued to shoot, and count, as he waited to hear from Kennedy's security chief. He squeezed the trigger for the thirtieth time and then dropped to his right knee, ejecting the magazine and reaching for a fresh one. He looked back into the apartment at Stilwell and saw him loading the squad automatic weapon. As Rapp slammed a fresh magazine into his M-4 he tried to visualize the battlefield and what was happening around the corner to the rest of Kennedy's motorcade. Rapp fought back a sense of doom. There was no time for that now. He needed to stay focused and try his best to hold them off until reinforcements arrived from the base.

He chambered a round, stood, found a new martyr trying to man one of the .50-caliber machine guns, and hit him in the side of his head. Rapp heard moaning over his earpiece.

"Mac, is that you? Are you all right?" Rapp searched for a new target, which wasn't easy. The cops had started to figure out that a good way to get killed was to try and man one of the .50-caliber guns. "Mac," Rapp called out again. He watched as two of the cops pointed down the street and then jumped in one of the squads and peeled out. Rapp's spirits soared for a second. He didn't think the Stryker column could have gotten here that fast, but it had to be why the cops were running.

As quickly as his spirits had soared, they sank like a rock in a pond when he saw a beat-up sedan race through the intersection toward Kennedy's motorcade. The vehicle was followed by two more, and then two vans and a truck that stopped in the middle of the intersection. Some of the cops took off while others stayed and began stripping off their uniforms. Rapp stopped shooting for a moment, not sure who he should target.

Stilwell joined Rapp on the balcony, and said, "We got some bad news. The quick reaction force has a problem."

Before Rapp could ask what the problem was, the Kurds entered the room just then and began shouting at their boss. Rapp noticed that several of them were wearing black balaclava hoods. He looked at all the firepower in the corner of the apartment and then the street that was suddenly crawling with hooded militia types.

Rapp yelled for everyone to be quiet and asked Stilwell, "What kind of problem?"

"I didn't get an answer out of them. All I was told was the base was under lockdown."

Rapp let loose with a string of profanity and then looked at one of the hooded Kurds. He stuck out his hand and said, "Give me your balaclava."

The man didn't respond quickly enough so Rapp screamed his order like a drill sergeant.

"What are you doing?" Stilwell asked.

"I'm going down there." Rapp took the black hood from the Kurd.

"Are you out of your fucking mind?"

"I don't want to talk about it. Open up those crates," Rapp pointed to the stockpile of weapons, "put half the guys up on the roof and the other half out on the balcony and start pounding the shit out of anything that moves except me."

Rapp put on the hood and looked at the Kurds. "Don't shoot me. Black pants, gray shirt, black hood." He touched each garment. "Everybody except me."

37

Imad Mukhtar looked through the dusty storefront window and surveyed the scene on the street. A block and a half away the police had set up their barricade just as they had told him they would. Mukhtar had leaned heavily on Ali Abbas. He'd handpicked Abbas two years earlier to be Hezbollah's commander in Mosul. During that time Abbas had built up a very effective network. He didn't have as many successes as his counterparts in other cities like Basra and Baghdad, but his job was much more difficult due to the large Kurdish population. He had been put here to collect intelligence and run limited operations against the Americans. One of the things they had discovered was the near-total corruption that was rampant in the Sunni-dominated police department. Virtually every man on the force had moved to the northern city on Saddam's orders as part of a plan to lessen the influence of the Kurds and Shiite populations.

Now that Saddam was gone, they were doing whatever it took to survive. In many ways they were more like local organized crime than a police force. If someone wanted protection, they had to pay for it. Even those who wanted to be left alone had to pay money. Getting the police to cooperate had required a lie, and a large portion of the $250,000 that Amatullah had given him. Abbas had told Mukhtar that the police would more than likely not be involved in the plan if they knew the intended target was someone as high-ranking as the director of the Central Intelligence Agency. A similar operation that they ran in conjunction with the Iranian Quds force had brought too much heat down on the police in the days that followed. So a convenient lie was constructed.

They told the police commander that the intended target was a Jewish banker from Switzerland. Mukhtar knew that both sides had agreed the local police would be hired for traffic and perimeter control only. It was agreed that they would not be told who was at the meeting. Mukhtar offered the commander more money; the man took the offer and then intimated that he would also like a cut of the ransom. Mukhtar acquiesced after another ten minutes of negotiating. The commander tried to negotiate further, but Mukhtar had had enough. He told the man his exposure was minimal. Mukhtar already had the men and the police vehicles. All the commander needed to do was keep his own men away until the dust had settled and the American military showed up. Then he could come in and act as if he knew nothing.

Mukhtar kept his eyes on Abbas. He was wearing a police uniform and standing at the next corner waiting to signal Mukhtar that the motorcade was about to move. Mukhtar had already called him and told him to tell the imbeciles in the pickup trucks to point their guns in the other direction until he gave the order to attack. The Americans were stupid but not that stupid.

Abdullah had made it clear that it was crucial that Minister Ashani make it back alive. For their plan to work they did not need the public embarrassment of such a high-ranking official caught meeting with the director of the CIA. In most cases Mukhtar thought people expendable, but not this time. He owed Ashani for saving his life. If it weren't for the minister he would have followed that idiot Ali Farahani down into that pit of radioactive waste. The thought of such a death caused his hands to tremble momentarily. Several years earlier during one of their brief wars with the Zionists, an Israeli bomb had found the building where he was staying and had almost killed him. Mukhtar had been trapped in an almost entirely collapsed basement for two days. He'd lost three fellow warriors on that one attack. Their dusty and mangled bodies were emblazoned on his memory. That and his near death at Isfahan had brought him to the conclusion that he would never again set foot in a bunker. He would take his chances aboveground.

Abbas moved closer to them and pulled a white handkerchief from his back pocket. He began waving it wildly, and then held up both fists, telling Mukhtar Kennedy was in the second Suburban. It was the signal they had been waiting for. Mukhtar turned to the fourteen men standing at the back of the shop.

"They are coming. Put on your hoods." The Lebanese terrorist grabbed his cell phone and hit the send button. Three rings later an eager voice answered. Mukhtar said, "It is time." He did not wait for a response. He dropped the phone to the floor and drew his Markov pistol. The one he had told each man he would use to kill them if they did not use proper restraint.

38

The orange-and-white taxi had been cruising the southern edge of the old city for the better part of an hour. One man sat in back and the other drove. They stopped for coffee once and at a newsstand a second time. Fifty minutes into their patrol they headed further south. They had selected their spots the evening before. The locations were some of their best. Both were within two miles of the base's main gate, which was crucial. Sahar and Ziba were Iranian revolutionary guardsmen who were now attached to the

Quds Force. They were part of a small cell whose specialty was mortar attacks. They'd been in Iraq for only five months, but they knew their way around well.

When they received the final call they were only three blocks from their first launch point. The small car sped down the garbage-ridden street and stopped next to a dilapidated warehouse. Both men jumped out. The car was left running and the trunk was opened. Sahar, the larger of the two, grabbed an M224 60mm mortar. Fully assembled, it weighed close to fifty pounds. He set the base plate down exactly in the middle of a chalk-drawn circle that he had put there the night before. He then moved the feet of the bipod so they were positioned directly on top of two marks. The elevation and traversing screws were already dialed and locked in. Sahar stepped away from the mortar and on his way back to the trunk passed Ziba, who was headed toward the tube with a round in each hand.

Sahar put on a pair of heavy leather gloves and grabbed two rounds for himself. They had done this dozens of times, but they had attacked the main base only once, and that had been months ago. They had found out the hard way that the Americans had very advanced, fire-finding artillery radar. One of their first missions had been to fire on the main runway as a cargo plane was coming in for a landing. They set up their mortar, got a shell, and then dropped it in the tube. With a thud and whoosh it was gone. They stood there waiting to hear the explosion. It came a few seconds later and they clapped and laughed with elation. Sahar was about to drop a second round in the tube when they heard the whistle of an inbound artillery shell. The only thing that saved them was a nearby sewage ditch that they reached as the first of six shells pounded their position. The car was completely destroyed. Sahar had lived and learned.

On this particular day Sahar and Ziba were less than enthusiastic about their job. The man from Hezbollah had told them what he expected of them, and it was too much. Six mortar rounds fired from one tube would take nearly twenty seconds. More than enough time for the Americans to fire back at them and with shells a hell of a lot bigger than the ones they were firing. They told him his plan wouldn't work and he immediately called their devotion into question. Even their manhood. Sahar and Ziba had taken the bait and had told the man they would do it. Neither man had slept well, and in the middle of the night they agreed that four shells would be enough. They would then drive to a second position and fire two more.

Sahar returned to the mortar tube and looked at his friend who nodded that he was ready. Sahar dropped the shell in the tube and each man took a half step back. There was a loud bang and whoosh as the shell was sent skyward. Gravity would play its role within a second and pull the round back down to earth, hopefully placing it near the front gate of the base. Ziba dropped the second round in the tube and off it went. The last two shells were launched, and Sahar grabbed the hot tube with one hand and the bipod with the other. He heaved the fifty pounds of metal into the trunk and ran for the driver's door. Just as he was sliding in behind the wheel he heard the bloodcurdling whistle of an incoming round. Sahar stepped on the gas with all his might and the small Toyota took off. A second later the first round hit causing the ground to shake for blocks in every direction. The rear window shattered from a piece of shrapnel, but the car kept moving.

Ziba was now sitting in the front seat with Sahar. The two men looked at each other and laughed nervously. At twenty-four and twenty-five, they still found humor in such things. Eight blocks later they pulled up to their second location. Again Sahar grabbed the mortar and Ziba grabbed two rounds. Sahar placed everything on the proper marks and then reached out for Ziba's second shell. He nodded for his friend to proceed. Ziba cradled the shell with both hands and tipped it until it slid backwards down into the tube. The 60mm shell boomed out of the tube with force.

This street had dirt and sand covering most of the asphalt. The launch kicked up a cloud of dust, which caused Sahar to lose sight of the tube for a second. Once he reacquired it, he rushed to load his shell. His nerves were frayed and the dust was making things difficult. Under better conditions he probably could have loaded the round without incident, but as soon as he heard the demonic shriek of multiple inbound shells, he panicked and missed the tube entirely.

The shell hit the ground with a clank, and Sahar thought for sure that it would explode. Both men froze for a moment, looked into each other's eyes and then without having to say a word, starting running like hell for their idling car. With every step Sahar was cursing himself for allowing the Hezbollah man to goad him into doing something so foolish. When he reached the driver's door, the first 155mm howitzer round impacted a mere seventy feet away. Razor-sharp shrapnel flew in every direction at more than 16,000 feet per second. The concussive blast and the molten hot shrapnel tore through both men in a flash.

39

Mukhtar kept his eyes on the street and said to Rashid Dadarshi, the Quds Force commander, "Bring up the first wave."

Mukhtar was referring to the RPG teams who were tasked with taking out the convoy's first two vehicles. Mukhtar and Dadarshi were in complete agreement that they had assembled more than enough firepower to handle the meager five-vehicle convoy. Dadarshi, however, had stressed that they would possess that advantage for a limited time. Maybe only minutes. He availed Mukhtar of story after story where the Americans had sent reinforcements, either by ground or air, within minutes of a fight starting. Mukhtar had worked to negate the American firepower from the start. He had instructed President Amatullah to make sure the Ministry of Intelligence made it clear the meeting would be canceled if any American units were seen within two miles of its site. The Americans appeared to be honoring the security agreement that both sides had reached. Dadarshi's scouts had reported that the city was quiet.

Mukhtar knew American military doctrine well. He had studied it for years. He knew they would have one of their quick reaction forces on standby. That was why he had deployed the mortar team. If the shells they lobbed managed to hit a few of the vehicles all the better, but Mukhtar's real intent was to create confusion and hopefully put the base into lockdown mode. Every second could prove to be crucial and his plan would hopefully gain them whole minutes.

Mukhtar was also willing to bet there were very few people at the base who knew that Kennedy was in Mosul. Whatever it was that the Americans wanted to talk about, they were certainly taking a huge risk to do it. That was why they were holding this clandestine meeting with spies instead of diplomats. They wanted deniability. While it suited their purposes, it also happened to suit Mukhtar's needs perfectly. The Americans could try to tell the world that it was Iranian insurgents who had destroyed Iran's nuclear facility, but Mukhtar knew better. The Americans were behind the attack. He had no proof, but his faith told him they were guilty. He was going to show them for the liars that they were, and with Amatullah's bold help they would begin driving them out of the region.

Mukhtar saw the police vehicles that had been blocking the street begin to move. He kept his eyes on the street corner and said, "Send them out, and move the next group up."

The Quds commander signaled for the first four men to move. They filed out the front door of the shop and turned left. They were working in pairs. All four were dressed in plain clothes and carrying backpacks, none of them wearing masks. Mukhtar watched them hurry up the sidewalk, the second pair trailing by thirty feet. He reached down and pressed the start button on his digital watch's stopwatch function just as the first white Toyota SUV rounded the corner.

"Easy," Mukhtar said loud enough for the second wave to hear. "I'll tell you when to move."

This second group was composed of six men. Four were holding RPGs and two were carrying 7.62mm Russian-made PKM light machine guns with bipods. They were all wearing hoods.

The first Suburban entered his view and then the second one with Kennedy on board. The lead vehicle began to pick up speed as did the others. The final SUV came into view and started to turn onto their street. Mukhtar stuck his right arm out and was about to tell the men to go when the first shot was fired by one of the big guns at the other end of the street.

"Go!" Mukhtar screamed. "Go! Go!" He stepped over and began pushing the men out the door. The idiot policemen were supposed to wait. The front of the convoy was supposed to be attacked first, not the rear.

The first man out the door sprinted across the street and stopped between two parked cars. By the time he reached his position the second man had already made it to his spot on the near side of the street. He hefted his RPG onto his right shoulder, took aim at the grille of the lead SUV, and fired. The 85mm rocket-assisted grenade belched from the smooth-bore tube and screamed its way down the street. The shaped-charge warhead slammed into the engine block of the Toyota, sending a fireball skyward. The vehicle swerved to its left sideswiping two parked cars before it was completely disabled by a second RPG.

Of the four men who had been sent out first, only three were standing. The last man had been knocked to the ground by one of the RPG blasts and was slowly struggling to get to his feet. The other three men already had their backpacks off and were moving between parked cars toward their targets. Each backpack contained a shaped satchel charge designed to breach the underbelly of armored vehicles. In unison, they each pulled the fuse cord on the charges and sent the backpacks sliding across the pavement. Two came to rest under the first black Suburban and the third stopped just under the front bumper of the second Suburban. All three men turned and ran for cover.

Mukhtar watched as the double blast of the first two satchel charges lifted the lead Suburban clear off the ground. Virtually every sheet of bulletproof glass on the vehicle was blown free, as well as one of the doors. The vehicle landed with a metal-crunching thud on its side. The blast stirred up so much debris that Mukhtar could not see how the second black vehicle had fared. He resisted the urge to rush outside and find out. They were not done. Mukhtar watched as the last satchel charge was thrown under the first vehicle, the one that had already been hit by two RPGs. The vehicle and everyone in it appeared to be out of commission, but the man was going to carry out his orders. The explosion ripped the Toyota to pieces.

With the column stopped and the lead vehicles destroyed, Mukhtar felt it was time to move. He turned to the Quds commander and said, "Let's go see what is left."

There was still a lot of gunfire. Dadarshi said nervously, "I would feel better if we waited a little bit longer."

As Mukhtar put on his black hood he asked, "Are you afraid to go out there?"

Dadarshi grinned and shook his head. "I was ordered to make sure nothing happened to you."

Mukhtar remained unflinching as he walked past Dadarshi. "Nothing will. Allah has plans for me." He stepped outside the building and began walking calmly up the sidewalk. The five men around him were all moving in a crouch. Gunfire was everywhere, but not so close that one could hear the supersonic snaps of bullets whistling past.

Through the settling dust, Mukhtar glimpsed the

other truck. Its hood was blown off and it looked to be resting on its fender, but other than that the passenger compartment looked intact. Mukhtar allowed himself a smile as he savored what was a sure victory.

Bullets thudded into a parked car in front of them, and before Mukhtar knew what was happening he found himself thrown to the ground.

He twisted his neck and found the dark eyes of Dadarshi peering through the two slits in his mask. "Get off of me," Mukhtar ordered.

"In a minute." Dadarshi grinned. "Allah wants me to keep you safe until things have settled down a bit."

In spite of himself, Mukhtar laughed loudly. There weren't many men who would have dared to defy him.

The Quds commander ordered his men ahead to clear the way. Mukhtar looked at his watch. Only a minute and forty-one seconds had passed. They were making good time, but they could not afford to get bogged down. Finally, after another twenty seconds they were up and moving. Mukhtar was even more pleased when he finally got a clear glimpse of the second Suburban. It was disabled, but not destroyed. The driver was slumped over the steering wheel, but the man in the front passenger seat was moving.

Mukhtar approached the vehicle to get a good look. Right there, in the middle of the back seat, he locked eyes with the director of the CIA.

"She is alive," he said loudly as he stepped aside and pointed at the driver's side passenger window. "Take it out."

One of Dadarshi's men shouldered a .50-caliber rifle and took several steps back. Everyone, including Mukhtar, covered their ears. The first shot splintered the glass and left a small hole the size of a quarter. The second shot took out a fist-sized hole. Mukhtar held up his hand, signaling the man to stop shooting. He approached the window with a smoke grenade in one hand and his Markov in the other. He pulled the pin with his teeth and stuffed the grenade through the hole. Another man was standing ready with an industrial saw in case they needed to cut into the vehicle. Mukhtar didn't think they would need it. These men would choose survival, even if it were only for a few more seconds.

As they waited for the smoke to build up, two cars skidded to a stop just short of the Suburban. These were meant to transport Mukhtar, Kennedy, and a security detail.

"Remember," Mukhtar yelled, "nothing happens to the woman." He stepped closer to the truck and made sure he stayed away from the opening in the window in case one of the bodyguards decided to fire out the hole. "Come out and no one will be harmed!" He waited a few seconds, checked his watch, and started to get nervous. He was about to tell the man with the saw to go to work, when the rear passenger door opened.

One of the security men stumbled out of the vehicle with his empty hands above his head. Coughing, he was immediately thrown to the ground. The director of the CIA came out next. Mukhtar grabbed her roughly and pulled her away from the smoky vehicle. Two more men came out of the truck also gasping for air and coughing. They were thrown to the ground next to the first one.

Mukhtar yanked the hijab from Kennedy's head and slapped her across the face. Her sunglasses went flying. She staggered for a moment and then slowly turned to face him. The man from Hezbollah looked into her eyes relishing the fear he would find, but instead was confronted with the blankest expression he had ever seen. There was no emotion in her eyes. In fact, she looked as if she had been drugged. Mukhtar slapped her again. She lowered her head for a second and then slowly regained her posture, standing up straight and staring back at him with the same flat, brown gaze.

Mukhtar forcefully grabbed her hair and dragged her back to where her bodyguards were lying on the pavement. He pointed his Markov pistol at the first man and squeezed the trigger. With all of the explosions and heavy machine-gun fire that had been going on, the relatively light report of the 9mm seemed ridiculous. The damage it caused, however, wasn't. A pool of blood began spreading beneath the man's head. Mukhtar forced Kennedy to look at the dead man and then held her firm while he shot the next two men in the head.

"You," Mukhtar growled in Arabic, "will do exactly as I tell you, or you will suffer the same fate."

Before Mukhtar could pull her head up to see if he had finally gotten through, two explosions rocked the intersection just to the north. Mukhtar looked up to see one of the police vehicles aflame and another car burning.

The Quds force commander grabbed Mukhtar by the arm and started pulling him away from the dead body-guards. "We need to leave," he yelled over increasingly loud gunfire.

Mukhtar did not disagree. He grabbed Kennedy and began dragging her toward one of the waiting vehicles.

40

Rapp rushed down the stairs with a loaded Glock .45 in his left hand. As much as he had wanted to bring his distinctly American M-4 rifle instead, he thought it best to leave it behind. Rapp hit the landing with a thud, grabbed the railing, and started down the next flight. He couldn't get the vision of the burning white Toyota SUV out of his head. The thing had been cut to shreds in a matter of seconds. Kennedy's armored Suburban would fare much better, but it would not hold up indefinitely. He needed to get out there and help them.

Rapp hit the first-floor landing and reached the front door. He looked out the small window and said, "Stan, are you guys ready?" He waited to hear Stilwell's voice over his wireless earpiece.

"Mitch, I think this is a bad idea," Stilwell said in a worried voice. "The base says they have air assets on the way, and the quick reaction force is rolling. The smart thing to do is sit and wait."

Rapp lowered his head. He knew this wasn't the brightest thing he'd ever done, but sitting and waiting for reinforcements to show up while Kennedy and her people were in all likelihood dying simply wasn't in his programming.

"Stan," Rapp said firmly, "we're done talking about this. On the count of three I'm coming out the door. Are you with me or not?"

"Yeah," Stilwell groaned.

"One," Rapp tugged on the black balaclava hood to get a better opening for his eyes. "Two," he took a breath and told himself he was crazy. "Three," he put his hand on the doorknob and waited to hear Stilwell and his men open fire. Right on cue there was a massive volley of gunfire. Rapp leaned his shoulder into the door, hit the small stoop, took a hard left, and started running for his life.

The first thing Rapp noticed were four men standing behind an old blue Chevy Impala that had been backed up on the sidewalk to form a makeshift barricade. All four men were pointing their rifles directly at him. Rapp had no choice but to keep moving toward them. If he stopped and went back they would shoot him for sure. If he kept rushing toward them they would hopefully think he was one of them.

As planned, two explosions rocked the opposite

corner. Rapp winced as tiny pebbles of debris pelted him. The men behind the car elevated their weapons and began firing at Stilwell and his men. Rapp reached the corner and hopped up onto the trunk of the car. He slid across on his butt and was helped to the ground by one of the men.

Rapp tried to steal a quick glance at the convoy, but the street was covered in smoke. Of the four corners of the intersection this was safest. The two just to the north were getting absolutely hammered by Stilwell and the Kurds, and the fourth corner, just behind him, had received its first incoming grenade. Bodies were everywhere and confusion was spreading rapidly.

Rapp had the .45-caliber Glock in his left hand and kept it up in the air so it was there for anyone to see who might be watching. His right hand slowly slid under his shirt and drew his silenced 9mm Glock from its paddle holster. Rapp moved up behind the first man and placed the tip of the silencer right between his shoulder blades and slightly to the left. At the same time he extended his .45 and aimed it down the street. Rapp fired the 9mm and slid his right knee under the man's butt to stop him from falling. He kept his left arm raised and angled the 9mm to the left. He fired one quick suppressed round, striking the second man in the head. He instantly collapsed. Rapp fired another shot into the third man's head and then finally the fourth.

Rapp dropped to his knee, as if he was seeking cover. He placed his back against the Impala, and for the first time he took in the full scope of the carnage. Through the billowing smoke he saw what was left of the vehicles. His heart sank. The fourth vehicle was as bad as the fifth. The white skin was riddled with blackened .50-caliber holes the size of fists. The lead vehicle was in flames and the first Suburban was in two pieces. The second Suburban was shrouded by white smoke, rather than the dark gray smoke caused by explosives. From what he could make out, Kennedy's vehicle looked pretty much intact.

Just beyond the Suburban, Rapp noticed some movement. There were men in black hoods moving around. He looked up and down the cross street. Stilwell and the Kurds were pounding the hell out of the militia and the few remaining cops. Rapp decided to move closer.

"Stan, I'm moving to take cover behind the last Toyota. Make sure your guys don't shoot me."

Rapp could hear Stilwell passing on the information to the Kurds. A moment later there was a slight lull in the shooting. Rapp stayed low and scrambled the thirty-odd feet to the front fender of the Toyota. The dead security contractor was lying a few feet away. From this new angle Rapp could see a group of the militiamen moving hurriedly toward two big late-model American sedans. There was a brief opening, and he got a glimpse of Kennedy. She was being forced into the backseat of the sedan by one of the men.

Rapp was on one knee; his eyes surveying the tactical situation. From left to right he counted eleven men, not counting the ones in the vehicles. They were all carrying machine guns. About half of them were in positions of cover, and they were alert. At best he could take down two or three. The rear door of the first sedan closed and the tires began spinning on the pavement. Rapp's hope sank as the vehicle took off. Through the back window he saw the man grab his boss by the hair and force her down.

"Stan," Rapp said tensely. "Irene is alive. I repeat Irene is alive. They just put her in the back of a gray Ford LTD. There is a second car following with a bunch of militia guys inside. It's a white four-door. Maybe a Chevy. I can't tell for sure." Rapp watched both vehicles take a right at the next corner. He passed the information on to Stilwell and then said, "Tell the base commander Kennedy has been kidnapped. He needs to get roadblocks set up ASAP, and I want every Predator and helicopter he has in the air immediately. Then call global ops and tell them to light a fire under everyone's ass."

Rapp had a vision of Stilwell having to explain the situation from start to finish with each call. Rapp realized he needed to speak to the president directly, so the orders could be issued from the top down—without question. He was about to tell Stilwell to get him a line to the White House when he noticed a police officer in a hood come running up to one of the men standing by Kennedy's smoking Suburban. The police officer pointed in one direction and then the other. The man he was talking to began barking orders to the men around him.

"Stan, I need three of your Kurds down here right now!" Rapp holstered the .45, scooted back a couple of feet, and lay down on his stomach. He was just behind the driver's-side front wheel of the Toyota. Looking under the SUV he could see both men from the knees down. Rapp switched the 9mm to his left hand and lined up the shot. The men were approximately fifty feet away.

"Tell them to hurry up," Rapp whispered and then gently squeezed the trigger. The bullet spat from the end of the circular suppressor, and seconds later the man on the left collapsed to the pavement. Rapp already had the sights trained on the second man. He fired again with the same results. The police officer joined the first man on the ground, both of them writhing in pain. Rapp stayed right where he was and waited for the inevitable. Two men appeared at the exact same time. They both bent over to grab the man Rapp guessed was their leader. These guys were well trained. Rather than administer first aid on the spot they were going to drag him to a safer location. Rapp dropped both men with shots to the head. They crumpled to the asphalt; the one on the left motionless, the one on the right twitching.

"Stan, where are those Kurds?" Rapp whispered as he searched for more targets.

"They're on their way, and the Stryker column is two minutes out."

"Tell your boys not to shoot me when they get here."

Another man showed up to drag his commander to safety and Rapp put a bullet through the top of his head. Knowing he was pushing his luck, he got to his feet and quickly moved to the rear fender of the Toyota. He leaned against the truck, ejected his magazine, and put in a fresh one. The cops and militia to the north were in full retreat. A block away he spotted a group of men disposing of their weapons and tearing off their hoods and uniforms. Rapp circled around the back of the Toyota and looked back down the street toward the two wounded men. Beyond them he found two militia members taking cover behind Kennedy's still-smoking Suburban and three more hiding behind parked cars. At the far end of the block there were more men fleeing on foot. As far as Rapp could tell, the five remaining men must have figured there was a sniper in one of the buildings across the street.

Rapp looked over his shoulder and saw four of Stilwell's Kurds approaching the Impala he had slid over when he'd first reached the intersection. Rapp waved his hand to get their attention and then motioned for them to stay put on the other side of the vehicle. He took one last peek around the fender of the Toyota and decided to make it quick. Rapp drew the .45-caliber Glock and put it in his right hand. With a gun in each hand he crouched and ran for the sidewalk. As he passed around the end of the first parked car, he hit the sidewalk and began sprinting toward the three men who were taking cover behind a parked car. They paid him no attention.

Rapp covered the ground in under two seconds. The men were talking among themselves, probably trying to figure out whether to grab their commander or abandon him. As Rapp drew almost abreast of the first man, he extended the silenced pistol, aimed it at the man's right temple, and fired at near point-blank range. Before the other two men even realized what was going on, Rapp fired two more quick shots hitting both men in the face. Never breaking stride, he cut between two parked cars and charged at the last two men. He lowered the silenced 9mm and raised the .45-caliber Glock. Both men were kneeling. The man on the right tried to swing his rifle around. Rapp fired from a mere ten feet away and kept charging. The heavy round snapped the man's head back into the Suburban. The man to the left was so startled by the shot he froze. Rapp closed the final few feet, and at the last second decided to take the man alive. He pivoted and snap-kicked the man in the side of the head, sending him tumbling to the ground. Rapp kicked his rifle clear and yelled for the Kurds to come over and help.

"Stan," Rapp said, as he did a 360-degree sweep of the area. He looked at his watch; it wasn't even noon. The president was more than likely in bed. "Send one of the Kurds down here with a satellite phone."

The scene had changed drastically in less than a minute. The police and the insurgents were all gone. The gunfire had fallen silent. All that was left were dead bodies and broken vehicles. It was the aftermath of battle. Rapp eyed the two men he had shot in the knees. The policeman had rolled onto his stomach and was trying to crawl away. Rapp then looked to his feet at the four men from Kennedy's security detail. They were all lying facedown with bullet holes in the back of their heads. McDonald wasn't one of them. Rapp turned and checked the front seat of the Suburban. There was a body in the front passenger seat, but it was missing a face. Rapp knew it was McDonald. That was where he'd been sitting when they'd left the café.

The anger came boiling up from deep in his gut. Rapp made no effort to control it. He turned and eyed the pathetic piece of shit in the police uniform who was still trying to crawl away. Rapp raised the .45-caliber Glock and fired the weapon. The heavy round hit the man in the ass and blew out a chunk of his right hip socket. The man may as well have been hit by a bolt of lightning. His entire body snapped rigid for a moment and then he began screaming in pain.

Rapp holstered the 9mm, but kept the .45 ready. He pulled off his own hood and yelled for the Kurds to do the same as he walked over to the man the police officer had been talking to.

Rapp reached down to yank off the man's hood. As he did so, the man's right hand lashed out. Rapp stepped clear as the tip of a knife sailed wildly past his abdomen. Before the man could take another swipe, Rapp brought his right foot crashing down on his shattered knee. As he convulsed in pain, Rapp found the hand with the knife in it and sent his left foot crashing down with bone-crushing force. The knife was instantly released. Rapp kicked it clear and snatched the hood off the man's head.

Rapp was not surprised to find a bearded man, with brown eyes, in his mid to late thirties. Wherever he had come from he was not Arabic. His skin was too light and brow too pronounced. He could be an Iraqi, but the pronounced brow and high cheekbones told Rapp the man was more than likely Persian or Kazakh.

"Where did they take her?" Rapp asked conversationally.

The man clenched his teeth and said nothing. Rapp stepped on his knee again. After a few seconds he released his foot and repeated the question, this time in Arabic.

"Fuck you!" the man screamed in English.

Rapp thought he caught a slight Persian accent. He answered the man in Farsi, saying, "I don't think so." Leaning in closer, he lowered his voice and asked, "Do you like being a man?"

The fierce brown eyes stared defiantly back at Rapp.

"The two of us"—Rapp pointed to himself and the man on the ground—"we're going to find out the hard way." Reaching under his shirt, Rapp drew his matte black ZT knife and dangled it in front of the man's face. "That woman you just helped kidnap . . . she means a lot to me." Rapp's eyes turned crazed. "Trust me when I tell you you're gonna tell me where she is."

The man twisted his face into a frown and spit on Rapp.

Rapp didn't even blink let alone bother to wipe the spit from his cheek. He took his knife and drove the four-inch blade into the man's right shoulder socket. With a violent jerk he twisted the knife a quarter turn.

The man gasped at the sheer pain and then let loose a stream of profanities, all in Farsi.

The words confirmed for Rapp that the man was Iranian. Rapp leaned hard on the knife, and when the man opened his mouth to scream again Rapp stuffed the barrel of his .45 into his mouth. Bringing his nose to within an inch of the other man's, he said in Farsi, "I don't care how tough you think you are, you Persian piece of shit. You'd better hope for your sake that she gets returned quickly and she better not have a single mark on her, or you're going to be eating your own nuts for dinner."

41

STRAIT OF HORMUZ

They'd lost the Iranian Kilo. Halberg stood in the combat and control center of his sub, sweating profusely. He took a drink of water and silently watched his men work. They'd lost plenty of contacts before, but never in a situation this tense. His steel blue eyes darted from one screen to the next. A digital readout on the plotting screen read 14:32 and counting. That was how long it had been since the Kilo had broken contact. They were nearly three months into a six-month patrol and the men had conducted themselves wonderfully, until now.

Halberg had been in the engine room hitting the heavy bag when the officer of the deck had sent word that the Iranian sub had vanished. Without saying a word, Halberg peeled off his boxing gloves, grabbed a towel, and headed to the CACC. His XO met him at the plotting table and played back the tactical information on the screen starting two minutes prior to losing contact. Ten seconds of footage told Halberg all he needed to know. He saw what the Iranian captain must have done. The man had timed things perfectly. Just as he finished one of his lazy figure eights, he had made a dash across the outgoing channel and the bow of a heavily laden supertanker that was making a lot of noise and churning up a lot of muck. When the supertanker had finally passed, the Iranian Kilo was gone. They did a quick sweep and came to the conclusion that she had headed back into the strait sandwiched between two container vessels that were separated by less than a mile. Halberg ordered a new course and they fell in behind the second container vessel. As best they could figure it they were approximately two miles back from the Kilo.

The executive officer finished speaking with the navigator and then walked across the CACC to where Halberg was silently standing watch. In a hushed voice meant for only the two of them Strilzuk said, "I'm sorry I lost her, Skipper."

"No need to apologize. She made a good move."

"You would have seen it coming."

Halberg shrugged. "Maybe."

"No. You would have seen it, and we both know it."

"You will too one day. You're almost there."

"I don't know about that." Strilzuk looked deflated.

"Stop beating yourself up, and tell me what he's going to do next."

Strilzuk looked down at the tactical screen and started weighing options. The Kilo really had only two choices. She could head back into port, which based on the fact that practically the entire Iranian navy had been put to sea, didn't seem very likely. The most probable scenario was that she would transit the strait and head back into the gulf.

"She's going to head back into the gulf, and make a sprint while we're stuck in the channel."

Halberg nodded. "How long will she run?"

Strilzuk checked his watch, and looked at the tactical screen. It marked the estimated location of the Kilo, the two freighters, and their speeds. Based on the Kilo's known top speed Strilzuk answered, "Roughly five and a half minutes."

"Any other possibilities?"

"She could head back into port, but I don't see that happening."

"Neither do I. What else?" Halberg asked in a tone that told Strilzuk he was missing something.

Strilzuk studied the tactical for a moment. He looked at the clump of islands off Bandar Abbas. "She might decide to partially surface, run to the leeward side of one of these islands, wait for us to pass, and then fall in behind us."

"That's possible, but not likely." Halberg hit a button and rewound the tactical to the point where they lost the Kilo. He pointed to the screen and said, "What if she ran clear across the inbound channel, looped around to the east, and headed back out, or worse, fell in behind us?"

Strilzuk looked embarrassed. "That's possible."

"But unlikely," Halberg offered in consolation. He read his friend's frustration and said, "Dennis, you're practical and straightforward. This guy," Halberg pointed at the screen, "is a little crazy. Running across the outbound channel that close to a fully loaded tanker with all this other traffic around is not exactly a conservative move. Would you ever try something like that?"

Strilzuk sighed, "Not under normal conditions."

"Which tells you?"

"This guy's either got a screw loose or these aren't normal circumstances."

"Exactly. Send a message to CTF 54. Let them know we lost contact."

"You sure?" Strilzuk studied his captain's face. "You don't want to wait and see if we reacquire her on the other side?"

Halberg clicked a button and the tactical zoomed out

to show the entire Persian Gulf and the northern half of the Gulf of Oman. The screen was filled with hundreds of contacts. The Eisenhower Strike Group was positioned smack-dab in the middle of the Persian Gulf with the bulk of the noisy Iranian navy headed her way. It was the perfect screen for a quiet diesel submarine. One missing Kilo was bad enough. Two could wreak havoc on the strike group.

Halberg decided to swallow his pride. "The sooner we let them know the better."

"I'm sorry, Skipper."

Halberg brushed off the apology. "I'm sure we'll find her when we clear the channel, and then we'll fall in behind her and make sure she behaves."

42

MOSUL, IRAQ

Rapp looked through the thick windshield of the up-armored Humvee as they rolled through the main gate. He had his satellite phone held to his right ear and a look of impatience on his face. The bulk of the quick-reaction force was still back at the site of the attack securing the perimeter and collecting bodies. Rapp had commandeered a Stryker and two Humvees to transport him and the three prisoners back to the base so he could begin interrogating them immediately.

"Chuck," Rapp said to the man on the other end of

the line, "it's the Wild West out here. I have no idea who took her. But I'm going to find out, and I can guarantee you it isn't going to be pretty."

"Mitch," said the deputy director of the CIA, "get her back, but I'm telling you this as a friend. This thing is going to attract a lot of heat. Every reporter and politician in Washington is going to want to dissect every aspect of not just the kidnapping, but the aftermath as well."

"And they can all go fuck themselves."

"Mitch," Charles O'Brien sighed, "that's the kind of attitude that's going to get you into a lot of trouble."

"Let me make this real clear for you, Chuck." Rapp's voice was tense. "I don't want to hear another word about my attitude. I don't want anyone looking over my shoulder, and I sure as hell don't want anyone second-guessing what I do. We've got maybe twenty-four hours before they break her. The rule book is out the window. This is gangland violence time. Don't send me any analysts from Baghdad. I need knuckle draggers. I need guys who are going to kick down doors and kick the shit out of people until they give us answers."

"Mitch, I think you need to take a step back and reassess how you're going to handle this. I'll be at the White House in . . ."

"They're going to torture her!" Rapp growled.

"Mitch," O'Brien sighed, "none of us want to see that happen, but you can't go running off half-cocked. You need to . . ."

"Don't tell me what I need to do!" Rapp screamed into the phone. "You and everyone else in Washington need to stick your fucking heads in the sand for the next twenty-four hours, and let me do whatever it takes to get her back."

"That's not going to happen. I can't let you do that."

"Then you'd better go on vacation."

"You're too close to this thing," O'Brien said forcefully. "You need to take a step back and cool down . . . remember that there are laws."

"Well, apparently the other side didn't get that memo, did they? You go ahead and cover your ass, Charlie." Rapp shook his head angrily and then added, "But I remember when you used to have a pair. Back when you were in the field. Now you've turned into just another wussified seventh-floor desk jockey."

There was a prolonged silence and then O'Brien said, "I'm going to ignore what you just said and write it off to the fact that you're under a lot of stress."

In slow, punctuated words, Rapp said, "I meant every word of it, Charlie. When this thing is over if the press comes down on you, I'll gladly fall on the sword for both of us. Now you'll have to excuse me. I need to put on my white gloves and ask these guys if they'd like to waive their right to an attorney."

Rapp's thumb stabbed the end button on the phone just as the Humvee was pulling up to the CIA compound.

The driver glanced over at Rapp and said, "This is my third tour over here." The vehicle came to a complete stop. "I wish more people in Washington had your attitude."

"So do I." Rapp got out of the vehicle and waited for the soldiers to unload the prisoner who had ridden with them. Rapp had separated the three men. He'd put the Persian-speaking commander in the Stryker vehicle, the cop was strapped to a stretcher and put in the back of the second Humvee, and the foot soldier who he'd knocked out rode with him. Rapp was already racking his brain for a strategy. He needed to squeeze information out of these guys as quickly as possible. Just beating them silly would probably fail. At least short term. If he had a few days he could wear them down, but time was a luxury. He needed to come up with something more creative.

He didn't know for sure how long Kennedy could hold out, and he didn't want to find out. This was personal. Rapp had been tortured years before. He desperately wanted to spare her the pain, suffering, and degradation. He started to think of the ways it would be worse for a woman and then forced himself to stop. He needed to focus on finding her, not worrying about her. And he needed to do it as quickly as possible.

Two Humvees came rolling up and stopped just short of Rapp and the prisoners. Rapp recognized the base commander, General Gifford, as he climbed out of the lead vehicle. He was in full battle gear—helmet and all. He walked right up to Rapp.

"My recon choppers are up, I've got three Predators in the air, and two Reapers are on their way up from

Baghdad. There's four main roads that come into the city, and six more secondary roads, the Hundred and First is in the process of setting up checkpoints on all ten of those roads between forty and sixty clicks."

"What about the river?"

"Covered to the north and south," he replied in his clipped military tone. "We're mobilizing every soldier we can and putting them on the street. Is there anything else you need from me?"

Rapp thought of the conversation he'd just had with O'Brien. "Yeah." He jerked his thumb over his shoulder at the three prisoners in black hoods. One was walking and two were on stretchers. "These guys with the bags over their heads . . . you never saw them . . . understand?"

Gifford looked beyond Rapp at the men. He hesitated for a moment as he thought of the obvious implication. He gave a quick nod and then said, "What men?" The general turned and marched back to his Humvee, over his shoulder he shouted, "You need anything, call me."

Just as the general was pulling away Stilwell arrived with his Kurds. Rapp told the soldiers to set the stretchers down and had the Kurds take over. He figured the less the GIs knew the better.

Rapp and Stilwell walked into the trailer that housed the offices and a reception area. "Do you have a camera?" Rapp asked.

"Polaroid or digital?"

"Polaroid."

Stilwell disappeared into an office and returned a moment later with the camera. As he handed it to Rapp he asked, "What else?"

Rapp flipped the camera around to see if it was loaded. "Yeah . . . find out where those bodies are."

"What bodies?"

"The ones that I asked that captain, from the QRF . . ." Rapp snapped his fingers while he searched for the name.

"Captain Jensen," Stilwell offered.

"Yeah, that's him. I told him I wanted all the bodies brought back here so we could identify them. Make sure they're brought here."

"Not the base morgue?" asked a confused Stilwell.

"Here . . . right here. I want them stripped naked and dumped in the biggest cell you have. I want every square inch of the floor covered with dead bodies."

"You're serious?" Stilwell asked with a questioning frown.

"Yes," Rapp barked.

Taken slightly aback Stilwell asked, "Anything else?"

Rapp was already halfway to the door. He stopped and asked, "What kind of sound tracks do you have to soften these guys up?"

Stilwell looked up at the ceiling and recited the list. "Barney, 'I love you, you love me,' 'The Macarena,' that obnoxious Nelly Furtado song, a lot of heavy metal . . . there's some Barry Manilow, which I personally think is bullshit. The guy's a genius . . ."

"No," Rapp yelled. "I mean soundtracks of people being tortured . . . screaming, yelling, begging for their life. Not the looped Barney shit. I don't have a week to wear these fuckers down."

"Oh . . . sorry. Yeah, we've got a few good ones."

"Put one on." Rapp left the office and walked across the compound. The interrogation containers were around back next to a massive tan hangar. The containers had been placed side-by-side and covered in three layers of sandbags. Only one door and an air-conditioning unit weren't covered. Rapp walked in the door and past a small desk and a bank of surveillance monitors. Twelve ten-inch screens. One for each cell. A man in jeans and a T-shirt was sitting behind the desk with his feet up reading a magazine.

Rapp stopped and pointed to the monitors. "You record what goes on in these cells?"

"Twenty-four seven. Mandated by Congress, courtesy of Abu Ghraib."

"Lovely," Rapp growled. "The recordings are stored on that hard drive sitting there?"

The guy looked at the computer sitting on the floor. "Yep."

"Excuse me." Rapp nudged past the man and yanked all the connections out of the back of the computer.

"Hey, you can't do that. That's against . . ."

Before the man could finish, Rapp grabbed him under the arm and yanked him to his feet. "Take a break."

Rapp pushed the guy outside and started for the cells. A hallway had been cut down the center of the three containers, halving them with six cells on each side. The doors and walls were all quarter inch steel with foam insulation in between. Rapp ran into one of the Kurds in the hallway and asked him where the guy was who they thought was the leader. The Kurd directed him to the last cell on the left. Rapp slid the spy hole to the side and saw the man lying on his stretcher in the middle of the cell. He undid the lock, entered the cell and stood next to him. Then he reached down and yanked the hood off the man's head.

The man opened his eyes for only a second, and then, unable to shield them from the overhead light because his hands were strapped at his sides, closed them. Rapp pointed the camera at the guy's face and snapped a shot. The Polaroid clicked and then whirled as it spit out the developing photo. Rapp leaned over and used his head to block the overhead light.

"Open your eyes." Rapp spoke in English this time.

The man slowly opened his eyes.

"Where did they take her?"

The man started to purse his lips like he was going to spit.

Rapp was ready this time. His right fist came crashing down and hit the man square in the mouth. The guy coughed and turned his head to the side, spitting out blood and a tooth. Rapp let a moment pass and then in a very congenial tone said, "All right, I guess we'll have to do this the hard way. You do know you're gonna tell me where she is, though."

The man spit a gob of blood from his mouth and then said, "Fuck you."

Rapp laughed and leaned in a little closer. "Let me tell you how this is gonna go. I'm gonna start by slicing off your left nut . . . and then I'm gonna slice off your right nut."

The man closed his eyes.

"And if you manage to make it that far without telling me," Rapp continued, "you won't get much further. Because trust me on this one . . . you're going to tell me what you know, because no man in his right mind wants to have his dick cut off and shoved down his throat."

Rapp stood up and when the man opened his eyes, he took another photo. Almost as if on cue, the voice of a man screaming in pain erupted from somewhere beyond the door. Without saying another word, Rapp turned and left.

43

STRAIT OF HORMUZ

Halberg sat in his elevated chair, an elbow on each armrest, his hands bridged under his chin. They were halfway through the channel and so far there had been no sign of the *Yusef*. Not that Halberg expected any. With a constant stream of supertankers coming and going the acoustics were horrible. Add to that freighter traffic of all shapes and sizes, fishing boats, and pleasure craft, and his sonar men were left with a din that was comparable to trying to listen to your cell phone while sitting in the front row of rock concert. Still no one complained. They simply did their best to sort it all out and make sure they didn't run into anything.

Halberg got up from his chair, walked into the sonar room and noticed a concerned look on the face of one of his operators. Each of the five men was wearing noise-canceling headphones so they wouldn't be distracted by the other conversations taking place in the CACC. The captain took a sip of coffee. His eyes stayed trained on Louis Sullivan, or Sully as he was called by the rest of the crew. He was by far the best sonar operator on the boat. If he looked concerned, that meant something unusual was going on outside the hull and that meant Halberg needed to be concerned too. He waited for Sully to start nodding. Waited for the smile to form on his thin lips. That's what Sully always did when he classified a particularly difficult contact.

One minute passed. Then two. Halberg remained motionless, other than to take an occasional sip of coffee. He noted the time, decided on how long he would wait, and then returned his attention to the tactical display. Before entering the Persian Gulf, the shipping channel turned almost due west forcing vessels to turn hard to port. Halberg had set a course for the inside edge of the channel. If the *Yusef* was trailing the first ship by 200 feet or more they stood a good chance of picking her up as she executed her turn and came out in front of the tanker that separated them.

Halberg glanced over at the sonar station just as Sullivan was looking over his shoulder back at him. This was not a good sign. Halberg stared intently at Sullivan who had moved the large, bulky headphone from his left ear.

"What's up, Sully?"

"We picked up the *Sabalan* heading out of port."

Halberg nodded; he'd already noted the ship on the broadband sonar. The *Sabalan* was a British-made Vosper Mark V–class frigate that had been commissioned in 1972. Back in 1988 an A-6 Intruder from the U.S.S. *Enterprise* dropped a 500-pound bomb on her in retaliation for an Iranian mine that had blown a fifteen-foot hole in the side of the U.S.S. *Samuel B. Roberts.* Instead of allowing the navy to finish her off, then–secretary of defense Frank Carlucci decided to spare the *Sabalan.* The ship was then towed back into port and repaired. By surviving the attack the ship had become an Iranian national treasure.

"Nothing unusual. Just cruising along at the standard fifteen knots. About five minutes ago, her Rolls-Royce turbines started howling. She's been steadily picking up speed, and if she holds her current course it looks like she's going to try and slide in between the two container ships."

"You think she's going to sit on top of the *Yusef* and help screen her when she clears the channel?"

"That's what I thought until a few minutes ago. It's hard to be sure, Skipper, with all that noise out there, but I think the *Yusef* has been blowing ballast. In fact I think her sail might be out of the water."

Halberg could not hide his surprise. "You're serious?"

"I know I'm a bit of a screwball, Skipper, but I would never joke about something like this."

Halberg glanced around the CACC. Strilzuk and the navigator were watching them. The captain looked back down at Sullivan and said, "Keep me posted." As he walked over to Strilzuk he wondered why in the hell the *Yusef* would be showing the top of her sail. Strilzuk glanced at the fire control panel and noted the assumed position of the other sub. In forty more seconds she would be clear of the container ship, and they could get a glimpse of her. Halberg was about to order the photonics mast raised when Sullivan called for him.

"Skipper, I've got her! She's taking on ballast and increasing speed."

Halberg quickly moved his attention back to the sonar monitor. He looked down at the updated location. She had been right where they thought she was. Halberg was in the midst of trying to figure out if he could pass the container ship on the inside turn when he noticed a commotion among the sonar operators.

The man to Sullivan's left announced, "Sir, the *Sabalan* is pinging the *Yusef*."

Before Halberg could absorb the comment, Sullivan announced, "The *Yusef* is flooding tubes."

"You're sure?"

Sullivan didn't bother to answer the question. "The *Yusef* is opening rear torpedo doors, sir."

Strilzuk joined Halberg at the tactical. "Strange place to be running a drill."

"I was just thinking the same thing."

"Torpedo in the water!" Sullivan said loudly.

"Battle stations," Halberg said without wasting a second. The order was repeated throughout the ship in a matter of seconds. Halberg was about to order the sub to flank speed when the bearing of the torpedo showed up on the tactical. The torpedo was clearly headed for the Iranian frigate *Sabalan*.

"Sully," said the captain, "confirm that bearing."

Sullivan reconfirmed the bearing of the torpedo. Strilzuk said, "Are we sure that's the *Yusef*?"

"It isn't one of ours."

"Twenty-one seconds to impact," Sullivan announced.

Halberg looked at Strilzuk. "I want visual."

Strilzuk ordered the photonics mast raised and joined Halberg in front of the color monitor. Sullivan began counting down from ten. As he reached two all five sonar men took off their headsets. Halberg increased the magnification on the camera and the *Sabalan* went from a spec to a clearly visible ship plowing through the water. As Sullivan's countdown reached zero, Halberg watched a geyser erupt from under the *Sabalan*'s bow. For a moment it looked like the entire ship had been lifted out of the water. As she settled down her back broke and the front third of the frigate started sinking.

"Send a flash message to CTF 54," Halberg said. He paused to look at the sonar monitor. The *Yusef* was passing the container ship in front of her and sprinting toward the Persian Gulf. "Set course to follow the *Yusef.*"

44

MOSUL, IRAQ

Rapp walked through the short sandbag tunnel and into the trailer that housed the offices. He was looking at the last of the six photos he'd taken. The colors were growing more vivid with each step. The castration speech had gone over swimmingly. He'd delivered it to each of the three men, and they all took it differently. The first one, the one who Rapp had punched in the mouth, went into shutdown mode. Before the speech the man had been cussing up a storm and acting as defiant as a teenager. As Rapp described how he would dissect the man's groin, he watched the fight drain out of him. He had either decided it was not wise to antagonize Rapp any further, or he was working to come up with a plan. More than likely a lie that would keep him firmly in the sexual category of his choice.

The second man, the policeman, was either a great actor or an absolute crazed lunatic. With each increasingly descriptive word about what Rapp planned to do, the man only laughed harder. He had a kind of crazy, bring-it-on attitude that Rapp had seen before. He was the type that either cracked right away or never did. There was very little in between. Rather than waste time, Rapp decided to find out if the guy was a pretender or a crazed, true believer.

The army medics had cut away the man's pants so they could bandage the bullet wounds to his knee and butt. He was still on a stretcher, his lower body covered with a drab green army blanket over which he was bound by restraints. Rapp yanked the blanket out from under the straps, exposing the man's genitals. He drew his knife and held it in front of the man's face.

"What's your name?" Rapp asked in an easy, even tone.

The man laughed hysterically and refused to answer. Rapp placed the tip of the knife against the man's left testicle and repeated the question. The man's laugh turned into a crazed cackle. Rapp forced the knife downward, twisted it and jerked it back up. A hunk of flesh flew from the tip of the knife and smacked against the cold, steel wall of the cell.

The man twisted back and forth on the gurney, struggling against his bonds and screaming at the top of his lungs. After ten seconds the man stopped his wailing, looked at Rapp through moist eyes, and continued to laugh maniacally.

Rapp looked down and simply said, "I'll be back for the other one in five minutes."

With that he left the cell and went to find the last

prisoner. This was the one Rapp had knocked out rather than kill. Rapp guessed since he was younger than the other two by at least ten years he would be the easiest to break. After delivering the castration speech, Rapp stood, took a second photo, and told the man he'd give him a few minutes to think about life without a pecker and then left.

Rapp entered the reception area and found Stilwell and Ridley standing behind a desk looking at a large flat-screen monitor. Rapp held up a photo of the man whose left nut he had just cut off and said, "There's no way in hell this guy is a cop."

Ridley pointed at the screen and said, "I just got off the phone with Chuck O'Brien, and I think he's right." Ridley pointed at the screen. "You've lost it."

"What in the hell are you talking about?"

"I'm talking about," Ridley pointed at the screen in front of him, "you cutting off that guy's testicle. You think we've only got one work station to keep an eye on the prisoners?"

"Oh . . . don't tell me you've gone soft too."

"It has nothing to do with going soft, although I'm not so sure about your methods . . . it's about the fact that this is a U.S. military base. This isn't some dark facility in the Stans. The military keeps records, they keep track of who comes and who goes, and these GIs gossip more than a bunch of goddamn sorority sisters. Then there's the press, and I don't even want to think about what's going to happen when that guy ends up with a lawyer someday."

"That guy is never going to end up with a lawyer," Rapp said forcefully.

"You don't know that."

"Oh, I sure do, because after I'm done cutting his dick off, I'm going to drag him into one of those other cells and I'm going to blow his brains out right in front of the other two."

"Mitch," Ridley screamed, "you can't do that. We have a team of interrogators on the way up from Baghdad. These guys are the best in the business. They will get every last ounce of information out of them."

Rapp folded his arms across his chest. "Great, why don't we just grab some lunch and a cup of coffee, kick back, shoot the breeze, and give these pros some room. That sounds like a hell of a plan. Then a week or a month from now when they finally squeeze the information out of these guys we can try to get Irene back. In the meantime I'm sure they'll treat her like a queen."

"It's not going to take them a month."

"It's not going to take me more than an hour."

"Mitch," Ridley sighed, "I personally don't care what you do, just so long as you don't leave any permanent marks on these guys."

"I personally don't give a shit what you think, Rob. We're not in Washington. We're in a fucking war zone where our boss, the director of the CIA, the person who knows every damn spy we have in every damn country, has just been kidnapped. You think those guys are flying in a team from Damascus. A team that's going to make sure they won't leave a mark." Anguish gripped Rapp's face and he screamed, "They're going to torture the shit out of her, Rob, and I'm not going to sit here and debate with you what I can and can't do."

Rapp took the six Polaroid photos and threw them down on Stilwell's desk. "Scan those into the system and see if you can find a match. Where's Marcus?"

"I don't know."

"Find him."

Stilwell picked up the photos just as the phone started to ring. He grabbed the handset with his other hand and said, "Chief of base, Mosul." He listened for a moment and then looked at Rapp. "Yeah, hold on." He held the phone out for Rapp. "It's the White House . . . the president wants to talk to you."

Rapp thought about not taking the call for a second. Most of his career had been based on asking for forgiveness rather than permission. But this was the president, not one of his colleagues from Langley. Rapp thought of the conversation they'd had on Air Force One. He didn't get the sense Alexander was the type of man who would try to put a leash on him. Even so, Rapp reluctantly stuck out his hand and took the phone.

45

The warning came in while the majority of Washington was asleep. The duty officer in the White House Situation Room received the call from the CIA Global Ops Center shortly after 5:00 a.m. Within minutes phone lines were buzzing around the capital and beyond. There were plans in place for such things. Security details were rousted, motorcades were sent out early, and key players in the National Security arena were told to get to their respective offices immediately. Secretary of Defense England was the first Cabinet level official to receive the bad news.

A former Merrill Lynch executive and the head of their London office, England rose at 5:00 a.m. every morning so he could spend some time monitoring the European markets before heading in to the Pentagon. He was sitting at his desk in his study when the call came in. The ring, two quick chimes followed by a third, longer one, was distinctly different from all of the other phones England's job required. At this early hour, England instantly knew the ring was a harbinger of bad news. As he eyed the secure telephone unit, his mind ran down a list of hot spots that could warrant the predawn call. Almost immediately his thoughts turned to Kennedy and her meeting. He picked up the phone, listened to the voice on the other end, and simply said, "I'll be there in thirty minutes."

England called his office and told the duty officer to roust the Joint Chiefs. He also directed the woman on the other end, that in twenty minutes, he wanted to talk to someone in Mosul who could give him an on-the-ground assessment of what had happened. Irene Kennedy may have been CIA, but Mosul was the domain of the Defense Department. He knew of Kennedy's meeting with her Iranian counterpart, but knew none of the details other than the disquieting fact that the Iranians had been adamant that no U.S. military personnel be present.

England raced upstairs, showered, threw on a suit, and grabbed his electric shaver. By the time he came back downstairs his full security detail was waiting in the driveway. England jumped in the back seat of the armored, black Suburban and started running the electric razor over his mostly gray stubble. His thoughts turned to Kennedy almost immediately. All he had been told by the situation room duty officer was that Kennedy's motorcade had been hit in Mosul. The director of the CIA was believed to be alive and taken hostage. Everyone else had been wiped out.

England liked Kennedy. He liked her style, the way she kept things brief and to the point. Washington, England had found, was a town with an inordinate amount of people who liked to hear themselves talk. Kennedy was a breath of fresh air, highly intelligent and as well versed in Islam and the Middle East as anyone he'd ever met. He had grown to depend on her input.

England was an old acquaintance of the president. He had no government service on his record—military or otherwise. As the president had told him at the time of his nomination, he wanted England for his analytical mind and his ability to not just win an argument, but get others to agree with him. He'd also spent decades trying to anticipate trends, constantly looking into the future, and attempting to predict how things would play out. As his vehicle moved through the predawn streets of DC, he tried to do the same now with this crisis. Unfortunately, the first thought that entered his mind were the tapes of Muslim extremists decapitating their prisoners. The beheading of the director of the Central Intelligence Agency would be a powerful piece of propaganda.

England pushed his personal feelings aside and played out parallel permutations in his mind. As harsh as it sounded, the quick beheading of Kennedy might not be the worst thing for America. The celebration among the Islamic radical fundamentalists would more than likely be short-lived. Europe, Australia, Japan, Russia, and possibly even China were certain to see in the end the beheading of a woman and the mother of a child, not the leader of America's chief spy agency. Such a barbaric move by the terrorists could end up harming them in the long run.

As cruel as it sounded, Kennedy knew too much. A drawn-out hostage situation would provide her captors with the opportunity to compromise America's national security on a scale that was almost unthinkable. Just the thought of having to advise the president in such a manner made England extremely uneasy. He was too positive a person to settle for such a dismal outcome so early in a crisis. There had to be a better way to resolution.

As England's Suburban passed through the Secret Service checkpoint on West Executive Drive, his secure phone rang. The duty officer at the Pentagon informed him that she had General Gifford on the line. England had met Gifford twice before on recent trips to the region.

"Tom," England said, "I'm walking in to meet with POTUS right now. Can you give me the brief version of what happened?"

England listened while Gifford passed along the condensed version of an already condensed version that had been given to him from the commanding officer of the quick-reaction force. When Gifford was done, England thanked him and told him to stay by the phone. There was a good chance the president would want to talk to him. England entered the West Wing and went straight to the Situation Room, where he found President Alexander, National Security Advisor Frank Ozark, and Attorney General Pete Webber. The three men were sitting at one end of the massive, shiny wood conference table. They all had their elbows on the table and were staring at a gray, star-shaped speaker phone.

"Mr. President, I'm afraid he's out of control."

England unbuttoned his suit coat and sat in the

leather chair next to Ozark. He recognized the voice coming out of the speaker phone as that of CIA Deputy Director Chuck O'Brien.

The president sighed and sat back in his chair. "Chuck, considering the situation, I think his rage is understandable."

"Sir, I'm as big a believer in Rapp's abilities as anyone. I just think that his judgment is clouded at the moment. He's too close to this thing."

England cleared his throat and said, "Chuck, Brad England here. What has he done that has you so worried?"

"Apparently several of the attackers were left behind and taken prisoner. One of the men, who we think may be a policeman, was wounded. After the attack was over, Rapp shot the man in the backside while he was lying on the ground."

"The policeman?" asked a surprised attorney general.

"Yes. We think local law enforcement may have aided the insurgents. Rapp then decided to conduct a battlefield interrogation with one of the other men. According to early reports he pulled out a knife and stabbed the man in the shoulder while he was subdued."

The attorney general looked extremely uncomfortable. "Were there witnesses?"

"This all happened in a residential neighborhood," O'Brien replied. "My guess is there were plenty of people who saw it."

"Oh God," the attorney general moaned. "Any reporters on the scene?"

"Not that I know of."

"Again," England said, "I apologize if I missed something, but why are we so concerned with how Rapp is handling prisoners? I just got off the phone with the base commander in Mosul. He says the local police didn't merely look the other way. He says they opened fire on Director Kennedy's motorcade."

"That's correct," O'Brien's voice sounded from the speaker phone.

"So let me get this straight. The director of the CIA has been kidnapped, her personal security detail was all shot execution-style, and we are worried about Mitch Rapp roughing up a few prisoners?"

"I personally could care less about these men, Brad, but mark my words, when the dust has settled, the hill is going to have a lot of questions. They are bound to launch hearings into how this happened and how all of us acted in the aftermath. Right now Rapp is out of control."

"Correct me if I'm wrong, but isn't he always out of control? Isn't that one of the reasons why he gets stuff done while everyone else sits around and talks about it?"

"Mitch Rapp is very good. But there have been plenty of times when he's gone overboard."

England looked at the president and then said, "Chuck, I'm going to try and be gentle here. You've got a lot of pressure on you right now. One of Director Kennedy's greatest strengths was that she got results. She also knew how to keep the president insulated from some of the less-than-civil stuff that is sometimes required in your covert world. Do you follow what I'm saying?"

O'Brien did not answer right away. After a moment he said, "Yes, but I still think it would be a good idea for the president to talk to him. Just briefly. My point is we can get answers out of these guys without cutting off appendages."

"I agree," the attorney general said forcefully.

President Alexander looked to England, who simply shrugged in a manner that said, what harm could it do?

"All right," the president said. "Have your people put the call through."

"Will do, sir."

There was a click as the line went dead. The president leaned forward and pressed a button on the speaker phone. He then looked up at his old friend England and asked, "Your thoughts?"

"My thoughts," the secretary of defense leaned back and sighed. "If we don't get her back soon . . . and I mean really quick, we are going to have some major problems."

The president rubbed his forehead. "How the hell did this happen?"

"Don't even go there, sir. It won't do us any good at this point. We have to deal with the here and now. Let's talk to Rapp, find out what he has, and then we can make some contingency plans."

The president nodded. A few seconds later a voice came over the speaker announcing that Rapp was on the line. The president leaned forward and stabbed the speaker button saying, "Mitch, it's the president here. Are you all right?"

"I'm fine, sir."

"Do I have this right that you saw Irene being put into the back of a sedan and driven away?"

"That's correct, sir."

"Any ideas who is behind this?"

"No, but I have three prisoners, sir. In fact I'm in the process of interrogating them right now. I'm confident two of them will talk. The third looks doubtful."

The president looked around the room. "Mitch, I've got Pete Webber with me, as well as Frank Ozark and Brad England. The rest of the National Security Council should be here shortly. There's been some concern that you're too close to this thing." The president paused and then added, "That you might be out of control."

A sigh of frustration could be heard over the speaker phone. "Mr. President, the director of the CIA has just been kidnapped. As per our discussion on Air Force One . . . I think now is the time to pull out all the stops."

Attorney General Webber had no idea what Rapp was talking about, but it didn't sound particularly thoughtful. "Mitch, Pete Webber here. We all know you and Irene are close, but you really have to take a few steps back and remember that you took an oath . . . an oath to protect and defend the constitution of the United States. We all took that oath, and that means none of us are above the law . . . including you."

There was a long pause and then in a voice filled with frustration Rapp said, "You have got to be kidding me."

Rapp's stark response caused everyone in the room to take a quick look at each other. "Excuse me?" the attorney general asked defensively.

"The director of the CIA was just kidnapped, and her entire security detail was wiped out, and you want to lecture me about an oath and a two-hundred-plus-year-old piece of paper?"

"Our entire country is based on that piece of paper," Webber responded defensively.

"You may have been thinking about defending a piece of paper when you took your oath, but I was thinking about protecting and defending American citizens from the type of shit that just happened. I apologize for my language, Mr. President, but this is ridiculous. If they haven't already started torturing her, they are going to shortly. And once that happens, sir, it is only a matter of time before she breaks. And when she does, we are screwed. She has a photographic memory. She knows every single spy and clandestine operative we have in the Middle East, and that's just the tip of the iceberg."

"There are legal ways to do this," Webber responded.

"This isn't a court of law," Rapp snapped. "We don't have a month to wear these guys down by asking them the same question five hundred times and waking them up twenty times a night. We don't even have a week. If I don't get answers out of these guys in the next twenty-four hours, we are going to have to start recalling every clandestine operative the CIA has in the region, and if we still haven't got her back a month from now, we'll have to recall the entire Clandestine Service. Every spy who has ever worked with us will be in danger of being exposed and executed. Our intel will dry up faster than any of us can imagine, and we will be flying blind."

England looked at the president and said, "I'm afraid he's right."

"Mr. President," Rapp said in a pleading tone, "all I'm asking for is twenty-four hours. Just let me do my job and I promise you, I'll find out who is behind this."

President Alexander looked directly at England, who in turn looked at the attorney general and said, "Pete, I'd like to have a word alone with the president and Frank. Would you excuse us for a moment?"

The look on Webber's face was one of dejection, but he understood. He flipped his leather briefing book shut with a snap and stood. He marched across the room and closed the heavy soundproof door behind him.

England knew the president well enough to anticipate what must be done. There was no need for further discussion. Alexander was the quarterback. Their job was to protect and shield him. Alexander had already communicated with his eyes how this thing should play out.

"Mitch," England said, "you have twenty-four hours . . . no questions asked. Just cover your tracks."

"I will."

"And, Mitch," the president said, "bring her back."

"I will, Mr. President."

"Even if she's dead, Mitch, I want her back."

"Yes, sir."

The speaker phone made a clicking noise as Rapp disconnected the call from his end. The president was about to say something when the door opened and Secretary of State Wicka entered looking very hurried.

"I'm sorry I couldn't get here sooner, sir." Wicka dumped her leather shoulder bag on the chair next to England and reached for one of four remote controls sitting in the center of the shiny table. "I'm afraid this situation has just gotten more complicated." Wicka pointed the remote at the large plasma TV on the wall across from her. "Sir, al-Jazeera is reporting that one of our subs has just sunk an Iranian military vessel in the Strait of Hormuz."

"What?" a shocked Alexander asked as images of a heavily damaged gray military vessel appeared on the TV. The president tore his eyes away from the TV and looked at England.

The secretary of defense was already reaching for the phone. "I'm on it, sir."

46

Irene Kennedy lay on the dirt floor and tried not to move. She was wearing only her bra and panties, and was partially covered by an itchy wool blanket. A foul, canvas bag was tied around her head. Even though she desperately needed to go to the bathroom, she was not about to ask her captors. They had already savagely kicked her for attempting to sit up. The man who had been watching her didn't bother to say a word. Just delivered a swift boot to the ribs. He didn't need to. The message was clear. Stay put. If we want you to get up we'll let you know. Kennedy's inventory of her surroundings was bleak. She was almost certain they had her underground. The floor was dirt, and even through the filthy canvas bag she could smell the must.

The attack had been horrifying. Kennedy saw the vehicles in front of them get blown to bits, and then her own Suburban was hit. She wasn't sure, but she thought the explosion might have knocked her unconscious. The next thing she remembered after the series of explosions was the vehicle filling with smoke. Her bodyguards on either side were yelling into their radios calling for help, but none came. She didn't know if the doors had been pried open or if her bodyguards, gasping for air, had decided they had no choice but to abandon the armored vehicle. She had been grabbed roughly and slapped the second her foot hit the pavement. She remembered having the presence of mind to at least look calm. And then the man who had hit her forced her to watch as he shot three of her bodyguards in the head.

They had traveled no more than a block when she was shoved down onto the floor. The hood was placed over her head, and the men went to work with knives, cutting away her clothes. After that they bound her wrists, knees, and ankles. A few minutes later, she guessed, they pulled into a garage where she'd been transferred from one vehicle into the trunk of another, although, it was possible they had simply moved her to the trunk of the same car. She guessed that for a good thirty minutes the car drove around the city. She could tell by the motion and noise that they were stuck in traffic. At one point she heard the men in front arguing. They were talking in Farsi. They said something about roadblocks and having to abandon their original plan. Shortly after that they dumped the car. The men wrapped her in a blanket and moved her from the trunk to her current location.

One man had carried her over his shoulder, and she got the sense they had walked down several narrow flights of stairs. Every time the man hit a landing, he would turn and the hood on Kennedy's head would brush against the wall. She'd heard an old door open with a creak and then she was dumped on the floor like a sack of fertilizer. Kennedy rolled onto her side and attempted to sit up. That was when one of her captors kicked her in the ribs and flipped her onto her back.

The pain of what she thought was most likely a broken rib was a bit of a blessing. It gave her something else to worry about. It had been nearly twenty-five years since she'd gone through her training at The Farm near Williamsburg, Virginia, but she remembered it very well. In fact one lecture stood out all too vividly in her mind. It was about the kidnapping of CIA Beirut station chief Bill Buckley in March of 1984. Buckley had been a Special Forces officer in the army before joining the CIA and was no wilting flower. One week after his kidnapping the first of dozens of CIA spies went missing. Buckley's Hezbollah interrogators broke him and began selling the information to Syria, Jordan, Egypt, and other countries in the region. They brutally tortured him for more than a year and then hanged him. The CIA had managed to get their hands on some of the tapes Hezbollah had made of the torture sessions. The instructors at The Farm made Kennedy and her fellow classmates watch the tapes twice—once before they started their classes on interrogation and again at its two-week conclusion. Showing Buckley's horrible experience was intended to make two simple points. The first was that everyone breaks. Even the toughest of the tough. All you can do is hold out as long as possible to give your colleagues time to move agents and operatives out of harm's way. The second lesson to be learned was simple yet important—don't get caught.

It was obviously too late for that, but Kennedy was attempting to order certain facts in her mind so as to protect the CIA's most important assets as long as possible. She knew, by both code name and real name, virtually every current spy on the CIA's payroll. For the moment Asia and Africa were of little concern. The two most immediate problems were the Middle East and Europe. Kennedy was going down a list in her mind, country by country, of who had been most effective and who had been the least valuable. She basically inverted the list, putting least helpful at the top. Then she added suspected double agents and those the CIA suspected to be on Russia and China's payroll.

By far it was more difficult to rank her own clandestine operatives—employees of the CIA who worked abroad without diplomatic cover. Some were more effective than others, but they were all her fellow countrymen. Kennedy attempted to compile a list, but didn't get far. They had told her all those years ago that everyone broke. She knew it was true, but she had to hold on to hope. She was still in Mosul, surrounded by the American military and sympathetic Kurds. And then there was Rapp. The thought of Mitch put a smile on her face. He would stop at nothing until he found her. Just the thought of him in the city put her momentarily at ease.

For a second she even pitied the men who had taken her. What if they were simply a band of local militia looking to collect some ransom? If that was the case, they were in way over their heads. For the first time since being attacked, Kennedy began to seriously question who her captors were, when she heard the muffled voices of two men talking. The squeaky wooden door opened with a bang, and Kennedy had the horrible feeling it was about to start.

47

Imad Mukhtar had changed into a suit and dress shirt. He had chosen not to wear a tie, however. He descended the ancient steps one at a time. The fact that they had not made it out of the city was not what was worrying him. He had felt from the beginning that it would be too difficult to make it the sixty-odd miles to the Iranian border, but it was worth a try. Even so the Americans had reacted far quicker than he had predicted. An advance team had been sent to an abandoned factory midway between Mosul and the border. As luck would have it, two American Blackhawk helicopters had landed and disgorged over twenty men a mere 100 meters from the factory. Mukhtar was forced to turn around after traveling nearly twenty miles, and then they had to face the gridlock that had been created by the American roadblocks.

Mukhtar had another backup location within the city. A place where the Americans were not welcome. He continued down the steps of the mosque to the dank basement, where the director of the CIA was waiting. Mukhtar had been very pleased with the attack up until just a few minutes ago. Kennedy had been plucked from her SUV without a scratch, and they had left the scene just in time. At least that was what he thought at the time.

He had just been given the bad news that they had lost thirty-four men. At first Mukhtar thought the information was surely inaccurate. How could they possibly have lost so many men? It started to sink in when he asked for Ali Abbas, Hezbollah's liaison in Mosul. Abbas was the man who had brokered the deal with the local police chief. When he was told that Abbas was one of the men killed, his first response was to make sure. If Abbas was alive everything was in jeopardy. He knew Hezbollah's entire infrastructure. Not just in Mosul, but back in Lebanon as well. He also knew they were working directly for the Iranian president which could complicate things. Abbas knew where each and every safe house was located and what local officials were on their payroll.

Someone needed to be dispatched immediately to the scene to find out if anyone had been taken alive. Next he asked for Rashid Dadarshi, the Quds Force commander. Dadarshi was extremely capable. He surely had a man who could go back and begin poking around. But the news only got worse. Dadarshi's second in command informed Mukhtar that his commander had not made it back.

Mukhtar could scarcely believe it. He had seen both men just seconds before he had left with Kennedy.

What could have possibly happened in such a short span of time? He reached the final step that led to a second basement beneath the Great Mosque and again wondered if he was doing the right thing by staying put. Abbas had been the one who had told him about the mosque—that it had an imam who they could trust with their lives. Dadarshi did not know that Abbas had told him about the mosque as a place of refuge and Mukhtar felt very confident that if by chance the Americans had taken Abbas alive, it would take them at least twenty-four hours to break him. He pitted that against the risk of moving Kennedy in broad daylight while the streets were buzzing with American military and police.

When the imam informed Mukhtar of the ancient tunnels beneath the mosque, he decided it was best to stay put, at least until nightfall. Mukhtar's orders were unfortunately specific in one regard. He was not to kill Kennedy unless given the order from Amatullah himself. The only exception was to be during the original attack. If that were to happen, her death could be blamed on Sunni insurgents and no one would be the wiser. He was tempted to walk through the door at the end of the narrow passageway and be done with the whole thing. Simply put a bullet in her head and then dump her body in the river, but he was equally tempted to interrogate her. That was why he was willing to risk the run to the Iranian border. She was a very smart woman, so it would take time to deconstruct her lies. Mukhtar had no doubt he could do it, but it would not be easy. It would require months of painstaking interrogation, but the information would be so valuable it could fund Hezbollah for the next decade, not to mention what it would do for their reputation. First things first, though. He had given President Amatullah his word that he would deliver a vital piece of propaganda.

One of the Quds Force commandos was standing guard outside the door. Mukhtar straightened his jacket as he approached and asked, "How is she?"

The man shrugged. "No problems so far."

"Let's keep it that way."

Mukhtar threw the door open and entered the dank, stone walled storage room. It was approximately ten feet wide by twenty feet long with a ceiling of only seven feet. A single lamp was plugged into an extension chord that ran back down the hallway. The stench of mold and stale air was oppressive. Mukhtar walked across the dirt floor to Kennedy and looked down at her bare legs protruding from the blanket they had thrown on her. Mukhtar bent down and pulled the canvas bag off Kennedy's head. She looked up at him with blinking eyes as he reached down and covered her legs with the blanket.

In English, Mukhtar said, "I'm sorry I couldn't get here sooner, Dr. Kennedy." Mukhtar was very proud of the research he'd done and the ingenious angle he'd come up with. He'd read in a *Washington Post* piece that she was referred to as *doctor* by her close friends. "I only found out thirty minutes ago that you had been taken hostage. Have they treated you all right?"

Kennedy stopped blinking and looked up at Mukhtar with searching eyes. "I'm sorry . . . you are?"

Mukhtar smiled and said, "Someone who would like to see this mistake rectified before anyone else gets hurt."

"That is very nice of you. Do you work for the regional government?"

"You could say that. I'm a freelancer of sorts."

Kennedy was well aware that kidnapping for ransom was rampant across all of Iraq. It had grown into a cottage industry complete with neutral negotiators who collected upwards of a third of the ransom. "I see," Kennedy said as she struggled to prop herself up on her left elbow.

"Here," Mukhtar offered as he grabbed her around the shoulders and helped her sit up. The blanket fell partially away exposing her bra and bound wrists. Mukhtar drew a knife and cut the plastic flex cuffs on her wrists and then her knees and ankles.

Kennedy clutched the blanket and covered her exposed skin. "Thank you . . . I'm sorry, you never told me your name."

"You may call me Muhammad."

"Of course," Kennedy replied a bit suspiciously. He might as well have said John Doe. "You said this was a mistake. I'm sorry, but I find that a bit hard to believe."

"I'm sure you do, but I think I can explain." Mukhtar glanced at the guard sitting in the corner and

305

in Arabic asked him if he could have a moment alone with the prisoner. The lumbering man slowly got off his chair and left the room.

"The police force here in Mosul is extremely corrupt. They were not told that you were in that convoy."

Kennedy knew they had not told the police for that very reason. "Then who did they think was in the convoy?"

"They are not telling me that. All they've said is that it was someone who they would be able to ransom for a lot of money."

"Have you contacted my government?"

"Not yet."

"Why not?"

Mukhtar glanced nervously over his shoulder and then in a much quieter voice said, "Some of them want to kill you, some of them want to negotiate with your government, and some of them would like to sell you to another government."

"Who are you talking about?"

"A local group, but very powerful. More like your Mafia than one of our militias."

"Sunni?" Kennedy asked.

Mukhtar shrugged off the question. "I cannot say, but I wanted you to know I am working on your release . . . and that I will do everything I can to make sure you remain unharmed."

"Thank you."

Mukhtar stood. "Now I must go, but first if you will allow me I need to take your photo."

Kennedy looked hesitant.

"It is for your own good. So I can prove that you are alive."

That sounded like a good idea to Kennedy. She clutched the blanket around her shoulders and sat up as straight as her broken rib would allow her.

Mukhtar snapped her photo with a digital camera and said, "I will be back to check on you in a bit. Is there anything I can get for you?"

There were a lot of things she would have liked, but she decided to keep it brief. "I need to go to the bathroom."

"I will see if I can arrange that. Anything else?"

"Some clothes would be nice."

"Of course. I will see what I can do." As Mukhtar left the room he gave Kennedy one more comforting smile and then closed the door behind him. He waved for the guards to follow him down the hallway.

When they were far enough away Mukhtar lowered his voice and in Farsi said, "Wait five minutes and then bring her a pot to go to the bathroom in. I want you to watch her do it. If she gets shy, rip her panties off, but do not rape her. At least not yet. When she is done you can slap her around a bit, but do not hit her face. Then put the hood back on her. Do you understand?"

Both men smiled and nodded.

"Good. I will be back in one hour."

48

Rapp stood behind Marcus Dumond and watched the younger man's fingers fly over the computer keyboard with the skill of a concert pianist. Dumond was by far the most accomplished hacker at Langley, and perhaps in all the U.S. government. The MIT graduate had scanned the photos Rapp had taken and was now running a search through multiple databases to see if he could come up with a match.

"How long will it take?" Rapp asked as he zipped up the khaki flight suit Stilwell had given him.

"It could take five minutes. It could take five hours. That's even if we have them in one of the databases."

"You talked to NSA?"

"Yep. They came up with nothing."

Rapp had asked Dumond to contact the National Security Agency and see if they could locate Kennedy's secure mobile phone. Even if it was turned off they should have been able to locate it. The fact that they couldn't meant her captors must have destroyed it.

"Any other ideas?" Rapp asked.

"Not really." Dumond kept working the keyboard. "I'll keep pounding away on this while you start pounding on them." Dumond nodded at the stack of photos.

"I want you listening to the interrogations. I'll try to do as much as I can in English, but if I switch to

Arabic or Farsi, Stan will be with you to translate. Once we find out where these guys are from, I'll need you to work your magic and try to confirm what they're saying."

"No problem."

"All right. Let me know the second you find anything."

"Will do."

Rapp walked down the short hallway and poked his head in Stilwell's office. It reeked of cigarette smoke. The chief of base was working his contacts, trying to find out where the local police commander had run off to. Stilwell interrupted the person he was talking to and told him to hold on for a moment. He covered the phone and said, "What's up?"

"I need a video camera and some rubber gloves. Some drugs too."

Stilwell held up a finger and put the phone back to his mouth, "Faris, I'm going to have to call you back." Stilwell tried to hang up, but it was obvious the man had more to say. "Yes, there will be money. Lots of it." Stilwell looked at Rapp and asked, "How much?"

"For the police chief or Irene?"

"Irene."

Without flinching, Rapp said, "A million dollars cash and a U.S. citizenship . . . no questions asked."

Stilwell repeated the information.

"Tell him the offer's only good until midnight," Rapp added. "And it has to lead to us getting her back."

Stilwell listened and said, "Yeah, tax free, Faris. Sure . . . whatever you want. Just find out who took her and where she is . . . Yes, your wife and kids can come with you. If you help get her back, Faris, I will personally find you a house and help you move in. Now get going." Stilwell stuffed the phone back in the cradle before the person could ask any more questions.

"Who was that?" Rapp asked as he examined some clothes hanging on a hook.

"One of my sources. He's pretty good. He loves money and his wife wants to move to the states so he's highly motivated."

"Send him the photos of the three guys we have in lockup."

"Good idea." Stilwell looked up Faris's e-mail address, typed a quick note and attached the photos.

"What are these?" Rapp pointed to the clothes.

Stilwell glanced up and smiled. "Those are my clerical robes. No better way to pick up women."

"You can't be serious."

"Not about picking up women, but you'd be amazed the doors those things open."

"What'd you find out about the police chief?"

"Fucking rat bastard is nowhere to be found. I hope someone put a bullet in his head."

"I'd like to talk to him first."

"You know what I mean."

"Yeah . . . What kind of drugs do you have?"

Concern on his face, Stilwell asked, "Are you hurt?"

310

"No. I want to soften these guys up before I start in on them."

Stilwell opened his desk drawer and grabbed a set of keys. He stood and said, "Follow me."

The two men left the trailer and stepped out into the bright afternoon sun. They were cutting across the courtyard, dodging satellite dishes and antennas, when they ran into Ridley, who was talking on a mobile phone. Ridley held up his hand to stop the other two men and said to the person he was talking to, "Of course I'm going to pay you. Just send me the damn photos."

Ridley stuffed the phone into his pocket and said, "Mitch, I know the president gave you a blank check, but I want you to at least consider something."

Rapp stepped around him and kept walking.

Ridley fell in line and followed the two men. "I think it's great that the president gave you the green light, but we both know if this thing ends badly, all of us are going to get thrown to the wolves. The damage to the Agency could be catastrophic."

"Rob, if we don't get Irene back alive, I really don't give a shit who's thrown to the wolves."

"You don't care if this mess sets the CIA back another twenty years?"

As Stilwell punched a code into a cipher lock on the door to the storage trailer, Rapp said, "How are we going to suffer any more under these idiots than we already have?"

"By you mutilating prisoners. Do you have any idea

how that will play with the average citizen? They're going to think we're a bunch of monsters."

"Right now I am a monster. Just like the guys who took Irene. That's how you fight this damn war. Not with politicians, reporters, and lawyers."

Stilwell opened a small refrigerator and started reading off labels. "Sodium pentothal, phenobarbital, lysergic acid diethylamide, heroin, speed . . . you name it, we've got it."

"Give the fake cop the sodium pentothal, and the other two the speed."

"Got it." Stilwell grabbed a bottle of each and a handful of syringes.

Ridley was still hovering. "Mitch, please, just don't do anything permanent. I mean, come on—you can't cut the guy's dick off. If that ever gets out, it's going to look so bad."

Stilwell was poking around the storage shelves. Without bothering to turn around, he said, "He's got a point, Mitch. I mean, you're just threatening to cut these guys, right? You're not actually going to do it, are you?" Stilwell found a box of latex gloves and handed a pair to Rapp.

Rapp took the gloves and thought about the question for a moment. He had absolutely no problem doing whatever it took to get these guys to talk, but he saw a possible middle ground that might work to heighten the anxiety of his prisoners. Looking at Stilwell he asked, "Did your Kurds get those dead bodies stripped and dumped in a cell?"

"Last I checked they were working on it."

"All right," Rapp said to Ridley. "For now, I won't cut their peckers off, but I'm not going to make any promises." Pointing to Stilwell, Rapp said, "Give each of them a healthy dose, and I'll be in there in five minutes."

49

Congressional oversight was a nuisance Rapp had been working feverishly to circumvent for the majority of his career. In theory it was fine; Congress doled out the money, and someone had to keep an eye on how it was spent. When it came to national security, though, things got a little more complicated. The number of elected officials who were willing to put the good of the country ahead of their own ego, and the success of their political party, was minuscule. Given the chance, they would tout freedom of speech, a person's right to privacy, and any other platitude they could come up with, rather than shut their mouths and grapple with the hard fact that they were fighting an enemy who didn't play by the rules. Invariably, only a small handful had the dignity to resist the call of the camera and personal fame. The politicians, for the most part, were lawyers; men and women who'd been trained to argue both sides of an issue with equal passion and vigor.

Rapp knew Ridley was right on this front. Washington was run by people like the attorney general, who had little if any practical experience with the war on terror. People who, if in Kennedy's perilous position, would be praying frantically that someone like Rapp would be there to do absolutely everything it took to make sure they were rescued. These were the same men and women who would eventually sit him down in a committee room and dissect every move he'd made to save his boss and protect America's most important secrets.

Rapp had no doubt they would be revolted by what he was about to do, but he didn't give a shit. When the time came, he would go to them, raise his right hand, swear to tell the truth, and for perhaps the first time in his entire career, he would do exactly that. And then he would ask them what they would want Rapp to do if they were ever taken hostage. Would they want the State Department to begin negotiations for an exchange that might take years, while they were tortured and tormented? While their teeth fell out and they lost a third of their weight? Is that what they would want or would they want someone like Rapp to throw away the rule book, climb down in the gutter, and begin bashing heads?

Kennedy was too important to him personally, and too important to the country, for him to get squeamish. The three men in the holding cells were not merely suspected terrorists who'd been turned in by their neighbors and snatched out of bed in the middle of the night. These three had been caught in the thick of it, and that made what Rapp had to do significantly easier.

The door to the first cell on the left was wide open. Inside, the floor was covered with naked hairy men, piled one on top of the other. Blood was everywhere; smeared across fleshy, pale skin and pooling on the uneven, dented floor. Most of the bodies had bullet wounds to the head or chest. A few had wounds beneath the waist as well. Rapp figured he'd killed a good number of them. He surveyed the scene with a flicker of reservation. He told himself that the task before him was necessary to convince the prisoners that his threat was real. Three tugs and three quick slices, and he was done.

Rapp left the cell, wiped the blood from the blade on the thigh of his coveralls and put the knife away. He walked all the way to the end of the hall and stood in front of the last cell on the left. Rapp slid back the metal cover on the peephole and looked at the youngest of the three prisoners. He was sitting in a galvanized metal chair, his ankles handcuffed to the legs of the chair and his hands cuffed behind his back. Rapp stepped to the side of the door, undid the lock, and then swung it open just enough to toss one of the severed appendages into the cell.

Rapp closed and locked the door and then moved back to the peephole. The prisoner looked at the hunk of flesh at his feet. A look of confusion quickly melted away as he realized what he was looking at. The young man shut his eyes and began shaking his head vigorously. Rapp closed the peephole and moved to the next cell. He undid the door, entered the cell and stood over the man he thought was the commander of the group. The man was still strapped to a stretcher.

Rapp held the severed organ in front of the man's face. He casually bent over, dropped it onto the man's chest, and said, "I found out this guy was lying to me."

Without saying another word, Rapp left and went to the last cell, where he did the exact same thing. He then found Stilwell and told him he wanted only audio recordings of the interrogations. Rapp checked the time and then continued back to the first cell. He grabbed an extra chair and brought it in with him. He positioned the chair four feet from the prisoner and sat. On the floor almost exactly between them was the severed penis. Rapp didn't speak at first. He looked at the severed organ, up at the man across from him, and then back.

The prisoner was sweating. His knees were beginning to tremble, and his eyes were darting all around the small cell. He took in everything except the hunk of flesh at his feet. Rapp studied him. He tried to lock eyes, but the prisoner wouldn't commit. The speed he had been given would only heighten his anxiety.

"I'm a soldier," the prisoner blurted out in a panicked voice. "I shouldn't be treated like this."

Rapp smiled. "A soldier. That's interesting. Most of the soldiers I know wear uniforms."

The man closed his mouth tightly and shut his eyes.

"That body part there," Rapp pointed to the organ on the floor, "belongs to one of your comrades. I told him not to lie to me. I told him I had plenty of ways to verify what he was saying. He thought he was smarter than me. Do you think you're smarter than me?"

"No."

"Good . . . then this should go much smoother. Let's start with your name, and look me in the eye when you answer." Rapp cocked his head slightly to the left and studied the man's face.

"Corporal Nouri Tahmineh."

"Where were you born?"

The man hesitated.

"This is the speed round, buddy. Rapid-fire. You don't have to think about these. Just answer. I got five guys in another room that can hack into any computer system in the world. I've got another room full of people back in Washington working the phones. We've got spies in every frickin' government in the region. Right now they're calling around about you and if what you say is true, and you're a soldier, we'll find your military records. If the photo doesn't match the name, or we can't find you, I'm going to cut off your left nut just like I told you I would. Your friend there," Rapp pointed to the object on the floor. "He gave me the wrong name, the wrong town, and a bull-shit date of birth. He made it real easy for me. I just cut everything off in one fell swoop. You probably heard him screaming like the peckerless little pussy that he now is."

Rapp pulled out his knife and extended the blade. "Here's how dumb the guy is. After all that . . . he's in so much goddamn pain he ends up telling me his name anyway. The point is, you're going to end up telling me everything, so you might as well hold on to your manhood." Rapp pointed the tip of the knife at the man's crotch. "Now, are you ready for the speed round?"

The prisoner nodded quickly.

"Name?" Rapp fired the question like a drill sergeant.

"Corporal Nouri Tahmineh."

"Place of birth?"

"Qom."

The only city Rapp knew of by that name was approximately 100 miles southwest of Tehran. "Date of birth?"

"Fourteenth of January, nineteen-eighty-two."

"You said you're a soldier. What unit?"

"Twenty-Third Special Forces Division. Jerusalem Force."

Rapp kept his emotions in check. The man sitting before him was not some insurgent volunteer. He was an Iranian soldier. A member of their elite Quds Force or, as some of the more anti-Semitic men referred to it, Jerusalem Force. His involvement in the kidnapping of Kennedy caused Rapp to see things in an entirely different light.

"How long have you been in Iraq?" Rapp asked while he tried to think of the implications of direct Iranian involvement.

"Almost two months."

"All of it in Mosul?"

"Mostly . . . and the surrounding area."

Rapp wondered if Minister Ashani had ordered this. Up until now, he had thought the man very reasonable. Now he wondered if the sincerity he had shown Kennedy was all an act. "You married?"

The man looked away nervously and hesitated.

"Don't lie to me."

"Engaged."

Good leverage, Rapp thought to himself. He unzipped the thigh pocket on his coveralls, and pulled out the stack of Polaroids. He flipped through until he found the one he was looking for. He held the stack in front of Tahmineh's face and said, "Careful on this one. Name and rank, just like it says in the Geneva Convention. Which also says you're supposed to be in uniform, but we'll talk about that later."

The young Iranian looked at the photo and hesitated.

"Your fiancée," Rapp started, "will never marry you if the goods are damaged." Rapp could tell the speed had taken full effect. Tahmineh's knees were shaking and his eyes were darting around the room. "Look at me!" Rapp screamed. "Is she pretty?"

"Who?" the man asked, genuinely confused.

"Your fiancée."

"Yes."

Rapp stuck the tip of the knife up against the man's crotch. "Then you're screwed. No way in hell a good-looking Persian woman is going to marry a guy without a dick. Now quit fucking around, and tell me who this is and remember I might already know his name. This could be a test and if you fail, off comes the first nut."

"Captain Rashid Dadarshi . . . my commanding officer."

Captain was the equivalent of a captain in the U.S. Army. "When were you told who you would be kidnapping?"

Tahmineh looked nervous. "I was never told."

"Never?" Rapp said forcefully.

"Never. We were only told it was an American, and that we were not to harm her."

Rapp looked at him skeptically even though he had a suspicion the man was telling the truth.

"We were only told yesterday of the plan."

"Who told you?"

"Captain Dadarshi, of course."

"No one else?"

Tahmineh shook his head.

"Then who the hell is this?" Rapp shuffled through the photos and held up the one of the man who had been dressed as a police officer.

Tahmineh took one look at the photo and his face twisted into a disgusted scowl. "That is a Palestinian dog. He is not part of my unit."

"Name?" Rapp barked.

"Ali Abbas," the man offered willingly.

"If he isn't Quds Force, then who is he with?"

"Hezbollah."

"Hezbollah," Rapp repeated as he stood. "What the fuck is Hezbollah doing in Mosul?"

"I do not know. I am only a corporal."

Rapp had a good sense that the man was telling him the truth, but he needed to keep him on the edge for a bit longer. He stuck his knife under the Iranian's chin and lifted it until he was looking straight into his eyes. "I'm going to go check your story, and if I find out you lied to me about a single thing, I'll be back for your nuts."

50

Rapp closed the door to the cell, and hustled down the hallway. The looped recording of a man being tortured was playing on the overhead speakers. Rapp ignored the agonizing screams and grappled with the implications of what he'd just learned. From the onset of the attack on Kennedy's motorcade he'd assumed it was Sunnis who were behind the plan. The Sunnis ran the police force and had been known to work with al-Qaeda in Iraq on a limited basis. Iranian and Hezbollah involvement brought things into a much more complicated light. At first Rapp couldn't believe they would be so reckless as to actually kidnap the sitting director of the CIA, but the more he thought about it, the less he was surprised. Clearly these were desperate men willing to take great risks to hold on to power.

Dumond had set up shop in the conference room. He had two of his high-powered laptops plugged into full-size monitors and was working both. Stilwell was sitting next to him taking notes and helping translate.

Rapp stopped in the doorway. "Any luck?"

"Not yet." Dumond didn't bother to look up from the screen. "I'm not sure the Iranian Army has these personnel records on their network."

Rapp was afraid of that. "What about public databases? Motor vehicle registry, utilities, birth records?"

"I'm searching all of them."

Ridley joined Rapp in the doorway. He was holding a stack of freshly printed 5x6 photos. "These just came in." Ridley handed the stack to Rapp, who began peeling through them. "That first one is of Minister Ashani right after he arrived."

Rapp reached the third photo and Ridley stopped him. The vantage was from the front of the helicopter and showed Ashani walking to the right. On the left side of the helicopter there was another man in a dark suit walking in the opposite direction. "Who's this?"

"I don't know."

Rapp flipped through a couple more photos and stopped on a head shot of the mystery man. The digital photo had been cropped and blown up. The quality wasn't perfect, but it was still easy to make out the man's features. He had a dark brown beard and even though he was wearing sunglasses there was something vaguely familiar about him. Rapp continued going through the shots and stopped on the second to last one. It showed the mystery man climbing into a police SUV that was bracketed by two police pickup trucks, both with .50-caliber machine guns mounted to the roofs.

Rapp quickly shuffled back to the best photo of the mystery man and handed Ridley the rest of the stack. "Charlie's in the Situation Room with the president, right?"

"Yes."

"Get on the horn with him and tell him we're ninety percent sure Iran is behind the kidnapping of Irene."

"Ninety percent?" Ridley questioned. "We haven't even verified that this Tahmineh is who he says he is."

"That's why I didn't say one hundred. Trust me, Rob, we need to get the National Security Council talking about this. If it is Iran, it'll take them half a day to figure out who the hell to even call." Rapp began moving toward the door. "Irene doesn't have that kind of time."

Rapp went straight back to Tahmineh's cell. He threw open the steel door, walked right up to the seated and handcuffed man, and thrust the photo in his face. "Who is this guy?"

The Iranian's eyes were literally bugging out of his head and he was sweating profusely. "I don't know."

"Bullshit!" Rapp screamed.

"I mean I don't know his name. I don't know him. I saw him for the first time today."

Rapp felt his jaw tighten. Through clenched teeth, he asked, "When and where?"

"It was this morning. Right before the attack. We had been moved into position before dawn and were waiting. He showed up maybe an hour before the attack and took over."

"Is he special forces?"

"No." The prisoner frantically shook his head. "I don't think so."

"He gave Captain Dadarshi orders?"

"Yes."

"Was he from the Ministry of Intelligence?"

"I don't know," the man pleaded.

Rapp eyed him. There were no signs that he was being anything less than truthful. "You have no idea who the man is?"

"No."

It would stand to reason that the mystery man worked for Ashani, and it would also stand to reason that a lowly corporal would have no idea who the man was. Rapp did not want to try to figure out his next move in front of the prisoner. He left the cell without saying another word and closed and locked the door. He began pacing up and down the hall while the torture track played as background noise. His mind turned the facts over and over, looking at each bit of information from every angle he could think of. He couldn't believe he hadn't seen it earlier.

Rapp snatched the two-way radio from his hip. He hit the talk button and said, "Rob, get me a number for Minister Ashani."

51

The helicopter ride from Mosul to the border had taken just twenty minutes. The Air Force had a relatively small Dassault Falcon 10 waiting to take him to Tehran. For most of the hour-and-ten-minute flight Ashani made notes to himself. They were cryptic so as to protect him if somehow they should fall into the wrong hands, which was doubtful since he planned to destroy them as soon as he got to his office. He'd hesitated even making the notes, but he wanted to organize his thoughts and be very clear about what Kennedy had offered on behalf of the U.S. government.

There was another reason he had opened the notepad. Ashani wanted to make a list of objections, or more precisely a list of who would object. There were more than a few people in Tehran whose power would evaporate if peace was made with America. It would make no difference that the American offer made complete sense. President Amatullah would do everything in his power to make sure the offer was rejected. That was why Ashani had opted not to call the president during his brief border stop. He needed to talk to Najar first. As head of the Guardian Council he could influence many people if he was persuaded. If Amatullah found out first, he would find some way to have his P.R. machine kill the offer before it was ever seriously considered.

Shortly after the plane landed in Tehran, Ashani looked out the window and got a sinking feeling in the pit of his stomach. In addition to his normal car and driver there were two additional vehicles and another eight armed men. Ashani looked at his security chief, Rahad Tehrani, who had the same look of concern on his face.

"Stay here," Tehrani said, "and I will see what the problem is."

Ashani glanced out the window and watched his security chief approach the group of men. At that precise moment he realized he had forgotten to turn his cell phone on upon landing. Ashani hit the power button and watched the color screen come to life. A picture of a spinning globe flashed on the screen before it changed to a list of icons and then the phone started to beep as it retrieved voice mails first and then e-mails. After a few seconds the beeping stopped, and Ashani saw that he had eight voice mail messages and twenty-three new e-mails. The amount was not unheard-of, but it was a bit high. He was about to begin scrolling through the e-mails, when the phone began ringing. The readout on the phone would tell him only that the information on the person who was calling was unavailable.

Ashani pressed the talk button and said, "Hello?"

"Minister Ashani?" the caller said in English.

"Yes."

"This is Mitch Rapp. I work for Director Kennedy. Do you know who I am?"

Ashani glanced nervously out the window and said as casually as he could, "I'm afraid everyone in our line of work is aware of your reputation."

"Good. Then you'll know how serious I am when I tell you that I'm going to kill you."

"Excuse me?" Ashani said in genuine surprise.

"I know what you've been up to. If Director Kennedy is not released in the next hour, I'm coming after you. And if, as you say, everyone in our line of work is aware of my reputation, then you know I will succeed. I will hunt your ass down and kill you, and no level of security will stop me."

"Mr. Rapp, I can assure you that I have no idea what you are talking about, and I do not take kindly to your threats."

"What are you going to do . . . take out a fatwa on me? Well, let me tell you something. I'm not some defenseless author who's going to go into hiding because you thin-skinned little pricks decide I've offended Islam. I bite back, and I'm going to hunt down every single one of you fuckers that had anything to do with this."

Ashani was literally speechless. He was all too well aware of Mitch Rapp's abilities. On at least two occasions the American operative had sneaked into Iran. Both times his targets were terrorists who had traveled to Iran in an attempt to avoid the reach of the U.S. government. Both men were extremely well protected, and neither had survived his run-in with Rapp.

Despite his dry throat and trembling hands, Ashani attempted to sound calm. "Mr. Rapp, I have no idea what you are talking about and, as I said, I do not appreciate being threatened."

"Well, you'll have to excuse my poor manners, but in light of the fact that my boss has been kidnapped and her entire security detail killed, I really don't give a shit what you appreciate and don't appreciate."

Ashani's mind was swimming. All he could think to say was, "In Mosul?"

"No, in Paris! Of course in Mosul."

"I can assure you that I have no idea what you're talking about."

"Well . . . I have a stack of photos, and three prisoners who say otherwise."

Ashani looked up as Tehrani came back on the plane. The security chief started to talk, but was silenced by Ashani, who waved him off the plane. "Mr. Rapp," Ashani said with as much sincerity as he could muster, "I do not know what you are talking about. I have a great amount of respect for Director Kennedy."

"Go sell your bullshit to some moron who's buying. I don't have the time for this, and if you want to live, you'll get your ass in gear and have her released within the hour."

"Mr. Rapp," Ashani said with a trace of panic in his voice, "I have no idea what you are talking about!"

"You're telling me that she left a meeting with you,

traveled a block and a half, and was attacked by a platoon of Quds Force commandos and you had no idea?"

"What?"

"And I suppose that guy who flew in with you on your helicopter . . . you have no idea who he is either . . . because I've got a bunch of Iranian soldiers in custody who are telling me he ran the operation to kidnap Director Kennedy."

Ashani's mouth was agape as he pictured Mukhtar blessing him and running toward the waiting police vehicles.

"What's wrong?" Rapp yelled. "You finally run out of fucking lies to tell me?"

Random pieces of information fell into place as Ashani replayed the events of the past several days. Ashani was left no other conclusion than the dreadful reality that he had been deceived by his own government. Amatullah and Mukhtar had clearly been conspiring, but to what end Ashani could not see.

"Mr. Rapp, I have not told you a single lie. I'm afraid this entire operation was kept from me."

"Well, you'll have to excuse me if I don't take you at your word," Rapp said sarcastically.

Ashani's chief of security was back in the door looking very nervous. Ashani waved him away. "Mr. Rapp, I am going to do everything in my power to make sure Dr. Kennedy is released safely."

"Who was that man who flew in on the helicopter with you?"

"I . . ." Ashani hesitated, "am going to have to get back to you on that."

"Bullshit! You've given me no reason to believe you. Give me one good reason why I shouldn't tell the president to proceed with the strike that the Joint Chiefs are recommending."

"What strike?"

"Operation Medusa. They want to cut off the head. Your homes, your offices, they're all in the targeting package."

"Mr. Rapp, I urge you to tell the president to give me time."

"Why the fuck should we trust you? You set us up. You kidnapped a sitting director of the CIA, the president's closest national security advisor. You think he's going to negotiate for her release? He's going to use this as an excuse to bomb you fuckers back to the Stone Age."

"I just landed in Tehran. Please give me some time to find out what is going on."

"You don't see what's going on here, do you. I'm in Mosul. President Alexander is sitting in a bunker right now surrounded by a bunch of generals who think this is a blessing. They've already launched the B-2s from their base in Kansas. They're on the way. You can help avoid this. That man who rode in on the helicopter with you . . . what is his name, and where did he take Director Kennedy?"

"That man," Ashani hesitated, "is someone I detest."

"Name!" Rapp shouted.

Ashani looked out the window at the waiting men and it occurred to him that they might be there to arrest him, or at a bare minimum keep an eye on him. This might be his last chance to freely discuss things with Rapp. "Imad Muhktar," Ashani said, with loathing in his voice.

"Imad Mukhtar!" Rapp practically screamed. "You mean Hezbollah's head of paramilitary operations?"

"Yes."

"Where did he take her?"

"I have no idea, but I am going to do everything I can to find out. Do you have a pen?"

"Yes."

"Take down my e-mail address and send me your phone number."

Ashani gave him the information and then promised he would get back to him within the hour. He ended the call before Rapp could threaten him again. He stood, his mind reeling with horrible possibilities. Amatullah had clearly not told him of this operation because he knew he would have never agreed to go along. The question now was, whom else had Amatullah recruited? Whom could Ashani trust, and how could he make things right without committing treason in the process?

52

The president was on his feet, his right hand stuffed under his left arm and his left hand up and supporting his chin. His jacket was off, and the sleeves on his crisp white dress shirt were rolled up. He was basically in a standing version of Auguste Rodin's statue *The Thinker.* Behind his chair at the end of the long conference table he paced back and forth. Four steps to one wall and then back again. In the far corner, Secretary of State Wicka was talking in hushed tones on one of the bulky secure telephone units. She was in the midst of calling a half dozen key allies and explaining to them that despite what they were seeing on TV, the United States had not attacked the Iranian vessel. The president would have made the calls himself, but they had decided until they received absolute confirmation from the navy that he would let others put their reputations on the line.

Secretary of Defense England was sitting near the president with a phone clutched tightly to his ear. His deep baritone voice had a tendency to carry, so most of the other Cabinet officials had either left the room or moved farther away like Wicka. From time to time England would raise his head and relay to the president what the Joint Chiefs were telling him. Everyone from the secretary of the navy down to the theater commander had denied the report of a U.S. submarine's being involved in the sinking of an Iranian frigate. Now, England was attempting to speak firsthand to the Task Force Commander for the subs in the region.

The door to the conference room opened, and Ted Byrne, the president's chief of staff, entered with a deeply concerned look on his face. He moved quickly around the far side of the table and intercepted the president.

"I just got off the phone with Mark."

"Mark?" the president asked.

"Stevens."

Mark Stevens was the president's treasury secretary. Alexander nodded for Byrne to continue.

"The European markets are in a free fall."

"Shit . . . I should have seen that coming. Oil futures?"

"Through the roof. They jumped to ninety dollars a barrel, and there's rumors that Iran is calling for an OPEC embargo of the United States."

Before the president could decide what assets to put on this new front, Secretary of Defense England's voice drowned out the entire room.

"You're sure?" England half yelled. "Have you seen the footage?" England looked at the president and smiled. "Great work, Captain. Send it." The secretary of defense slammed the handset back into the cradle and said to the president, "You're not going to believe this. We had a sub in the strait when the Iranian frigate was torpedoed."

"Why would we find that hard to believe?" the chief of staff asked in a sour tone. "That's what the Iranians are claiming."

"They're claiming we sunk their ship, and they're full of it. We had the U.S.S. *Virginia* tasked to follow the *Yusef*, one of Iran's three Kilo-class subs. The *Virginia* followed the *Yusef* into the strait and has the sonar tapes of the *Yusef* firing on its own ship."

"Why on God's green earth would they fire on their own ship?" Byrne asked.

"Because they want to make it look like we did it," the president answered.

"Exactly," England agreed. "The task force commander is sending the contact tapes as well as footage of the Iranian ship being hit."

CIA Deputy Director O'Brien entered the room looking harried. "Mr. President, I just spoke to Rapp. He has confirmation that Kennedy's kidnapping was an Iranian operation."

The room went silent. The president asked, "What kind of confirmation?"

"One of the prisoners has confessed that he's a member of the Quds Force. For lack of a perfect analogy, that means he's Iranian special forces. He identified one of the other prisoners as his commanding officer, and the third he says is a member of Hezbollah."

The president looked around the room at the other members of his National Security Team. "So this was no random attack by local insurgents?"

"No, sir, in fact we have an even more damning piece of evidence." O'Brien looked over his shoulder and nodded to a tech who had followed him into the conference room. A series of photos appeared on one of the large plasmas. O'Brien pointed to the photo in the upper left corner and said, "These were surveillance shots taken of Iranian Intelligence Minister Ashani as he landed in Mosul this morning." The deputy director pointed to a second photo. "Here he is shaking hands with our deputy director of operations, Near East Division. On the far left of the frame you can see a man walking in the opposite direction." O'Brien's finger moved to the second row. "This man walking right here toward the police vehicles."

"Rapp took this photo," O'Brien said, pointing to the last one, "and showed it to one of the prisoners, who did not know the man's name but said he arrived in Mosul this morning and took over the operation to kidnap Director Kennedy. The man Rapp has been interrogating"—O'Brien looked down to consult a piece of paper—"a Corporal Tahmineh, says he was not told who they were kidnapping. Only that this man was adamant that it was a woman and she be taken alive."

The president looked angrily at the screen. "Who is he?"

"It's Imad Mukhtar, sir, the head of Hezbollah's paramilitary wing."

The president stared at the screen in absolute disbelief at the Iranians' audacity. "You're sure?"

O'Brien looked at the president with a partially dazed expression. "Well, sir, this information is coming in pretty fast, so we haven't had the chance to source it properly. In fact the only photo we have of Mukhtar is nearly thirty years old."

"So you're not sure," the president said with no attempt to hide his irritation.

"Let me explain further. Mitch called Minister Ashani and asked him who . . ."

The president interrupted, "Mitch called Minister Ashani directly?"

"Yes, sir." O'Brien cleared his throat and said, "After the prisoner," the deputy director stopped to consult his notes.

An irritated president Alexander said, "Corporal whoever . . . I don't care what his name is. Tell me about Mitch's conversation with Ashani."

O'Brien looked extremely nervous about his next words. "Mitch told Ashani he was going to hunt him down and kill him unless Irene was released within the hour."

"Good," Secretary of Defense England announced.

Other members of the National Security team looked less enthused.

"How did Ashani react?" the president asked.

"This is where it gets a little tricky. Mitch said Ashani seemed genuinely surprised by the whole thing."

"What do you mean, surprised?" The president pointed at the screen. "He rode in on the same heli-copter as this Mukbar, or whatever his name is."

"All I'm doing is relaying what Mitch told me. He thinks there's a chance Ashani was kept in the dark."

"Or he's trying to save his own ass," England said.

"Maybe," replied O'Brien, "but he's the one who identified the man as Mukhtar."

"Can we corroborate that info with another source?" asked the president.

"Mitch is working on that right now."

The president was about to ask how, and then he thought better of it. Instead, he clenched his jaw in anger and said, "I can't believe they had the gall to launch this operation right under our noses, and think we wouldn't find out."

"I'm not sure we would have found out, sir, if Mitch hadn't taken those prisoners." This was O'Brien's way of attempting to say he had been wrong about trying to put a leash on Rapp.

"Maybe not," the president mused. Turning to the secretary of defense, the president asked, "What's their endgame? What are they trying to accomplish?"

"I'm not sure. This isn't exactly rational behavior."

"Sympathy, sir," announced Secretary of State Wicka as she walked up to the group, twirling her trademark reading glasses in her right hand. "I just had a very enlightening conversation with France's foreign minister. He says he received a call from Iran's foreign minister claiming that his country is under attack by the U.S. He requested that France sponsor a resolution in the UN condemning the attack and asking that the U.S. pay reparations for both the vessel and the nuclear facility at Isfahan. He urged that the UN Security Council hold an emergency session to vote on this issue. He said if the UN didn't take care of the problem, OPEC would."

"Oh God," Byrne moaned. "We'd better find a way to defuse this before oil prices shoot past a hundred dollars a barrel."

"Prices will snap back as soon as this thing is over," England said dismissively. "The important thing is to make sure this damn Iranian sub doesn't sink any of our ships, and that we get Director Kennedy back as soon as possible. I think the way to do that is to turn up the heat on these guys. I think you should hold a press conference and put the facts out there, and I think you should consider laying down an ultimatum for the release of Kennedy."

"What kind of ultimatum?" the president asked.

"I would consider calling her kidnapping an act of war."

"Whoa . . ." Byrne put his hands up in a cautionary manner. "I know this is going to sound callous to some of you, but it has to be said." The chief of staff looked at the other key advisors. "Maybe this is the price we have to pay for taking out their nuclear program."

"Ted," England sneered, "we had nothing to do with taking out that facility."

"I know . . . but we benefited from it." Byrne could tell by the expressions on everyone's face that they were not buying his rationale. "All I'm saying is that before we rush off to war, we take a look at the big picture. Losing one person in exchange for making sure Iran doesn't get the bomb is not a bad deal."

Secretary of State Wicka's normally calm demeanor turned to one of overt irritation. In a voice laced with sarcasm, she said, "I think that is great advice, Ted. In fact maybe I could call Iran's foreign minister and work out a prisoner exchange. You could take Irene's place, and then we could just write you off."

Before Byrne could respond, the White House press secretary entered the room and announced that President Amatullah was about to begin a press conference. The attention of everyone in the room shifted to the wall of large plasma TVs. All but one showed the bearded and tieless Iranian president stepping to the podium.

53

Mosul, Iraq

Rapp walked the hallway in front of the cells in an attempt to jog loose a strategy that he could use to interrogate the other two prisoners. Just knowing their names went a long way toward getting some honest answers out of them, but there was a bigger problem. If either man knew where Mukhtar planned to take Kennedy, the odds were that she was no longer there. Mukhtar would surely know by now that the two men had not made it back to the rallying point, which in turn would alert him to the possibility that his location was soon to be compromised.

The Iranian connection had been passed on to General Gifford, who felt that there was little chance Mukhtar could have gotten her across the border into Iran. The military units handling the border had shut down the crossing points less than thirty minutes after the attack. Still, Mosul was a large, sprawling city of close to two million people. The odds of finding Kennedy without some hard intelligence were not good.

Rapp looked at the black rubber dive watch on his wrist and felt his chest tighten. He knew it was the first sign of an oncoming anxiety attack. He'd gone through his entire life without suffering one, and then with the loss of his wife they had started to pop up. He told no one. Not even Kennedy. He figured with the passage of time they would lessen. And they did to a degree, but he could still count on a night or two a month during which he would lie in bed and feel as if an anvil had been placed on his chest. The attacks were characterized by a feeling of overwhelming failure. Failure as a man, that he had not been able to defend his own wife. Failure that he had been so selfish as to ever marry her in the first place.

Rapp held no illusions about who he was, or what he did. He'd been at war with radical Islam a good ten years before the country even knew there was a war. He'd threatened, beaten, tortured, and killed so many men it was hopeless to even attempt a tally. During all of that, though, he'd clung to the conviction that he was very different from the enemy. As strange as it would seem to many in a civilized society, he was able to live with what he did because of whom he did it to. Unlike the people he hunted, Rapp made every effort to make sure noncombatants stayed exactly that. Women and children were strictly off-limits. Thankfully, in the chauvinistic world of radical Islam, this was far easier to accomplish than one would think. The men Rapp hunted, however, made no such distinction. In fact, they sought out the innocent to amplify their terror.

Imad Mukhtar was such a man. Rapp knew the story of Mukhtar all too well. The highly reclusive leader of Hezbollah's security section had cut his teeth in Beirut in his late teens. He was rumored to be behind the suicide attacks on both the U.S. Embassy and the marine barracks. What worried Rapp most about the man, though, was his involvement in the kidnapping of CIA Station Chief Bill Buckley. Mukhtar and his compatriots had squeezed every last bit of information out of Buckley over the course of a year and then hanged him. The thought of Kennedy suffering at the hands of such an animal was agonizing. With each passing minute, he feared his ability to save Kennedy was slipping away.

Rapp had waited long enough. Strategy or not, he needed to begin breaking these two and hope whatever he got out of them remained current. Rapp yanked open the cell door and approached the man on the stretcher.

As he pulled out his knife, Rapp said, "Name and rank?"

The man looked up at him with dilated pupils and a sweat-drenched face. The severed sex organ was still on his chest. "I don't know what you're talking about."

"Fine." The man's right pants leg had been cut away above the knee by the army medic who had treated his bullet wound. Rapp stuck the tip of the knife under the remaining portion of fabric and began slicing away. Rapp intentionally dug the blade into the man's inner thigh just enough to draw blood. The prisoner yelled and jerked against his bonds.

"Sorry about that," Rapp said as he cut away the rest of the pants, exposing the man's underwear. "Do you have a preference . . . left nut, right nut . . . it doesn't matter to me."

"What are you talking about?" the man said with genuine horror.

"Which nut would you like me to cut off first? Your left nut, or your right nut?" Rapp fished the tip of the knife under the elastic band of the man's briefs and with one yank, shredded the underwear.

"Wait!" the man screamed. "What do you want to know?"

"Your name, Captain. That's right," Rapp said in response to the look of shock on the man's face. "I know quite a bit about you, so don't even think about lying. Now tell me your name."

"Captain Rashid Dadarshi, and I demand to see a representative from the International Red Crescent."

Rapp laughed. "You demand?"

"Yes, it is my right!"

"And how is it your right?"

"My country is signatory of the Geneva Convention, as is yours."

"Listen, if you had been wearing a uniform and fighting U.S. troops, I would be more than happy to call the International Red Crescent, but you weren't. You're just another piece-of-shit terrorist."

"I am not. I am an officer in the Iranian Revolutionary Guard."

"Where's your uniform? You didn't wear it to work today?"

"I demand . . ."

Before Dadarshi could finish the sentence, Rapp stepped on his wounded knee. Dadarshi screamed in pain, and Rapp said, "I don't want to hear that word come out of your mouth again. In fact, if you say it, I'll carry out my threat, and if you don't believe me, you can ask your friend from Hezbollah." Rapp saw the admission on the man's face and said, "That's right. Your buddy Ali Abbas has been singing like a little girl. I actually had to cut one of his nuts off to get him to talk. Since then the guy's been very helpful, giving me the location of your safe houses, and who your local contacts are. We've got people checking on them right now, and if it turns out he lied to me about a single location I'm going to cut off the other one. Now how about you?"

Rapp reached into his pocket and pulled out the surveillance photo of the man who had ridden in on the chopper with Minister Ashani. "The trick here is that I know a hell of a lot more than you think I do, but I don't know everything. So if you feel like gambling with your family jewels, you go right ahead and try to lie to me. The man in this photo," Rapp held it up, "who is he?"

Dadarshi closed his eyes and said, "Imad Mukhtar."

"Good answer, captain. And how do you know him?"

"I met him for the first time this morning."

"Where?"

"At one of the safe houses."

"And why did he come to Mosul?"

"To oversee the operation."

"The attack on the motorcade?"

"Yes."

"And who was the target of that attack?"

Dadarshi hesitated and looked to his left.

"Not a good question to gamble on."

"The director of the CIA."

"And where were you planning on taking her?" Rapp asked as casually as possible.

"We were going to try and make it across the border."

"Where were your backup locations?"

"There was a warehouse, approximately halfway between Mosul and the border."

"You're going to have to do better than that."

"You will have to get me a map."

Rapp thought about it for a second and then grabbed

the two-way radio. He pressed the transmit button and said, "Stan, did you hear that?" Rapp released the button and moved the radio away from his mouth.

"Yep."

"Bring me some maps." Rapp lowered the radio and studied the Iranian officer lying on the stretcher. "While we wait for the maps, I want you to tell me about the backup locations you have in the city."

54

TEHRAN, IRAN

Based on his conversation with Rapp, Ashani had been certain the extra men at the airport were there to arrest him, but he soon learned he was wrong. An American submarine had sunk the *Sabalan* in the Strait of Hormuz. President Amatullah had declared a state of emergency and called for a meeting of the Supreme Security Council. Under normal circumstances Ashani would have had little difficulty believing that the Americans had acted so recklessly. All he had to do was revisit the tragedy of Iran Air Flight 655. On Sunday, July 3, 1988, the commercial airliner left Bandar Abbas for a short flight to Dubai, when it was shot down by the U.S.S. *Vincennes*. The Americans reacted to the tragedy by giving their cowboy captain a medal. In light of Rapp's phone call, however, Ashani had his doubts as to what may have led up to the *Sabalan*'s being sunk.

This time, however, Ashani got the feeling that it was Amatullah who was acting like a reckless cowboy. He remembered the first meeting they'd had in the wake of the disaster at Isfahan. How Amatullah had come strutting in with General Zarif and General Sulaimani in tow. His promises of making the Americans and the Jews pay. Ashani had never encountered a more duplicitous man than Amatullah. He was a master manipulator of public opinion.

Ashani looked out the window of his barely moving sedan at the sea of bodies marching rowdily toward the old American Embassy. Apparently, Amatullah had closed the schools and ordered mass protests against America's aggression in the Strait of Hormuz. It was very convenient for Amatullah that Ayatollah Najar was in Isfahan with the Supreme Leader, meeting with aggrieved families from the tragedy at the nuclear facility. Ashani had so far been unable to reach Najar and was growing increasingly nervous. If Amatullah was crazy enough to kidnap Irene Kennedy, what would stop him from killing Najar, his chief rival?

The three-car motorcade finally reached the gates of the Presidential Palace. The normal security detail had been augmented by tanks from the Revolutionary Guards' 18th Armored Division. As the soldiers made way for his sedan, Ashani got the sinking feeling that Amatullah would not hesitate to use these shock troops to seize power. He would feel much better when Najar and the Supreme Leader returned to the capital. After entering the palace Ashani was escorted to Amatullah's office suite, where he found Foreign Minister Salehi, Brigadier General Sulaimani, Major General Zarif, and a handful of aides. They were all gathered around a large television watching a news conference, or so he thought.

As Ashani drew closer he could see that their focus was on President Amatullah, who was in the midst of delivering one of his impassioned speeches. He was dressed in his signature boxy tan suit with a dress shirt and no tie. Ashani found the fact that he was making a statement a bit odd since he had yet to meet with the Supreme National Security Council to discuss the situation, but then again, the man had a history of not letting facts get in the way of his message.

Amatullah was going through a timeline of the events that led up to the sinking of the *Sabalan*. Apparently two separate ships reported picking up a submarine on surface radar as well as visually confirming the vessel only minutes before the *Sabalan* was torpedoed. Amatullah was adamant that the *Sabalan* had done nothing to provoke the attack and called it a blatant act of war by the Americans.

"This act of barbarism is bad enough, but Iran's security agencies have uncovered something more treacherous. Over fifty years ago the CIA launched a plot to remove the rightfully elected Dr. Mohammad Mossadegh from office in my country. For the next thirty years the CIA backed the criminal Mohammad Reza Pahlavi and continued to meddle in the affairs of the Iranian people until we rose up in revolution and threw both the shah and the Americans out of our country. For more than twenty-five years now, we have been vigilant in our fight to remain independent from the corruption of imperial America."

Ashani glanced to his left and then right as Amatullah continued his litany of American deception and manipulation against the people of Iran. The generals and the foreign minister seemed excessively pleased with Amatullah's words. Most of his complaints were old accusations; more than a few of them complete falsehoods, but that did not stop these men from paying rapt attention. Ashani got the sense that the master manipulator was building toward something even bigger.

"As the entire world knows, earlier this week my country's nuclear facility in Isfahan was destroyed. The American secretary of state went before the United Nations and offered so-called proof that the facility was destroyed by Iranian saboteurs. She made it seem to the world that the United States had no hand whatsoever in the attack against my country. That it was simply average Iranians who were rebelling against an oppressive government. What she intentionally chose not to tell the world was that those saboteurs were recruited and funded by the CIA.

"For months now various intelligence services in my country have been tracking the movement of this dissident group of mercenaries. That investigation culminated in Mosul, Iraq, this morning when the group's leaders met directly with CIA Director Irene Kennedy." Amatullah held up an enlarged photograph of Kennedy.

Ashani noticed immediately that she did not look herself. Her straight brown hair was matted down and one side of her face looked red, as if she'd been hit. She had a blanket wrapped around her shoulders and her expression was far from her usual calm demeanor. Ashani felt ashamed for his country and embarrassed for Kennedy.

"In Director Kennedy's possession was this." Amatullah held up a second enlarged photograph. "This briefcase and several others like it contained more than a million dollars in cash that the director of the CIA was delivering to her spies as a bounty for destroying Iran's quest for energy independence and self-government. I ask the world to stand up for what is right and help my country stop Imperial America's aggression. It is time for us to come together and stand up for true democracy and freedom and to fight against the capitalist pigs of America.

"Iran will not pump another drop of oil"—Amatullah shook his fist defiantly at the camera—"until every American warship has left the Persian Gulf. I call on my OPEC brothers to do the same. Together we will send a message to America that we are done being bullied. We have already demanded compensation of ten billion dollars for the destruction of the Isfahan facility and the hundreds of Iranians who were killed in this attack by America and her spies. With the sinking of the *Sabalan* and the escalating cost to clean up the disaster at Isfahan we are now demanding that America pay a total of fifteen billion dollars. In addition America must also apologize for what they have done and make a commitment in front of the United Nations General Assembly that they will cease meddling in the affairs of Iran."

Amatullah paused and folded his hands in front of him, adopting a less aggressive pose. "Until such time as America fulfills these obligations, we will keep CIA Director Kennedy as a guest of the country of Iran. And I can assure the international community that we will treat her with more respect and dignity than America has treated my Muslim brothers that have been captured on the battlefield."

With that parting shot, Amatullah turned and walked off camera. Ashani stood among the other advisors absolutely thunderstruck by what he had just heard. The mad genius and sheer audacity of Amatullah knew no bounds. The idea that the *Sabalan* had done nothing to provoke being torpedoed seemed a bit ridiculous, but what Amatullah had just accused Kennedy of was an outright lie. Only several hours earlier he had sat across from a very sincere and believable Kennedy and listened to her offer an aid package worth billions of dollars. She hardly seemed like a woman plotting the overthrow of the Iranian government.

Ashani looked around the room at the faces of the other men and got the uneasy feeling that they all knew something that he did not. The door to Amatullah's office opened, and the president burst into the room like an actor arriving backstage after delivering the performance of his life. Amatullah stopped triumphantly in front of the group with his chin held high. The generals offered their exuberant congratulations on a brilliant speech. The foreign minister, whom Ashani had forgotten about, was now standing in the corner behind him talking to someone on the phone. He began thanking the person loudly and then hung up.

"Wonderful speech, sir," Salehi said enthusiastically as he returned to the group. "That was Foreign Minister Xing. The Chinese have agreed to bring our grievances before the UN Security Council, and put pressure on the Americans to make reparations."

"Excellent," Amatullah said with more relief than surprise. Almost as an afterthought he noticed that his intelligence minister was now present. Amatullah looked at him with a hint of suspicion and then said, "Azad, you have made it back safely. I would like to have a word with you in private." Amatullah gestured toward his office and began walking.

Ashani did not move right away. His head was spinning with plots and deceptions. Defying the request would undoubtedly lead to bigger problems. With reluctance, he followed Amatullah into his office, and tried not to flinch when the door was closed behind him. Amatullah ordered the TV crew out of his office so he could have a word alone with his intelligence minister.

"I am sorry," Amatullah started the conversation, "that I did not let you know about this sooner, but I did not want you tainted by it until the intelligence proved to be accurate."

Ashani said nothing, but nodded as if it was a reasonable precaution even though it wasn't.

"Imad and his people have been working on this for months. I wanted to bring you in on it, but Imad feared that the Intelligence Ministry had an unacceptable number of people who were sympathetic to the MEK and other resistance organizations."

This was such an outright lie that Ashani could barely conceal his growing anger. In a measured voice he said, "I think I know my organization better than Imad Mukhtar."

"I will not argue with you on that point, but we have arrived here nonetheless, and your skill and support are greatly needed to help us get through this crisis. Can I count on you?"

Here it is, Ashani thought to himself. *A test of loyalty.* He contemplated the two generals in the other room, both fiercely devoted to Amatullah, neither of them afraid to use violence to get what they wanted. Less than a second passed as Ashani's thoughts raced to his wife and daughters and back again. Now was not the moment to take a stand against the madman.

"Of course you can," Ashani answered in his most sincere voice. "I know better than perhaps anyone, other than yourself, that this nonsense with America must stop."

"Good," Amatullah said as he clapped his hands together. "Now as you can imagine, I am going to be very busy. The Supreme Leader is on his way back from Isfahan, and I must prepare to brief him as well as continue to lobby our allies to support us against this American aggression."

"How can I help?"

Amatullah led him across the office to his desk. "Imad is in need of desperate assistance. I'm afraid his network of agents may have been compromised. He has Kennedy in a safe location for the moment, but he thinks he might have to move her." He opened his desk drawer and withdrew a sheet of paper. On it was a handwritten list of ten phone numbers. The first two had lines through them.

"I have spoken with him twice. After each call move onto the next number."

Ashani took the sheet and looked at the numbers.

"If you go through all of them, start over at the beginning."

"What would you like me to do?"

"Call him. You will refer to him as Ali and he will refer to you as Cyrus. Find out what he needs. The last time we spoke he was confident that he could get Kennedy to confess, but he said the city is crawling with American and Iraqi military units."

Ashani felt a knot in his stomach. Mukhtar was a brutal thug. "Did he say where he was holding her?"

"No." Amatullah shook his head. "I asked, but he did not want to talk about it on the phone." He handed

Ashani a mobile phone. "If there is an emergency, he will call you on this phone."

"Is there anything else?"

"Yes. If there is any way to get her across the border without being caught I want you to do it."

Ashani nodded dutifully and said, "I will look into it immediately."

55

MOSUL, IRAQ

Kennedy lay naked on the floor. Salty tears streamed down her face and mixed with the puddles of urine on the dirt floor. Her panties and bra lay shredded a few feet away. The musty blanket that had given her a sense of security had been torn from her hands and tossed to the far corner. Her captors stood over her and laughed while they described in graphic terms how they were going to rape her. That had been about the only indignity she'd been spared thus far.

All she had done was ask to go to the bathroom. A simple function that she had taken for granted her entire life. The man who called himself Muhammad had made it sound as if it would not be a problem. Instead of taking her somewhere, though, the guards brought her a rusty bucket and stood a few feet away leering at her. Kennedy squatted over the bucket and used the blanket to try and maintain a modicum of privacy. When she was in the middle of relieving herself one of the men gave her a kick that sent her sprawling. The second man then joined in as they tore the blanket and her undergarments from her. The men pawed at her bare skin; slapping, punching, and kicking her. Kennedy attempted lamely to fight back, but they were too strong and far too vicious.

In the end all she could do was curl up in a defensive ball and hope they would tire. When they finally did, they dropped their pants and urinated on her. That was when they began to describe in gruesome detail how they were going to rape her. Kennedy did not scream or cry out loud. She simply lay there and let the tears flow. She thought of her son, Tommy, her mother, and a life she had devoted to her country. She did not ask "Why me?" or drown herself in pity, she simply accepted her fate for what it was—a very nasty ending to an otherwise wonderful life.

She had surrendered herself to the idea that it would be better to die than give up the most closely guarded secrets of her country. She owed that to the men and women of the CIA, and the spies they had recruited. She knew she would not be able to endure many more beatings like the one she had just gone through, so her mind began searching for a way to end it all. The tears stopped and in a strange way the thought of taking her own life gave her strength.

A loud clang of the metal latch being lifted and squeaky hinges announced the presence of a visitor. Kennedy did not attempt to lift her head and look. She stared beyond the feet of her tormentors at the blanket in the corner as if she could will it to come to her.

"In the name of Allah, what have you done?"

Kennedy recognized the voice as belonging to the man who called himself Muhammad.

"You fools!" he yelled.

Kennedy saw him push his way past the two men and retrieve the blanket on the far side of the room. He came back and draped the blanket over her naked body and then turned his anger on the men. He screamed at them and ordered them out of the room. When they were gone he returned to Kennedy and squatted down at her side. He started to move a strand of hair from her face and then stopped when he realized it was soaked with urine. He stood quickly and marched into the hallway.

Kennedy could hear him yelling at the guards and telling them to bring fresh water and a first aid kit. There was more shouting and more demands. Kennedy went numb and stopped listening. The man came back into the room several times to check on her, each time apologizing for what the men had done. Kennedy never acknowledged his presence. She simply kept staring off into space.

At some point a chair was brought into the room and the man helped her up so she could sit in it. She was beyond caring that she was naked under the blanket. The man tried his best to keep the blanket wrapped around her chest, as he took the bucket of water and began rinsing the urine from her hair. He then wet a washcloth and cleaned her face.

When he got to her shoulders he stopped and placed the washcloth in Kennedy's hand. "I will get you some clothes. Please finish cleaning up. We need to discuss your release."

Kennedy blinked for the first time in minutes. Her head slowly turned and watched the man leave the room. The door closed behind him and she realized she was alone. Looking down at the white washcloth, she had the strangest feeling that she must have been dreaming. Her eyes moved slowly over her arms, noting the scrapes and bruises. She took the water-soaked cloth and ran it along the inside of her left forearm. The blood and dirt came off. She bit her tongue to make sure this was really happening and upon feeling the pain realized it was. Kennedy stood and draped the blanket over the back of the chair and then set about bathing. She doused herself with handful after handful of water until the blood, dirt, and stench were gone. A good five minutes later there was a knock on the door. Kennedy grabbed the blanket and held it in front of her.

Muhammad entered the room with a towel, a stack of neatly folded clothes and some sandals. He set them down on the chair and said, "Please put these on. We have much to discuss."

After he left, Kennedy slowly got dressed. The clothes were all slightly too big for her but she was grateful nonetheless. She put on the blue dress pants, brown sweater, black hijab, and finally the sandals. There was another knock on the door and then

Muhammad entered carrying a video camera and a tripod. Kennedy was instantly suspicious.

"I am sorry for the behavior of those two animals. They were not raised properly."

Kennedy only nodded.

The man set the camera down and asked, "How do your clothes fit?"

"Fine." Kennedy clutched at the hijab.

"Good. Now I have been talking to many people about your release, and I think we have something arranged. The men who took you . . . I can't tell you who they are, but they are a nasty lot. More than half of them want to kill you because of what you have done to their country and who you work for. There are a few, however, who think that this is a waste. They are split. Half of them want to torture you and sell the information to the highest bidder and the other half want to ransom you and be done with it. I think I have them convinced to ransom you, but before I can do that they want you to read a statement."

"What kind of statement?" Kennedy asked in a guarded tone.

"I want to remind you they are only words. Once you are free, you may say whatever you'd like." The man handed over the sheet of paper and then busied himself with the video camera. "Smile for me, please," he said as he pressed play.

Kennedy looked down at the double-spaced typed words and began reading. He heart sank with each sentence. Thirty seconds later she was done. She handed the paper back to the man and said, "I can't read that."

"Yes, you can." The man handed the paper back. "All you need to do is read it and you will be free to leave with me."

"Those are all lies. My country had nothing to do with the destruction of the Isfahan nuclear facility. We did not invade Iraq for oil, and we are not plotting to invade Iran to steal their oil."

"I am not arguing with you." The man said with his hands held up. "And when you are set free you can scream from the mountaintops that you were forced to read this statement at gunpoint."

Kennedy knew there would be no taking it back. There were too many in the Middle East and beyond who thought it was true to begin with. Her reading this prepared speech would be used for decades to come as proof of America's imperial ways. "I can't read it."

"You must, or they will kill you."

There was something in the way the man said "kill you" that gave Kennedy concern. It occurred to her that the most logical move by her captors would be to kill her after she read the statement. With no denial by Kennedy it would go down as fact. "I'm sorry, but I cannot read that statement." Kennedy sat down in the chair and folded her hands across her lap.

The man moved with great speed from behind the camera. He slapped Kennedy across the face three times, knocking the hijab off her head. He grabbed a handful of hair and yanked her head back. Looking down at her he yelled, "You have exactly one hour to change your mind, and if your answer is still no, I will leave you to your fate. Do you want that to happen?"

"No," Kennedy answered.

"Twenty men!" he screamed. "They will line up to rape you for a week straight. Is that what you want?"

"No."

"Then read the statement." The man let go of her and handed her the piece of paper again.

Kennedy took it, looked down at the words, and thought of how the tape would be used against her country. She would be considered a traitor. She could never live with herself. Without having to think any further, she opened her hands and let the paper fall to the floor.

The man stepped away from the camera and help up a finger. "You have one hour to reconsider, and if your answer is still no, there is nothing I can do to help you."

56

WHITE HOUSE

Ted Byrne stayed on the president's left elbow, matching him step for step, which was not easy, considering he was almost a foot shorter. The debate had been as heated as anything Byrne had ever seen in his nearly twenty-five years of politics. He'd known Josh Alexander since he was a little tyke. Byrne had played high school football for Alexander's father and had coached for the father after college. When Alexander looked at him with those same dead, serious eyes that his dad used to shoot him when he'd pushed an issue as far as he could, Byrne knew he'd lost the battle. It didn't help that the majority of the National Security Council, as well as the Joint Chiefs, had sided against him.

Even so, Byrne felt so strongly that the president was making a mistake that he had to give it one more try. "Josh," he whispered so no one else could hear, "I really think you need to sit on this one for an afternoon. Probably a whole day, but at least an afternoon."

"Too late, Ted. They're all up there waiting for me."

"So give a brief statement like I said. A blanket denial. Then we can send others out to argue the details. Don't lower yourself to the guy's level."

The president hit the steps that led from the basement to the first floor of the West Wing. "I've made up my mind."

"I know you have and that's why I'm trying to talk you out of it. That's my job. When you're about to run off a cliff, I'm supposed to stick out my foot and trip you."

"I'm not in the mood for any jokes right now."

"It never hurts to take a breath and collect yourself."

"And sometimes he who hesitates gets his ass handed to him." They reached the first-floor landing and the president stopped. A cortège of aides and advisors piled up behind him on the stairs. "If I had the time, we could sit here all afternoon and throw sayings back and forth at each other, but it comes down to this, Ted. If you don't confront a lie, people will believe it. Now I'm done talking about this. Are you done?"

Byrne hesitated and then reluctantly nodded.

"Good." The president turned and strode into the White House press room. Secretary Wicka and Secretary England joined him on the small dais, taking up positions behind him, one off each shoulder. The president placed both hands on the edge of the podium and looked out at the reporters and photographers. He made no attempt to hide the fact that he was not happy.

"I'm about to give you a lot of information. The press secretary is preparing briefing books for you. You may pick them up when I'm finished." The president paused for a moment and consulted an outline that he had written on a piece of paper. "I'm sure by now you've all had an opportunity to review President Amatullah's remarks. I am here to openly refute his two main accusations. The first, that a United States submarine sank the Iranian vessel *Sabalan*, is an outright lie. The U.S.S. *Virginia*, a nuclear-powered submarine, was in the vicinity and tracking the Iranian submarine *Yusef* as it proceeded through the Strait of Hormuz earlier today. The *Virginia* recorded the *Yusef* flooding her rear torpedo tubes and firing one torpedo against the *Sabalan*. That torpedo hit the *Sabalan* and sunk it. The *Virginia* reported this incident immediately, and followed the *Yusef* through the strait and into the Persian Gulf. The *Yusef* is now on an intercept course with the Eisenhower strike group, as is much of the Iranian navy. I have ordered the strike group to engage and sink any Iranian vessel that attempts to close within fifteen miles of the U.S.S. *Eisenhower.* I repeat, if any Iranian vessel attempts to close within fifteen miles of the aircraft carrier *Eisenhower* it will be engaged and sunk."

Alexander glanced down and then said, "Knowing President Amatullah's penchant for rhetoric and obfuscation, I feel it is my duty to provide hard evidence of what I have just told you. Against the advice of the secretary of defense and the Joint Chiefs, I am going to allow representatives from Great Britain, France, Russia, and China to review the contact tapes made by the U.S.S. *Virginia.* These tapes will prove beyond a shadow of a doubt to any naval officer with sonar experience that it was the *Yusef* that fired on and sank the *Sabalan.* In addition, I am offering to make the U.S.S. *Virginia* available for immediate inspection by representatives from Great Britain, France, Russia, and China. Upon boarding the *Virginia,* they will find that she is still carrying her full complement of torpedoes. I challenge President Amatullah to also make the *Yusef* available for inspection, although I doubt you will find him so accommodating. As to why President Amatullah would order one of his submarines to sink an Iranian frigate, I have my theories, but I will leave it up to you, the press, to try and get an honest answer from him.

"Now on to the second point of contention between our two countries. CIA Director Irene Kennedy did in fact have a meeting in Mosul this morning. It was with this man." The president nodded to one of his aides and then gestured toward the flat-panel TV that sprang to life with a head shot of a bearded man in his mid fifties. "Iran's Minister of Intelligence. In recent years Director Kennedy and Minister Ashani have met on several occasions to share information that would help combat terrorism. I directed Dr. Kennedy to sit down with Minister Ashani and discuss the possibility of our two countries restoring limited diplomatic relations. Upon the conclusion of this meeting Minister Ashani was escorted to his helicopter and is now safely back in Iran. Director Kennedy was not so fortunate." The president gestured to his aide yet again, and a new photo appeared.

The photo showed charred vehicles and bodies littering a street. "This is Director Kennedy's motorcade. After parting with Minister Ashani, Director Kennedy's motorcade made it exactly a block and a half before it was ambushed." A new photo appeared. It was of four men lying facedown on the street. Pools of dark red blood could be seen by each man's head. "These were members of Director Kennedy's security detail. They all lived here in the Washington area. All of them were married, and they all had children. I spoke with each of their wives over the past hour and offered my condolences."

The president lowered his head and consulted his

notes. "Eighteen men died in the attack on this motorcade. A secondary CIA security team was nearby and fought their way to the site of the attack in time to see Director Kennedy being forced into a car and driven away. The CIA security team took three prisoners."

The president paused and the photos of three men appeared on the screen with their names and affiliations listed. "The man on the left of the screen is Ali Abbas. He is a senior member of the terrorist organization Hezbollah and has been in Iraq recruiting and arming terrorists for more than a year. The next man is Captain Rashid Dadarshi of the Iranian Revolutionary Guard Corps."

Gasps and murmurs erupted from the seated reporters. Alexander stopped until he had their undivided attention. "Captain Dadarshi has admitted that he received orders from his superior officers in Tehran to participate in the kidnapping of Director Kennedy. The last man is Corporal Nouri Tahmineh, also of the Iranian Revolutionary Guard. All three of these men identified the next man," a new image appeared on the screen of a man in a suit wearing sunglasses, "as the one who ran the operation. This is Imad Mukhtar, the head of Hezbollah's Security Services and the mastermind behind the U.S. Marine barracks bombing, the U.S. Embassy bombing in Beirut, and many others. He is also believed to be behind numerous kidnappings and assassinations committed by Hezbollah over the past three decades."

Several photos appeared showing Mukhtar and

Ashani exiting the same helicopter from different sides. "These photos were taken this morning when Minister Ashani arrived in Mosul on an Iranian Army helicopter with Imad Mukhtar. Note the briefcase in Mr. Mukhtar's right hand." An enlarged image of the briefcase appeared and then, next to it, a second photo of an open briefcase filled with cash. "The photo on the right is the one that President Amatullah showed the world only an hour ago. President Amatullah claimed that Director Kennedy was in possession of this cash when she was supposedly caught meeting with an Iranian opposition group. I find it a bit too coincidental that Imad Mukhtar arrived in Mosul this morning carrying a briefcase that looks exactly like the one President Amatullah claims was found in the possession of Director Kennedy."

The president stopped and shook his head sadly. After a long pause he said, "This might be humorous if it wasn't for the fact that so many people have died today. I refuse to speculate what it is exactly that President Amatullah is up to, but I will not tolerate such brazen aggression. Director Kennedy is one of my closest advisors and the head of one of America's most important national security agencies. I consider her abduction an act of war by Iran. I have directed Secretary of Defense England to put all U.S. forces at Defense Condition Three. I have also ordered the U.S.S. *Reagan* strike group, which is conducting operations off the east coast of Africa, to proceed at top speed to the Gulf of Oman, where she will join the

Nimitz strike group already on patrol. Other assets are also being rushed to the region.

"I want to be very clear on something. I will not negotiate with terrorists, and I will not get drawn into a debate with a man who is so desperate to hold on to power that he would kill his own people in order to drum up support. I am giving the Iranian government two hours, and not a minute longer. If Director Kennedy is not released within that time, I will order offensive operations to begin against the Iranian military and the country's leadership."

The president took a second to look around the room at the shocked faces of the reporters, and then said, "That is all I have to say, for now."

57

MOSUL, IRAQ

Rapp was seated on a metal folding chair. Next to him, lying on a stretcher, was a drugged-up Ali Abbas. The CIA interrogation team had arrived from Baghdad, and were busying themselves with the other two prisoners. Captain Dadarshi and Corporal Tahmineh had given up the location of three safe houses and the warehouse halfway to the Iranian border. An army unit patrolling near the warehouse was dispatched but found nothing. This did not surprise Rapp. A man like Mukhtar didn't stay alive all these years by making mistakes. The Quds Force safe houses in the city were tempting though. Rapp had to fight the urge to head into the city and participate in the safe house raids. As much as he wanted to be on the street doing something, however, he knew he needed to stay put until they had some solid intel. The safe houses would no doubt be an intelligence boon, but they would not find Kennedy in them.

Rapp's hope for that crucial piece of information was lying at his feet, and with each passing minute he became more doubtful that he would learn anything from Abbas. From Rapp's prior experience sodium pentothal worked differently with each subject. The drug always elicited conversation, but not necessarily meaningful conversation. Typically, the more logical and ordered the person's mind the better the answers. Conversely, the more scatterbrained or dim the subjects were, the more likely it was that they would string unconnected thoughts together like a radio stuck in scan mode. Five seconds on one subject and then on to the next. After twenty minutes with Abbas, Rapp was wondering if the man was clinically insane.

The terrorist's train of thought bounced from one subject to the next, and the only common thread had to do with a comment Rapp had made about the seventy-seven virgins that were supposedly awaiting Abbas in paradise. Abbas had been rambling on and on about how he was not afraid to die. Allah had a special place for him. He would have his pick of the finest seventy-seven virgins. Rapp told Abbas it was too bad he wouldn't be able to have sex with them. When

Abbas asked why, Rapp told him because he was going to cut off his dick. This one comment sent the thirty-some-year-old terrorist into a fit of blubbering tears. Some twenty minutes later he was now trying to engage Rapp in a theological debate over whether or not his penis would magically reappear when he reached paradise.

Rapp decided that giving the man sodium pentothal had been a mistake. He stood and looked down at Abbas. "It doesn't matter."

"Of course it does," Abbas replied with tear-filled eyes.

Rapp thought about telling the man the virgins didn't exist, and even if they did he would undoubtedly be on an express elevator to hell, in which case his penis wouldn't matter, but he decided it wasn't worth it. It was time to call Ashani again and put more pressure on him. He left the interrogation trailer and went back to the office trailer, where Dumond, Stilwell, and Ridley were holed up in the conference room working the phones and computers. Rapp felt a wave of hopelessness. They were not making anywhere near enough progress.

He looked across the room at Stilwell and asked, "Anything new?"

"Yeah. Come here and look at this photo."

Rapp walked around the conference table and looked at the computer screen. On it was the photo of Kennedy that President Amatullah had shown during his speech.

Stilwell clicked on the wall behind Kennedy and zoomed in on that part of the photo. "They're holding her underground, and I'm pretty sure she's in the city. This type of limestone is quarried near the river. You can find it in cellars all over the city, but it's predominantly found in the old section of the West Bank."

Rapp studied the photo. Bands of green and black mold streaked the rocks closest to the floor, and white clumps of calcification could be seen near the corner. "He's making mistakes."

"How so?"

"Terrorism 101, cover the walls with sheets, so you don't give up clues like this." Rapp felt a glimmer of hope. "He's someplace he wasn't planning on, and my guess is, he's short on people too."

"Really," Stilwell said with feigned surprise. "You only killed about twenty of his men this morning."

Rapp ignored the comment and said, "Make copies of this section of wall and get it to all the military units. Also, track down any local stonemasons and see if they can give us a better idea of where this might be."

Moving on to Dumond, Rapp asked, "Any luck with Ashani's cell phone number?"

"Nothing. The only thing we came up with today was the call you made to him, and a call he made to his wife."

"Shit." Rapp ran a hand through his thick black hair. "Is the NSA giving you everything you need?"

"And then some. With all the drones up in the air

and the satellites overhead we're picking up so much stuff, the translators are having a hard time keeping pace. If we had a sample of Mukhtar's voice it would help."

"I'll see what I can do." Rapp grabbed his cell phone and scrolled back a couple of calls until he found the one he was looking for.

58

TEHRAN, IRAN

With the blessing of Amatullah, Ashani had rushed back to the Ministry of Intelligence. He had told Amatullah it was not wise to conduct such a risky operation from the Presidential Palace. Ashani now sat at his desk with the piece of paper Amatullah had given him resting squarely in the middle of his leather desk pad. Next to it was a small index card with the number and e-mail address Rapp had given him. Across the room, sitting atop a credenza, a TV replayed the speech of the American president.

Ashani watched at first with his usual analytical detachment. He did not know a great deal about President Alexander, but he had a general feel for the man's speaking style. Like most politicians, he talked a lot, and when he talked about Iran, Ashani's people made sure he received a DVD of the speech. He could tell from the first line of this speech that Alexander was not going to roll over.

By the time Alexander got to the part about the *Yusef* sinking the *Sabalan*, Ashani feared the worst. It all came back to him now. The knowing glances between the generals at the Presidential Palace during Amatullah's speech, Amatullah ordering Mukhtar to accompany him to Mosul—it was all a deception, and the madman actually thought he was going to get away with it.

As the American president continued to lay out the facts, Ashani grew increasingly anxious. What path were these supposed leaders leading them down? Then the photo of Ali Abbas appeared on the screen along with those of the two Iranian Republican Guardsmen. Right when Ashani thought things couldn't possibly get any worse, the president showed a photo of him and Mukhtar arriving together in Mosul.

Ashani was so distraught he almost missed the closing part of President Alexander's speech. As it was, the ultimatum couldn't have been more clear. Ashani thought of Alexander's words yet again. *I am giving the Iranian government two hours and not a minute longer. If Director Kennedy is not released within that time, I will order offensive operations to begin against the Iranian military and the country's leadership.*

Ashani knew with a discomforting level of certainty that the very office he was sitting in would be decimated by the first wave of cruise missiles. Before he could even attempt to think what his next move would be, his office door burst open. His deputy minister for covert activities wanted to know why he had not been consulted. Within seconds, the deputy minister in charge of Hezbollah was in front of his desk demanding to know the same.

Ashani attempted to explain to them that he had also been kept in the dark. It was obvious from the looks on their faces, though, that they did not believe him. Then the phones began to ring and ring; office phones, cell phones, secure phones—every single phone he had. His wife reached him on his personal cell phone after trying to get past his secretary. She was in a panic and wanted to know if she should load up the girls and leave the city. Ashani told her to stay put and tried to reassure her. Before getting off the phone he promised he would call within the hour.

Then he kicked everyone out of his office, told his secretary to hold all calls, and closed and locked the door. After a moment's hesitation he decided to ring Ayatollah Najar's private line. For the third time in as many hours he was told by his assistant that Najar was unavailable. Ashani hung up the phone and began to wonder if Najar and the Supreme Leader being out of the capital hadn't been planned. What if they had given Amatullah their blessing?

The possibility shook Ashani's faith in the leaders of his country. What if they had all been in on this plot from the beginning? What if they had knowingly sent him to meet Kennedy, knowing full well that she would be kidnapped? Ashani stared down at the list of phone numbers on one piece of paper, and Rapp's information on the other. With one phone call he could defuse the entire situation. If for a second he thought that either Amatullah or Mukhtar possessed the ability to do what was right, he wouldn't even think about passing along this information, but he had his doubts. In the end, Amatullah was likely too much of a narcissist to risk the full might of the U.S. armed forces, but he might be able to convince himself that their planes would never find him. In the end, America would never invade. They had neither the troops nor the stomach for what would be a very costly battle on both sides.

But Mukhtar was an entirely different matter, a true believer, with a martyr complex. Mukhtar could not be counted on to turn Kennedy over. Since their close call at Isfahan, the man seemed hell-bent on plunging the region into conflict. He had made it abundantly clear that Iran had not sacrificed enough blood in the war against the Jews and the Americans. Ashani decided Mukhtar could not be trusted.

Would he be committing treason, or would it be an act of patriotism? Ashani believed the American president when he said if Kennedy was not returned safely in less than two hours he would declare war. Despite the bravado of the generals and admirals, every Iranian pilot who took to the sky would be downed, and those planes that stayed on the ground would be blown to bits. Every ship and sub foolish enough to try to engage one of the mighty strike groups would be sent to the bottom of the Persian Gulf. It would be recorded as the most lopsided naval engagement perhaps in history. Thousands would die, and that was before the Americans turned their bombs on the civilian leadership.

Ashani shook his head at the heartbreaking thought of all the chaos and destruction. The loss of life. And for what? So a group of men could say that they refused to back down. Ashani knew the nonsense had to stop.

He picked up the list of numbers that Amatullah had given him, as well as Rapp's information and moved his chair over to his computer. He quickly composed an e-mail to Rapp listing all of the numbers. Even the two that had been used. Afraid he'd lose his nerve, Ashani hit the send key. He then grabbed his satellite phone and dialed Rapp's number. After a few rings a man answered on the other end.

Ashani recognized Rapp's voice. "I just sent you an e-mail. It contains a list of numbers that I was given so I could reach the man you are looking for. Do you understand?"

"I think so."

"The first two numbers have already been used. I am going to call the third one in two minutes. Is that enough time for you to make the proper arrangements?"

"Yes."

"Good. There's one more thing."

"I'm listening."

Ashani glanced nervously at his door, half expecting it to be kicked in at any moment. "I want to be clear that I had nothing to do with this. I am acting on my own right now."

"Why?"

"Out of respect for our mutual friend, and my hope that we can avoid further bloodshed."

"I appreciate that. I'll be waiting for your call."

Ashani set the phone down and looked at his watch. He was only halfway there. In two minutes time there would be no turning back.

59

MOSUL, IRAQ

Rapp paced anxiously behind Dumond, as the younger man worked feverishly to make sure everything was in place. The eavesdropping assets in, around, and over Mosul comprised an all-encompassing net. The mobile phone networks were tapped, as were the fiber optic lines running in and out of the city. Keyhole and Voyager satellites circled far overhead in geosynchronized orbit snapping images and sucking every desired signal from the air. Predator drones hovered above to provide real-time imaging as well as radio intercepts. There wasn't a call made in the city that wasn't intercepted.

The complicated part lay in sifting the valuable calls from the 99.999 percent of them that were absolutely worthless. To do that normally required the deciphering of the signal and then the translation and analysis of the conversation. The National Security Agency in Fort Meade, Maryland, accomplished this by employing complex voice recognition software and more sheer computing power than any other entity in the world. So much information was collected that the analysts at the NSA were the modern-day equivalent of the prospectors who worked the rivers and streams of the California Gold Rush. Except in this case, intel intercepts were like produce in a grocery store. Each bit of information came with a "best if used by date." Provided that Minister Ashani had really given them the numbers that Mukhtar would use, all of these hurdles could be avoided.

Dumond pounded on his keyboard with a final few strokes and then pushed his chair back, removing his headset. He looked over his shoulder at Rapp and said, "It's all set to go. We're at the top of the list on every system. The numbers are programmed in. The second they go active we'll be able to isolate them." Dumond pointed at the screen on the far left and said, "The two numbers that you said were already used . . . We're mining the records right now, to see which towers relayed the most recent calls."

"What about the third number?" Rapp asked. "If he has the phone turned on, can't we pick it up?"

"He doesn't even have to turn it on."

"I know," Rapp said with frustration in his voice. "Now's not the time to get technical with me."

"Sorry. We're searching for it right now. As you know, it's standard field practice to turn these on sparingly. It greatly reduces the risk of being tagged."

"I know, but ten phones is excessive."

"He's probably just switching out SIM cards."

"Marcus," Rapp shot him a cautionary look, "I'm well aware of how it works. Can we please focus on what is important and stop talking about semantics."

Dumond nodded quickly and swore at himself for being so stupid. He'd known Rapp for a long time. Had worked with him on a lot of operations. Kennedy was like family to Rapp. The stress of this situation understandably had shortened his already short fuse.

Dumond pointed at the middle screen, which had a map of the greater Mosul metropolitan area. "These red dots represent mobile phone towers."

Rapp noted that there were easily more than a hundred dots on the screen.

"Now if Mukhtar is using a satellite phone," Dumond continued, "he'll bypass these towers and the big bird up in space will get him."

"Do you have Ashani's voice programmed into recognition software?"

"Yep," Dumond pointed at the third screen. "It's all set to go. As soon as he comes online. I'll have verification for you in ten seconds or less."

"And Mukhtar?"

"We have no known samples, but we'll be able to use this print and run it against everything we have in the archives."

"How long will that take?"

"Even if we prioritize it, the search might take weeks. We're talking about a lot of phone calls."

"There's got to be a way to speed it up."

"If we get lucky and find a hit, we can narrow the search to a specific time frame and region. That would help."

The door to the trailer opened and General Gifford entered with two other officers. All three were in full battle gear with sidearms strapped to their right thighs.

Gifford took off his helmet and said, "Mitch, Stan called me and said you guys might be close to finding a location."

"That's right, General."

"How good is the intel?"

"We have Mukhtar's mobile phone number, and we expect him to be receiving a call any minute."

"We've got a hit on one of the previous numbers," Dumond announced excitedly. He pointed at the middle screen. "This tower about ten miles east of town. My guess is he was traveling on this road right here."

General Gifford hurried around the table and looked at the screen. "That's Highway Two."

"Hold on," Dumond said, "the second number just came in." He pointed to a tower near the Tigris. "This one was made after the first."

Rapp looked at the new location and then checked the spot on the map where the ambush had taken place. "Based on the calls it looks like they tried to take her out of the city and then ended up coming back."

"That's assuming she's still with this Mukhtar fellow," Gifford said.

Rapp considered his point for a moment and said, "I don't think he'd take his eyes off her."

"The third number's up."

Rapp leaned over Dumond's shoulder and looked as he pointed the same tower near the Tigris. "Stan," Rapp yelled, "get in here!"

A moment later Stilwell emerged from his office and joined Rapp and Gifford. Rapp pointed at the middle screen. "Is this the part of town you were thinking of when you were talking about the stone in the photo?"

"It's exactly where I was thinking."

Gifford grumbled, "That's the heart of Indian country."

"Yeah," Stilwell agreed. "Shiite central."

"The streets are really narrow," Gifford said with a wary expression. "We've had more than a few patrols ambushed in there."

Rapp noticed Dumond touch his headset and then watched him reach for his mouse. After a single click a man talking in Farsi came over the speakers resting on the table. Rapp immediately knew the voice belonged to Ashani. Only he and Stilwell spoke Farsi.

"Ali, is that you?"

There was an unnerving pause and then another voice said, "Cyrus, you sound different."

"That must be Mukhtar," Rapp said to Dumond.

"I'm on it."

From the speakers came, "I was asked by our friend to call and see if there was anything you might need. He is stuck in a very important meeting."

"There is much that I need." The man they assumed was Mukhtar made no attempt to hide his irritation. "Things are not progressing the way we had planned, and I have only a handful of men to assist me."

"Can I send you some help? I have men in the area."

There was a sigh followed by silence and then, "At the moment, I fear it would only draw more suspicion."

"Then what can I do to help?"

Dumond announced, "We've got him." He clicked the mouse and the middle screen zoomed in on a four block area of downtown Mosul. A blinking red dot marked the location of the call.

"Nothing at the moment," Mukhtar replied.

"Our friend would like a progress report," Ashani stated.

There was another long pause and then, "Tell him the videotape he requested is taking more time than I anticipated. The actress is not cooperating."

"What are you going to do?"

"I think if I employ some harsher methods, she will perform."

Rapp's gut twisted upon hearing the words. He pointed to the screen and asked Stilwell, "Where is that?"

"That's the Great Mosque."

"Oh shit," Gifford moaned.

"What's the problem?" Rapp asked.

"We can't go in there."

"What do you mean, you can't go in there?" asked an irritated Rapp.

"The city would explode in violence."

Rapp heard Ashani warning Mukhtar not to harm the actress. The words caused him to put aside what Gifford had just said and focus on Ashani and Mukhtar's conversation.

"I have come too far to fail," Mukhtar said. "I will do whatever it takes to succeed. Tell our friend I will have the tape for him within the hour."

The call went dead. Rapp immediately told Dumond to get him a live overhead shot from one of the Predators. He then turned to Gifford. "You can't go in there, or you won't?"

"If the president tells me to go in there, I will go in, but I'm telling you, if American military forces surround and enter the holiest mosque in Mosul we will incite an all-out rebellion in the city and possibly the country."

"He's right, Mitch," Stilwell said.

Rapp didn't like it, but he knew they were right. "Then we need to go in low profile."

"That's fine, but the Great Mosque has some pretty serious security."

"Local militia."

"Basically."

As Rapp struggled to find a solution he was

reminded of something he saw in Stilwell's office. "How well do your Kurds know this area?"

"Like the back of their hands."

"All right, tell them we're moving in five minutes, and tell them to bring everything they have."

60

TEHRAN, IRAN

Only minutes after concluding his forced conversation with Mukhtar, Ashani was informed via intercom that Ayatollah Najar was holding on line one. Ashani greeted his old mentor with a mix of relief and panic. Before he could say a word, Najar ordered him to get to the Presidential Palace immediately for a meeting of the Supreme Security Council. Ashani found his friend's brevity very unsettling, but after a moment he concurred that in the wake of the American president's speech, it could simply be that Najar was in a rush to get a handle on the situation.

Five minutes later Ashani was in President Amatullah's conference room with all but a few members of the Security Council. They were all waiting for the arrival of Najar and, they assumed, the Supreme Leader. While they waited, Ashani paid close attention to Amatullah. At present, he was standing in the corner talking with General Zarif and General Suleimani. All three men looked worried, but then again everyone in the room looked worried. Ashani tried yet again to figure out how far-reaching this plot was. Did Ayatollah Najar and the Supreme Leader know, or were they simply duped? Did they leave the city to distance themselves from any accusations should the plan fail or did they simply travel to Isfahan to offer aid to the families of those lost?

Ashani desperately wanted to believe that Najar was incapable of such foolish and deceitful behavior, but the man had been avoiding his calls all morning, and if Ashani had to guess why, it was because he was not prepared to answer any difficult questions. Nonetheless, here they were, on the brink of war, and a meaningful discussion of the facts had yet to take place. Something that had to happen if there was any hope of releasing Kennedy before the deadline.

Ashani had no doubt Amatullah and his cronies would argue that the Americans were making empty threats. That they would never attack. Ashani was actually listening to General Zarif parroting that very statement to President Amatullah when the door to the room burst open.

Ayatollah Najar strode into the room with six large men all wearing either dark blue or black suits. Ashani recognized several of them as belonging to the Supreme Leader's security detail. Ashani expected the Supreme Leader to follow, but instead the last man closed the door and locked it. The already tense mood in the room worsened. Ashani shifted nervously in his seat and felt his throat tighten.

Najar walked straight for President Amatullah and

the two generals who were still standing in huddled conversation. Najar adjusted his thick glasses and asked, "Which one of you ordered the sinking of the *Sabalan*?"

Amatullah demurred and said, "I don't know what you are talking . . ."

"Lies!" Najar screamed. "Lies! Lies! Lies! I am sick of the lies."

The entire room was taken aback, but Amatullah quickly rebounded. With a dismissive half smile, he said, "I can assure you that I am not lying."

"And I can assure you that the Supreme Leader is certain every word that comes out of your mouth is a lie," Najar spat back. He turned his glare on the two generals and screamed, "Which one of you came up with the idea to sink the *Sabalan*?"

Amatullah took a half step forward and said, "The Americans . . ."

"The Americans did nothing," Najar snapped. "I know when I'm being lied to, and as much as it pains me, it was brutally obvious that President Alexander was telling the truth. You, on the other hand, have built your entire career out of lying, so I am left with only one conclusion. Now for the last time, which one of you ordered the sinking of the *Sabalan*?"

Both Amatullah and General Zarif glanced at General Sulaimani and took a half a step away. The leader of the Quds Force found himself deserted. He looked at his two coconspirators and shook his head in disgust. With his chin help high he said, "I am proud of what I have done. It is time to stop running from the Americans. The men aboard the *Sabalan* will be remembered as martyrs for the cause."

"And so will you," Najar said as he drew a pistol from under his robes. He pointed it at the general's face and squeezed the trigger of the .357 revolver. The large-caliber bullet blew chunks of brain and flesh against the white plaster wall, and General Sulaimani's lifeless body slumped to the floor. Before anyone had time to react to the shock of what had just happened, Najar turned back to Amatullah and yelled, "And now on to the issue of the kidnapping of the director of the CIA."

Ashani noticed that the Supreme Leader's body-guards had all drawn their weapons.

"Who," Najar shouted, "was the fool who came up with this plan?"

Ashani's ears were ringing as he watched Amatullah squirm. The man's eyes were desperately darting around the room in what looked like a plea for help. Amatullah then locked eyes with Ashani and slowly raised his right hand. Ashani sat in horror as he realized Amatullah was pointing at him. Before Ashani could defend himself, Amatullah said, "It was Minister Ashani's idea. I only found out about it in the last hour."

"Liar," Ashani shouted as he rose out of his chair.

"Sit," Najar commanded in an authoritative voice. He turned back to Amatullah and asked, "What proof do you have?"

Amatullah seemed momentarily stymied and then

he said, "He brought Mukhtar with him on his trip to Mosul. They have been conspiring for a way to get back at the Americans after they were almost killed at Isfahan."

"He accompanied me on your orders," Ashani yelled back and then looked to Najar. "Ahmed, you know I would never do something so foolish."

Najar nodded in agreement and then looked back to Amatullah. "That is hardly proof."

Amatullah appeared to struggle for a moment to come up with something else and then his face lit up. "He showed me a piece of paper with ten numbers that he is using to stay in contact with Mukhtar. And he has a phone. I saw it on him only an hour ago. Search him," Amatullah ordered. "I tell you he has it on him."

Ashani's fear showed on his face. The phone and the list of numbers were in fact on him. "You gave me the list and the phone when we were in your office." Ashani looked at Najar for help.

"Empty your pockets," Najar ordered as he walked around the table.

"That is why I have been trying to call you," Ashani pleaded. "To tell you about this and try to defuse the situation before it is too late."

"Empty your pockets!"

Ashani did as he was told. He placed the phone on the table and slowly unfolded the sheet of paper and set it next to the phone.

A gloating Amatullah smiled and said, "I told you he had them."

Ashani watched as Najar raised his gun and pointed it at him.

Najar looked extremely disappointed. He pulled the hammer back on his revolver and said, "Do you have anything to say for yourself?"

With a sad shake of his head Ashani looked back at Najar and said, "In all the years we worked with each other, have you ever known me to be so careless with operational information? Have you ever known me to write it down in such a straightforward, careless manner?" Ashani gestured to the piece of paper and looked at the numbers written in black ink. After a second his shoulders shook, and he began to laugh.

"I fail to see the humor," Najar said, deadpan with the pistol still pointed at Ashani's head.

"I'm sorry," Ashani said, still laughing, "but that isn't my handwriting." He looked up slowly from the paper and pointed across the room at Amatullah. "It is his."

Najar grabbed both the phone and the piece of paper. He walked around the table and handed them to Amatullah. "Call Mukhtar right now, and tell him to release Director Kennedy."

Amatullah did not move fast enough, so Najar pointed his gun at his head and said simply, "I am going to count to five."

61

R app sat in the back of the blue Chevy Caprice with Stilwell. One of Stilwell's Kurds was driving, and another one was literally and figuratively riding shotgun, with a twelve-gauge Mossberg in his lap. The other five Kurds were following in the beat-up Ford Crown Victoria. The two vehicles topped 90 mph as they screamed north on the main road from the airport back to the heart of the old downtown, a mere five miles away. Two Predator drones patrolled high overhead offering continuous coverage of the Great Mosque and the tangled neighborhood that it dominated. They had a little more than an hour before the afternoon call to prayer. Stilwell made it clear that they needed to get in and out before the men started to file into the mosque. If they didn't, there was a good chance they would be torn to shreds by the mob.

General Gifford and his staff were busy repositioning units so they could create a buffer zone around the Great Mosque by sealing off the streets. The catch was to wait until the last possible minute so that they wouldn't tip off the terrorists and rouse the neighborhood. Rapp would let them know as soon as he was inside the mosque, and then the units would move into final position, setting up a one-block perimeter in every direction. The locals would be told that there was credible intelligence that Sunni insurgents were going to attempt a car bombing during evening prayer. This would allow the army to control the neighborhood and hopefully drive down attendance for afternoon prayer.

An Iraqi army mechanized company was also being mobilized at their base eleven miles away, but they were not told why. The last thing Rapp wanted was a leak that would tip Mukhtar off that they were coming. It was decided that if things got out of control the Iraqi army unit would be called in to secure the mosque itself. Contingencies were being put into place for a helicopter evacuation and medical personnel were put on high alert.

All of this was background noise to Rapp. He knew the contingencies were important, but he couldn't get his mind off Mukhtar's words. *"Tell him the videotape he requested is taking more time than I anticipated. The actress is not cooperating . . . I think if I employ some harsher methods she will perform."*

The good news was that Kennedy was alive. The bad news was that harsher methods meant brutal torture. Contingencies took time to put into place. Rapp didn't have the patience to wait for everything to be perfect, and if American forces were shy about entering the mosque, Rapp had no such qualms. In fact, thanks to Stilwell, Rapp was wearing the perfect solution to their problem.

Stilwell's clerical robes, vest, and turban fit Rapp almost perfectly. He even had a pair of nonprescription glasses to make Rapp look more learned and less threatening. Under his gold silk vest, Rapp was wearing a level-three body armor. A secure Motorola radio was clipped to his belt and was in sync wirelessly with a tiny ear bud that provided communications with Dumond, Stilwell, Ridley, and General Gifford. His .45-caliber Glock was in a paddle holster on his left hip, and his 9mm was in a paddle holster on his right hip—both had suppressors attached. He had four backup magazines for each gun.

Rapp sat silently in the back of the sedan and listened to Dumond relay an update.

"The fourth number just went active, Mitch."

"Location?" Rapp asked as the vehicle got off the highway and headed into the old section of the West Bank. Shortly after the call between Mukhtar and Ashani ended, the signal on Mukhtar's phone went dead. That had been almost ten minutes ago.

"He's still at the mosque."

"Do you have us on visual?"

"That's affirmative."

"What are you seeing at the mosque?"

"There's still a group of maybe a dozen armed men out front, but there's only two guys at the entrance to the madrasa."

"Thanks for the info. Let me know if anything changes."

It had been Stilwell's idea to enter from the religious school that was adjoined to the mosque. That was where Imam Husseini kept his office and were he spent most of his time between prayers.

Stilwell was on his phone. "I will tell you when I get there. We're about a minute away." He listened to the other person for a moment and then said, "Faris, just stand on the fucking curb and wait for me. When we get there I'll tell you what's going on, and yes, I'm going to pay you a shitload of money. Just tell Husseini's guy that you have someone who would like to sit down with his boss and discuss a large donation to the mosque. I'll see you in a minute." Stilwell stabbed the end button and put the phone back in his suit jacket. "Faris is a good man, but he can be real pain the ass."

"Will they trust him?"

Stilwell nodded. "Faris has made a lot of money for a lot of people."

Rapp stared straight ahead and asked, "What about this Imam Husseini?" Rapp was referring to the head Imam at the Great Mosque.

"What about him?"

"Can you trust him?"

"I told you, the only people I trust in this town are my Kurds, but"—he shrugged—"the guy is a whore, so if we show him enough cash, I think he might look the other way and stay out of our hair."

"And if he doesn't?"

Stilwell winced. "Try not to kill him, Mitch. If you do, we're going to have a whole lot of pissed-off Shiites on our hands."

"At this point, I really don't care how many Shiites I piss off."

Stilwell was about to tell Rapp that was the kind of attitude that might get them all killed, but he decided to bite his tongue. The car turned hard left at a stoplight and then took the next right.

"There it is," Stilwell said as he pointed. "Straight ahead on the left. One more block."

The street was blocked with big concrete Jersey barriers to prevent suicide car bombers from getting any closer to the mosque. The sedan swung left and stopped in front of the main door of the madrasa. Two men were waiting at the curb, both in business suits. Stilwell quickly exited the car with a small attaché case and shook Faris's hand. Faris in turn introduced Stilwell to Imam Husseini's personal assistant. The three men exchanged brief pleasantries and then Stilwell motioned for Rapp to join them.

The Kurds piled out of the two vehicles and formed a loose circle around Rapp, Stilwell, and the other two men. Stilwell lifted the thin attaché case and popped the two clasps. He opened the case just enough for the imam's assistant to get a glimpse of the cash.

Stilwell moved closer to the man and whispered, "The Supreme Leader would like to show the imam his appreciation."

The assistant smiled knowingly and motioned for them to follow. Stilwell had told Rapp how Imam Husseini frequently traveled to Tehran; especially when ethnic conflict flared up within the city. The imam of the Great Mosque was a ripe target for the Sunni terrorist groups. The assistant opened the door and held it for his visitors. When he saw that the body-guards were trying to follow, he shot Stilwell an extremely dissatisfied look.

Stilwell turned and motioned for the Kurds to stay put. This had been anticipated. If things got hairy inside, he would radio them for backup. Stilwell then handed Faris an envelope stuffed with hundred-dollar bills, and thanked him for arranging a low-key visit with the imam. Faris turned and left while the other three entered the building.

The assistant led the way down a wide hallway. Rapp and Stilwell followed a pace behind. Behind the closed doors students could be heard reciting suras from the Koran. At the end of the hallway was a stair-well that went down or up a half flight. Rapp noted a side entrance on his right as they went up the steps and straight ahead to another building that connected the madrasa to the mosque.

At the end of the hallway they turned right. Rapp saw a man up ahead standing guard in front of an office door. Rapp's left hand moved to the hilt of his .45-caliber Glock. His movements were concealed under the black clerical robes. His index finger depressed the release on the holster and he drew the weapon. His right hand reached over to casually adjust the folds of the robe to make sure the gun was fully concealed. As they drew closer to the office door and the bodyguard, Rapp grew increasingly suspicious. The man was wearing the exact same boots as the two Iranian prisoners he had been interrogating and his tactical vest was also identical. The man was holding a black AK-74 across his chest. When they drew within ten feet, he stepped forward and blocked the door.

The assistant said something that Rapp didn't quite catch. The guard shook his head in response and said, "I have to search them."

"These are emissaries sent by the Supreme Leader." Rapp adopted the haughty attitude imams were known for.

The bodyguard was not intimidated. He stepped forward and motioned for Rapp to raise his hands. At that exact moment, Dumond's voice came over Rapp's earpiece.

"Mitch, we've got a call being made to the new number."

Rapp began raising his arms and in clear unaccented English, replied to Dumond by saying, "Patch it through."

The words spoken not in Arabic or Farsi, but Americanized English caused the bodyguard to pause for a second as his eyes and ears attempted to reconcile the diverging facts. Rapp pulled the trigger on the silenced .45-caliber Glock. The hollow-tipped bullet hit the man in his bulletproof tactical vest like a sledgehammer. He dropped his rifle as he stumbled backward two steps and fell. Rapp swung his cloaked arm around and brought it to bear on the assistant. He grabbed him by the back of the neck, and in Arabic hissed, "Do what I tell you and you will not be harmed."

Rapp pushed him toward the door, past Stilwell, who was throwing a pair of white plastic flex cuffs on the gasping bodyguard. The assistant opened the door without having to be told, and he and Rapp spilled into the room. The imam was straight ahead, sitting behind his desk, frozen with a pen in one hand and the other draped on top of the desk. Rapp did a quick check to his left and right, and when he put his eyes back on the imam, he saw the gray-bearded man reaching for something under the desk. Rapp took aim and fired, sending a bullet thudding into the top of the heavy wood desk. Splinters flew and the elderly Husseini jerked backwards, rolling away from the desk in his chair. Rapp raised the pistol up above his head and brought it crashing down on the base of the assistant's neck. The man's legs turned to rubber, and he collapsed to the floor.

Rapp rushed around the desk and kicked the side of the imam's leather office chair, sending him rolling across the wood floor and away from whatever it was that he had been reaching for. The chair skidded to a stop against a bookcase.

Rapp looked under the desk and found a gun set inside a small shelf. He left it there and moved to the imam while Stilwell dragged the bodyguard into the office and then went back for the rifle. "I've been told you're a reasonable man, and I'm a little short on time. So I'm going to make this quick. I've got a briefcase with fifty grand in it. You tell me where you've stashed Imad Mukhtar and CIA Director Kennedy and the money's all yours. If you don't, I'm going to start by shooting you in the foot and then the knee. Both places that really hurt. So what's it going to be . . . the money, or a bullet?"

62

Stilwell closed the office door and slapped flex cuffs on the ankles and wrists of the unconscious assistant. The bodyguard was lying on the floor writhing in pain from what Rapp guessed was a broken sternum.

Rapp pointed at the bodyguard and said to Husseini, "He's with Mukhtar, isn't he?"

The imam nodded.

Rapp thought of Kennedy's bodyguards all lined up and shot in the head. He then considered how eliminating this problem might motivate Husseini to be a bit more forthright; both in the sense that there would be no witnesses to talk about the deal Husseini had made, and by serving as a stark example of how serious the situation was. Rapp extended his wrist, squeezed the trigger, and a heavy bullet spat from the end. The man's head bounced off the floor, and then the blood began to flow in an expanding pool of crimson.

Imam Husseini looked on in shocked horror. Rapp was about to tell him that he was now free to talk when he heard President Amatullah's voice emanate from his tiny earpiece.

"Ali, this is Cyrus."

"Marcus," Rapp said in hushed English, "is he still in this building?"

A couple seconds later Dumond said, "We have his signal isolated to a four-by-four-meter area in the southwest corner of the mosque."

"Stan," Rapp commanded, "show him the cash."

"*Where are you?*" Rapp heard Amatullah ask.

"*I would rather not say,*" Mukhtar answered.

"*Well, there has been a change of plan.*"

"*I am close to getting you what you asked for.*" Rapp could hear the frustration in Mukhtar's voice.

"*You need to release the hostage,*" Amatullah said.

Rapp literally froze in mid stride.

"*Why?*" Mukhtar hissed.

"*Because I am ordering you to.*"

"*I do not take orders from you.*" Rapp noted the anger in Mukhtar's voice.

"*Well,*" Amatullah sighed, "*the Supreme Leader has decided that she should be released.*"

"*Why? Is this because of the ultimatum the American president has given you?*"

There was a long pause and then Amatullah said, "*Yes.*"

Mukhtar started laughing. Rapp knew instantly there was a problem. He took two quick steps and placed the tip of the silencer against Husseini's knee. "Change of plan. We're going to start with the knee. I need a quick answer. Fifty grand, or more fucking pain than you've ever imagined in your entire life."

The imam looked at the cash, and then the dead

man on the floor and said, "I will take the cash."

"Good choice. Let's go." Rapp grabbed him under the arm and yanked him from the chair. Over his earpiece he heard Mukhtar say, *"It is time for the war to begin. It is time for you arrogant Persians to sacrifice for Allah."*

"Fuck," Rapp mumbled under his breath as he pulled Husseini toward the door.

The imam resisted, saying, "I will tell you where he is. He's in the old catacombs under the mosque."

"You will show me," Rapp kept moving, "or I'll fucking blow your head off."

Stilwell opened the door, and Rapp rushed through it with the imam.

"Stan, grab the back of his robes. If he makes a wrong move kill him." Rapp drew his silenced 9mm with his now free hand. With the .45 in his left hand he grabbed the extra fabric from the robe and draped it over the gun so all but the last few inches of the silencer were concealed. In his ear he could hear Mukhtar droning on about the struggle to cleanse the cradle of Islam of all infidels.

"How many men does he have?" Rapp asked Husseini.

Husseini straightened his glasses as they hurried around the corner for the stairs. "Eight, I think."

"Are you sure?"

"I don't know. I didn't count . . . maybe ten."

"What about your men?" Stilwell asked. "The ones from the local militia."

"They are guarding the three main entrances to the mosque, but that is normal. We do not like the guns inside if we can avoid it. They do not even know she is here," Husseini added as an afterthought.

Rapp felt like asking him, "So you're the only rat bastard who is helping him," but since Husseini was cooperating, he thought it was best to keep things as positive as the situation would allow. Rapp heard a new voice come over his earpiece. The man was speaking Farsi and was very angry.

"Imad," the man barked, *"you are to release her unharmed, and you are to do it immediately!"*

As they hit the first-floor landing that led back to the madrasa, Stilwell asked in Arabic, "Do you want me to get the Kurds in here?"

"Ayatollah Najar," Mukhtar said, *"knowing your disdain for the CIA, I would have thought you'd approve of my actions."*

"No," Rapp said to Stilwell's question. "Give them an update, but tell them to stay put."

Husseini led them down another half flight of stairs. "The mosque is straight ahead."

"Where does he have his men?" Rapp asked Husseini.

"Some of them are upstairs sleeping."

"Back in the madrasa?"

"Yes."

"How many?"

"I think three."

"And the rest of them?"

"He has two out front with the militia, and then two more guarding the stairs that lead to the catacombs."

"And in the catacombs?"

"I think two. Maybe more."

Counting the man he'd already killed, Rapp had the number at ten, which fit with Husseini's earlier statement. Mukhtar and Ayatollah Najar were now in a full-fledged argument. Rapp wanted to concentrate on what they were saying, but he needed to gather more information about how Kennedy was being guarded. Husseini was describing for him where she was being kept at the end of a narrow passageway when they entered the mosque. As they traveled across the centuries-old heaved stone floor another cleric saw them and began walking toward Husseini.

"I am going to kill her, and there is nothing you can do to stop me," Rapp heard Mukhtar say.

"Keep walking," Rapp whispered to Husseini. "You are going to be greatly rewarded for this. The Supreme Leader wants her released, and Mukhtar has refused."

Husseini waved off the younger cleric, and they moved around a series of columns to a long gallery that ran along the south side of the mosque. Much farther down, light streamed into the shadowy space through a series of narrow windows. Rapp got a quick glimpse of a man passing between two columns and back into the large open part of the mosque that was covered in prayer rugs.

"A little further," Husseini said. "The door is on the right."

Rapp could see a single boot resting on the square base of one of the round columns. In his left ear he could hear Mukhtar and Najar yelling at each other, and in his right ear he could hear the echo of someone talking loudly in the mosque. Farther down the gallery, at least seventy feet away, the man who he had glimpsed just a moment earlier walked back between the columns through a patch of sunlight. It wasn't so much that the man was talking on a cell phone, as much as it was the sudden immobility of Husseini that caused everything to click into place for Rapp.

Rapp and Mukhtar noted each other at the same moment. Both froze for what was only a fraction of a second but seemed like at least five.

"That is him," Husseini whispered.

Rapp was already moving. He saw Mukhtar pull back his suit coat and reach for a radio. Rapp raised the .45 and fired two rushed shots as Mukhtar jumped behind one of the large columns. The bullets sailed past and thudded into the next column, sending shards of rock to the floor. Two steps later Rapp saw movement on his right. He brought his 9mm up and kept his .45 pointed in the direction of Mukhtar. A man in a tactical vest holding a machine gun came into view. Rapp fired a single shot from the 9mm, striking the man in the head. He could now hear Mukhtar barking commands into a radio. Rapp didn't have to hear the words. He already knew what they would be.

In a split second Rapp made up his mind. He turned to the right and burst through the doorway as the man he had just shot was coming to a rest on the floor. A second man was sitting on a chair inside the small vestibule. He barely had the chance to open his tired eyes to see what was going on.

The 9mm bullet hit him in the center of the forehead. Rapp tossed off his black robes and yelled for Stilwell to stay with Husseini. As he ran into the vestibule, he could hear Mukhtar's voice coming over the radio clipped to the dead man's tactical vest. While still holding on to his .45, Rapp reached out and snatched the radio with his thumb and forefinger. He pressed the transmit button and countermanded Mukhtar's order as he started down the stairs three at a time. He reached the first basement in just a few seconds and made sure to keep his finger on the transmit button so that Mukhtar couldn't relay any more commands.

The door that led to the second basement was right where Husseini said it would be. Rapp yanked it open with no concern for his own safety and rushed into the significantly more narrow passage. A thought occurred to him and he brought the radio to his mouth. In a gruff voice, he barked. "I'm coming down. Don't do anything until I get there."

Rapp momentarily lost his footing on the smooth narrow treads and skidded into the wall at the switchback. A third of the way down the last, small flight he leapt and hit the dirt floor. He glanced to his left. There was nothing but darkness. He wheeled to his right, dropping the radio and bringing both guns to bear on the wood slat door thirty feet away. Lines of light cut through the cracks, and a man's voice could be heard on the other side asking someone to repeat what they had said. Rapp charged forward, picking up speed. Lowering his shoulder he plowed through the ancient dry wood like it was made of twigs.

Two men stood no more than eight feet away. One in front of the other. The closest one was holding a radio in front of his mouth and in the other hand a pistol dangled lazily at his side. Rapp fired the 9mm, hitting the first man in the side of the head. As he sank to the floor, Rapp got a full look at the other man, and his first glimpse of Kennedy. She was tied over the back of a chair and bleeding profusely. Her shirt was lying in shreds on the floor, and her back was covered with long red welts from being whipped. The other man was shirtless, covered in sweat and holding a double length of electrical cord in his right hand.

The man shrugged, dropped the cord to the ground, and raised his hands in the air.

Rapp took one more look at Kennedy and then the man who had been beating her. He could feel the bile rising up from deep within.

The man looked at Rapp and said, "I was only following orders."

"So am I." Rapp pulled the trigger on the 9mm and shot him in the chest.

EPILOGUE

Ashani was driven straight to Langley by Rob Ridley and brought into the Old Headquarters Building via the executive underground parking garage. Before entering the director's private elevator he'd been roughly searched by two of Kennedy's bodyguards—an indignity that he would have not tolerated a week earlier; but now, considering all that had happened, he didn't dare complain. He'd spoken with Rapp twice in the past week. The first conversation didn't go all that well. In fact it consisted mostly of Rapp threatening him and telling him to pass along threats to other Iranian officials. Ashani had learned a great deal about the man in the past week, and nearly all of it was unsettling. He was not someone they could afford to take lightly or ignore.

Ashani had discussed the problem with Najar, who was not pleased to be threatened. His curt response was that they should hire someone to kill the American agent. Ashani, who hated the idea, dissuaded his mentor by explaining that others had tried to do the same thing and had failed. "In fact," he added, "they are all dead."

Ashani used that anecdote to help pitch his proposal. He explained in detail what he proposed to do and how it would both solve a problem and satisfy Rapp.

405

It was the classic killing of two birds with one stone. With Najar's blessing, Ashani had called Rapp and told him he would like to sit down and discuss a very important matter. Rapp pressed him for more information, of course, but Ashani just repeated that he was willing to share some very important information with him. Rapp agreed to the meeting, but refused to do so anywhere other than Langley. Ashani reluctantly agreed, and now he found himself entering the belly of the beast.

As he was escorted through the door by Rob Ridley, he laid eyes on Kennedy for the first time since their meeting in Mosul. She was sitting in a chair next to a couch with an expression that was devoid of emotion. Ashani averted his eyes, feeling an overwhelming sense of shame. He noticed someone approaching from the far end of the large office and turned to see who it was. The man was around six feet tall and had longish, wavy black hair and a beard—both with flecks of gray. He was wearing dark slacks and a white dress shirt that clung to his broad shoulders and tapered down to a narrow waist.

Ashani knew it was Rapp by the photos in his dossier, but seeing him in person was an entirely different matter. It was like looking at a photo of a lion as opposed to standing only a few feet away from one of the Creator's most efficient predators. He had expected him to be more rigid, like the former army officers who worked for him, but he wasn't. He had a relaxed, athletic grace in the way he moved. Ashani thought of the threats Rapp had made over the phone, and it sent a shiver down his spine.

Rapp pointed at the couch next to Kennedy and said, "You can sit over there."

There were no pleasantries. No hellos, or would you like anything to drink. Ashani moved around the glass coffee table and sat on the couch. He looked at Kennedy and with all the sincerity he could muster said, "I am so sorry for what happened to you, and my country offers its sincerest apologies."

"Bullshit," Rapp said in a menacing tone. He took up a position on the other side of the coffee table and remained standing. "There's people in your government who were behind the whole thing."

Ashani looked up at Rapp and noticed a large-caliber automatic holstered on his left hip. He turned back to Kennedy and said, "He is right. Most of them have been punished. Some have paid with their lives."

"What about Amatullah?"

"As I have already told you," Ashani said to Rapp, "his term is up in less than a year. He will not be running for office again."

Rapp stood there and shook his head in disgust.

Ashani found the man very unsettling, so he turned his attention back to Kennedy. In a soft voice he said, "I wish there was a way I could prove to you that I had nothing to do with this crazy plot. I have four daughters and a wife. I would never have participated in something like this."

"Yeah, you just help fund and train Hezbollah suicide bombers so they can blow themselves up in supermarkets and kill pregnant women." With a sarcastic sneer Rapp added, "That's much better."

Kennedy looked at Rapp and cleared her throat. It was a signal for him to back off. She then looked at Ashani and said, "It is my hope that this experience will serve as a lesson that our two countries need to open relations. The lack of communications only allows the zealots to advance their ideas."

"I agree," Ashani responded.

Rapp made a face like he might get sick.

"Now, why did you travel all this way?" Kennedy asked in a congenial voice.

"The short answer . . . Imad Mukhtar."

"What about him?" Rapp said.

"He is back in Lebanon." Ashani placed a thick manila envelope on the glass table and slid it toward Kennedy. "I have prepared a dossier for you."

Kennedy opened the package and began flipping through the pages. "This is a lot of information." She looked at him with her searching eyes and asked, "Why?"

"Because he wants us to clean up his mess," Rapp said.

Kennedy held up her hand, signaling to Rapp that she would like him to butt out for a minute. "Why?"

"Ayatollah Najar has asked the senior leadership of Hezbollah to arrest Mukhtar and send him to Tehran. They have assured him that they would put their full resources behind it."

"Let me guess," said Rapp, "they're not putting a lot of effort into finding him."

"They are putting *no* effort into finding him. They are putting all their effort into *hiding* him."

"Where?" Rapp asked.

"North of Tripoli."

"Lebanon?"

"Yes." Ashani pointed to the file in Kennedy's hands. "It is all in there. Bank records, known associates, et cetera . . ."

"There's a lot more than that in here," Kennedy said.

Ashani shrugged sheepishly.

Kennedy studied his face for a moment and in search of a more full answer, repeated her question. "Why?"

"Only one other person in my country knows about my trip to see you. That person and I agree that Iran's future would be better served if we were to cut our ties with Hezbollah."

"And by giving this to us you hope to accomplish . . . what?"

Ashani thought about his answer carefully and then said, "I think it will help us close a very ugly chapter in our shared history, and hopefully give you personally a sense of justice."

Kennedy considered the thick file for a moment and said, "Thank you."

"You are welcome." Ashani stood and said, "Thank you for taking the time to meet with me."

"You are welcome. Please excuse my not getting up, but I'm still a bit sore."

Rapp escorted Ashani to the door and handed him off to Ridley. He closed the door and walked back to Kennedy, who was staring out the window lost in thought. Rapp stood there for a moment and then asked, "What would you like me to do with Mukhtar?"

Without looking, Kennedy handed the file over her shoulder to Rapp and said, "Kill him."

TRIPOLI, LEBANON

The G-5 landed shortly after midnight. Rapp looked out the window and was pleased to see that the police escort was there as promised. It had taken Rapp three hours to read the file from cover to cover, and by the time he was finished, he knew exactly what he was going to do. He had his secretary make two copies of the file. He sent one to Marcus Dumond with instructions to scan everything into the system, so they could begin the collection of intercepts, and the other file went to Kennedy with instructions for it not to be distributed until he gave the okay. The last thing he needed was some gung-ho analyst, or worse, someone from the Justice Department getting in his way before he had a chance to permanently resolve the outstanding issue.

The next thing he did was call a certain Middle Eastern monarch who had a deep fondness and respect for Kennedy. This monarch had called in the aftermath of Kennedy's kidnapping and offered to do anything to help bring Imad Mukhtar to justice. The king also happened to be from the Sunni sect of Islam and despised the Shiite terrorist group Hezbollah. Mukhtar himself had been behind a plot to kill one of the king's brothers. Rapp explained the situation, and told the monarch what he would like to do. The monarch did not hesitate to offer his significant assistance, and in fact told Rapp he would like to incur the costs the operation. This actually became the stickiest part of the conversation. Rapp had to eventually invoke tribal honor to get the monarch to back down.

Operations like this were often very tedious and drawn out—usually taking months and sometimes even years. Every so often, though, a shortcut presented itself. The trick was to know when to take it. In this instance, Rapp was influenced by several factors. The first, simple fact was that every government and organization, with the exception of Hezbollah, had turned its back on Mukhtar. And according to Ashani's information there were even a few high-ranking members of Hezbollah who thought it was time for the man to simply disappear. The second reason why Rapp was willing to take the shortcut was because he knew if anything went wrong, the president would have his back. Alexander had told him personally that he wanted Mukhtar's scalp and he didn't care how long it took. The third and final reason Rapp decided to take the quick route was simple poetic justice.

Rapp looked at his satellite phone and punched in a number from memory. After a few rings someone answered on the other end and gave Rapp the confirmation he needed. Rapp thanked the person and put the phone back in his pocket. He unbuckled his seat belt, and opened the storage closet near the cockpit. After putting on his suit coat he grabbed a large, heavy black duffel bag and threw it over his shoulder. On his way past the cockpit, Rapp poked his head in and told the pilots he would likely be back in an hour. Rapp walked down steps and across the rain-slick tarmac. Two police officers were standing by the squad car; one a detective and the other a patrolman. Rapp shook hands with the detective, who informed him that the chief was waiting for him at the station.

Rapp climbed into the backseat and they were off. Where Beirut was a city of mixed religions and sects, Tripoli was predominantly Sunni. They arrived at the station a few minutes later. Rapp lugged the heavy bag up two flights of stairs and was shown immediately into the chief's office. Introductions were extremely brief. Neither man wanted to get to know the other. They simply wanted to complete the transaction and go their separate ways.

"Is that what I think it is?" the chief asked, pointing at the bag on the floor.

Rapp nudged it with his foot. "Sure is. Would you like to take a look?"

The chief nodded eagerly.

"Before we do that I want to verify one thing."

"What is that?"

"You spoke to his majesty directly?"

"Yes."

"And I assume he told you that I am the last guy you want to double-cross."

The chief grinned uncomfortably. "Yes, he did. He actually said you are the second-to-last guy. He is the last guy."

"Whatever works," Rapp smiled amiably. He bent down and unzipped the bag, revealing five tightly shrink-wrapped packets of money. Stepping back, Rapp said, "Five million dollars." Rapp figured it was cheap. The leadership of al-Qaeda all had price tags of twenty-plus million on their heads. Mukhtar at five million was a bargain. Especially when one took into consideration that based on Ashani's information, they could easily clear that much, once they started raiding the Hezbollah accounts they now knew about. If Mukhtar could bribe Sunni cops in Mosul, Rapp saw no problem in offering a cash reward for one of the most-wanted terrorists in the world.

The chief clapped his hands together, and could barely contain his glee. "Oh, this is wonderful."

"Yes, it is. Now, may I please see the prisoner?"

"Of course. Please follow me."

The chief led Rapp down to the first floor. At the back of the station were a series of holding rooms with one-way glass. The chief stopped in front of one and said, "Everything has been arranged just as you asked."

There sat Imad Mukhtar handcuffed to the metal table. His shoes, belt, watch, money, and cell phone were all on the table in front of him. He had shaved his head in an attempt to disguise himself. It didn't matter, though. Now that they had his voiceprint and the home where he was staying it had been easy to find him.

"What about the security camera?" Rapp asked.

"This one is not working."

"All right. You have the key for the handcuffs?"

The chief gave it to him. "I will wait right here until you are done."

"Thanks." Rapp grabbed a handkerchief, twisted the knob, and entered the ten-by-ten-foot interrogation room. Without turning around, Rapp flipped the handkerchief up onto the security camera directly above him. The chief seemed like a nice guy, but there was no reason not to be thorough. He then snapped on a pair of latex gloves.

Mukhtar looked up with tired bloodshot eyes and asked in Arabic, "Are you my lawyer?"

Rapp laughed, and as he pulled the curtain across the viewing window and said, "No, I'm your proctologist, you idiot."

Hearing the visitor speak Americanized English caused Mukhtar to grow deeply concerned. "Who are you?"

"Who I am doesn't matter, Mr. Mukhtar." Rapp circled around him.

"I do not know who you are talking about."

If all they had to go on were the photos taken in Mosul, there might have been a sliver of doubt, but

Ashani had provided them with sixteen different quality shots. Those, combined with the voice analysis, guaranteed that the man he was looking at was Imad Mukhtar.

Rapp grabbed the belt off the table and stood directly behind the prisoner. Mukhtar sensed he was in some serious trouble and began yanking violently against the handcuffs. It was a waste of his energy. The metal table was bolted to the floor. Rapp slid the belt around Mukhtar's neck and threaded it through the buckle. Mukhtar started screaming and thrashing even harder. Rapp put his left hand on Mukhtar's shoulder and gave the belt a good yank with his right hand. Mukhtar began gasping for air and making choking noises.

Rapp leaned in close, his mouth hovering mere inches away from Mukhtar's left ear and said, "This is for Irene Kennedy, you piece of shit."

Rapp put his left foot in the center of Mukhtar's upper back and grabbed the belt with both hands. He leaned back and yanked with everything he had. Mukhtar's windpipe collapsed like an aluminum can. His eyes nearly popped out of his head, and his limbs went rigid. Rapp held the belt tight for another ten seconds to make sure, and then let go. Mukhtar slumped forward, his head thudding to a rest on the table. Rapp undid the handcuffs and leg restraints and tossed them on the floor. He then took the tail end of the belt, tied it around the metal bar that Mukhtar's right handcuff had been attached to, and pulled the chair away.

Mukhtar's knees hit the ground and his head slid off the table. The belt caught and stopped his face a foot short of the floor.

Rapp took one last look around and then opened the door. On the way out he reached up and collected his handkerchief from the security camera and then took off the latex gloves.

The chief was waiting. "How did it go?"

"Exactly as planned." Rapp thanked the police chief, turned, and walked straight out the front door.

Center Point Publishing
600 Brooks Road • PO Box 1
Thorndike ME 04986-0001 USA

(207) 568-3717

US & Canada:
1 800 929-9108